Available in from Mills & Boon Intrigue

Secrets in Four Corners
by Debra Webb
&
Profile Durango
by Carla Cassidy

Mountain Investigation
by Jessica Andersen
&
Priceless Newborn Prince
by Ann Voss Peterson

Set Up with the Agent
by Lori L Harris
&
Terms of Attraction
by Kylie Brant

Cowboy Commando
by Joanna Wayne

"I requested your reassignment," Mark clarified.

In the middle of the night? Normally a transfer didn't happen instantaneously and the idea that this one had left her feeling uncertain.

Beth's eyes narrowed. "Why would you do that?" It didn't surprise her that he had pull, but that he would use it to get her transferred did. What could be that urgent?

His eyes met hers, but there was a disconnect in them that hadn't been there earlier tonight. A sense that he saw her, but that he was no longer emotionally involved with her on a human level.

She had suddenly become a means to an end. An instrument he could use. That he could exploit.

She jerked off her mask, dropped it on the pile of rubble. "So you want to use me as bait?"

His mouth tightened. "Sweetheart, you *are* bait. I can't change that. But I fully intend to take advantage of that fact."

TERMS OF ATTRACTION

It was all too easy to imagine lying on that bed with Ava beside him.

He could still recall the feel of her supple muscles and soft curves.

As if recognising his thoughts, she took a step back. "No." Her voice was firm. But in her expression he saw a reflection of the desire he was trying desperately to stem in himself. "We aren't going to make the same mistake twice."

"That's good to hear." His mind splintered into duelling parts: logic and temptation. His hand reached out, as if devoid of conscious decision, and cupped her jaw.

Her hand came up as if to push his away. Lingered to stroke. "You don't trust me," she said.

The skin beneath her ear was baby soft. When he brushed his fingertips over it she shuddered.

"I can't."

"So why should I trust you?"

He replaced his hand with his lips, tracing her delicate jawline with a string of whisper-soft kisses. "You shouldn't."

First published in Great Britain 2010
Harlequin Mills & Boon Limited,
Eton House, 18-24 Paradise Road, Richmond, Surrey TW9 1SR

Set Up with the Agent © Lori L Harris 2008
Terms of Attraction © Kimberly Bahnsen 2009

ISBN: 978 0 263 88248 3

46-0810

Harlequin Mills & Boon policy is to use papers that are natural, renewable
and recyclable products and made from wood grown in sustainable forests.
The logging and manufacturing processes conform to the legal environmental
regulations of the country of origin.

Printed and bound in Spain
by Litografia Rosés S.A., Barcelona

SET UP WITH THE AGENT

BY
LORI L HARRIS

TERMS OF ATTRACTION

BY
KYLIE BRANT

MILLS & BOON

SET UP WITH
THE AGENT

BY
LORI L HARRIS

Lori Harris has always enjoyed competition. She grew up in southern Ohio, showing Arabian horses and Great Danes. Later she joined a shooting league, where she competed head to head with police officers – and would be competing today if she hadn't discovered how much fun and challenging it was to write. Romantic suspense seemed a natural fit. What could be more exciting than writing about life-and-death struggles that include sexy, strong men?

When not in front of a computer, Lori enjoys remodelling her home, gardening and boating. Lori lives in Orlando, Florida, with her very own hero.

For Bobbie Laishley and Bill Laishley
And for the Harris Family: Trip, Kathy, Gracie, Mike, Nichele, Brett, Connor, Dillon, John, Billy, Patsy and, most of all, for Bobby. Love You All!

Prologue

FBI Special Agent Mark Gerritsen ripped his shirttails from his trousers. It was just past 3:30 a.m. on a hot July night, and he was standing on the street in front of a modest home in a quiet Frederick, Maryland, suburb.

"Has the lab determined how much of the chemical weapon is missing?" Mark kept his voice low. As he stripped off his shirt, he glanced at Special Agent Colton Larson, who stood several feet away.

Larson was also down to his T-shirt. "They're calling it sizable."

Mark offered a terse smile. "In other words they don't know, and they're trying to cover their asses."

He suspected it was also the reason the FBI hadn't been alerted of the theft until the middle of the night—because those in charge of security, of protecting the people from the kind of occurrence that had just taken place, had been scrambling to protect their jobs instead of the American public.

Leaving his shirt hanging over the open car door, Mark grabbed the heavy body armor off the seat and settled it over his shoulders. He shrugged the protection into position before pressing down on the Velcro straps. The rest of the counterterrorism unit had been contacted but was unlikely to arrive in time, which meant Mark and Larson would be working with a local SWAT team.

The target was a home two doors down from their current location. Mark scanned the front of the residence. Except for the dim front porch light, the small, brick ranch house with peeling trim paint had been dark when they'd arrived and remained that way.

The owner, Dr. Harvey Thesing, made a good wage, but from the brief background information Mark had obtained en route, over the past year Thesing had been spending his money on environmental causes. Which should have tipped off his superiors that no matter what his credentials were, Thesing wasn't the best chemist to work on MX141.

Along with the rundown on Thesing, Mark had also received one on the chemical weapon. Though fairly stable in the powdered form, once dissolved in a liquid and vaporized, its lethal power was immeasurable.

Bottom line, they were talking some nasty stuff.

Mark checked out the surrounding residences. "How are those evacuations coming?" While he had been meeting with the SWAT guys, Larson had been seeing to the perimeter.

Larson looked up. "Local cops have cleared a block in all directions and are in the process of closing off roads."

Mark would have liked to ask for a larger area, but there just wasn't time for that luxury right now. It was a decision that he hoped he didn't end up regretting. "Make sure they stick close by in case we need to get more people out."

A SWAT team member rounded the front end of Mark's car, striding soundlessly toward them. "Car's in the garage. Bedrooms appear to be at the back."

Mark grabbed the olive drab hazmat suit and stepped

into it. Because he'd been assimilating a lot of information when they'd met five minutes ago, it took him a second to recall the officer's name. Rogers?

Mark slid his arms into the sleeves of the suit. "But you don't know which one Thesing is using? Or if he's even in that area of the house."

"No. We're not picking up any sounds inside."

Which meant they might find an empty house. That Thesing could already be putting his plan into motion.

Mark zipped up the lightweight suit. But what was Thesing's agenda? What in the hell did a tree hugger do with a chemical weapon that he'd been instrumental in developing?

"What about a basement?" Mark asked.

"There's one."

"Any type of entrance?"

"Two well windows that are boarded up from inside."

Was it possible that Thesing was sleeping down there? Perhaps because with the recent heat wave it was cooler?

Mark grabbed his holstered weapon and strapped it on. "Any word on whether Thesing owns a gun?"

"Nothing registered."

Which, given current gun laws, didn't mean a whole hell of a lot. Thesing could be sitting on a whole arsenal.

Rogers scanned the area quickly and then returned his attention to Mark. "How do you want to do this?"

"Covert entry through the front door. I'll need for one of your men to handle the pick gun, then hang around long enough to offer some initial cover. Once Larson and I are in, though, your man needs to back off immediately. Best-case scenario, we reach the chemist before he has time to get to the stuff."

Mark looked up, his gaze connecting with Rogers's. "No one goes in without full hazmat gear, understand?" He waited until the officer nodded before continuing. "Have the rest of your men keep the windows and doors under hard surveillance, while still maintaining a safe distance."

"Does this stuff have a name?" Rogers asked.

Larson had just stepped past Mark to grab a hazmat suit. "Yeah. Scary."

Even as Rogers offered a tight nod and turned away, Mark sensed the local cop's frustration at being asked to respond to a situation where critical information was being withheld.

Not that Mark had any choice in the matter.

They were under orders to avoid full disclosure of MX141's capabilities, something that made him extremely uncomfortable. But if everything went well in the next few minutes, if the MX141 was recovered without incident, the decision to withhold certain facts could turn out to be the right one.

At least, that's what he was hoping.

Grabbing the twelve-gauge he'd left on the sedan's floorboard, Mark spilled the box of shotgun shells onto the floor mat. After collecting six of them, he backed out of Larson's way and then waited while the other man did the same. They'd worked together often enough that there was no need for discussion.

With his chest already beginning to tighten with tension, Mark glanced across the hood of the Taurus and toward the residence. Still no sign of life. Maybe he should at least be thankful for that.

Mark took the lead, and by the time they reached the front door, a SWAT officer was already in place. Mark and Larson tugged down their night-vision goggles and adjusted their breathing apparatuses before lowering their hazmat hoods into place.

At Mark's nod, the officer inserted the pick gun into the first of two locks. In seconds the door was unlocked, but it took another few to dispense with the safety chain.

As the SWAT officer stepped out of the way, Mark moved inside, intent on reaching the bedroom hallway as quickly and as soundlessly as possible.

The door to the first bedroom was open. A home office. Unoccupied. The doors to the other two remained closed. Mark stopped next to the nearest of them, and then waited for Larson to reach the other one.

At Mark's signal, both men checked to see if their door was unlocked. Larson offered a slight nod, indicating that his was. Mark did the same. On Mark's next signal they entered their assigned rooms as silently as possible, twelve-gauge shotguns leading the way.

Mark did a quick sweep before focusing on the double bed covered in unfolded clothes. He made sure Thesing wasn't buried beneath the laundry, and then did a fast inspection of the closet. He hooked up with Larson in the hallway again.

Taking the point position, Mark moved cautiously toward the living areas. The element of surprise was off the table now. If Thesing was in the house, even if he was in the basement, it was unlikely that he'd still be unaware of their presence. Which made it more likely they'd be facing an armed suspect.

Motioning Larson to hang back, Mark skirted the dining room table. Cardboard moving boxes sealed with tape surrounded the table, and a mountain of newspapers covered it.

Because of the hazmat gear, Mark was drowning in

sweat, but his breathing was still slow and easy. Like the bedroom he'd just left, the kitchen was a mess. Trash overflowed the fifty-five-gallon waste can in the center of the room, and a healthy roach population was chowing down on the food remnants covering pots and pans and plates. For a man worried about the environment, it looked as if he was well on the way to creating his very own toxic-waste site.

The family room was just beyond and appeared to be in the same condition as the rest of the house.

Backtracking, Mark returned to the kitchen where he waited for Larson to get into position before opening what Mark had correctly assumed would be the door to the basement.

Positioned just to the left of the opening, he peered into the lower level, looking for any hint of movement. Seeing none, he slowly lowered his foot onto the first tread, allowing the wood to absorb his weight.

As he continued to work his way down the stairs, his breathing became less smooth, less even. He kept his back pressed to the wall. Larson was covering him from the head of the stairs, but Mark was still in a very exposed position.

Halfway down, a single tread gave under his weight, the resulting sharp squeal enough to wake anyone. Seeing it as his only option, Mark took the remaining steps quickly and noisily. At the bottom, he dropped into a crouch next to the wall.

The conditions in the basement were even worse than those above stairs. Along with stacks of junk, there were more piles of newspapers and cardboard boxes and bags of trash. Why in the hell would Thesing hoard garbage? What kind of nut case were they dealing with here?

Larson had made it to the bottom of the steps and spread out slightly to Mark's left as both men moved forward cautiously.

A workbench stretched along the closest wall and was the only relatively neat area. A washer and dryer occupied the opposite wall. In between was a gauntlet of every type of imaginable junk—a tricycle, a dollhouse, an old sewing machine. A rolling cabinet for tools. More sealed plastic bags.

It wasn't until Mark got past them that he saw the bed tucked back in the far corner. And Harvey Thesing's body on the floor next to it. Even from his current position, Mark was fairly certain the chemist was dead, but kept his weapon leveled on him as he closed the distance.

It looked as if a shotgun had been used, the blast to Thesing's midsection nearly cutting him in two, while the one to his head had taken off half his skull.

Knowing it was a waste of time, he checked for a pulse and found none. But as he started to pull his hand away, he realized that, given the cool conditions of the basement the body was warmer than he would have anticipated. He checked the facial muscles—the first place that any signs of rigor mortis would appear—but found no rigidity.

"How long?" Larson asked.

"If I had to make a guess?" Using the method to determine time of death was risky at best. "I'd say only a short time—possibly less than an hour."

Mark desperately wanted to plow his fist into something—into anything. If the damn lab hadn't been trying to cover their asses… If they'd made the call an hour earlier…

Talk about being screwed. Even the relatively short lead

time wasn't going to help them. For the moment at least, they were chasing a ghost.

A ghost armed with the most lethal chemical weapon ever developed.

Chapter One

Four Months Later

Leaving her dark, wool coat and white scarf draped across the chair, FBI Special Agent Beth Benedict paced to the bookcase and scanned the titles. *Experimental Psychology, Evaluation of Sexual Disorders, The Problem of Maladaptive Behavior*—a bevy of volumes detailing human psychoses. Exactly what she would expect to find on a psychologist's shelf.

As with her previous two sessions, she was the last patient of the day. The receptionist had shown her into Dr. Carmichael's office, indicating that she should take a seat in one of the high-backed contemporary chairs. Dr. Carmichael would be with her shortly.

But since Beth had been released from the hospital, she'd found it very difficult to sit still for any length of time. Another reason that she needed to be out in the field and not trapped behind a desk.

She took a deep breath in preparation for the coming confrontation. The FBI had trained her how to deceive criminals, how to gain their trust, so scamming one psychologist shouldn't be all that hard. She just needed to stick with the plan, with her "blueprint of progress."

This week she'd remain calm and in control, no tears, no outbursts. And no more stony silences that suggested she was bucking authority. By her next appointment, the claustrophobia issue would be nearly resolved.

As with any type of deception, the key was to keep it believable.

When she heard the office door open behind her, her shoulder muscles tightened, and the headache that she'd been coping with exploded at the base of her skull.

Dr. Samuel Carmichael paused momentarily in the opening. He was somewhere in his late forties, with thick, prematurely gray hair and a quick smile. Because any good con required that you know your mark, she'd done her homework. He liked to sail and was on his second marriage, this one to a law student half his age.

"Sorry about running late," the psychologist offered as he pushed the door closed.

"No problem." Beth took a seat and settled back, giving the illusion that she was comfortable.

"Can I get you some water before we get started?"

"No. Thanks."

Taking the chair opposite hers, Carmichael propped his right ankle atop his left knee before resting the legal pad in his lap. "So how do you think you're doing?"

"Actually, a little better."

"What about the nightmares? Are you still experiencing them?"

"Occasionally." She kept the confident and somewhat bland smile on her face. Though this was only her third session, she knew the routine, so she waited for the psychologist to pursue the current subject.

"Are you saying there's been a decrease in their frequency?"

"Yes. Some." In reality, the opposite was true. Every time she was lucky enough to fall asleep, it was only a matter of time before she sat straight up, her heart pounding, the scent of spilled gasoline so real that it usually took her several seconds to realize that the smell was a remembered one, a cruel joke played by her own mind.

Dr. Carmichael scribbled a note. "And when they do occur, would you characterize them as any less vivid than when we started meeting?"

"Definitely." She knew she needed to start offering more than short responses, but despite her earlier resolve, she was finding it surprisingly difficult, her emotions already bubbling to the surface. Her palms were now damp and as she met Carmichael's gaze, her respiration quickened, almost as if he had leveled a gun at her chest.

But in some ways, the situation she found herself in now was just as much a life-or-death struggle as the event that had landed her here. Dr. Samuel Carmichael held her career in his hands. And since her career was her life....

Carmichael leaned back in his chair. "What about the claustrophobia?"

"It's better." Another short response. "I'm back to riding elevators. Wouldn't you say that's a pretty major step?"

She managed a slight smile, but when she tried to force it a bit wider, she felt her facial muscles freeze. And knew that she'd made a mistake. She could see it in his washed-out blue eyes and in the way his mouth tightened.

"Beth." Carmichael uncrossed his legs. "I've been in

practice for a lot of years. I know when I'm being manipulated. I can't help you unless you're open with me."

She kept her gaze level. How should she respond? Pretend confusion? Try a small amount of honesty?

Taking a deep breath, she let it out slowly, having decided the latter was going to be the best course of action.

"You're right. But you have to understand what I need to get better. I need work. Real work. I've been pulled out of the field and assigned to administrative duties. Do you have any idea what that includes? I run a copier. I collate reports for other agents. I answer the phone."

"You do recognize that your boss, that Bill Monroe is concerned that the incident has left you—"

Irritation kicked in. "Incident? Isn't that a slightly benign description for being locked in the trunk of a burning car? The fact that I have some difficulty sleeping, that I've had occasional problems handling tight spaces isn't all that unusual, is it, given the circumstances?"

"No. What you're feeling is quite normal." Holding a pencil in one hand, he ran the fingers of the other one up and down the length as he studied her. "So you believe that you should be put back out into the field? Where your failure to function at a crucial moment could possibly endanger your life or the life of an innocent bystander or coworker?"

She held on to her irritation. "I recognize that I do have issues at the moment, but I believe they are temporary and controllable. I don't feel they undermine my ability to do my job."

"So, if you don't believe you need help, why are you here?" He paused before adding, "My understanding is that these sessions are voluntary."

"That is what the manual says," she agreed. Unable to sit still any longer, she got up and paced to the window. Even though her SAC—Special Agent in Charge—had characterized the counseling as voluntary, she knew better.

"Don't you want to improve?"

"Sure." And she wanted to keep her job, too. She looked out at the dark night. The window overlooked the parking garage across the street where she'd left her car.

"Of course I want to get better." She just couldn't see how dwelling on problems could be therapeutic. That wasn't the way she'd been raised. You get knocked down, you get back up. End of story.

With her carefully constructed blueprint of progress a bust, she decided maybe it was the right time to put at least a few cards on the table. And at the same time momentarily steer the conversation away from her. "You attended University of Maryland, didn't you?"

"That's right."

She faced him. "And graduated the same year as Bill Monroe?"

It was Carmichael's turn to look uncomfortable. "So you think you're being set up in some way? That I'm your boss's hit man?"

"It crossed my mind." Having given up all attempts to control her body language, she tightened her arms in front of her. "I suppose after that remark, you'll be adding paranoia to the list."

Carmichael's eyes narrowed and his lips thinned. "Do you consider yourself to be overly suspicious of the motives of people around you?"

She pretended to consider the possibility. When she'd been doing the background check on Carmichael, she'd done a little self-diagnosing while she was at it. She might be experiencing a sense of fatalism where her job was concerned, but it was fully grounded in cold, hard facts.

Beth realized the psychologist was still waiting for an answer on the paranoia issue. "No. I don't consider myself to be paranoid."

Even if Carmichael didn't know the real reason she was undergoing counseling, the only reason she still had a job, she did. She was the prosecution's only witness on the Rabbit Rheaume money laundering case, and they were worried that she'd fall apart during cross examination. These sessions were meant to keep her functioning until after the trial—until after she'd taken the stand and the feds had their conviction.

But once they did, all bets would be off.

For more than two years now, since she'd gone over his head, Bill Monroe had been looking for a way to get rid of her—not an easy task considering the previous glowing evaluations he'd given her.

The knot in her gut tightened. Even before she'd gone in undercover, landing a position as Rabbit Rheaume's assistant, she'd been trying to hold on, to play Monroe's game. She was hoping that those above him would somehow miraculously recognize that he was conducting a witch hunt against her. But even from the beginning she'd known that her survival was unlikely. That even though she'd managed to survive Rabbit's car trunk, it was unlikely she'd survive Monroe. He was a twenty-two-year veteran of the Bureau. Part of the men's club. And the FBI historically tended to protect those in higher positions, sacrificing lower-ranked employees.

Realizing Carmichael was watching her again, she

slammed the door closed on that line of thought. She couldn't afford it right now. "Maybe I'm a little lost at the moment, that's all."

"We all are sometimes. But none of us has to remain that way." Carmichael crossed to his desk, opened the top drawer and pulled out a prescription pad.

She found it difficult to hide her exasperation. What kind of pill would it be this time? She'd tried taking what he'd prescribed on the first visit, something for anxiety, but when the drug had interfered with her ability to function, she'd quit taking it. She'd needed to stay clear-headed, keep her wits about her.

When he finished writing, he ripped off the top sheet and handed it to her. Even though she had no intention of having the prescription filled, Beth glanced down at the writing. The name Harriet Thompson was followed by a local phone number.

"She's a colleague of mine. She didn't attend Maryland and doesn't know Bill Monroe."

Her eyes narrowed briefly as she wondered if she was in fact paranoid.

"You're a very strong woman, Beth, but you still need to talk to someone."

She glanced up. "Are you firing me?"

"No. I just want to be sure that the next time we meet, you're here for the right reasons. I can help you, but only if you let me."

ONLY MINUTES LATER Beth buttoned the heavy, wool coat over her navy-blue suit and pulled on gloves before pushing open the office building's exterior door and stepping out into the cold night. As the early-November wind cut through her, Carmichael's words lingered in the back of her mind.

She'd always considered herself to be tough and competent. During the sixteen weeks at Quantico, she'd physically and mentally outperformed most of her class, even those with military or law enforcement backgrounds.

But in a single night, that had all changed. She'd gone from tough to frightened. And now, nearly four months after she'd escaped the trunk of a burning car, she still felt trapped, as if everything around her was going up in flames. Her career. Her relationship with her father.

She couldn't afford to look weak, though. Not if she wanted to keep her job. And not when she took the stand at the Rheaume trial. If the prosecution lost there, getting a conviction on the connected attempted-murder charge was going to become even tougher. How was she going to live with herself if the man who had tried to kill her wasn't made to pay?

She crossed the now-deserted street. Though it was just past seven-thirty, there were few lights on in the surrounding buildings. Which wasn't surprising since most of them were private medical offices.

Her footsteps rang out sharply. The little bit of snow they'd had earlier had melted, but now with nightfall, the moisture had refrozen, creating an extremely thin shield of ice. Not enough to make driving dangerous, but enough to make walking a little trickier, especially in pumps.

She headed into the parking garage. During normal business hours there was an attendant at the entrance, but the enclosure was now deserted.

As she stepped around the barrier bar, a red Beemer came down the ramp, headed for the exit. Out of habit, she reached inside her jacket to check her weapon, but then remembered she'd locked it in her trunk.

Seeing the woman behind the wheel, Beth relaxed. For the past few months, she'd done a lot of looking over her shoulder, waiting to see if Rheaume would try to stack the deck in his favor. It was just another reason that she was constantly on edge, and why she refused to take the anti-anxiety medication. And the reason she'd be armed at her next appointment despite Carmichael's office policy. There was a difference between paranoia and vigilance.

As she passed the elevator doors, she glanced at them but didn't slow. She'd managed to ride up in the one at the office two days ago, but at the moment she didn't feel like trying it again.

If the outside temperature had seemed frigid, inside the garage was even worse. She slid her gloved hands into her pockets. A few cars—a green Taurus, a blue Explorer and a white Escalade were clustered near the entrance—but the rest of the lower level had cleared out. Unfortunately, it had been full when she'd arrived, so she'd been forced to leave her car on the second level. She hiked up the ramp.

Several of the fluorescent lights overhead were out. As quickly as she looked up, she diverted her gaze from the reinforced-concrete ceiling. For some reason even in this reasonably wide-open space, she felt as if all that weight was pressing down on her, as if she'd be buried beneath it. Inhaling sharply, she forced her hands a little deeper into her pockets.

She was fine. Absolutely fine. The claustrophobia was getting better. Maybe it was resolving more slowly than she wanted, but she just needed to keep pushing herself.

Reaching the top of the incline, she spotted her red

Taurus off to the right, but instead of walking toward it, she stopped in her tracks. A white Chevy van with heavily tinted windows had been backed in next to the Taurus. Her fingers closed around the car keys in her pocket. There had been a maroon Honda in the slot earlier and quite a few empty spaces near the elevator.

She scanned the rest of the second level and, finding it deserted, studied the van again. Something just didn't feel right. With this level pretty much empty, why would the driver choose to park there? And more important, why go to the trouble of backing in?

The front seats were empty, but that didn't eliminate the possibility that someone was in the backend, waiting to roll open the side door, waiting to pull her inside when she tried to reach the driver's door of her car.

Should she bail?

And do what, though? Use her cell phone to call a cop? What if she was wrong about the van? What if in this one instance she actually had taken that downhill slide from cautious to paranoid?

If so, calling Baltimore PD would have been a bad idea. Once the cops realized she was a fed, there was very little chance it wouldn't get back to Monroe. Or that he wouldn't use it against her, claiming that the incident further demonstrated her inability to do her job.

She took a deep breath and let it out slowly. *Think.* No one had followed her here. She was certain of that. And for the past few months she'd been careful to avoid any hint of a pattern in her activities—she never took the same route, never scheduled an appointment on the same day. But all three of her sessions with Carmichael had come at the end of the day…

And then she realized if Rheaume had sent someone after her, bailing now wouldn't stop them. There would be a next time. One she might not see coming until it was too late.

Better to confront it now.

As a blast of frigid air screamed through the garage, she strode purposefully toward her car, a plan already formulated. She wasn't going to let them win—not the Monroes or the Carmichaels, and definitely not the Rabbit Rheaumes.

Keeping her eyes on the van, her thumb worked the automatic trunk release on the key fob. If anyone was in the van, they obviously were waiting until she walked between the two vehicles. Otherwise they would have already made their move.

The raised trunk would offer some protection while she grabbed her weapon. And if she was wrong, if the van was empty, she'd just get in her car and go home. Soak in a hot bath. Forget she'd nearly made a fool of herself.

She was already leaning into the trunk when she heard the nearly silent footsteps behind her. Her fingers closed around the holstered SIG-Sauer, and she had it free of leather when the sharp pop echoed. White-hot heat streaked just above her right temple.

Diving toward the side of the car, hoping to use it as cover, she brought the SIG-Sauer up, getting her first look at the shooter—a stocky male in dark clothing. She fired two quick rounds. Both slammed into his chest.

He kept coming.

A loud crack sounded. The taillight next to her shattered. Small bits of plastic exploded, some of it hitting her in the face, causing her to blink. Causing her third shot to miss.

As a bullet punctured the fender next to her, she squeezed the trigger again, this time going for a head shot.

Like a tethered pit bull hitting the end of its chain, the guy's forward momentum vanished, and for the briefest of moments it was as if both time and motion stood still. His expression changed, bloomed from one of aggression to chagrin and then to stunned disbelief.

And then time kicked in again, and he was flying backward.

Chapter Two

Beth got to her feet, her weapon trained on her attacker as she checked out the darkened garage for additional signs of danger.

Nothing.

No hint of movement or sound. But then, she hadn't heard her attacker until it was nearly too late. Where had he come from? Why hadn't she seen him sooner?

Her pulse scrambled uncontrollably. No matter how fast her lungs worked, she remained winded, gasping for air.

Keeping her weapon leveled at the body on the ground fifteen feet away, she forced herself to focus.

Part of her training had involved role-playing, learning how to survive a situation like the one she'd just been involved in, one where taking the time to weigh options could get you killed. And it was that same training she fell back on now, her attention flipping between her attacker and her surroundings.

She kicked aside the weapon he'd dropped—a .45 Smith & Wesson automatic—before closing the last few feet and getting the first clear look at his injuries. His right eye was gone.

As she reached down to check for a pulse—something she knew was a wasted action even before she did it—the warm scent of fresh blood reached up and grabbed her. Swallowing the bile that piled in her throat, she straightened.

He was younger than she'd first thought, midtwenties maybe. He wore a black ski cap pulled low over his ears. Seeing no sign of hair, she assumed his head was clean shaven. The rest of his clothing—jeans and sweatshirt—were also black.

When her gaze made it as far as his feet, she realized the reason she hadn't heard him. He wasn't wearing shoes. Who goes barefoot in November? In freezing temperatures?

Still facing him, she backed away, fumbling for the cell phone at her waist. She couldn't stop her hand from shaking, so it took several tries to disengage the phone from the clip.

After placing calls to 911 and to Bill Monroe, she sat on the bumper of her car to wait. It was unlikely that Monroe would show up. When she'd reached him, he'd been at some type of social function.

For the first time, she allowed herself to really think about what had just taken place. She'd taken a life. And no matter how prepared she'd thought she was to do it, how certain she'd been that she could live with it, she suddenly realized she might have been wrong.

Inhaling sharply, she tried to dislodge the growing tightness in her chest. She couldn't fall apart now. Deep breaths. Cleansing breaths. She'd killed a man, and there was no going back.

An hour later Beth was still sitting on the bumper of her car, but she was no longer alone. Minutes after she'd placed the 911 call, the first responding officer—a street cop—had secured the area and taken down an initial report.

Two Baltimore detectives and the crime-scene unit were the next to arrive. And less than two minutes ago, three FBI special agents from the Baltimore office had shown up. At one time she'd considered them office allies. But ever since Monroe had tagged her for termination, they'd distanced themselves from her.

It was always the office relationships that were the first to go. Next would come the stripping of security clearances. So far she'd dodged that bullet, for the same reason she still had a job—because they needed her testimony. Testimony that would carry more weight coming from a special agent whose security clearance hadn't been downgraded or revoked.

She lowered the wad of fast-food napkins she'd found in her glove box and had been pressing to the side of her head. The gash just above her right temple was a minor one, but like most head wounds, it had bled pretty profusely at first. She glanced down at her shoulder. The white silk scarf was probably a lost cause, but because the coat she wore was navy-blue wool, the bloodstain wasn't particularly noticeable and would probably clean up okay.

Her gaze returned to the three special agents and two detectives who were still conversing near the ramp. What were they discussing now? Just the shooting? Or were her coworkers eagerly explaining to the detectives that her appointment tonight had been with a shrink and not some other type of doctor?

Beth shifted her attention away from them and onto the dead man. His body remained uncovered. At least the shooter had a name now. Leon Tyber. The shoeless hit man. But even if he'd forgotten footwear, he'd remembered to wear body armor, the reason the first two shots to his chest hadn't stopped him.

He'd come prepared to take me down swiftly and effi-
ciently. But instead, I killed him.

As another sharp breeze blew through the structure, she
shivered. She wasn't really dressed to hang out in a cold
garage. Like everyone else at the scene, she was waiting
for the medical examiner to show up and release the body
for transport to the morgue. Until he did, she couldn't
move her car without destroying evidence. Of course, if
she'd been really eager to go home, she could have called
a cab and come back tomorrow to pick up her car.

Hearing footsteps, she glanced up. Special Agent Tom
Weston, a seventeen-year FBI veteran, walked over and
propped his backside next to hers. He was tall, well built.
In her early days in Baltimore, he'd been somewhat of
a mentor to her. Up until a year ago, she'd considered
him a friend.

Hands clasped in front of him, he looked over at her and
then motioned at her injured head. "Maybe you should
consider a trip to the emergency room to get that checked out."

"It's just a crease. I'm fine."

"What you are," Tom said, "is lucky."

Frowning, she refolded the napkins and rested them
against her scalp again, trying to ignore the now throbbing
headache. Tom's comment didn't surprise her. It did
however sting more than she would have expected. "What
I am is good at my job."

"I didn't mean to suggest—"

Her eyes narrowed. "Of course you didn't." But they
both knew better. Recently her accomplishments and skills
had increasingly been downplayed. "And the fact that I'm
not included in the Friday-night get-togethers doesn't mean
a damn thing, either."

Beth knew she was venturing into areas that would only serve to further damage her relationship with Weston, a man she had once held in great respect.

"You're shutting me out," she said, and glanced down; not wanting to meet his eyes, not wanting him to see how much his actions had hurt her. "I didn't expect that." She looked over at him. "I actually thought you would be the only one in the office willing to back me up."

"Damn it, Beth." Tom grimaced. "I have two kids already in college and another one starting next year. I'm not about to put my job in jeopardy."

"There's a name for that, Tom. Careerism. The practice of protecting one's career. At the cost of one's integrity."

When Tom shifted his gaze to the group of men near the ramp, Beth sensed he was looking for a reason to leave her, to rejoin the others. And at the same time she realized even if he'd been going about it very cautiously, he had been trying to be somewhat supportive. At least for tonight.

"I'm sorry, Tom. I'm not being completely fair here."

He rubbed his face, suddenly looking even more exhausted than when he'd sat. "You have nothing to apologize for." He studied her, a deep furrow between his brows. "But why didn't you come to me before going over Monroe's head?"

She balled up the bloody napkins. "Like you said, you have kids in college. I don't."

"But you had to know that you were risking your career. That Monroe wouldn't hesitate to blow you away if you said anything about his screw-up."

"He didn't give me a choice." Even she heard the edge of anger in her voice. "It was a viable lead, and he didn't assign it. And because he didn't, terrorism got another payday." Beth realized the other men were watching them now, and lowered her voice. "I took an oath to protect and defend this country," she said. "Not keep my mouth shut."

Tom nudged her shoulder with his. "You always were a damned idealist."

"So were you," she offered with a sad smile.

He nodded. "Back when I could afford to be."

"What did Monroe have to say when he called you tonight?"

"Just that I was to head up the investigation and he'd talk to you in the morning. There's nothing for you to worry about. It was obviously self-defense."

He glanced toward where the other men were still talking. This time she didn't think it was because he was looking to escape her. But then his facial expression suddenly changed, went from one of fatigue to near anger. "What in the hell is Mark Gerritsen doing here?"

Surprised to hear the name, Beth followed Tom's gaze, certain he must be mistaken. Unfortunately, he wasn't. At six-three and deadly handsome, Special Agent Gerritsen was easy to recognize even from where she sat. Currently he was talking with the other two FBI special agents and the two detectives.

She frowned. Why would the FBI's leading counterterrorism specialist have any interest in what had taken place here tonight? In a simple shooting?

Mark suddenly broke away from the other men and walked toward Tom and Beth. When he reached the dead shooter, he stopped to examine the body.

Beneath the beige trench coat, Mark Gerritsen wore a dark suit. The collar of his white oxford-cloth shirt was open, and his hair looked as if he'd plowed his fingers through it more than once.

Not so amazingly, as she watched the FBI's best-of-the-best straighten and walk toward them, her thoughts had nothing to do with national security, and everything to do with the last time they'd met. A meeting where she had come off as completely foolish and sophomoric. A meeting she was hoping he didn't recall.

But it probably hadn't been all that memorable for him. During her sixteen weeks of new recruit training, he'd been her counterterrorism instructor. There hadn't been a female in the class who hadn't been in lust with Mark Gerritsen, her included. After all, when it came to aphrodisiacs, power coupled with intellect, looks and honor was damn potent.

Back then he'd been newly divorced and had a couple of kids. Was that still the case?

Tom had stood as soon as he'd seen Gerritsen, but she waited until he reached them to get to her feet.

Tom held out his hand, his expression anything but welcoming. "Gerritsen, let me introduce—"

Mark's gaze connected with Tom's briefly before immediately shifting to Beth. "We've actually met."

It was only when he extended his hand to her that she realized she still held the bloody napkins. After quickly shoving the wad into her pocket, she shook his hand, lifting her gaze to his face at the same time.

His eyes were brown, and at the moment the brows were drawn down tight over them. There was a rawness to his features—eyes that were deep set, a nose that wasn't quite straight, a mouth that rarely smiled. But when it did, there was a dimple just to the left of it. She'd seen it on only one occasion—the one she was hoping he'd forgotten.

"I hear you had a rough night," Mark said.

"Oh, I don't know." She tried for a confident tone. "All in all, I'd say mine was better than Leon Tyber's."

Mark's lips shifted toward a smile, but it never actually appeared. He now glanced over his shoulder at the body, too. "At what point did you discover he was wearing body armor?"

"When my first two shots didn't stop him." If he was impressed, it didn't show.

"How many rounds total?" He seemed to be studying her a little too intently, and she again wondered what his interest could be in the shooting. She couldn't imagine Tyber having any connection to terrorism.

"He got off three, I fired four." She was aware that Tom still stood beside her and that there was some animosity between the two men. She wondered about its origin.

"And you think Rheaume hired him?" Mark asked.

She paused. How would he have known that? Then she realized the other agents had undoubtedly filled him in. What else had they said? "It went down like a hit." She took half a step backward. Somehow it suddenly felt as if he'd invaded her space. "Not to mention the fact that street punks don't usually carry twelve-hundred-dollar weapons and wear body armor."

"What makes you so certain it isn't linked to another case?"

"Because the Rheaume case is the only one I'm involved with." She wasn't about to elaborate on the reason that it was her only one. If he didn't already know about her current employment problems—something she figured was fairly unlikely since that kind of thing tended to get around the Bureau pretty quickly—she saw no reason to enlighten him. To make herself look worse in his eyes.

"What brings you here?" Tom asked.

Mark's mouth tightened. "Perhaps you could excuse us, Tom. I need to speak with Beth."

Those words took her by surprise. Especially since she'd assumed he was there to see one of the other agents or even Tom. What would Mark Gerritsen need to discuss with her that he wouldn't want to talk about in front of Tom Weston?

Tom glanced at her. "Are you okay here?"

What was he asking? Why did he seem so hesitant to leave her with Mark? Was it concern for her? Or was he simply worried she'd do something to make their boss look bad? And that as the senior special agent at the scene, he would somehow be held responsible?

"I'm fine." Those two words were quickly becoming her new mantra.

Mark waited to speak until after Tom walked off. "*Fine* might be an overstatement. If you haven't already had someone look at your head, maybe you should."

"Thanks for the concern, but I'm okay. And I'm curious about what would bring you here tonight."

Mark turned his back to the breeze. "I just came from trying to see a friend of yours."

Hands shoved deep into the pockets of her coat, she leaned against the car fender, even more perplexed. "What friend?"

"Rabbit Rheaume."

The name took her by surprise. "Really?" Glancing down, noticing the ripped-out knee on her pantyhose, she immediately lifted her gaze again. She wanted to look more confident, more together than she felt. "I plan to pay him a visit tomorrow. To give him the good news about Leon Tyber."

Mark stared at her. "You'll find him at the morgue."

Chapter Three

Mark followed Beth into her small bungalow. It hadn't taken much to convince her to let him bring her home. Or to control the conversation during the drive. They'd covered the recent weather and a number of other unmemorable topics. And the only time she'd brought up Rheaume's death, he'd suggested they wait until they reached her place. Her agreement had come in the form of silence.

Just inside the door, she stopped to disarm the security system and to turn on the foyer and living room lights, but then kept moving. "Make yourself comfortable. I'm going to put on some coffee."

"Sure."

As she walked on through to what he assumed was the kitchen, he didn't follow. He wanted to give her some space. Even if she wasn't displaying any of the obvious signs of distress, she was still coping with it internally. He recalled the first time he'd used lethal force, the way his hands had shaken for hours afterward. How, for nearly a week following the incident, even when he hadn't been thinking about the shooting, his hands would suddenly start to tremble again.

Turning, he checked out the living room. Though the house and neighborhood dated before the 1940s, the inside of the home had been decorated with an almost loftlike starkness. Lots of metal and wood and bright colors.

He glanced at the red chair and hassock in front of the unlit fireplace and found himself wishing he could afford the luxury of just sitting, of sharing a cup of coffee with a woman without having to interrogate her.

Unfortunately he couldn't do either of those things. He had a meeting in Boston in the morning, and in the meantime he had a job to do.

The kitchen light went on and then there was an extended stretch of silence where he was left to wonder what she was doing.

After several minutes, he finally took half a step toward the kitchen. "Can I help?"

"No," she answered in a voice that was an octave higher than usual. "That's okay. I've got it."

"How long have you lived here?"

"Three years," she said over the soft thump of a cabinet door closing. "I bought it as soon as I was assigned to the Baltimore office."

Hearing the kitchen faucet run and figuring that she'd be busy for a few minutes more at least, he stepped across the foyer and into the darkened home office. At one time the space would have been a formal dining room. Like the living room, the furnishings were also contemporary. He took off the khaki-colored trench coat and folded it over the back of the desk chair, before turning his attention to the wall of family photos.

She was the only daughter of a diplomat. Geoffrey Benedict had done stints in both France and Turkey, which accounted for Beth's proficiency in Turkish and French. And for the numerous black-and-white photos with European and Middle-Eastern backgrounds.

Though she held a degree in accounting, he suspected the FBI had been more impressed with her language skills. Since becoming a government employee, she'd added Farsi and Spanish to the list. And with the global environment out there now, that ability would only become more important as time went on.

So why was Bill Monroe so determined to terminate her? Was she really the loose gun her personnel file suggested? Unwilling to follow orders? Unable to function as part of a team? That wasn't the recruit Mark remembered.

He'd first noticed her in his class because, even at twenty-three, she'd been a standout. Not only physically but also intellectually. Her questions had demonstrated an awareness of world views that most of the other recruits had yet to recognize. She had intrigued him then. And she intrigued him now. Perhaps more than was wise.

Suddenly the overhead light went on. "Make yourself at home."

Glancing over his shoulder, he didn't miss the slight rebuff. Or that she'd taken off the coat and scarf, but didn't appear to have checked the head wound. If she had, she would have wiped away the dried blood on the side of her neck. She had dark-gray eyes and nearly black hair that was on the short side. And if anything, she was more attractive than she'd been three years ago.

"Coffee will be a few minutes," she offered as she took an additional step into the room. "Maybe while we're waiting on it, you could tell me what this is about. Why you went to see Rheaume? And why you came to see me?"

He turned and faced her. "What I'm about to say can't leave this room." He held her gaze. "You understand?"

"Okay." She crossed to the desk chair and sat, looking up at him, her hands resting palm up in her lap. She wanted to look at ease, but he sensed she wasn't.

Maybe he was making a mistake here. Several members of the task force, men he trusted, had questioned the advisability of approaching Beth Benedict. But given the situation, he didn't feel he could ignore any lead.

"Nearly four months ago, despite tight security, a canister of MX141 was taken by Harvey Thesing, a chemist who had been instrumental in its development. He not only managed to circumvent the stringent safeguards that were in place, he was also able to conceal the theft for several days."

"And what exactly is MX141?"

"The next generation chemical weapon. So deadly that exposure to the vaporized form kills in less than a minute. With other types of exposure, either to the skin or ingestion, you're looking at five minutes tops."

He grabbed the remaining chair. It didn't surprise him that she didn't know anything about MX141. Currently, because there was a very real concern of a full-scale panic should the public learn about the theft, only key members of the administration, the defense department and Mark's unit knew anything about it.

"By the time the theft was noticed, Thesing was dead and the container was missing. The assumption at the time was that the weapon had changed hands, and Thesing's buyer had decided it was cheaper to pay with a bullet than with cash."

"I'm assuming his bank account supported the theory." He nodded. "No unusual activity."

She shifted her hands in her lap, the motion drawing his gaze down. She'd removed her damaged stockings. Her legs were now bare, her skin pale and smooth and…

"Any theory on who the buyer was?"

"No. We've been looking at a number of groups, both foreign and domestic. Thesing had recently aligned himself with environmental causes."

"And that was four months ago?" Beth clarified, obviously trying to figure out the connection between what he was telling her and Rabbit Rheaume and even herself. And also possibly recognizing that for months now the terrorism alert level had remained in the elevated level, when, given the situation, it should have been much higher.

Mark straightened. "We've been chasing leads with little progress. Recently, because continued Intel hasn't picked up any mention of the theft or the weapon, we had started to theorize that Thesing may have had second thoughts and either destroyed the MX141 or possibly hidden it somewhere. That his death had been a result of his refusal to turn it over to the buyer."

Leaning forward, he propped his elbows on his knees and met her gaze. "And then just this morning I received a call from Rabbit Rheaume's attorney. Rheaume claimed to have been approached in early July by a man looking to sell MX141. In exchange for the prosecution dropping a number of charges, Rheaume would give us his identity."

Her shoulders dropped slightly. "And now Rabbit is dead?" As if she'd noticed his previous interest in her legs, she tugged at the hem of the navy-blue skirt, tucking one ankle in even more tightly behind the other.

It was a prim-and-proper pose that he suspected she'd

perfected during the years when she'd acted as her father's unofficial hostess following her mother's death.

"And you don't really think it's a coincidence. You think whoever has the chemical weapon knew Rheaume was about to give him up?"

"The timing and the way it went down certainly leaves open the possibility."

Her eyes narrowed. "How did it happen?"

"An inmate using a shiv got Rabbit in the jugular. He was dead before prison guards could get to him."

"And the inmate? Did you question him?"

"Didn't get the chance. A guard shot him." Mark clasped his hands in front of him. "Right now we're interviewing any recent visitors the inmate had, but there's only a few and none of them look promising."

Her eyes narrowed. "If it was a hit, someone would have needed to contact him to set it up, wouldn't they?"

"Sure. But it looks as if there may have been a middle man, another inmate who was involved. A go-between. Who, even if we're lucky enough to ID him, obviously isn't going to talk. At least not right away."

She nodded. "So you're hoping I can help in some way?"

"At the time of the theft and the possible contact between our unsub and Rheaume, you would have still been working the money laundering case. Any chance you saw or heard anything?"

Beth's mouth tightened briefly before she answered. "I saw and heard a lot during those eighteen months as Rabbit's assistant, but unfortunately, none of it pointed to Rabbit's involvement in the sale of any type of weapon, even assault rifles. And certainly nothing like a chemical weapon."

Obviously it wasn't what he wanted to hear. "You're certain?"

"Absolutely certain?" She hedged. "No. Of course not. Even though I was involved in most aspects of his business, I imagine there were instances where that wasn't the case. Rabbit was the cautious sort. He built himself a pretty good niche business laundering money for half a dozen mid-level drug traffickers. He wouldn't do business with large ones because they were the ones the feds were after. And he refused to take on a partner. Which is why he managed to fly under the radar for so many years and why it was so difficult to get the evidence needed to prosecute him. All that being said, though, I just can't see his having the type of contacts who would deal in chemical weapons."

She leaned back. "My guess, for what it's worth, is Rabbit somehow heard about the theft and decided to use it to his advantage."

This time when her mouth tightened, his gaze lingered on her lips for several seconds before he caught himself and forced his eyes to meet hers again. "A deal would have been contingent on the info panning out."

"Even if it didn't, he would have had some fun messing with the feds. Rabbit likes—" She broke off to correct herself. "Rabbit liked to mess with people. He really enjoyed watching them squirm. He was cruel like that."

She glanced away, her voice dropping. "One minute he'd be chatting you up, the next he'd have your face in the dirt and a gun muzzle planted against the back of your skull."

Because he'd read her file, he knew she was speaking from personal experience.

Getting to her feet, she motioned toward the kitchen. "The coffee should be ready by now. If you're in a hurry," she said over her shoulder, "I can put it in a to-go cup."

She wanted him gone. Unfortunately, there was at least one more thing he needed to discuss with her. "No. I'm not in any hurry."

After pouring two cups, she handed one to him, then retreated with the other to lean against the opposite counter. The harsh fluorescent lighting revealed the shadows beneath her eyes. She'd had a rough night, maybe a couple of rough years. Eighteen months undercover, constantly on edge, continually fearful of taking a wrong step, would have been a difficult assignment for even a seasoned agent, let alone one with just over a year's worth of experience.

Why had she been chosen for the assignment?

He set his cup on the counter. "I think there may be one possibility you haven't yet considered."

"What's that?" She blew on her coffee.

"If Rabbit Rheaume wasn't lying, if he was killed to keep him from talking… Maybe it wasn't Rabbit behind what happened to you tonight."

Something flashed briefly in her eyes. Renewed fear maybe, but then it was gone. She took a quick sip and then lowered the cup. "So you're theorizing that whoever silenced Rabbit is now trying to do the same to me? Because he believes I know something?"

"I think you have to consider the possibility. Especially given that Rabbit contacted us today and not a week from now. Why, after arranging your death, not wait to hear if Leon Tyber was successful? If he had been, there'd have been no need to contact us. To get messed up in any of this.

At least, that's my understanding. That without your testimony there was a good chance the prosecution wouldn't get a conviction."

She seemed to contemplate what he'd said for several seconds, and then just as quickly discarded it. "Thanks for the warning, but I'm putting my money on Rabbit. And even if I'm wrong, whoever your unsub is, he's not stupid. He's got to realize that if I did have any information, I would have already shared it. If not before tonight, certainly during this visit."

Looking down at her coffee, she pushed away from the cabinetry before lifting her chin, meeting his eyes. "Besides, nothing has really changed. I've been looking over my shoulder for months now. I'll just keep doing it."

Her calm composure didn't particularly surprise him. In essence, she was right. Nothing had really changed for her. "It still might be a good idea to stay with a friend for the next few days. Or maybe even your father. If you want, I could talk to Bill Monroe about a few days—"

She cut him off, her voice sharp. "I'll be fine." Her mouth briefly tightened as if she regretted her tone. "Now, if you don't mind, I'd like to get some sleep."

"That's not a bad idea. For both of us. I have an early flight tomorrow, and I'm sure after everything that's happened, you must be beat."

She remained silent. He'd been about to suggest he could sleep on her couch, an offer that, given everything he'd seen and heard to date, she wasn't likely to appreciate.

He dumped what remained of his coffee into the stainless steel sink. But when he turned back to her, something in her expression stopped him from heading for the door. "What is it?"

Beth's eyes narrowed. "Did Rabbit say he'd actually met with the seller?"

"Why?"

"There was one call." She started to bring the mug up to her lips again, but then suddenly lowered it. "It came in on July fifth. The man wouldn't give his name, insisted on talking only to Rabbit."

Mark noticed that her voice shook slightly now and that the knuckles on the hand grasping the mug were pale. As if it wasn't just the cup she was trying to hold on to, but her composure, too. It was a definite departure from her behavior of several seconds ago. As much as he would have liked to be concerned about the emotional shift, he couldn't be right now.

"Did he take the call?"

She nodded. "In his private office. Afterward, when he came out, he was in a mood and said something about having limits." She put the mug down and crossed her arms in front of her. "And that some things weren't for sale."

The fifth… The theft had occurred on the second, so the timing made it possible. And since she'd provided a date, going through the calls from that day wouldn't take much effort. But why would she find a discussion about a phone call from four months ago unsettling? Maybe when he heard it, he'd have a better understanding.

"I'll need you to listen to the recordings from that day. Tell me which—"

"There aren't any."

"What do you mean? Certainly if there was an ongoing investigation—"

"There was a problem with the phone taps. I'd just been alerted to the situation and assumed the call, the one we're talking about, was somehow connected to the problem. That my cover had been blown." She grimaced. "Which turned out to be true, but not until much later."

"But you're fairly confident now that the call wasn't related to your cover, but to something else?"

"I'm not certain, no. But looking back, recalling Rabbit's behavior, I don't think he knew until that afternoon that I was a fed. He wasn't usually the patient sort."

"You mean because he didn't confront you until later."

She offered up a wry smile. "Yeah. Because the *incident* didn't take place until later." Her emphasis on the word seemed to suggest something, but he didn't allow himself to get sidetracked.

"I assume the phone company had a trap on the line, too?"

She offered a stiff nod. "Sure. And we got a phone number. Unfortunately, it belonged to a public pay phone outside a laundromat."

He inhaled sharply. Jesus. He couldn't recall the last time he'd worked a case like this one, where he was thwarted at every turn. "I know I'm talking a long shot here, but is there any possibility that you could recognize the voice if you heard it again?"

For several seconds she continued to meet his gaze and then, tightening her arms in front of her, she closed her eyes. Her brows drew down over them, her head cocking ever so slightly to the left. As if she listened to something only she could hear.

Waiting for her response, his gaze dipped to her mouth. Her lips were softly full, the remnants of lipstick clinging to the shapely outer edges. As he watched, they parted, the tip of her tongue running along the lower one briefly before disappearing again.

His pulse had immediately accelerated as he watched, but it was several seconds before he realized that more than just his heart had been impacted. Fighting the tension in his lower body, he averted his eyes.

He found himself recalling the last time he'd reacted similarly to a woman. It had been nineteen months, three days and counting.

And because he'd allowed himself to get distracted, she was dead. It was that final memory that destroyed whatever sexual tension remained, leaving behind the cold emptiness he'd come to accept as a necessity. Because it allowed him to do his job.

When he lifted his chin, his eyes met her slightly narrowed ones. He got the oddest sensation that she somehow knew where his thoughts had gone.

She inhaled sharply, looking slightly unsettled. "Would I recognize the voice? Maybe."

LESS THAN SEVEN hours later at 4:30 a.m. Mark was in the hotel exercise room, wrapping up mile four on the treadmill while Colton Larson sat on the edge of a bench working with free weights. Because of the early hour, they had the relatively soundproof space to themselves.

A television mounted high in one corner was tuned to CNN, but the volume was turned off, the closed caption scrambling across the bottom of the screen. Mark read the story covering a congressional investigation. "Another lobbyist bites the dust."

Larson was still too focused on what they'd been talking about before, though, to show any interest in the Carson scandal.

"I can't believe you're even considering this," Larson

said. "Adding Beth Benedict to the team." The dumbbell he'd been using made a soft *thump* and *clang* as he exchanged it for a heavier one. "I'm not downplaying her language skills. Or suggesting that they aren't ones that we're in need of since Ledbetter was pulled off the team. But her background is in forensic accounting, for godsake, not counterterrorism."

"She was at the top of her class three years ago. She impressed not just me but her other instructors, too."

Larson's mouth tightened. "I'm just questioning if she's the best we can do. If one of us has to break pace to bring her up to date on four months of investigation, you're not really adding manpower, you're losing it. At least temporarily."

Mark upped the treadmill speed, lengthening his stride into a full sprint. He understood Larson's reservations because he shared a number of them. "I haven't made any kind of decision yet."

With an intense expression, Larson pumped away. Sweat collected at the end of his nose. He blew out, dislodging it. "Bill Monroe isn't an idiot. If he's limiting her to administrative duties and has her seeing a shrink, there's a reason." Larson released the twenty-pound weight and straightened. "And from what I hear, she was so spooked by getting locked in that car trunk, she can't even get on a damn elevator. You're going to have a hard time finding anyone who wants her covering their back."

Everything Larson said was true. She wasn't an ideal choice. In fact, when Mark had been working his way down the pro and con list at 3:00 a.m., the cons had been a runaway train. Her emotional health was questionable; she didn't have a background in counterterrorism; not one of his agents would be eager to work with her.

And as far as recognizing the voice on the phone that day, even if she had the ability, it wouldn't do them any good until they had a suspect in custody, and even then it was unlikely to be admissible in court. On top of all those things there was nothing to say with any certainty that the call was even related to the current situation.

In the pro column, though, she would bring something to the table that no other candidate could.

Mark adjusted the treadmill speed downward, slowing his pace. "I think you're overlooking one crucial fact. She may be the only connection we have to our unsub. If it wasn't Rabbit who hired Leon Tyber, but our unsub, there's always the possibility he'll come after her again."

"I agree. Use her as bait. But that doesn't necessarily require that she be part of the team. If the unsub wants her dead, he's just as likely to go after her here in Baltimore. Ask that she be placed under constant surveillance."

Larson was right. Mark could handle it that way, but he wouldn't. He grabbed a towel from the basket next to the door and wiped down. He'd request that Beth be added to the team this morning before leaving Baltimore.

As it had several times since he'd left her place last night, his mind drifted slightly off-topic and into more personal avenues, where he wasn't so much thinking about her as an agent but as a woman. Even during their short conversation, he'd found himself distracted more than once by her attractiveness. It seemed reasonable to assume her presence would impact at least a few members of his team in the same way.

He had just draped the towel around his neck when his cell phone went off. Even as he reached for it, he and Larson glanced toward the television, focusing on the closed caption, looking for the kind of bad news that would lead to a predawn call, but the text at the bottom of the screen still dealt with the lobbying scandal.

The ringer sounding a third time, Mark checked the number to the incoming call. It was his SAC, special agent in charge, David Daughtry.

As he listened to what Daughtry had to say, the knot in Mark's chest—the one he'd been battling recently—tightened. He sank onto the closest bench. Larson sat only a few feet away having abandoned his weights, his elbows propped on his knees as he listened.

Even from the one-sided conversation, it would be obvious to him that after months of chasing a ghost, they'd officially run out of time. The investigation had suddenly rocketed into a whole new phase. With even higher stakes.

Disconnecting less than three minutes later, Mark dragged the towel from around his neck and tossed it toward the hamper. Bellingham, North Carolina. He'd never heard of it, had no idea what larger, more-familiar city it was located near. He soon would.

When was the last time he visited a city, a town, a destination where something bad hadn't just happened? When was the last time he'd climbed onto a plane with a bathing suit and not a business suit packed in his luggage?

Larson's face had gone from flushed to pale. "It's finally happened, hasn't it?"

"Too early to be certain. Call came in just over an hour ago, requesting our assistance."

"Where?"

"Bellingham, North Carolina." Mark tried to breathe past the knot. "A high school."

Larson swiped the sweat from his face with a single hand. "How many casualties?"

Mark climbed to his feet. "Two."

Still sitting, Larson looked up in surprise, his eyes narrowing in disbelief. "Only two?"

Two casualties. Mark knew he should be relieved by the number, but somehow it didn't make any difference. Even two was too many.

Taking a deep breath, he then let it out slowly. The maneuver didn't help. The tightness in his chest was still there. "Obviously, if it was MX141, it's just a warm-up exercise."

Chapter Four

Breathing hard, Beth hefted the sledgehammer to waist level, her right hand choking down near the steel head, her left one sliding to the very end of the wooden shaft before tightening. A radio tuned to a rock station blared in the background, and construction dust floated around her. Good thing her neighbors were out of town.

The decision to take out the wall between her kitchen and the small breakfast room had been a spur-of-the-moment one when she couldn't sleep. Perhaps it was a bigger project than was sensible to take on like that, but she'd needed some kind of physical activity to block out the nonproductive thoughts that had been plaguing her since Mark's departure.

When she'd last checked it had been 4:00 a.m., but that probably had been more than an hour ago. In another thirty minutes or so, she'd need to shower and get dressed. Start psyching herself up for another round of questioning by some of Baltimore PD's finest and for a face-to-face with Bill Monroe. The first wouldn't require much in the way of preparation, but the latter would. Undoubtedly, Monroe would find some way to turn last night's attempt on her life to his advantage.

She nudged aside the two-by-four that had fallen, widening her stance once more as she studied the framing above the doorway. She'd been at the demolition for possibly three hours now and her muscles were beginning to slow even if her mind wasn't.

"Name three things—" she heaved in a breath "—that are deader than a doornail."

She'd lost track of the times she'd ticked off the first two. Leon Tyber. Rabbit Rheaume. And since it was only her testimony during Rheaume's upcoming trial that had been keeping Bill Monroe in check, her career was likely to be number three on the hit list.

Unless Mark intervened.

But that still didn't justify what she'd done. She'd intentionally misled him when she'd said she might be able to recognize the voice if she heard it again—an exaggeration born of a desperate desire to save her career. A prime example of careerism.

Her gut roiled with guilt. She'd sat there in the garage tonight with Tom, acting as if she possessed more integrity, pretending that her principles were superior to his, when in reality they weren't.

Her biceps and shoulder muscles tensed as she lifted the sledgehammer higher still, taking careful aim. She put all her weight and upper-body strength into the swing, but as soon as iron struck wood, she quickly stepped back. The loosened chunk of framing slammed to the floor, kicking up a small cloud of plaster dust.

What if Mark had known he was being manipulated? And even if he hadn't, even if he bought the idea that she might recognize the voice, would he be likely to go to Bill Monroe?

If not, her awkward attempt to save her job wasn't going to be worth squat. It would be only a matter of time before she was sent for a fitness-for-duty exam. She wouldn't be surprised to learn that Bill Monroe was already making the arrangements. Which meant that in a matter of weeks, even before Christmas rolled around, she could be out of a job.

The idea left her feeling as if she'd been sliced open, twenty feet of gut pulled out and run through a meat grinder. From the time she'd been eleven and had written to the FBI, asking for a silhouette target, she had dreamed of becoming an agent. She had worked hard, acquiring skills to give herself the all-important leg up over the competition.

And now it was very likely going to be taken away from her. Just like that. Because she'd confronted Bill Monroe. Because she'd believed the oath she'd taken to protect the American public was a sacred one—more important than anything else…even the survival of her career.

Recognizing that she'd allowed her thoughts once more to get bogged down in things she had no control over, she shifted her grip on the sledgehammer.

Maybe what she needed to worry about was how she was going to live with herself if Mark did believe her. She'd lied to a man whom she held in great respect. She was intentionally trying to use him to save her ass. Both of which made her extremely uncomfortable.

She heaved out a breath. "Let's not pull punches here. Everything about the man makes you uncomfortable." That damn intense gaze. Those probing questions. And that lean body was pretty damn hard to ignore, too. All those lovely muscles…

She suddenly realized she was about to start down yet

another wrong road, one with even less value than the previous one. What she needed to do was remain completely focused on the really important things right now.

"Name four things that are deader than a doornail…Leon. Rabbit. Your career." Ducking her head, she used her forearm to wipe sweat from her forehead. "And coming in at number four on tonight's big countdown…what's left of your integrity."

Negotiating around the debris, she raised the sledgehammer into position again, her shoulder muscles fighting to retain control.

"Name five things that are deader than a doornail…"

Here was where it got scarier. At least on a personal level. If Mark was right, if it hadn't been Rabbit behind the attempt on her life tonight, there was every possibility that she'd be number five on her own list.

When Mark had first posed the potential risk, it hadn't really unsettled her. Because it had seemed as if nothing had really changed. For four months now she'd been looking over her shoulder, believing Rheaume might try to have her killed. But now that she'd given it some more consideration, she realized that it was different. Seriously different.

As crazy as it was on a subconscious level at least, she hadn't been overly afraid of Rabbit. Because she'd survived his first attempt to kill her, she felt more confident that she would be victorious again if put to the test.

But they were no longer talking a midlevel money launderer out to get her. They were talking terrorists here. The real deal.

Definitely not a comfortable thought.

Dropping the sledgehammer, she left it standing on its

head as she stepped around the fifty-five-gallon trash can to reach the bottle of water on the counter. She tugged off the face mask, leaving it dangling around her neck.

It was as she took the first swig that the room's condition registered fully. Believing her safety glasses responsible for most of the fuzziness, she removed them. The haziness remained. And that was only the beginning. Dark electrical wires dangled from the ceiling like long tentacles, their safely capped ends of neon yellow and orange swaying slightly. Pebblelike chunks of plaster had fallen out of the lath as she'd ripped the ceiling down and now resembled gravel strewn across the old floor.

Reaching over, she turned down the radio. What in the hell had she been thinking? Starting a demolition when there was a chance that she'd have to put her house on the market? No job, therefore no money for mortgage.

But as with most things in her life right now, there obviously was no turning back.

As she reached for the sledge again, someone pounded on the front door. She glanced at the clock—5:55 a.m. Who the hell…?

Dread beginning to pool at her core, she shed the safety glasses and retrieved the .45 automatic—her home-protection weapon—from the counter.

Maybe it was just a neighbor in trouble, but she didn't think so. Given the past twelve hours, she felt fairly certain Mark had been right. That Rabbit had nothing to do with the attempt on her life. That someone had come to correct Leon Tyber's mistake.

Flicking off the safety, she pulled aside the plastic sheeting she'd used to seal the kitchen from the rest of the house and stepped into the hall. There were no lights on in this part of the house, and she left it that way, preferring not to give whoever was out there a heads-up.

She took up a precautionary position just to the right of the door and out of the direct line of fire in case the person on the other side was planning to pump a few rounds through the solid wood panel. Whoever it was had finally located the door buzzer and punched it a dozen times in rapid succession. Her already fatigued muscles contracted as if the zaps of sound were short blasts of electric current.

Taking a deep breath, she shifted her index finger from the trigger guard to the trigger. "Who is it?" she called through the door.

"Mark Gerritsen."

The sound of his voice only served to make the adrenaline kick a little faster. What would he be doing here at this time of morning? She hadn't anticipated any additional contact with him, at least not right away. As she'd shown him out last night, he'd mentioned having to catch an early flight to Boston.

"Beth?"

"Give me a sec." Still holding the automatic, she punched in the security code to the alarm system and then worked the dead bolt.

As soon as she had the door open, almost before she had time to move aside, he slipped past her, accompanied by a gust of frigid air.

He was dressed in a suit and an overcoat. If not for the fact that he was clean shaven and that he smelled of soap, shampoo and cologne, she might have questioned if he'd been to bed since she'd last seen him.

In sharp contrast to his impeccable grooming, she wore

paint-spattered, low-rise sweatpants, an old FBI T-shirt that she'd long ago cropped and a face mask clogged with construction dust. And since she hadn't bothered to brush her hair when she climbed out of bed it was matted to her skull. Not exactly how any woman wanted to be caught. Especially by an attractive, well-dressed male.

"You should try answering your phone," he offered tersely, his brows drawn down tight over his eyes.

What in the world was with him? Just because she hadn't answered her phone at an unreasonable hour, he decided to drive all the way out here at this time of morning? And then is irritated...? She frowned. Was it possible that when he hadn't been able to reach her, he'd grown concerned? She found the possibility that he might have been checking on her intriguing.

By the time she turned around again, he'd wandered as far as the kitchen doorway and was pulling aside the plastic sheeting. Before she could stop him, he ducked through.

Obviously, he expected her to follow. For a brief moment she debated staying where she was, forcing him to return to the foyer, but then decided playing power games with Mark as an adversary was stupid at best. Mostly because she was unlikely to win, and it would eat up time better spent getting ready for work.

She jerked off the face mask and then, tugging up the neck of her T-shirt almost as if she was stripping it off, she used the less dusty inside to wipe her face before following him into the kitchen. "What's going on?"

"I could ask the same thing." He glanced at her. "Is this your idea of midnight therapy?"

Midnight therapy? For the second time in a matter of minutes, she scanned the mess she'd created, recognizing how it must appear to an outsider. To Mark. As if she'd lost her mind. And maybe she had.

Screw it. He was going to think what he was going to think.

Stepping past him, she turned off the radio. "I hadn't planned to start demolition until this weekend." The lie came with surprising ease. "But physical activity helps me think."

She folded her arms across her, her forearms settling against her bare midriff. "Now what's going on?" she repeated. "I know you're not here to discuss my renovation schedule."

She saw indecision in his eyes, as if he was wondering the same thing—why in the hell he was there. Or maybe he actually had been concerned about her, but for obvious reasons was now hesitant to admit it.

"You've been assigned to the task force, and there's been a development. You need to get packed."

"I've been what?" She managed to keep her voice in check, but certainly not her thoughts.

She hadn't given any consideration to the possibility he might actually request her transfer. The most she'd anticipated was a reprieve. One that would give her some time and a shot at another investigation where she could shine in her field—in forensic accounting. Which wasn't likely to happen in a counterterrorism outfit where the other team members would have been handpicked because of their extensive knowledge of terrorist groups and activities.

"I requested your reassignment," he clarified.

In the middle of the night? Had he awakened Bill Monroe? Or someone at FBI headquarters? Normally a transfer didn't happen instantaneously, and the idea that this one had left her feeling uncertain.

Her eyes narrowed. "Why would you do that?" It didn't

surprise her that he had pull, but that he would use it to get her transferred did. What could be that urgent? Then she replayed everything in her head a second time. "You said there's been a development. What kind?"

His eyes met hers, but there was a disconnect in them that hadn't been there earlier tonight. A sense that he saw her, but that he was no longer emotionally involved with her on a human level.

So it hadn't been concern for her after all. She was caught off guard by the level of her disappointment.

"I'll fill you in on the plane. Right now you need to get cleaned up and packed."

Tightening her arms, she lifted her chin. "I think you need to know that I may have misled you somewhat about my ability to recognize the voice."

"That has nothing to do with the reason I made the request."

"Then what does?"

"Whoever wants you dead... If they sent someone after you once, they may do it again. If they do, we've got a shot at getting to them before..." Mark didn't finish the thought.

Why not finish it? What exactly had happened? And then the last pieces fell into place.

"It's happened, hasn't it?"

"Maybe. We're waiting for the FBI lab to make the confirmation. Now get dressed."

Beth shoved the gun into her waistband. At least now she knew why he hadn't finished his earlier statement. And the reason for the disconnect in his eyes. She had suddenly become a means to an end. An instrument he could use. That he could exploit.

She jerked off the mask, dropped it on the pile of rubble. "So you want to use me as bait?"

His mouth tightened. "Sweetheart, you *are* bait. I can't change that. But I fully intend to take advantage of it."

Chapter Five

Ducking because of the limited headroom, Mark walked up the tight aisle of the Cessna Citation. The pilot, a man in his early thirties, glanced up from the instrument panel. Seeing Mark, he flipped the mike away from his lips.

"We'll be taking off in the next ten to fifteen minutes. We've got some more weather coming in from the west, so the ride's going to be bumpy. You might want to grab coffee and a doughnut from the beverage center before we get in the air." He motioned to the magazine rack. "I shoved a *USA TODAY* in there somewhere, too. Help yourself."

"Thanks." After digging out the newspaper, Mark bypassed the first seat because it faced backward. He preferred to see where he was going.

Larson had followed him onboard. Still talking on a cell phone, he dropped down into the seat facing Mark's, leaving Beth five more to choose from.

She hesitated just inside the door, one hand resting on a seat back as she gave quick consideration to her options. Mark saw her gaze briefly connect with Larson as she took the seat across the aisle from Mark's.

When she and Larson had met fifteen minutes ago, he

hadn't bothered to hide his opinion of her. Or of Mark's decision to add her to the unit. She'd handled the rebuff surprisingly well, and had maintained a professional aloofness since.

It was the third time in twelve hours that she'd remained cool in the face of significant pressure. It wasn't enough to allay all his concerns about her mental fitness—he still intended to monitor her every move—but it did make him wonder if Bill Monroe might be after her for more personal reasons.

There was a slight bang and thump as the outside door was sealed and then the usual fuselage shimmy as turbo-props were revved. Because of the frigid outside temperatures, the interior was cool and would probably remain that way through much of the flight.

After buckling up, she retrieved the case notes he'd given her earlier from her briefcase. It wasn't a particularly detailed breakdown of the investigation, but it did provide the basics on the dead chemist Harvey Thesing's background and a brief recap of his known associates, including business ones past and present, friends, family and fellow tree huggers.

All of them had been interviewed at least once and several of them had received repeated visits from the task force.

Along with those notes were the ones on MX141. She'd still be at a disadvantage, but it was the best he could do. As Larson had noted, Mark couldn't afford to waste manpower bringing her completely up to speed.

Besides, ask anyone in law enforcement—being a good investigator was as much about gut instinct and reading people as it was about anything else. From what he'd seen to date, she was well equipped in both departments.

As Larson ended his call, turning off the phone before clipping it to his belt again, Mark motioned toward the refreshment center. "There's coffee and doughnuts."

Larson grimaced. It was the reaction Mark had expected from the other man.

A year ago Larson wouldn't have passed up a doughnut or two or three. That had changed after his divorce. He'd suddenly gone healthy. Not just with his eating habits but with a strict exercise regimen, too. Which wasn't easy to maintain in the midst of a major investigation.

Mark turned to Beth. "What about you? I didn't give you much of a chance to get breakfast."

She shook her head and offered a vague smile, followed by a polite "No, thanks."

Settling back, she opened up the report. She was trying to appear at ease, but she wasn't. And if he had to make a guess, he'd have said it was the plane making her that way. Had small planes always bothered her, or was it something to do with the more-recent issue of claustrophobia?

Larson rubbed his hands together. "A bit chilly in here, isn't it?" He glanced over at Beth with a too-eager smile. "You okay?"

She looked up with a frown. "Sure. Why wouldn't I be?"

"I don't know. Some people have problems with small planes. With tight, confining spaces and nothing but empty air under their asses. It's sort of like an elevator," he said, smiling, "only there're a lot more floors between you and the basement."

She offered up a bland expression. "Interesting analogy." Without waiting for a response, she went back to the report.

Despite the continued tension between them, Mark

didn't plan to interfere. He suspected Beth wouldn't appreciate it if he did. And she might as well get used to it. Most of the unit wouldn't see her as a welcome addition. If she wanted their respect, she was going to have to earn it the same way the rest of them had. With her performance.

Crosswinds made taking off tricky, but once in the air the ride smoothed out some.

"What's the status?" Mark asked. He wanted to find out what Larson had just learned, but because the pilot might overhear them, he needed to keep the conversation as oblique as possible. "Has HMRU reached the scene yet?"

Even if the FBI lab's toxicology report had yet to be completed, the Hazardous Material Response Unit would be able to do a field verification. It wouldn't be extremely accurate, but at least they'd know if it was a nerve agent that they were dealing with and not some other compound.

"They're set to arrive in Bellingham before us. If we're lucky, we'll know something by the time we're on the ground, but no promises. And if we're really lucky, the medical examiner got it all wrong."

Mark nodded. As much as he would have liked the medical examiner to have made a mistake, Mark doubted that was the case. Even medical examiners in rural areas would recognize the differences between pesticide poisoning and one caused by a nerve agent.

Mark shifted the conversation. "Any news on Becky's application?" Larson's sister was nearly nine months into the FBI's rigorous application process.

"She just heard yesterday. Starts training next month. She wanted me to thank you for writing that recommendation."

"Sure."

"Know anything about Bellingham?" Larson asked.

"I know the local airstrip is on the short size and can handle only turboprops."

Normally Mark would have obtained at least a minimal amount of information on their destination. It tended to help in determining the best approach for establishing rapport with local law enforcement.

Large urban departments tended to be better organized and their personnel to be more highly trained. He found that with them he didn't have to watch what he said. They were up-to-date on current techniques and common law enforcement acronyms and oftentimes provided excellent reports and Intel.

On the other hand, with rural departments he tended to stick to more layman-type terms. The last thing he wanted to do as an outsider was to make a local officer feel dumb and get less cooperation.

Without looking up from the MX141 report, Beth said, "Bellingham's population at the last census was eight thousand. They're mostly an agricultural community, with some light industry. Bellingham Police Department's current roster includes seven deputies who respond to calls within the city limits. Unincorporated areas are patrolled by the county sheriff's department. Statistically they're a low-crime area although they had one murder last year. The police chief is Ramsey Livengood. Given the time constraints, I wasn't able to locate anything on his credentials."

Though pleased that she'd done so well, Mark was careful to keep the smile off his face. "Anything else?"

Beth still didn't look up. "The local high school basketball team, the Bellingham Bullets, won the state championship last year and hall-of-famer center Scotty Tiles is from Bellingham."

She flipped the page on the MX141 report. "As far as accommodation there's one chain hotel located in town. It even has an on-site health spa." She glanced up, hitting Larson with a neutral expression. "Should I schedule a seaweed wrap for you?"

Larson's gaze flicked between Mark and Beth, before settling on her face. His brows dropped over his deep-set eyes and he served up a stiff smile. "Thanks. But I can make my own appointments."

"Suit yourself."

Obviously her intention had been to return the favor—to get under Larson's skin some—but she'd been smart enough not to use anything connected to the investigation. Instead she'd utilized something that Larson wouldn't willingly repeat to the rest of the team.

Even after she returned her attention to the MX141 report, Mark continued to study her. She had an almost straight nose and a determined chin with the faintest of clefts. It was a strong profile for a woman. And at the same time, her dark hair somehow managed to soften the effect, as did her lips. It was a face that Mark found arresting. And not just because the bits and pieces made a pretty picture, but because of the intelligence and the resolve he saw in her gray eyes.

She'd cost him quite a bit of sleep last night, trying to decide what to do about her. The phone call this morning had effectively resolved the issue, though. Up until then he'd been trying to factor her best interests into the equation. But with the possible tragedy in Bellingham, he could no longer afford to. It was the country's interests, its safety, that came first. Personal sacrifice was expected. She'd taken the same oath that he had.

So why did using her as bait make him so damned uneasy? Especially when she seemed onboard with it?

Out of his peripheral vision, he caught Larson watching him speculatively. As if he recognized Mark's interest was more personal than it should be. Closing his eyes, Mark rested his head against the seat back, intent on getting a couple of hours rest.

But no matter how hard he tried to concentrate on the faint drone of the engines, he was unsuccessful. As soon as his eyes had shut, another sense kicked into hyperdrive, the scent of her perfume reaching him. At first it was a seemingly subtle one—clean, slightly floral. But then as he sat there, he picked up an underlying layer, one that wasn't quite so innocent. Slightly musky. Sensual.

He found himself wondering where she placed it. Behind the ears? Did she use a finger to dab it there before dragging it slowly forward along her jawline, canting her head slightly, exposing the pale skin of her neck…an offering…

He swallowed roughly.

Or did she put it in the hollow at the base of her throat, trailing it downward across velvety skin… He recalled how she'd been dressed this morning—the toned, bare midriff bisected by a line of perspiration. Suddenly he was envisioning the perfume trail dipping even lower… His chest tightened and his respiration quickened.

Straightening in his seat, he glanced out the window.

What in the hell was wrong with him?

BELLINGHAM HIGH SCHOOL was a large brick structure, the architecture reminiscent of Ivy League colleges. The school stood four miles outside of town and on a slight bluff overlooking fertile lowlands. At this time of year only the remnants of recently harvested crops remained, waiting for spring when they would be tilled back into the black soil, adding nitrogen.

Larson and Beth had already reached the front door when Mark turned and hesitated on the wide granite steps, the duffle containing his hazmat gear almost forgotten in his hand as he studied the picturesque town in the distance. Two church spires, nearly side by side, rose up through the scrabble of bare-limbed trees and into the cloudless sky. It was the type of scene that almost made it possible to believe everything was right in the world. But it wasn't.

Since that hot July night when he'd first learned of MX141, Mark had been waiting for the call. He just never expected it to bring him to someplace like Bellingham.

To make matters worse, some higher-up, citing concerns of a public panic, had ordered the Hazardous Material Response Unit to stand down until either the FBI lab or Mark verified a credible threat.

A mixture of frustration and anger pumped through him. Only minutes ago he'd received the detailed toxicology report on his PDA. There was no longer any doubt. Whoever had acquired MX141, they'd chosen Bellingham as their first target.

The federal Hazmat Response Unit and the task force were now en route, but critical time had been wasted.

Shifting his gaze, he stared at the county road where media vans were beginning to stack up. A television cameraman had now climbed onto the roof of his vehicle, his camera briefly aimed at the front of the school. At Mark.

In a matter of hours he would have to do the impossible—compose a statement that wasn't going to send the whole nation into a panic. And at the moment he still had no idea if they were dealing with home-grown terrorists or foreign ones.

Statistically, terrorist activity within U.S. borders was more likely to be carried out by extremists. By antigovernment groups. Animal-rights activists. Abortion opponents. And hard-line environmentalists. Since, in the months prior to the theft and Thesing's murder, the chemist had aligned himself with the latter, Mark kept coming back to that possibility. Because it made the most sense.

"Gerritsen?" Larson prompted.

Turning away from the view, Mark jogged up the remaining stairs. "No guard."

He'd expected to find the site sealed up, but so far the only form of security they'd encountered was the barricades across the entrance road. They'd easily driven around them. It wouldn't be long before the media did the same.

As Beth reached for the door, Mark took her by the elbow, urging her back to the edge of the landing.

"Why only two victims?" Mark asked as he released her. "Why here?"

She didn't appear to catch on to the reason he'd dragged her out of the shadows next to the building and into the sunshine where she could be seen, could be filmed by the cameraman below.

If the attack last night had been ordered by whoever had the MX141, the more exposure she had, the more likely they were to come after her again.

"Why would a terrorist choose Bellingham?" he prompted.

"Because…" Her eyes narrowed, traveling the same path his had moments earlier, taking in the setting, the crisp, beautiful day. The sound of crows cawing as they settled over the closest field like black snow. "Because no one would anticipate it happening here. Because the terrorists would know that even if the federal government hasn't announced anything to the American people, Homeland Security and the FBI are functioning at high alert, watching the high-profile targets like the New York Stock Exchange, the New York subway system, the White House…" She paused. "And because it buys them time."

A slight breeze lifted her dark hair, a section catching on her lips, forcing her to reach up in an unsuccessful attempt to capture the strands before the wind could again. Last night her hair had appeared to be nearly black, but in the sunlight it came alive with streaks of auburn and gold. And as with most things about her, he noticed more than he should.

"What do you mean?" He fought the urge to offer assistance as she tried to restrain her hair.

She shifted her duffle bag to the opposite hand. "If this had been a large metropolitan city, local law enforcement would have been all over it. It wouldn't have taken days for us to be brought into the investigation, it would have been only hours. Because big-city PDs train for this kind of thing. Places like Bellingham don't."

She impressed him with both the analysis and the way she handled herself. "And the additional time is important because it buys them a window of opportunity, the ability to deliver a second strike almost before we're aware of the first," he added.

"So you're suggesting we should be expecting another one almost immediately?" Larson asked from just behind them.

Mark's mouth thinned. "Yeah. My guess is that we're on borrowed time here. And I think the scope of the next incident and the target will depend on if they view what happened here as a success. Or if they feel their delivery system, or some other aspect needs refinement."

He could think of one more reason that Bellingham might have been chosen, a reason that in many ways was even more sinister. What better method to destroy the last of this country's false sense of security, than to strike middle America? To demonstrate that no one was truly safe. Truly beyond harm's reach?

Larson opened the door and held it for Beth and Mark, before following them into the large, dim space. Glancing up at the fluorescent fixtures more than twelve feet overhead, Mark realized that it wasn't so much a matter of poor lighting as the dark-oak trim and brown floor tiles soaking up the illumination.

The deputy sitting on a folding, metal chair just inside the door lurched to his feet, the heavy leather of his duty belt creaking as if brand-new. It wasn't unusual for police departments in small, rural towns to hire younger officers, and this freckle-faced, rawboned kid looked as if he should still be in high school.

Mark flashed his badge. "I'm Special Agent Mark Gerritsen, and this is Special Agent Colton Larson and Special Agent Beth Benedict. I'd like to see Chief Livengood if he's available."

The young officer lifted his radio to his mouth and made the request. Lowering it, he said, "The chief will be with you in a sec."

Mark nodded. "How much of the building has been sealed off?"

"The gymnasium and the locker rooms."

"But nothing else?" He tried to maintain a conversational tone. It wasn't easy given the situation. The whole structure should have been locked down immediately, no one allowed in. Of course, to be fair to the police chief, initially he'd thought he was dealing with an accidental death and not one caused by a nerve agent. And even now the FBI's soft response to the situation was probably leading him to believe the risk was minimal. Especially after thirty-six hours.

"No, sir." The officer looked slightly nervous now, as if he'd picked up on Mark's disapproval. "But it's only the principal and her secretary who's been in, and they go straight to their offices."

"Both of them are in the building right now, though?"

"Yes…um…yes, sir."

When Mark had walked away, beyond Kid Deputy's hearing, Larson followed. "They have no idea what they're dealing with," he offered quietly. "Shouldn't you order them to evacuate?"

"After the handshake. I prefer not to cut the local police chief off at the knees unless I have to. And you're right, he doesn't have any idea what he's dealing with. Because he and everyone else has been kept in the dark."

It wasn't until he heard the edge of anger in his own voice that he fully realized just how much that infuriated him.

Larson nodded. "I suppose the only danger at this point is if there's more of the stuff on school property that hasn't been discovered."

"If any of it remains in the building, it isn't in the administrative offices. It's in areas frequented by students, the kind of victims who will make people take notice."

While Mark had been talking to the officer and then Larson, Beth had wandered to the long display case stretching along one wall. As she studied the trophies, game balls and team photos, Larson studied her with a shuttered expression. Was it possible that, as much as he might not want to, Larson found her attractive? He'd been divorced for more than a year now, which made it likely that he was dating even if Mark hadn't heard Larson mention a specific woman.

But then, Mark couldn't recall the last time he himself had gone on a second date. Usually by the end of the first one most women were clued in on the type of relationship he was offering—one without expectations on either side.

As his ex-wife had so succinctly put it, absence didn't make the heart grow fonder, it just led to apathy. And as far as he was concerned, there was too damn much of that in the world already.

Larson's eyes continued to track Beth's progress as she followed the display case, pausing every few feet.

"She definitely has a good ass."

The comment irritated Mark. "That's not all she has. She's sharp. Her analysis of why a small town had been chosen was a good one."

Frowning, Larson placed his duffle on the floor. "Maybe she's having a good day."

"Or maybe she has what it takes."

"If you think so, then you should let her watch your back. Because no one else will want her watching their's. Not when it really counts."

It was the second time Larson had brought it up, which bothered Mark to a certain extent. He knew Colton Larson well enough to know that when it really counted, Larson would do the right thing. But when Mark saw Beth's shoulders stiffen as if she'd heard the exchange, it kicked his annoyance to the next level.

"We watch each others' backs. All of us. That hasn't changed. You don't like it…"

"Whoa." Larson held his hands out, palms down. "I just meant that right now her record seems to suggest that she's—"

"Let's stay focused on what's important here. On a good day we're all coping with a hell of a lot of pressure, we don't need to be manufacturing it for each other."

Hearing Chief Ramsey Livengood's approach even before the local cop came into view at the end of the hallway, he chose not to pursue the discussion any further. Larson no doubt had finally gotten the point. They were a team, and as a team they worked together. Seamlessly. Anything short of that wasn't good enough.

The police chief strode toward them, a large manila envelope in his left hand. Mark put his age somewhere in the late fifties, and the combination of high, flat cheekbones and the slightly broad base of his nose suggested Cherokee blood.

Livengood stuck out his right hand. "First off, thanks for coming. Second, I'd appreciate it if you kept me in the loop. This is my beat, my town, you know?"

Mark offered a sharp nod. "Sure. This is Special Agent Larson and Special Agent Benedict."

Even before Livengood's fingers closed around Beth's, he was already staring at her. And then, as if remembering himself, he offered a smile. "Sorry, ma'am. I don't mean to be rude, but you remind me of someone."

"Have you made any additional statements to the press?" Mark asked, wanting to get back on point.

"No. Last one was noon yesterday. I hadn't gotten the call from the ME yet, so we were still calling it accidental." Livengood's mouth flattened. "Once we started thinking about the possibility of a homicide, I figured the less said to news types, the better."

"Good call. Is it possible for me to get a copy of the medical examiner's report, as well as the autopsy findings, any photos taken at the time the bodies were discovered, any background information you have on the victims? And any notes on the case that your men have generated?"

With a smug look, Livengood passed the envelope to Mark. "It's all there. If after you look it over, you need anything additional…"

"I'll be sure to ask," Mark finished. "Now then, I guess the next thing we need is to see where the bodies were found."

"Sure. This way."

As Mark turned to walk with Livengood, Larson and Beth fell in behind. Mark passed the envelope to Beth. "I want the autopsy report on top and the crime-scene photos just beneath. Leave everything else in the envelope for now. I'll take a look at them later." He returned his attention to Livengood. "Maybe you can give me a brief rundown."

"T. J. Duke was a local plumber and the second victim was his helper, Tee Woods. Found them Tuesday close to midnight."

"Who was the first officer on the scene?"

"I was." His expression suggested a wallet or driver's license hadn't been necessary to make the ID.

"And you had no problems with shortness of breath or rapid heart rate?" Beth asked.

Glancing over his shoulder, Livengood shook his head. "No. Nothing like that, ma'am."

The lack of symptoms suggested a significant time lapse between the death of the men and the discovery of their bodies—enough time for the MX141 to have evaporated. Given the closed environment, Mark would estimate three to four hours. Which put the exposure some time before nine o'clock.

"Any idea what they were doing in the building at that time of night?" Mark asked.

"Not for certain. T.J. had been contracted to replumb the showers over the Christmas break, so possibly he'd decided to do some preliminary work."

"But no one saw them arrive?" They were walking past darkened classrooms of empty desks.

"Kids were sent home around ten that morning. Heating system had gone down overnight and the building was too cold to keep them here. Repair people didn't have it up and running again until early afternoon." Livengood slowed. "That was one of the reasons we figured a gas leak of some sort, that the heating guys might have cut a supply line or something."

"What changed your mind?"

Livengood grimaced. "When the medical examiner saw T.J. and Tee—I guess it would have been around three or four in the morning by the time she made it here—she thought it might be some kind of insecticide poisoning. Which got us looking at it as a homicide."

Mark didn't find it surprising that the medical examiner's first thought had been pesticide poisoning. Quite a few of them acted on the nervous system. And with Bellingham being a farm community and with the law of commonality—common things occur commonly—thinking Malathion and not a nerve agent would have been the most logical on-scene assessment.

Livengood jabbed a thumb over his shoulder. "You'll find a breakdown in the packet of T.J.'s and Tee's movements."

Mark scanned the timeline Beth passed to him. At 12:00

p.m. the two men had lunch at Rosie's Lunchbox—the meat loaf special and coffee for the older victim, two slices of apple pie and a milkshake for the younger one. Scanning the rest of the report, Mark realized it was pretty much the same.

As he handed the report back to Beth, Mark kept his expression neutral. There was nothing to be gained by telling Livengood the carefully constructed time line was a waste of time. A couple of plumbers hadn't been the intended target. They'd just been unlucky enough to be in the wrong place at the wrong time.

"It would be helpful to have a list of teachers, the office staff, and anyone who does any type of maintenance for the school. And the name of the outfit that did the heating repair."

"Sure."

Crime-scene tape, stretched between a pair of folding chairs, blocked the entrance to a short hallway and a set of double doors. Livengood scraped one chair aside. "Gymnasium and locker rooms are through there. T.J. and Tee were found in the boys'."

"School was canceled for Tuesday," Mark said. "What about other activities?"

"The basketball team was supposed to have a game. It got rescheduled for tonight."

Mark turned to Beth, retrieving the crime-scene photos and the toxicology report from her. He scanned the toxicology results first, focusing in almost immediately on two key details. The older victim's pant leg and the underlying skin had come into direct contact with a significant amount of MX141 while the younger man's clothing showed no such signs, his death most likely a result of fume inhalation alone.

Mark turned his attention to the top photo.

Livengood started to back away. "I'm late for an appointment with the principal and a couple of school board members. But if you need anything…"

Mark looked up with a frown. "Where's the meeting?"

"The principal's office."

"You should hold it elsewhere." Mark said. "And the game too. Otherwise…"

He held up the photo of the two dead men. "You could have several hundred more bodies like these two."

Chapter Six

Beth studied the crime-scene photo on top of the stack. Two men, one in his early twenties and the other older, were sprawled on a ceramic-tile shower floor, vomit covering their faces and upper bodies, their pants darkened with their own urine.

Her fingers trembled as she imagined the terror they had experienced in the last minutes of their lives. The loss of muscle control. Trapped inside unresponsive bodies. Tortured by the knowledge they were dying, but unable to help themselves.

How could anyone create a chemical that killed so viciously, so quickly? And having created it, how could they fail to keep it safely locked away?

It could have been worse, though.

If the heating system hadn't broken down. If school hadn't been canceled. If the basketball playoff game hadn't been rescheduled. How many more casualties would there have been? A hundred? Several hundred?

The possibility left her shaken.

"Benedict," Mark's low voice interrupted her thoughts. She inhaled past the tightness lingering in her chest.

Flipping the photo to the bottom of the stack, she looked up, surprised to find he'd peeled off his coat, and his duffel stood open at his feet. She obviously knew what he was doing. He was stripping to put on his hazmat suit.

His long fingers dragged the necktie knot steadily downward, finally freeing the tail end. And she'd seen plenty of men remove their neckties…

So why was it that she couldn't seem to treat it like all those other times? And then she realized that it was because there was something almost erotic in the way he did it. Suggestive.

Leaving the tie hanging around his neck, he went to work on the buttons of his conservative shirt.

She desperately needed to turn her attention else-where, before he realized the type of thoughts filtering through her mind.

"Get suited up, Benedict," Mark said, glancing up this time. "If you need some help with the gear, Larson will give you a hand."

"No." She managed to slide the photos back into the envelope. "I've got it."

Even if she'd needed help, she wouldn't have accepted it. Not from Larson. She removed her weapon and dropped down, unzipping the canvas satchel. Catching some motion in her peripheral vision, she looked over at Larson. Though he was already in his hazmat suit, he'd yet to close the front zipper, the gaping material revealing his bare chest.

Beth silently cursed her stupidity, her shortsightedness. She should have known she might have to change into gear, but beneath her conservative and heavy navy-blue suit jacket, she wore a barely-there silk camisole and nothing else. No T-shirt. Not even a sports bra.

Maybe she could just leave the coat on beneath the hazmat gear. But even as she considered the option, she knew it would be a mistake. That, at the very least, she'd look stupid. Overly modest.

Larson was already out to get her. And even though the rest of the counterterrorism unit had yet to meet her face-to-face, they would have heard the same rumors—that she was seeing a shrink and wasn't a team player. So the only hope she had of getting the all-male unit to accept her was by proving the rumors wrong. By being the epitome of a team player. By not requesting any type of concession—even one as simple as asking Larson and Mark to turn their backs while she climbed into protective gear. By being "one of the guys."

She dragged the hazmat suit out of the satchel. When Mark had told her about the reassignment, she hadn't known how to feel about it. Reading the report on the plane had changed that, though. She'd joined the FBI because she wanted to make a difference, and the counterterrorism unit was her second chance, her only chance to save her career.

And a little bare skin and some personal embarrassment sure as hell weren't going to stop her.

But a simple gas mask might, she realized.

As far as defining moments went, to anyone not coping with claustrophobia, donning a mask wouldn't seem like much, but to her...

She'd rather face Leon's .45 automatic again.

She tried to calm herself with the knowledge that there was only thirty minutes of air in the preloaded breathing apparatus and that with any luck they might get what they were after even faster than that. But just surviving the thirty minutes wasn't going to be good enough. Somehow, she was going to have to make herself an active participant.

Leaving the protective gear still partially folded at her feet, she straightened and immediately started unbuttoning her jacket. The higher she got, the more her fingers wanted to stumble.

Focus, Benedict.

As she undid the last of them, she heard Larson's zipper scrape upward, the sound climbing her spine like screeching metal. The muscles in her shoulders went tense and there was little hope of relaxing them anytime soon.

Lifting her chin slightly, she shrugged out of her jacket as if she undressed with male agents on a regular basis. The hairs on her arms and her nape lifted as cooler air reached the newly exposed skin. She didn't dare look down. The action would only serve to draw attention to the situation. But she did make the mistake of glancing over as Mark was shedding his shirt. Her breathing took an emphatic, unannounced hitch.

Even in a business suit, it had been obvious that he was well built, but stripped to the waist…

He had broad shoulders and well defined biceps, the kind that would make a woman want to run her hands over them, seeking to feel their resilient strength before moving on to hard pecs and tight male nipples…

It was only when her own abs contracted hard that she managed to look away. Even after she had, keeping her actions unhurried and natural was a challenge. And then as she bent forward to retrieve her gear, the top of the camisole gapped open, her breasts swaying slightly. Maybe it was the cool air reaching them, or the sensation of silk shifting across them. Whatever it was, their tips hardened.

She quickly grabbed the gear and stepped into it. The protective suit was intentionally roomy, but getting it up over her hips without doing the usual female waggle was nearly impossible.

Out of the corner of her eye, she saw Larson strap his weapon back on and grab a handful of evidence bags. She didn't see anything to suggest that he'd noticed her predicament.

Of course, it wasn't as if she had the type of figure that made men sit up and take notice. In fact, the last man she'd dated more than two years ago had summed it up pretty well—firm straight-aways with enough curves to make the trip interesting. Not exactly how any woman wanted to be described.

"All we're looking for at this point," Mark said, "is the method of delivery. How the victims were exposed to the chemical." He looked up from what he was doing, his gaze briefly crossing with hers before shifting to Larson. She realized that even if Mark had glanced at her for a split second, he wasn't actually talking to her. And he wasn't actually expecting anything of her. As far as he was concerned, she was just a piece of frilly bait.

The idea that she was being used wasn't exactly one she was fond of, and something else had been weighing on her mind since this morning, since the reassignment. What if Baltimore PD managed to link Rabbit and Leon? What if it was discovered that it had been Rabbit behind the garage shooting? If that happened, she became useless to Mark for all intents and purposes. She had no reason to believe that he wouldn't see her as dead weight on his team.

But would he immediately cut bait, or would he give her the chance to prove herself?

The next time she looked over, Larson was grabbing his gas mask. Turning he seemed to check out Mark's progress.

"Why don't you go on in, Larson?" Mark said simply as he zipped up and reached for neoprene booties to slide over his shoes. "We'll be there in a minute."

"Sure." Larson slipped on the gas mask with practiced ease, making the adjustments to the fit, checking to be sure that the personal breathing apparatus was working correctly. As he reached for the door handle, he looked back, his eyes skimming both of them. "I'll see you in there."

As she was shoving her arms into the sleeves, her gaze connected with Mark's. Even though it lasted only a second or two, there was no denying the awareness she saw, or the strong ripple of the same springing back to life deep inside her as he continued to study her.

Or the knowledge that if even one member of the task force saw it, there would be no hope of ever gaining their acceptance—the one thing she desperately needed if there was going to be any hope of resurrecting her career.

Grabbing her weapon and mask, she started to follow Larson through the double doors. By now he'd be in the shower room and not in the gymnasium. With any luck she might have a few moments alone to deal with the mask before Mark caught up.

"Aren't you forgetting something, Benedict?"

She managed a quick rundown of equipment before turning to face him. "Such as?"

He tossed her what resembled an oversize ballpoint pen.

Catching it, she realized that it was an autoinjector. And that she had forgotten a critical item. Because she wasn't ready to meet his eyes, she rolled the preloaded dose of antidote back and forth between her fingers and thumb for several seconds as if examining the external markings on the side. "Is it atropine?"

"No." He walked toward her. "It's been specifically developed for MX141." Stopping in front of her, he shoved a second autoinjector into the lapel pocket of the suit. "Do you remember your training? Where to inject yourself if it becomes necessary?"

Her breathing had taken another intense hitch as the pen hit the bottom of the pocket over her right breast. Fighting to control it, she lifted her chin. "Upper thigh muscle."

He stepped back half a step. "Use a smooth thrust and be sure to leave it in place long enough for the antidote to be delivered. From here on out, keep both injectors on you at all times. And if not on you, then within easy reach."

She wanted to be able to tell him that she hadn't suddenly gone stupid, that she recalled most of what she'd learned in his class, and that she was aware of what they were dealing with here, but she obviously couldn't.

"Now get your mask on." He pulled on his own and like Larson made several quick adjustments.

Left with no choice, she took a subtle but fairly deep breath, dragging in as much oxygen as possible. It still wasn't enough. As soon as the mask slid completely over her head, her chest went tight and her breathing became strained. Desperate to short circuit the panic attack, she inhaled slowly and pretended to check out the rest of her gear.

Breathe, Benedict. Suck it up. You'll be out of there in less than thirty friggin' minutes.

She didn't dare glance at Mark. It would take only one look at her eyes for him to figure out what was going on inside her head.

His gloved fingers closed on her right shoulder, the contact startling her more than it normally would have.

"If you can't do it, just say so. Larson and I can handle it."

He was giving her an out. As desperate as she was to take it, she couldn't afford to.

"I don't know what you're talking about." She reached for the door. He was right on her heels through the opening, but she kept going. Weak light drizzled through the windows high on the gymnasium walls, creating a grid pattern on the floor.

Sweat beaded on her forehead and her upper lip, and a small river of it ran down her rib cage, collecting at the waist-line of her slacks. Without exposed skin, there was no way for her to tell if the cavernous space was cooler than the rest of the building, but she suspected it was. Livengood had ini-tially thought the two deaths might be related to the heating repairs done on Tuesday morning, so it seemed only reason-able that he would have ordered the heat shut off to the area.

There was no door on the boys' locker room, only an arrangement of walls providing privacy, and just beyond, a room filled with lockers and benches. The attached shower room was fairly large but not particularly well lit.

Pale-yellow tiles—a washed-out Easter egg shade—covered the walls and floors and were bisected by a wide stripe of black tile that ran horizontally around the room about four feet above the floor. A dozen showerheads lined three of the walls.

As Larson looked up from where he was examining the central drain, Beth turned to check out the fourth wall where someone had used black paint and stencils to paint Go Billingham Bullets. Having managed to get her breath-ing somewhat under control, she tried to focus on what they were looking for.

Mark squatted opposite Larson. "Did you find some-thing?"

As Larson shook his head, Mark got back to his feet and immediately moved to the farthest corner where he seemed to study the vent in the center of the ceiling.

Noticing Mark's interest, Larson left the drain cover off and, straightening, backed away to get a better perspective. "Looks like an air return and not a vent."

"It's recently been removed."

"There was a crew working on the heating system that morning," Larson suggested. "They could have done it."

"But why mess with a return vent if the furnace wasn't working?"

"I'll grab the ladder," Larson said.

Shifting to one side, Beth allowed Larson past her, then turned her attention back to the room. Even if she wasn't all that sure what she was looking for, there weren't that many places to search. Besides the vent overhead and the drain, the showerheads appeared to be the only other possibility.

She walked to the closest of them and peered up at it the best she could. Protective suits were not only hot and airless, even the best ones tended to distort things some and to mess with the field of vision.

Mark walked toward her. "What do you see?"

"There was a toolbox in one of the photos. As if they were planning to take something apart."

Reaching up, she tried loosening the connection between the head and the stub pipe. "I'm not a plumber, but the first thing I do when I have to work on any type of plumbing is check the water pressure."

When the showerhead didn't budge, she moved counterclockwise to the next one, immediately closing her hand around the connection, the thick neoprene gloves making it easier to get a firm, nonskid grip.

She was working on the assumption that if any of them had been removed recently, they might be only hand-tight.

"MX141 was found—" She broke off, suddenly feeling somewhat winded. After taking a deep breath, she continued. "The right pant leg of the older victim, of T. J. Duke, came into contact with heavy concentrations of MX141. If he'd turned on one of the showers without paying attention to where the head was directed, that could explain…"

She gritted her teeth as she tried the third one. *Please let the damn thing turn. Let me have contributed. And let me get the hell out of here.* But like the other two it was on tight.

Stepping past her, Mark reached for the next one in line. It turned readily in his grasp.

Chapter Seven

Mark removed the showerhead cautiously. Adrenaline had already begun to spread through him, his muscles contracting, his respiration quickening ever so slightly. He'd long ago come to accept that he was a junkie when it came to excitement, to pushing the limits.

As he started to lower the showerhead, an inch-long cylinder constructed of what looked to be some type of metal mesh dropped from inside the stub pipe.

Despite the thick gloves, he managed to catch it in his free hand. After passing the showerhead to Beth, he examined the cylinder.

The lower edges appeared to be covered in solder remnants, as if the cylinder's end had been sealed closed at one time.

What in the hell was he looking at? Some type of filtering device or an ingenious and low-tech method to deliver MX141?

Mark glanced over at Beth who was busy checking out the showerhead he'd handed her. The room hadn't offered all that many options, so he hadn't been surprised when she'd gone for the first showerhead. What had impressed him was the way she'd managed to pull herself together, effectively dealing with her personal demons when it had become crucial.

"Do you see anything that shouldn't be there?"

"There's a circular piece of screening and what looks like red neoprene or latex." She tipped the threaded connection to catch the light better. "The mesh could be legit, some kind of filter, but the bits of neoprene or latex definitely aren't."

Mark passed the cylinder to her. "What about that?"

She rolled it around on her palm for several seconds. "The construction is too crude to be manufactured." Picking it up, she held it between her index finger and thumb as she checked out the open ends. "Without using calipers to get an exact measurement, I'd say the diameter matches that of the circular screen, as if the two were originally soldered together."

Her eyes narrowed. "If it was soldered together, creating a type of miniature cage, that was then filled with a neoprene balloon loaded with MX141... When the water was turned on, the pressure alone would have been enough to rupture the neoprene."

Mark looked around as Larson returned with the ladder. "Go ahead and check out the return vent, but I think we've found what we came for."

Less than five minutes later they were changing out of the protective gear. As Mark pulled on his jacket, he glanced over and found that Beth was already dressed and Larson wasn't far behind.

"Benedict, you're with me. We'll sweep the building to be sure it's been evacuated and catch up to Livengood to get that list. Larson, locate the main shut-off valve for the water and close it. Do the same with the hot-water tank. I assume the devices weren't just planted in the boys' showers, that there are other ones that haven't been set off yet. If water gets to any of them…"

Larson nodded, his expression grim as he hurriedly swung the chair with the crime-scene tape back in front of the gymnasium doors to block them.

As all three of them hurried toward the front of the building, Mark ran down the mental list of things that needed to be handled immediately to maintain public safety.

He glanced at Larson. "When you have the water shut down, contact the Hazmat Response Unit and give them a heads-up on what we've found and pin them down on their ETA. For now you'll be working with them, collecting any additional devices."

"Got it," Larson said before leaving to locate the water valve.

Beth's cell phone went off. Without breaking stride, she jerked it from her waistband and checked the screen.

When she hesitated to answer it, he wondered if it was because he was there. "If you need to take that…"

With a slight shake of her head, she clipped the phone to her waistband again. "It can wait."

"You undoubtedly need to make a few phone calls, tell family and friends where you are."

Her only response to the statement was to adjust her jacket to cover the phone.

He actually knew very little about her personal life. Which wasn't so surprising given that less than twenty-four hours ago there'd been no reason for him to. And even now there were certain aspects he technically didn't need to be aware of, but those were the very ones that made him the most curious.

Was she currently seeing anyone?

Until the first week of July, she'd been undercover. In his experience, even if she'd been involved with someone when she'd been assigned to the Rheaume investigation, few relationships managed to survive eighteen months with little or no contact.

But what about the past four months?

There hadn't been any obvious signs at her place to suggest she'd recently hooked up with someone. No framed photos on the mantel. No extra coffee mug in the sink or toilet seat left up. Of course that didn't necessarily mean she wasn't involved. In fact, other than the old family photos hanging in her office, the place hadn't revealed much about her as a woman.

But then, his condo said even less about him. Or did it? Perhaps it was exactly the opposite. Maybe the futon in the middle of the living room where he'd slept most nights when he was home, the large coffee table loaded with terrorism reports, the fifty-two inch television and the king-size bed that only got used when he brought home a date, pretty much said everything about him.

It had been four years since his divorce, and he still hadn't gotten around to really furnishing the condo. The weekends and holidays when he had his daughters he took them to the lake cabin. Because they liked it there, and because it was the one place where he seemed to be able to block out what he did on the days when he didn't have them.

As he'd done often over the past few years, he tried to avoid adding up the days and weeks since he'd seen them last. Was it six or seven weekends now?

Looking to shift his thoughts away from his shortcomings, Mark glanced over at Beth. Her dark hair had been smooth this morning, but now curled at her temples where perspiration had dampened it. The bullet graze was also more visible. Back there in the showers, she'd surprised him. Where had a woman with a privileged upbringing, a diplomat's daughter, learned about plumbing and swinging a sledgehammer?

Maybe it was time to find out.

"Tearing out walls and taking apart plumbing. Where did that come from?"

"My grandfather was always doing something around the house. I spent a lot of time with them as I was growing up, and there wasn't much I could do when I was there, so he'd let me help him. Taught me things." She glanced over at Mark. "And then during college, I did some community work. Inner-city revitalization. Habitat for Humanity."

When her mouth tightened again and she abruptly changed the subject, he wondered if she felt she'd divulged too much about herself. And if it had been the months undercover that had made her so cautious with personal information or if, like him, it was just part of who she was.

They'd reached the administrative offices and did a quick search to be certain no one remained. They met in the hall again seconds later.

"The device we just found," Beth said as they headed for the front entrance. "Obviously it's something you haven't come across before."

"No. And I had hoped retrieving it would at least tell us if we're dealing with a foreign or domestic threat."

"But it didn't," she supplied.

"Unfortunately, no. Choosing Bellingham and not a

large city like Los Angeles or Chicago is the only break we've had so far."

There was no need to spell it out. She was already aware of the advantages of an incident occurring in a small, somewhat isolated area of the country where there were a limited number of motels and restaurants and modes of transportation. And where an outsider was more likely to be noticed. The person or people they hunted would have undoubtedly crossed paths with at least one of Bellingham's eight thousand residents.

He just needed to find that one citizen.

"The rest of the unit will arrive by two, and I'll be requesting additional agents to help with the investigation. It's unlikely that Bellingham's police station has a space large enough to handle that many. You mentioned a motel out on the highway. If they have a spa, they probably have meeting rooms. And we'll need thirty motel rooms to start with."

He'd already mapped out who would be handling which aspect of the investigation. He knew his men, knew their strengths and liked to utilize them fully. The trick was going to be finding something to keep Beth busy once she'd made all the arrangements he'd just assigned her.

"Livengood will want in on the investigation," Mark said. "And we need him. Like he said, this is his beat." He glanced over at her. "As the liaison, you'll be expected to keep him in the loop."

Seeing her shoulders tense, he knew she wasn't happy about the assignment. He hadn't expected her to be.

"Look, Benedict, you did better than I expected this morning. But both of us know you were struggling back there and that it could have gone either way. And even if that wasn't the case, even if I believed you were ready to

be out in the field—which I don't—I'd have to put someone working with you."

"To protect me? Because you believe last night's
shooting makes me a target?"

"Maybe it does and maybe it doesn't. But until I know
for certain, you'll be working the command center. Got it?"

She didn't break stride. "Got it. But if that wasn't the
case, if it turns out that Rabbit and not some terrorist hired
Leon, will I still be riding a desk?"

They were still thirty-five feet from the front entrance,
but, wrapping his fingers loosely around her wrist, he
forced her to stop and face him. She immediately stiffened
at the unexpected contact, her chin popping up and her gray
eyes meeting his.

He'd planned to tell her that he was a fair man. That if
it turned out she wasn't at risk, then of course he would be
utilizing her in the field.

But as her dark hair slid back, exposing her throat, his
thoughts derailed. His gaze followed the pale skin
downward, his fingers tightening around her wrist,
enough that he could feel her pulse slamming hard
against the pads of his fingers. Could feel a similar throb
in his own veins.

And then he was recalling the silky thing she wore
beneath the heavy jacket, the way that when she'd changed
out of the hazmat gear moments ago, perspiration had
glued it to her rib cage and toned abdomen. To her breasts.
Before he could stop himself, he was imagining what it
would be like to touch her in all those places.

Suddenly remembering himself, he let her go and even
stepped back half a pace, eager to put some space and
sanity between them.

"Sorry," he offered. He could only imagine what she must be thinking.

Crossing her arms, she met his gaze. "I'm asking you to give me a shot. I want a chance to prove myself."

"For the record, I think Bill Monroe is full of crap."

She offered a sharp nod of understanding.

Both of them looked over as the front door suddenly opened, sunlight briefly cutting the gloom of the unlit hallway. They were too far away for Mark to tell much about the first man who stepped inside. But when he saw the television camera balanced on the shoulder of a more burly man, he realized the media had found their way around the unguarded barricades.

"Why in the hell was that door unlocked? And where's Kid Deputy?" Mark glanced down the hall, hoping to see the local cop. Or even Livengood.

Having spotted Mark and Beth, the reporter started toward them.

"How do you want to handle this?" she asked.

Mark frowned. "To be honest, the last thing I want to do right now is give a damn statement. Or play school bouncer, for that matter, but ejecting these two will be easier before a dozen of their colleagues show up. And as far as a statement is concerned, I don't see that I have much choice now. That's one bell that can't be unrung."

Reaching for his badge, he walked toward the two men. "Sir. The building is off-limits. You'll have to leave immediately."

As if he hadn't heard Mark, the reporter, dressed in dark slacks and a blue oxford shirt with the sleeves rolled back, continued to stride toward them. Without looking over his shoulder, he motioned for his cameraman to roll tape. "Is it true that the two victims didn't die of pesticide poisoning, that—"

"Sir," Mark tried again and this time held up his badge. "As a federal agent, I'm ordering you to leave this building. Now! Otherwise I'll have you arrested for impeding an investigation."

The reporter again ignored the request.

Mark was taken off guard when Beth suddenly swore. "We've got even bigger problems than these two. What if Kid Deputy didn't just wander away? What if he went looking for a restroom or a drink of water? If Larson doesn't have all the water shut off yet and the wrong faucet gets turned on…"

Mark knew she was right. That things could easily go from in-the-toilet to in-the-sewer in the next few seconds.

When Beth suddenly turned and plunged toward the closest restroom, one they'd just passed seconds earlier, he wanted to go after her, but his first priority was to protect the public. Even if they were undeserving pricks like these two.

Once he had these two out of here, he could catch up to her. She had the autoinjectors, knew how to use them. But even the chemist who'd developed the antidote had no idea just how effective it was. It had never been tested on a human being.

The reporter shoved the mike in Mark's face. "Why would the FBI get involved in the poisoning of two men?"

Barely retaining his temper, Mark sidestepped the reporter, grabbing the cameraman by the back of his sweatshirt instead and manhandling him toward the front door. It was a well-known fact that a television reporter was dead in the water unless film was rolling. "You are placing yourself in danger, sir."

He had the cameraman more than halfway to the exit when it was jerked open again. This time it was held wide as more than a dozen men and women plowed in, jostling and elbowing like a bunch of third-graders.

Not slowing and with his fingers twisting even tighter into the neck of the cameraman's sweatshirt, Mark pushed forward into the crowd, his badge held where everyone could get a good look at it.

"Listen up, people! I'm Special Agent Mark Gerritsen with the FBI. I'll have a statement for all of you shortly. If anyone prefers not to cooperate and move back outside, they will be arrested."

Most promptly turned toward the door to comply. Of course there were always a few who didn't.

Appearing at that moment, Larson grabbed one of them. "Move it!" Larson shot a look at Mark. "Where the hell is Benedict? Is she already outside?"

Mark ignored the question. "Did you get the water cut off?"

"The main valve, yes. I was on my way to take care of the hot water tank."

Mark released the man he held. "You handle this, I'll get the tank. And Benedict."

He rushed back the way she'd gone. Even with the water turned off, there might still be enough residual pressure in the lines to set off a device.

Chapter Eight

As Beth jerked open the door, Kid Deputy's unfazed gaze briefly met hers in the mirror above the sink, but then he immediately looked down and reached for the faucet handle. "You shouldn't be in here."

"Don't touch that!" But he already had, his fingers now choking the faucet handle. "If you turn on that water, we could both be killed."

His eyes popped up, meeting hers in the mirror again. He'd finally recognized that she hadn't just stumbled into the wrong bathroom. That she was there for a reason. To stop him from turning on the water.

She had the autoinjector out of her pocket and the cap off. If it happened… If he turned the handle and it set off another device, she'd inject herself first and then go after him.

But how much time did she have before she became incapacitated? Enough to reach him with the second autoinjector?

"Just let go of it," she said as calmly as she could, but even she heard the fear in her voice.

Mutely he looked down at the hand still covering the handle, almost as if it had become something foreign.

Something that shouldn't be attached to the end of his forearm. Why wasn't he releasing it?

Someone opened the door behind her. She didn't glance to see who it was. It wasn't until Mark's image was briefly reflected in the mirror next to the deputy's that she was certain who it was. The kid's color wasn't so good—his freckles more pronounced, his lips looking pale and dry in the harsh fluorescent lighting.

"It's going to be okay," she said evenly. When the kid looked over at her, she offered a confirming nod and tried flashing a smile to go with it. "Just take it easy. Just open your hand carefully."

Slowly he released the handle.

It was only then that she allowed herself to briefly focus on Mark's face in the mirror. She'd planned to play it loose, pretend that she'd been unaffected by the past few seconds, but as soon as their gazes connected in the mirror, she realized she'd never be able to pull it off. That her own coloring was nearly as bad as the kid's and that the hand holding the autoinjector was shaking. She recapped and slid the antidote into her pocket.

"You okay?" he asked quietly, taking another step into the space. Was the concern she saw on his face for the situation or for her? Or both? And what did it matter at the moment which it was?

Closing her eyes for the first time since she'd stepped into the bathroom, she took a deep breath and let it out slowly.

"Beth?"

It was only as she opened her eyes that the use of her first name really registered with her. "I'm okay." Avoiding Mark's gaze, she glanced at the kid, noticing that he hadn't moved.

"Did you get the press handled?" she asked, attempting to achieve a casualness that she still wasn't feeling.

"Larson's taking care of it."

"That's good." Reaching out, she wrapped a hand around Kid Deputy's upper arm. "Come on. Let's get you out of here."

TWENTY MINUTES after walking out of the school, Mark sat in the back of the rental SUV. Even though Livengood's men had cleared the school grounds of media, the reporters hadn't gone far and were now camped out on the road.

Waiting for him.

Mark scanned the carefully worded and brief statement again. The media wasn't going to find it particularly satisfactory, but that really wasn't his goal at the moment.

For now he just needed to give them something, and at the same time soft-sell the situation. Not because he felt comfortable with that approach, but because those were his orders. And because, as much as he didn't like misleading the public, it was probably in their best interest.

With no idea who they were dealing with, whether it was a domestic or foreign threat, there was no way to make even an educated guess about the next possible target. Or if the same delivery method would be used. So what in the hell good would it do to warn people about a danger that they couldn't hope to protect themselves against? How could you tell a whole nation that simply turning on a faucet could kill them?

Feeling completely exhausted and at the same time frustrated, he ran a hand over his face, trying to clear those thoughts from his mind. What he needed right now was a cup of strong coffee and to have the next fifteen minutes behind him. Once he'd made the statement, he could get back to the more important work—hunting down the people who had done this.

Looking through the windshield, he spotted both Larson and Beth. Larson was talking with two of Livengood's officers, and Beth was still on her cell phone, probably making motel and meeting-space arrangements.

As he watched, she paced to the edge of the parking lot, her stride somewhat aggressive, but he couldn't find fault with the way her ass moved. Or the way he liked watching it.

Back there in the bathroom, he'd called her by her first name. So, when was it that he'd stopped thinking of her as Benedict? Stopped seeing her strictly as another member of the unit?

Mark rubbed his forehead. It couldn't happen again. If she was to be accepted by the other agents in the unit, he couldn't afford to treat her any differently. Despite the fact that in two very key ways she was different from the rest of them. She was female and someone had tried to kill her seventeen hours ago.

And as bad as it sounded, he needed to pray that they'd try again.

Because in the long run, even though it put her at risk, it might possibly save countless lives.

Acceptable casualties. He wondered who'd coined the friggin' phrase. It damn sure hadn't been someone with a gun leveled at his head. Or the head of someone he cared about.

There were aspects of his job that he truly despised. And what he was about to do to Beth—pinning a bull's-eye to her chest—was definitely one of them.

Showtime, he thought with harsh resignation. As he

climbed out, he grabbed his suit jacket and pulled it on. Beth ended the phone call and, turning back, spotted him.

The wind had picked up enough that it now harvested the last of the fall foliage, sending those leaves and the ones already on the ground rushing past her and toward the front of the school.

Clipping the phone to her waistband, she headed back toward him. When she was close enough, she said, "The motel is in the midst of renovations, so all I could reserve were nineteen rooms. No problem with the meeting space, though. Or with providing food."

He started to replace the tie he'd taken off earlier, then decided against it and tossed it into the back seat instead. "We'll still need more rooms. See if there is anything close by."

"Already did. There's a bed-and-breakfast almost across the street and one a few miles down the road. They're holding whatever rooms they have available and they're willing to accept a discounted rate, but there's a three-night minimum and I couldn't get them to budge."

"That's not a problem. At least some of us will be here longer than that." He glanced down at the speech a final time before pitching the pad onto the back seat with the tie. He wanted to keep it relaxed and flowing, make the press believe that they didn't have a lot of answers yet.

"Come on, Benedict," he said, and motioned with his head. "My job is to give them a white-bread version of what happened here, and yours is to be as conspicuous as possible standing next to me."

IN A MATTER OF HOURS the motel meeting room had morphed into a command center for Mark's eleven-member team and the seventeen additional agents who had arrived since this morning. Because the recently remodeled space smelled heavily of fresh paint and new carpet, a pair of exterior doors leading to the unfinished pool deck had been propped open.

As the night had cooled down into the forties, so had the room. Which wasn't a bad thing since the frigid temperature along with an overload of caffeine were at least partly responsible for keeping them all functioning.

It was after 10:30 p.m. when Mark placed his laptop on the table closest to the open doors. He'd just come from a meeting with the medical examiner, the last in a long line of interviews.

After shedding his coat, he dropped into a chair and flicked on the computer. As he waited for it to boot up, he caught sight of Beth standing next to a table across the room and in deep conversation with Travis Mickels and Scott Duzenberry, both his agents, and Jenny Springer, a veteran agent and an information bloodhound on loan from the Atlanta field office. He'd worked with Springer before, had always found her to be both competent and diligent.

Even though he'd had to be in and out all day, he hadn't been overly concerned about Beth's safety. As long as she was surrounded by three or four agents, he didn't expect the unsub to go after her. He still had asked Jenny Springer to keep an eye on Beth, though. To make sure that she was never left alone.

When he'd asked about Beth's investigative skills, Jenny had been reasonably complimentary—which for Jenny was highly unusual. Given Jenny's remarks and the way Beth had handled herself at the school this morning and during the noon press statement, he wondered if somewhere along the line she had stepped on the wrong toes. Either Bill Monroe's or the toes of someone even higher up the food chain. She wouldn't be the first agent to find herself in that position. Or once in it, the target of an unfair and unjustified witch hunt.

So, what was he going to do if he found out that was the case? Was he going to stand by and do nothing? Or get involved and in the process place his own career on the line?

Almost as if she'd felt that she was being watched, Beth's eyes lifted, connecting with his. Maybe it was only the lighting, but she looked tired. She couldn't have gotten much sleep last night and today had been a tough one for all of them. And on top of that, she was having to cope with the reassignment and suddenly finding herself a possible target. All in all, given the pressure, though, she appeared to be holding up okay.

She suddenly broke eye contact and, stepping back half a step from the group, grabbed her cell phone and twisted away. As she had earlier in the day, she checked the screen and then reclipped it unanswered to her waist.

Was it the same caller?

As she rejoined the group, she shot a glance across the room, but avoided his gaze. He got the impression that it was intentional, that she was ducking him for some reason, but he couldn't imagine why. But then, maybe he was reading too much into absolutely nothing.

Mark refocused his attention to the computer screen and the reports he needed to compose.

When his cell phone went off several seconds later, he didn't hesitate to answer.

"Special Agent Gerritsen, this is Geoffrey Benedict." The booming voice on the other end wasn't a familiar one but the name certainly was. Why would Beth's father be calling him?

"Yes, sir, Mr. Benedict. What can I do for you?"

"I'm sorry to disturb you, especially at this time of night, but I've been trying to get in touch with my daughter. I understand from Bill Monroe that she's been reassigned and is now working with you."

"Yes, sir. As of this morning." Mark split his attention between the phone call and the computer screen. "Have you tried calling her cell phone?"

"Yes. I've left messages."

Were those the phone calls that she hadn't taken, then? But why wouldn't she want to talk to her father?

"She's been quite busy," Mark supplied. "We all have been. Is there some kind of emergency, sir?"

Geoffrey Benedict cleared his throat. "No. I don't suppose it's an emergency." The retired diplomat's voice faded some, sounding older and maybe a little less certain. "Bill assured me that he had made sure you were aware of my daughter's current situation."

"Mr. Benedict, as I said before, we're in the midst of an investigation."

"Could you at least tell me how long she'll be reassigned there with you?"

"You'll need to take that up with her, sir. I'm sure if you've left messages, she'll contact you as soon as possible."

The silence was especially heavy this time as Mark waited, and then, "Is there any possibility that I might speak with her now? I mean, if she's there with you?"

Mark glanced to where Beth and the rest of the group clustered around a computer screen, discussing some aspect of the investigation. If she hadn't returned the calls, there was undoubtedly a reason, and Mark had no right to intrude into her personal life.

"No, sir. I'm sorry. She isn't available. But I'll make sure she gets your message."

He was still frowning when Larson found him several minutes later.

Because Larson had nearly as much experience with counterterrorism as Mark, he always made a point of reviewing developments with him. They'd talked several times over the past nine hours, but it was the first time they'd been in the same room together since this morning.

"So, what's the status?" Mark asked.

Larson grabbed a chair and sat, placing his coffee cup on the table. "The Hazmat Response Unit has checked every bit of the plumbing, and they'll be starting the room-by-room search in the morning, but so far they've found only one additional device and it was in the boys' shower room."

Why just the boys' shower room? Why not the girls', too? Because there was some kind of interruption?

"The time frame for when the chemical could have been placed has been narrowed some," Mark said, "to between 10:00 p.m. on Monday night and Tuesday night when our vics showed up. Which still leaves a sizable window of opportunity."

Mark ran a hand through his hair. "The heating repair crew has been interviewed. Not one of them saw anything unusual. Springer and Beth are running more-detailed background checks on them and on the school faculty. Maybe they'll turn up a connection with an extremist group."

"So you think it's more likely a domestic situation and not a foreign one?" Larson asked.

"I'm not eliminating anything, but it seems to be

shaping up that way. After nearly a hundred interviews, we've got nothing. No eyewitness that can put a stranger in that school or anywhere else in town. So either our unsub is able to blend in or he's local."

After four months and two more deaths, it didn't feel as if they'd gained much ground. And in the back of his head, he couldn't ignore the similarities to another case. It had been nearly seven years since the first anthrax-tainted letter arrived in Florida. After countless man hours and a multi-agency investigation, no arrest had been made. And while the investigation was ongoing, there were fewer agents working it now.

Mark booted down the computer. "We've pretty well covered local businesses and have moved on to the charge slips on self-service gas pumps, but I bet we won't find anything there, either." He was beat. All of his people were quickly becoming that way. He couldn't afford for them to burn out too soon.

"There's not much more to be done tonight," Mark said. "Maybe you should get some sleep."

As Larson got to his feet slowly, he motioned with his head. "How's Benedict doing?"

"Fine." Mark had noticed Larson watching her closely several times.

"So no fallout from the press statement? No attempts to get to her?"

"No. But then, she's been under constant surveillance. Not exactly an easy target to hit."

"And whose watchful eyes will be on her tonight?" Larson asked, but it was plain in his tone that he already knew.

"She's my responsibility," Mark said. "So she's in the room next to mine."

Larson's mouth tightened, but he obviously knew enough not to say what he was thinking.

As Larson left, Mark grabbed a cup of coffee and walked outside to clear his head. Even though the pool appeared to be mostly complete, bright-orange mesh fencing kept people from getting too close.

Several large pines stood between the pool and the building, the breeze sighing in their branches. Keeping to their shadows, Mark wandered twenty-feet from the door before turning and checking out the lit interior. The room was still filled with agents, Beth among them, but one or two agents were beginning to gather up their laptops and briefcases, exchanging good-nights. Possibly making plans to meet for breakfast. A few would hook up for drinks in someone's room before turning in. Perhaps catch the end of a televised basketball game.

As he was watching, Beth turned to Scott Duzenberry and first said something and then smiled. At least some members of the team seemed to be accepting her well enough. Mark knew what Larson had wanted to say. That Mark shouldn't feel any more responsible for Beth than he did for any other agent assigned to the unit. Nineteen months ago, when Nidia Turner had been killed, he'd blamed himself. Still blamed himself for sending her into the situation that day.

When his phone went off, he unclipped it, but this time checked the caller ID. Even when he recognized his ex-wife's phone number, he debated taking the call. But he did. Because in the back of his mind he was always worried that something had happened to one of his daughters, to Gracie or Addison.

"Hi."

There was a pause on the other end, long enough that Mark started to grow uneasy. After setting the cup of coffee down on the window ledge in front of him, he turned his back to the window. "Is everything okay, Traci?"

"Yeah." She sounded tired or worried. He couldn't tell which. Her moods weren't really his responsibility anymore, but some habits were harder than others to break. "I just needed to know what time you were going to pick up the girls tomorrow."

He ran a hand through his hair. "Look, Traci. I'm not going to be able to make it."

There was a longer silence this time. "I can't believe you're doing this to the girls again. Not after what Gracie went through the last time."

"I'm sorry. Obviously it can't be helped."

"It never can be. Have you noticed that?" Her sharp exhale buffeted the receiver. "They're your children, Mark. It wasn't immaculate conception. You were there when they were conceived. And even managed to be there when they were born. But sometimes it feels as if that was the last time you were there for any of us."

It was an old argument. And tonight of all nights he wasn't up to going over it yet again. "The divorce was your decision, Traci. Not mine."

"You left us long before I ever contacted the attorney."

"I had a job to do."

"And you had a family, too."

"I know," he said quietly. "Do you want me to talk to Gracie? Maybe if she heard it from me it would be easier."

"No. I'd rather not tell her tonight. She's got a test in the morning, and I don't want her thinking about…"

"What if I call back tomorrow? About the time I would

normally be picking them up? I can explain. Maybe that way she wouldn't worry so much."

"Don't bother. I'll tell her when I pick her up," Traci said, anger creeping into her tone again.

"It's not a bother. And I think it might help her—"

"Having you around more often is what would help her. Not getting a phone call telling her why you can't show up. Again."

"Look. Just because I can't be there doesn't mean I'm not concerned."

She'd never been able to understand that the job he did, he did partly for his girls. Because he wanted them to feel safe at night and not afraid. Because he didn't want their futures to include another 9/11. All she'd ever been able to see is that it took him away from them.

"Do you have plans?" he asked, calmly. "Do you want me to call my dad? See if he can keep them?"

"I don't think that's a good idea."

The words and even the tone of her voice struck an uncomfortable chord within him. Traci had often dropped the girls off at his dad's. What was different about this time? Had something happened recently while they were there? Had his father forgotten about Gracie's peanut allergy?

Or was Traci just trying to make things harder on him?

"Why wouldn't it be a good idea?"

Traci lowered her voice. "It's not something I want to discuss over the phone, or in front of the girls. They're just in the other room and could walk in at any moment."

Which meant she was calling from the bedroom and could easily close the door, but he knew not to make the suggestion.

What in the hell was going on? He and Traci had talked

earlier in the week and everything had been okay. She hadn't mentioned any problems with his dad.

"When do you want to talk about it, then?" He was finding it difficult to keep his growing frustration under wraps and knew it came through in his voice.

"When do I want to talk about it? Never! So maybe you should call your attorney and let him fill you in."

"I'd rather talk to—"

She disconnected.

"You," he finished.

He started to hit the recall button, but knew it would be a waste of time. Traci wouldn't answer. That's how she'd handled most things during their marriage and the habit had only become more pronounced recently. She'd drop a bomb and then make herself unavailable.

He inhaled sharply and turned to check out the command center again. Only a few agents remained and most of those were packing it in, too.

Mark rubbed his jaw. What in the hell had she meant about contacting his attorney? What could she want? He was already giving her double the amount of child support that he was required to pay, and since the divorce, he'd periodically bailed her out when she'd gotten herself in trouble with credit cards, so it couldn't be about the money. Which left what? Visitation? Is that what she was going after? Nearly a year ago she'd threatened to take him back to court. To ask for sole custody.

His gut tightened. Not his girls. Traci could have anything of his that she wanted, his retirement, what was left of his savings account. Anything but sole custody.

Some sound behind him made him realize that he was no longer alone. Turning, he sensed more than saw someone standing in the shadows beneath the trees. He realized it was Beth.

Obviously, she'd used another exit, and more than likely had overheard at least part of his conversation with Traci, so there was no reason to pretend otherwise. "I have two daughters, nine and eleven. Gracie and Addison."

She cocked her head to the side, as if she were studying him. He realized it was something she did often.

"And this is your weekend to have them," she said simply. "And for obvious reasons you can't be there." She crossed her arms in front of her, the bottled water she held half-empty and dangling from the fingers of her left hand.

"Yeah." He put his phone away. "Everyone is calling tonight, it seems."

Her eyes narrowed. "What do you mean?"

"Your father called a few minutes ago. He's been trying to reach you."

"So when he couldn't, he phones you." Her mouth tightened and then she looked away for several seconds. She lifted the water to her lips and took a hurried sip. "Perfect."

The tone of her voice made it clear that she considered it anything but perfect.

"I told him that I'd see that you got the message."

"And now you have. I'm sorry. I'll make sure he doesn't call you again in the future."

"It's fine," he assured.

"No. It's not."

She looked more upset than the situation warranted. After all, it was just a phone call.

"Want to talk about it?" he asked.

"Not any more than you want to talk about what went wrong in your marriage."

Touché.

She took another swig of water. "I also got a call a little bit ago. An interesting one."

"From?"

"A detective with Baltimore PD. They've identified the connection between Rabbit Rheaume and Leon Tyber, including a paper trail."

"So I was wrong. You're not a target." The news didn't strike him as he'd expected it to. He found himself more relieved than upset.

But what about Beth? Had her reaction to the detective's call been the exact opposite? Had she been more upset than relieved? Did she find being a terrorist's target easier to face than possibly finding herself under Bill Monroe's control again?

Mark could ask her, he supposed, but he already knew that she wouldn't answer. Just as she'd refused to discuss her father's call.

"And you're wondering if, because you're no longer bait, I'll be sending you back to Baltimore?"

Chapter Nine

"Yes." The water bottle crackled as Beth's fingers choked it too tightly, the sound setting her nerves even more on edge. Loosening her hold, she tried to block out just how much rode on Mark's answer.

From the moment she'd stepped off the plane this morning, she'd been desperately trying to make herself an asset, a task made more difficult by the assignments she'd been given—making motel reservations and arranging meeting space; running background checks on teachers and hardworking trades people; running a list of names supplied by agents out in the field against a variety of federal databases. It was busy work. The kind that could be done by anyone. The type that wouldn't be enough to guarantee a permanent spot with the unit.

She fought to control her growing frustration. Not just with her situation, but with her father, too. Maybe she should consider herself lucky that he'd only asked for a message to be relayed. That he hadn't decided to fill in Mark the same way he'd filled in Bill Monroe.

She'd been so focused on her own thoughts that it wasn't until Mark moved toward her, stepping into the shade beneath the tree, that she realized she still stood mostly in the shadows.

"Tell me, Beth. I'm curious." He leaned toward her, his voice dropping. Not quite a whisper but low enough to give the illusion of intimacy. "How long did you think about just keeping the detective's call to yourself?"

He'd intentionally invaded her space, his crisp, white shirt only inches from her nose. As she took a shallow breath, it wasn't just the scent of his cologne that reached her, but that of laundry starch and warm male skin.

"I'll admit to being human," she said. "To wanting to make the transfer permanent." She met his gaze. "So. Should I be packing my bags?"

"Not tonight," Mark said simply as he shifted backward half a step.

Not tonight? It wasn't much of an answer. There wasn't a whisper of a promise in it, but she still felt as if she'd dodged a bullet. At least temporarily.

There was an awkward half second when both of them seemed to be waiting for the other to say good night.

It was Mark who made the first move, walking to where he'd left his coffee on the window ledge. "Since it was Rabbit who hired the hit and he's now dead, there's no longer any reason to worry about your safety, is there?"

"No."

"Good night, then," he said as he dumped the coffee on the ground.

"Yeah," she said. "Good night."

As she watched him walk away, she admitted that not wanting to be attracted to him and not being that way were two entirely different things. Every time he was within a few feet of her, every time that sizzle of awareness flooded her system, she lost track of everything else.

Especially her resolve to keep her distance.

HOURS LATER the phone next to the bed awakened her from what felt like a drug-induced coma. She groped for it, undecided about whether, when she finally found the phone, she was going to answer it or hurl it across the room.

Who in the hell would be calling at this time of night? And then as her head cleared some, she thought she knew.

Her father.

If he could get Mark's number, finding out where she was staying would be easy by comparison. And her father was nothing if not persistent. And as far as taking *no* gracefully, well, it just didn't happen. Stubbornness and determination were two things she and her father had in common.

Sitting on the edge of the bed and still in the dark, Beth dragged the phone toward her. As it rang again, she picked up the receiver, uncertain what she was going to say to her father once they got past the prerequisite hello.

"Is this Beth Benedict?"

She didn't recognize the male voice, but assumed it belonged to someone on the motel staff or to one of the other agents. "This is she," she mumbled.

"Your voice. I like it. Is it always that husky?" As he made the last statement, his had dropped.

Originally relieved when she realized the caller wasn't her father, adrenaline now hit her system. "Who is this?"

"Let's just say that when I saw you on television today, I became an admirer of sorts." She could hear piano music in the background. "How's your room there at the Laurelwood Inn and Spa? Did they get rid of the bedbugs?"

The wording of his last question pretty much did away with the possibility that the caller was any type of motel employee. A crank call, then? But how had they gotten her name? Her room number?

"It's a little late for a survey, so I'm hanging up now."

"I wouldn't do that."

Something in his tone kept her on the line. "Why not?"

"Because I'm the reason you're here in Bellingham."

It was as if someone had slapped her hard across the face, finally doing away with the last traces of sleep. The reason she was here in Bellingham? There were a lot of nutcases out there. Even during the short course of their investigation, it wouldn't be unusual for several to have been unearthed. But was this one of them?

"You don't believe me, do you?" There was obvious amusement in his voice.

"I didn't say that," she said cautiously, trying to plot the best course, the right questions to ask.

"But you were thinking it. You were trying to figure out if I'm for real."

"Why not convince me, then?" She turned on the lamp, squinting against the sudden glare. "If you are who you say you are, it shouldn't be difficult."

"Because that's not the reason I called, and because you'll have all the proof you need soon enough."

"What exactly does that mean?"

"That I'm not done in Bellingham." Something in his voice, the confidence coupled with the choice of words sent a chill through her and persuaded her that he wasn't some harmless creep. That there was a good possibility he was the real deal.

But why call her instead of the lead investigator? What was he after?

"What kind of proof am I going to have?" she asked. Keeping him on the line forever wasn't going to help. Not unless the call was traced. But for that to happen, she needed help.

Mark had contacted her several times during the day. His cell number would be stored on the incoming call log. But where in the hell had she left her cell phone? Her purse?

"What kind of proof?" There was more amusement in his voice now.

She'd briefly lost track of the conversation. Something she couldn't afford to do if she wanted to keep him on the phone. "That was my question."

She anxiously scanned the room for her handbag. Where in the hell had she left it?

"Why the undeniable kind of proof, of course. You're sounding a little breathless. I hope I haven't upset you."

"No." She didn't need anyone to tell her that she wasn't really equipped to handle this call. That there were people far better trained at this type of thing. No doubt Mark was one of them.

She spotted the purse on the dresser. By grabbing the base of the motel phone in one hand and taking it with her, she was able to stretch just far enough to reach the strap. She jerked the bag off the dresser, the contents spilling on to the carpet. After seizing her cell phone, she retreated to the bed again and immediately went to the incoming log.

Even as she keyed in the text message to Mark, she needed to continue asking questions. Draw out the conversation and keep the caller on the line as long as possible.

He'd called to tell her something. So maybe the key was not to let him get to it too soon.

If she could force him slightly off topic, without actually pissing him off and having him hang up on her, she might buy some time. "Is it true, what they say? That television adds ten pounds?"

He gave a fast chuckle. "You're wondering if maybe I saw you somewhere besides TV, whether our paths crossed today. You're quick. I like that. It'll make the game more interesting."

Why hadn't he answered her question? Because their paths had crossed?

She hit the Send key. "What game?"

"The one we're going to play, you and me. Just to make the roadtrip interesting."

"What makes you think I'll play along?" she asked, her gaze cemented to the lighted screen of her cell phone. *Come on, Mark.*

"Because if you don't, lots of people will die."

Beth climbed to her feet, the tightness in her chest increasing. "And if I do, they won't?"

When the soft knock on her room door came, she was already in front of it. She flipped off the security latch and the night bolt, the sound of the latter louder than she would have liked. But at that moment she would have been willing to tear down the door with her bare hands just not to be alone.

"No. That's not how the game works."

"Then maybe you should tell me how it does work. I mean if you expect me to play."

"People are going to die either way."

Beth moved backward, allowing Mark to step inside, but

she only gave him a cursory look, her attention completely focused on the caller.

"So if people are going to die, no matter what I do," she canted the receiver away from her ear, enough that Mark could listen. "Why should I play?"

"Because if you play well enough, I might just let *you* live."

Chapter Ten

Mark took the phone receiver out of her stiff fingers as soon as the call was disconnected. "You okay?" he asked. He was watching her closely.

"Sure. I'm fine."

Snugging her arms in front of her, she tried to pretend she felt calm. "He just took me by surprise."

Only hours ago she'd believed that she *wasn't* being hunted by terrorists and now… Beth uncrossed her arms. "What time is it, anyway?"

"Just after four."

He dropped the phone receiver back onto the base and pulled out the desk chair. "I need you to write down everything that was said and in as much detail as possible. Don't leave anything out. Include any thoughts you may have had at the time. Anything and everything, you understand?"

"Sure." She sat and picked up the pen supplied by the motel and the small notebook she'd left on the desk. As she started putting words to paper, though, the choppy hand-writing didn't look like hers. Because it was so scratchy and difficult to read, by the time she flipped to the second page, she'd finally given up and switched to block letters.

She knew it wasn't fear making her hand shake, that it was just the adrenaline, but would Mark know that? Or would he see the unsteady handwriting as a sign of weakness?

It was only as she jotted down the last few exchanges that she realized just how short the conversation had been. Probably no more than two or three minutes, but at the time it had seemed much longer.

She ripped off the four pages and passed them. "I'm afraid there's not much there."

Because the bed provided the only other seating in the cramped room, he sat on the edge of it, facing her. He'd pulled on pants but hadn't bothered with a shirt.

She could barely recall the last time a half-dressed man sat on the edge of her bed. During the eighteen months undercover, she'd avoided anyone from her previous life—for their protection and for her own.

And during the four months since the investigation had ended, she'd been screwed up just enough that she'd been leery of letting anyone get too close. In the end, having grown tired of being scared, and feeling so damn alone, she'd gone home to Virginia. To the family estate with all the high-tech security. To the only family she had left.

To the one person who should have been loyal to her. Her father.

But he hadn't been.

Taking a shallow breath, Beth pushed the thought aside. Right now there was something much bigger on her plate that needed her attention.

When she shifted her focus back to Mark, he was frowning. "Sorry about the writing."

"No problem." He continued studying the pages, and, because she wanted to avoid thinking about both the caller and her father, she watched Mark, ostensibly to offer answers if he had any questions.

A new-growth beard shadowed his jaw. On some men, the I-need-to-shave look suggested late-night bars and too much drinking. On Mark, the shadowed jaw when coupled with bare chest and bare feet, with rumpled hair and rumpled sheets, looked a whole lot more dangerous… It evoked images of another type of bingeing. The sexual kind.

The room's heat shut off. When chill-bumps immediately broke out on her arms, they were enough to remind her that she wasn't exactly dressed for company. White boxers and a T-shirt might technically cover her body, but because the material was on the thin side, they weren't exactly concealing.

Not that he seemed to have noticed.

Mark glanced up at that moment. "He made no attempt to disguise his voice. I assume because he's not concerned about you recognizing it?"

"And I didn't."

"So there's no chance that this is the same caller who contacted Rheaume in July? The phone call you thought might be connected to MX141?"

"And the voice I thought I would recognize if I heard it again? No. This guy sounds as if he might have either been raised in the Midwest or spent a considerable amount of time there."

When he glanced at her quizzically, she explained, "He speaks with what's called a lower vowel back merger. He loses a vowel when he says certain words."

Nodding, Mark glanced down at the pages again. "He makes no attempt to justify his actions. There's no mention of a grievance or some type of cause. But he refers to bedbugs?"

The area between Mark's dark brows puckered. "It's an odd question to ask. Maybe it wasn't a random one. Maybe he's trying to tell us that he stayed here at some point in the past or lived in the area and knew the motel had a reputation."

Getting to his feet, he paced to the center of the room. "How did he act when you said you were hanging up?"

"As if he wanted to be sure I didn't."

"But not desperate?"

"No. Not desperate," she agreed. "Confident was more like it. He knew what it would take to keep me on the phone." Recalling the chilling effects of his words, Beth folded her arms in front of her again.

"And yet there's nothing here to suggest that he'd done any homework on you. That he knew anything more than your name. If he had, I don't think he could have resisted using it."

"Why do you think that?"

"He does everything he can to keep you off balance. He wants to be in control." Mark ran a hand through his short, dark hair. "When you tried to change the course of the conversation by asking about the camera adding pounds, he never actually responds to your question. Instead he takes back control by hitting you with the game he wants to play and with people dying."

He was frowning again. "He needs someone to appreciate his cleverness, what he does. And he's chosen you. Because he saw you this afternoon." Mark's eyes narrowed. "Because I made it impossible for him not to—"

"He says he isn't through in Bellingham," she said solemnly.

"I suspect he is and just wants us to believe if we hurry

we can save lives here. But it's more likely, if there are additional victims, they're already dead. The 911 call just hasn't gone out yet."

She'd been sitting, but now climbed to her feet. What was he suggesting? "So we're going to do nothing?"

"No. We do what we've been doing from the start. We do everything we can."

As MARK STEPPED out of the rental SUV four hours later, he scanned the area surrounding the white clapboard farmhouse.

He'd received Livengood's call only a short time ago, but five local PD cars as well as one of the Hazmat Response Units and Larson's car were already in front. Not seeing Larson, Mark assumed he was inside. Walking the scene. Gathering evidence.

Counting the dead.

Every man drew some satisfaction from being good at his chosen profession. From reaching a level of proficiency. But there were moments when Mark would have liked to be proven wrong, and this was one of them.

The weather was probably typical for the area, overcast and with temperature in the low forties.

He glanced across the roof of the SUV as Beth got out the other side. "Nice place."

"Pretty," she agreed. "And remote." Turning, she seemed to briefly study the tree-covered mountain behind the farmhouse.

She'd managed to tame her dark hair again, smoothing it so that it hung sleekly. She wore trim-fitting slacks and a black blazer now, but as much as he might want to block out the image of her sitting at the desk a few hours ago in a thin T-shirt and boxer shorts, he couldn't. Nor could he recall the last time he'd wanted to touch a woman quite as much as he wanted to touch her.

Three years ago, when he'd been her instructor at Quantico, he'd known she was beautiful, proficient with a firearm and intelligent. In short, she'd impressed him more than any other new recruit he'd taught. But in the past thirty-six hours he'd learned several more things about her—that she was strong and courageous.

And because of him, she was in extreme danger.

His gut tightened in remorse. But what was done was done, and no matter how much he wanted to send her someplace safe, he wouldn't. Because as long as she was with him, there was an outside chance this madman could be stopped. And because he suspected even if he tried to send her away, she wouldn't go.

As she suddenly faced him, he forced his attention off her and onto the property again.

Besides the large home, there were three outbuildings: a barn, a lean-to with two tractors parked beneath it, and a chicken coop. All of them had been built on the downslope to ensure that groundwater runoff from livestock didn't contaminate the drinking well.

The only livestock he saw, though, were some free-range chickens and a small herd of cattle clustered beneath a large oak in a nearby pasture.

She closed the car door. "Seems like an odd target for a terrorist, doesn't it?"

"You're right. He's not acting like a terrorist. He's acting more like a spree killer. One with the most deadly weapons at his disposal, capable of easily taking out thousands. But he doesn't."

Which didn't mean he wouldn't. That Bellingham

wasn't what Mark had originally labeled it—a warm-up exercise. Maybe the more telling questions that needed to be answered were why the school, why only the boys' shower room, why those who lay dead in this farmhouse. How were they connected to each other?

If they knew why, they'd stand a better chance of learning who.

As he rounded the front end of the car, another SUV pulled in behind, loaded with two more agents. Mark continued toward the house where he saw Livengood and his deputies waiting on the large wrap-around front porch. Beth fell in beside him. As they passed a group of chickens scrabbling at the ground, she paused, so he did, too.

"They're Rhode Island reds," he supplied.

"They're beautiful."

"Maybe, but you might want to be careful around them."

Looking up, she appeared surprised. "Why?"

"Because they're territorial as hell." At her questioning look, he added, "I spent the first fifteen years of my life on a farm."

Continuing toward the house, he lengthened his stride, wondering why he'd shared that piece of information with her. As he climbed the front steps, he checked out the somber faces of the waiting deputies and Livengood.

"What can you tell me so far?" Mark asked as he hit the top tread.

Looking down at his feet briefly, Livengood smoothed the rim of the hat he held. "Names are Richard and Sally Ravenel and their seventeen-year-old son Kenny. Found them in the upstairs bathroom."

Mark could hear the shock in the police chief's voice. "How'd you find them?"

"A 911 call."

"Who phoned it in?" Beth asked as she reached the porch and stood beside Mark.

"The call came from here. It was a man's voice, but he wouldn't give his name and hung up fast." Livengood continued to manipulate the hat rim.

In a place like Bellingham, a neighbor wouldn't hesitate to identify himself. Out of the corner of his eye, seeing Beth's mouth tighten, he suspected that she'd come to the same conclusion he had. That the 911 caller had been the same man who'd phoned her at 4:00 a.m.

"I'll need a tape of the call," Mark said.

"Sure." Livengood nodded. "I'll see that you get it right away."

Even if the call had been placed on the home phone, because of the MX141 that had been used, it was unlikely the caller would have done it from inside the house.

Mark motioned toward the barn. "Is there a telephone out there?"

"Maybe." Livengood's eyes narrowed suddenly and he glanced over at his deputies. "Anyone seen or heard Max?"

"Who is Max?" Beth asked.

"Richard's dog. A shepherd mix. Big thing, but harmless. He's usually locked up in the barn at night. With all this commotion he should be going crazy by now."

Mark assigned the task of checking the barn for a phone and locating the family dog to the agents in the second car, then returned his attention to the police chief. "So tell me about the Ravenels."

"Up until three years ago, when Richard remarried and moved out here with Sally, he was the coach down at the high school."

"Any other children?" Mark asked.

"Kenny was actually Sally's son. Richard had a daughter. She died about nine years ago. A hunting accident."

"Where are Kenny's father and the first Mrs. Ravenel?"

"Dead. She died in an auto accident and Kenny's dad had cancer."

Livengood tossed his hat onto the seat of the rocking chair behind him and used both hands to wipe his eyes. He immediately looked away, tightening his jaw in an effort to stem his emotions.

Mark didn't need to be told that there was more to the story—there always was. But early in his career he'd discovered that knowing too many personal and inconsequential details about the dead not only made it harder to sleep, it also made it more difficult to do his job.

After giving Livengood a few seconds to collect himself, Mark continued, "Can you think of anyone who might want them dead? Anyone who Richard, Sally or Kenny had a run-in with?"

"Recently? Not that I know of. There might be a few who remember Richard from his years of coaching, though."

"Meaning what?" Mark asked.

"He was ex-military and tended to work his kids pretty hard. Most of them respected him for it, but a few didn't."

"Any names come to mind?"

"No. But I'll check with the principal and do some asking around." Livengood looked like a man who'd been knocked down one too many times over the past few days. "You think it's possible this guy is local?"

"I think it's a possibility. Any idea if the Laurelwood Inn ever had a problem with bedbugs?"

If the question surprised the police chief, he didn't show

it. "Maybe in the past. Place was pretty bad at one time, but it's been cleaned up for five or six years now."

Mark filed the information away, uncertain where it fit into the puzzle. Had Beth's caller used the bedbug question to mislead them, to convince them that he was either local or had lived in the area at some time?

At that moment the first body bag appeared. Livengood and his men shuffled backward, watching in grim silence as the bag was carried past the large baskets of orange flowers on either side of the door and then down the wooden steps.

Beth had followed Mark to the railing and now stood next to him.

As the body bag disappeared into the back of the waiting vehicle, his gut tightened. Had it been the seventeen-year-old kid with his whole life ahead him? Or had it been one of the parents who'd rushed to help their son?

Instead of turning back to watch the remaining two Ravenels carried out, Mark stared at the rolling farmland, wondering how many more porches he'd have to stand on, how many more people would die before it was over.

No one spoke until the third and last Ravenel had been slid into the back of a waiting vehicle.

Larson emerged right behind the bleak procession, stripping off his mask and gloves as he stepped out into the fresh air.

"Same type of dispersal device. Looks as if the son went in to take a shower and the parents came running when they realized something was wrong."

"Fingerprints?" Mark asked.

"Not on the showerhead. We'll collect what we can from other surfaces."

"Were you able to narrow down the time frame?"

"There are hamburger patties made up on a plate next to the sink. Looks as if they've been there a day or two."

Livengood shifted forward. "My deputies made some calls. Last time anyone heard from any of the Ravenels was Thursday afternoon."

"Timing sounds about right," Larson said.

So if the family had been dead since Thursday, why hold off on the emergency call? Because he'd expected them to be found before now? Because he'd grown tired of waiting? Something didn't quite add up.

"Any signs of forced entry?" Beth asked.

Her question had been directed at Larson, but it was Livengood who answered. "There's a basement entrance around back. It wasn't locked when my deputy arrived."

"Would you consider that unusual?" Beth asked.

"No. Folks around here aren't always so cautious, and having a dog sometimes makes them even less so."

Mark's phone rang. Glancing down, he recognized the cell number of one of the agents he'd sent down to the barn. "What did you find?"

"Dog's been shot. The phone is the cordless variety and the handset is missing. There's another structure with some tractors just below this one. We're going to head down and check it out."

Mark dropped the cell phone back into his pocket.

When he looked around, Beth had walked to the farthest corner of the porch and seemed to be studying the steep incline behind the house. It was the second time she'd shown more than casual interest. Did she see something?

Taking several quick steps back from the rail, she then hurried the length of the covered side porch.

By the time he reached her, she stood at the back railing. "What's going on?"

"There's someone watching us from up there," she tossed back as she jumped over the rail.

Mark vaulted after her. As soon as his feet hit the hard-packed red clay, he reached for his weapon.

Within three or four strides, he'd caught up to her. "You actually saw someone?"

"I saw binoculars aimed at us. They were there when we arrived. Considering the kind of community this is, I would expect a neighbor to come down to check things out. And if it's a hiker, they should have moved on by now."

Was it possible that it was the killer?

Was that the reason the killer hadn't called 911 until this morning? Because he'd wanted to be able to catch the show?

Mark grabbed his cell phone and hit the speed dial for Larson. "There's someone up on the mountain showing a lot of interest. Might be our guy. Benedict and I are going up to check it out."

"Tell me where, and I'll—"

"No. Stay put. I need you to give him something to look at. Something to focus on down there so that he doesn't start looking elsewhere."

"Are you talking a diversion? Like what?"

"Drag the dead dog out in front of the house for starters. That will keep him busy for a few minutes."

"And after that?"

"Get creative if you have to. He sees us coming, he'll bolt."

Mark disconnected and reclipped the phone to his waist. He'd been letting Beth lead the way, but now increased his pace, overtaking her. "I go off course, you let me know."

He didn't like the whole setup. Being on the downgrade made them vulnerable, made them easy targets for anyone above them. He wasn't wearing a protective vest. Neither was she.

Which meant the only thing between them and a bullet might be Larson's diversion.

For more than five minutes they moved upward, negotiating the expected gauntlet of dense undergrowth and roots and logs. But then when they were a hundred yards into the trees, the trunks suddenly seemed to close ranks and the light that had previously penetrated the nearly nude branches overhead, leaked away, leaving them in damp shade. And from there, the going only got tougher, until they were limited to pushing forward single file.

Suddenly, still behind him, Beth veered to the right, planting her back hard against the trunk of the closest tree, motioning him to do the same.

Once he had, she pointed upward, indicating that she'd seen something or someone above them.

As Mark edged out, the material of his jacket scraped across the rough bark. At first, the only thing he could sort out was the lighter color of the bluff's rock face. It wasn't a huge outcropping, but enough that anyone on top would have a clear view of not only them, but also of the farmhouse below.

And then just when he became certain that there was nothing there, he saw a flash of red. A shirt maybe.

Ducking back behind the tree, he used hand signals to instruct Beth. He'd go in first. She'd hang back to provide cover.

Trying to limit his exposure, he advanced in a partial crouch. His first course of action was to get in as tight as possible to the rock formation. Once he had, whoever was up there would have to lean out far enough to also become exposed.

Once Mark reached the rock face, he glanced back, trying to determine Beth's position. As he watched, she scrambled almost silently to a location that would allow her a better angle in case she needed to lay down some cover fire.

His phone vibrated in his pocket. He ignored it.

Keeping his weapon pointed slightly upward, he stared at the ledge above as he continued to place one foot in front of the other.

From here on out, even with careful foot placement, there was no way his movements wouldn't be heard by whoever was up there. But large game was common in these woods, so there was always the chance he'd be mistaken for a deer or a bear crashing about in the underbrush.

Of course, some people shot those, too.

Chapter Eleven

Another burst of adrenaline hit Mark's system as leaves suddenly exploded over the edge, cascading down the rock face. The exodus was accompanied by scrambling foot-steps overhead.

He'd obviously been spotted. And whoever was up there was either rushing to reach a more defensible position for a standoff or, even worse, attempting to escape.

Mark attacked the steep grade, the sound of his move-ments making it impossible to hear what was happening above him now.

Even as he climbed, he looked back once or twice, hoping to catch a glimpse of Beth somewhere behind him. But he couldn't.

Which didn't mean she wasn't there.

One moment he was dealing with the undergrowth and the next he was standing ankle-deep in loose rubble at the base of a thirty-foot rock wall. He could either swing left, hoping to find another more-passable route to the top, which would eat up time and might not result in a better option, or he could holster his weapon and, using two hands, start scaling.

If he could catch this guy, it could end right now. They could stop the killings.

He glanced over his shoulder. If Beth wasn't back there, wasn't in a position to cover him when he started climbing, he'd be shit out of luck.

Did he trust her with his life?

Did he believe what was in her personnel file, or did he trust his own assessment?

Deciding to go with what his gut told him, Mark tucked the automatic away, kicked out of his hard-soled shoes and, tying the shoelaces together, hung them around his neck.

Hurriedly scanning the wall, he searched for the best route, and then stretching for his first handhold nearly eight feet overhead, started the ascent.

Rock climbing required strength and skill and a certain amount of finesse even when using equipment, and without ropes and pitons, the sport quickly became more difficult and more deadly. It had been years since he'd attempted free climbing, but in most ways it was like riding a bike. Of course, if he fell off, the landing was going to be a hell of a lot harder.

Halfway up, his left foot suddenly slipped. The muscles of his fingers and hands and arms locked. With his face plastered to the rough stone, he fumbled, desperately trying to locate the foothold before his muscles gave out or the single foothold that was currently holding him up gave way.

When he finally recaptured the small edge of stone that was no more than an inch in depth, he shifted so that his weight was equally distributed over both feet. He slowly used his legs to push his body upward, reaching overhead for the next handhold, repeating the process over and over.

It wasn't until he got to within two feet of the ledge that

he stopped briefly to catch his breath. Glancing down and to the left, the only direction he could look given his current position, he scanned for Beth again, and then when he didn't see her, checked out the edge above. He listened intently for any sounds of movement, unable to quite shake the feeling that when he finally did reach the top, the only thing waiting would be a bullet.

But the odds of surviving a gunshot were probably better than those for a thirty-foot fall.

As he hoisted himself up and over, the first rifle crack rang out. Mark didn't see where the bullet struck the rock, but he felt the shards sting his right cheek. Two more shots rapidly followed.

And then, from somewhere below, came several answering rounds. Beth watching his butt, thank God. Mark dove toward the only cover he could reach, a log a dozen feet away. His shoes were ripped free.

Drawing his weapon, he listened in frustration as the shoes landed in the rubble below. In a standoff, being barefoot wouldn't matter. But in any type of pursuit, he damn sure was going to be screwed, and he could pretty well guarantee that's what they were looking at here. Otherwise, the shooter would have taken Mark out before he reached the ledge.

As far as the weapon the shooter was using, it had sounded like a twenty-two caliber rifle. A varmint weapon. Perhaps not the most deadly firearm out there, but at anything less than eighty yards, a well-placed shot could take down a man.

Had Beth actually seen the shooter, or had she just been firing blind, trying to make her presence known? Trying to give the shooter something to worry about?

Mark jerked the cell phone off his belt. As soon as he got a look at it, he realized he wasn't going to be reaching Beth or anyone else on it. At some point during the climb, he'd managed to trash it.

"Benedict?" Mark called.

No response.

Shit! Now what? Was she trying to find a way up?

Mark found himself wishing that it had been Larson and not Beth covering his back. Not because he didn't trust her to do her best, but because he wasn't completely sure how she'd handle the current situation.

Forced to consider his options, he stared up at the dirty gray clouds. The temperature was dropping. Or maybe it felt that way because his feet were bare, and he was stretched out on a cold slab of granite that suddenly seemed to offer all the comfort and warmth of a morgue table.

Doing a partial sit-up, he tried to see over the log while still maintaining a low profile. Another crack sounded. Mark dropped flat again as the bullet removed a chunk of log only inches from where his head had been seconds earlier.

A close miss by the shooter, or an intentional display of skill?

Either way, the round had come from the trees above him, from somewhere to the right of the wide strip of cleared land that was a utility easement.

He shifted sideways, enough that he could get a view of the top of the mountain, and quickly realized that he was screwed. That the shooter's position would make it possible for him to continue up the mountain while keeping Mark pinned down.

Mark grappled with his growing frustration.

Having heard the shots and now unable to reach Mark, Larson and the two agents down at the farmhouse would already be on their way up, possibly accompanied by Livengood and his deputies. But it would take them too long. At least ten minutes. With that kind of lead, the shooter could reach the summit. And the backdoor to an extensive forest.

So where in the hell was Beth? Where was his backup? He didn't like leaving her behind, but unless she showed in the next sixty seconds, that's exactly what he was going to be forced to do.

Hearing something scrabbling at the rock just below his position, he shifted sideways again so he could get a look over the edge. Though she sounded winded and was struggling, she was already within several feet of the top. As she settled into her current position on the wall, the shoes draped around her neck from the front thumped against her back. Not one pair, but two.

That he felt relieved to see her didn't surprise him. What did catch him off guard was the level of his relief.

As she looked up for her next handhold, she saw him and offered a tense smile.

"You're doing fine," he said.

"Yeah, well, I'm not so sure about that."

As she reached for the ledge, Mark quickly switched the SIG-Sauer to his weaker hand, leaving the stronger one free to grab the back of her jacket. "On the count of three you get your butt up here while I lay down some cover."

She gave no indication that she'd even heard him.

"One. Two." Mark lifted his weapon, squeezing off two rounds toward the trees while hauling her up next to him.

She collapsed in the dirt. Her chest continued to rise and fall rapidly as she tried to catch her breath. She'd shed her jacket before making the climb, so was down to a pink short-sleeved T-shirt.

As it had yesterday, her hair had begun to curl and the makeup she'd been wearing earlier was gone, revealing flushed, glowing skin. The bullet graze above her right temple was more pronounced, a visual reminder of what she'd faced during the past forty-eight hours. It was also an unpleasant reminder that he was solely responsible for making her this killer's target.

When she looked over at him, though, she was smiling and her eyes were bright.

He caught himself returning the smile. "Let me see your phone."

She passed it without comment. Mark punched in the only number he could recall off the top of his head. Larson answered on the second ring. "What in the hell's going on up there?"

"Right now? He's got us pinned down."

"Pinned down where?"

"You probably don't have a good visual of the bluff yet, but can you see the utility easement?"

"Yeah."

"He's on the right of it and headed to the top. In a few seconds we'll be going up the left-hand side." The cleared easement running up the mountain made a decent buffer and at the same time nearly eliminated the possibility of their walking into any type of ambush.

"Why don't you hang tight? We'll be there in five minutes, ten at the outside."

"Too long. He reaches the top, he's got a half-million acres to disappear into. Alert the park service. Have them shut down all roads. And get us some bloodhounds."

"Okay. Is Benedict there with you?"

"Yeah. She's fine."

As Mark ended the call and shoved the phone into his pocket, Beth passed him his shoes.

"Larson worried about me? Or is he concerned that I'm not taking good care of you?" she asked.

"He's a good agent."

"Didn't say he wasn't."

Mark worked at undoing the laces. "How are your legs holding up?"

"Better than my scraped-up feet." Rolling awkwardly onto her side, she shoved her shoes back on. "How do you want to do this?"

"We'll go together, but I'll take the lead. Try to stay behind me, okay?"

"I don't think he's looking to kill me. At least not yet. Where's the fun in that?"

He glanced over at her, surprised by just how loose she sounded. And just how comfortable he was having her as his backup. He motioned with his chin toward the top of the mountain. "There's a large pine leaning out into the utility easement. He's somewhere just below it."

Mark took off running, Beth only steps behind. A single sharp crack shattered the stillness.

Reaching the relative safety of the trees, Mark immediately set a grueling pace, this time unsurprised when she managed to stay with him.

Why only one shot when the shooter could have gotten off several more while they'd been out in the open?

Because the shooter felt his current lead was sufficient to guarantee his escape?

Or because he was low on ammo?

Or maybe killing them just wasn't on today's agenda.

Everything up until this morning had suggested an organized offender. The type of perp who carefully chose his targets in advance, spending weeks or maybe months researching them, planning for every contingency. And most important, always covering his tracks thoroughly.

So why had he allowed them to get so close this morning?

Mark scanned the opposite edge of the easement for their shooter.

"Do you see him?" Beth asked.

"No. He's probably moved back into the trees some, but it's unlikely he'll actually change his course." Grabbing a sapling, Mark used it to pull himself up the three-foot-high washout.

"So do you think this is how he came in? Through the forest?" Beth used the same small tree as a climbing aide. "That he has a vehicle waiting?"

"Even if he doesn't have one stashed somewhere in there, even if he hadn't planned to be spotted and now finds himself in need of an escape route, he might be planning to lose himself in there for a few days."

"He'd have to know the place will be crawling with law enforcement almost immediately."

"And he'd also know there's no way to completely secure five hundred thousand acres. If he's spent any time around here, which I suspect he has, chances are he'll know the area better than most of the manpower we bring in to find him. It wouldn't be all that difficult for him to slip by us."

Mark glanced up at the darkening sky. "Best chance we have of capturing him once he reaches the refuge is the dogs. That's assuming the weather holds off. If we get a good downpour, we might as well pack it in and wait for the next call, the next incident."

Not pushing quite so hard for a split second, he again searched for some movement in the trees above and to the right of them. This time he thought he saw something. Back in the shadows. And if he was right, the shooter had ditched the red shirt or jacket for one that was camo.

"Do you see anything?" Beth asked.

When Mark had slowed, she'd kept going and was now slightly above him. As she negotiated the loose soil and scrambled up the steeper grade, the muscles of her buttocks bunched and released rhythmically, the sight causing him to lose his concentration momentarily.

Because he wasn't a masochist, he lengthened his stride until he was shoulder to shoulder with her again. He'd always been an ass man. And even though he had no intention of acting on the attraction, there was no reason to pretend that it didn't exist. That he wasn't a man with a man's needs. Needs that hadn't been met in quite some time.

"He's still there," Mark said. "We may have gained some, but not enough."

"Must…must be in good shape."

He didn't comment on her observation. Mostly because he didn't want to waste the air in his lungs. He could do six miles on a treadmill with a twenty-degree incline, but the current grade was closer to fifty.

And the shooter was having no problem handling the steep and rough terrain while maintaining the pace. Which, at the very least, suggested that he was an outdoorsman. Someone comfortable in these mountains.

Was it someone who had shared Thesing's environmental concerns? Some extremist who hadn't shown up on the list they'd found in the chemist's home?

Beth nearly tripped on a root. Mark reached out to steady her, but she'd already caught herself.

She swiped at the sweat dripping in her eyes. "So do you think…it's possible…the reason he hung around… Because he wanted to see the body bags…hauled out? Proof of…of his success? Of…superiority?"

"Maybe." Mark's gut tightened as yet another thought entered his mind. One that now seemed to make complete sense to him.

Perhaps the reason the shooter had been on the bluff this morning had nothing to do with gloating or with watching body bags loaded into the backs of vehicles. Maybe the reason they'd managed to get so close was because the shooter didn't have time to plan things out quite as thoroughly as he normally did. Because up until 4 a.m. when he'd gotten off the phone with Beth, he hadn't intended to be anywhere near here this morning.

"Or maybe after calling you this morning—" He broke off long enough to drag in more air. "He wanted another look at you."

Out of the corner of his eye, he saw her lips tighten. Four months ago Rabbit Rheaume had tried to kill her. Two nights ago, he'd paid for a second attempt on her life. And now, only hours ago, she'd learned that she was again a marked woman.

No matter what the freak had said about letting her live, Mark didn't believe for a moment he would. Given the opportunity, this guy wouldn't hesitate to kill her. But in order to do it, he was damn well going to have to go through Mark.

Even as winded and leg weary as they were when they saw the first forest sign marking the western boundary of the Nantahala, they kept moving.

From here on out, things were only going to get more dicey. Gone was the easement's buffer of barren land that had made an ambush nearly impossible. Gone also was the dense underbrush that had provided at least some cover for them. All they had now were old-growth pines that towered above the ground.

He glanced down at the brown carpet of pine needles. With every square inch of ground covered by them, there weren't going to be any bootprints to point them in the right direction. And forget about hearing any sounds of movement this asshole might make.

Mark moved forward cautiously. Between the cloud cover and the tree cover, it looked like dusk, and if that wasn't bad enough, the tree trunks were big enough that a man could easily hide behind any one of them and step out at the last second.

As Beth started to spread out, moving away from him, he said, "We stay within ten feet of each other. No more."

She offered a silent nod.

Maybe he was just being paranoid, but he couldn't quite shake the feeling that instead of their chasing the shooter into the forest, they'd been skillfully led here by him.

How far behind were Larson and the rest of them at this point? From previous experience Mark knew that less time had passed than it felt like. Maybe only five or six minutes now. Time enough for Larson to reach the bluff, but not enough to get up the mountain.

There was a subtle sound to his right, like a twig cracking as it was stepped on. Mark motioned Beth to drop back some while he checked it out. As he got within five feet of the tree, a fox darted past him.

As Mark circled around the trunk, he first saw the rabbit's body at its base and then a few feet away the head that had been twisted off. Not by any fox, but by a man. His father had taken him hunting once or twice, so he'd seen the technique used, but he still found the sight slightly disturbing.

Backing away, he rejoined Beth.

"What did you find?"

"Dead rabbit."

"The fox?"

"No."

The scent of rain had been growing steadily stronger, but now so was the breeze. Pine needles floated down as the branches overhead swayed.

Mark glanced upward, briefly studying what he could see of the sky. "Weather doesn't look good."

Beth looked up quickly but didn't comment. But then she didn't have to. Because they both knew they were quickly running out of time. That rain was their enemy.

They managed to move carefully downslope for nearly a minute before it finally hit. But when it did, it was vicious. It pounded through the canopy, instantly soaking them as if buckets of water were being poured over them one after the other.

He wiped a hand down his face and then shoved the hair off his forehead. Talk about bad luck. "Whatever evidence there was, it's gone now. And after this, it's unlikely that even a bloodhound will be able to pick up anything."

Beth's mouth thinned. "We could continue in the direction we're headed for a few more minutes," she suggested. "We might get lucky."

He was beginning to believe that she didn't know how to stop. Though he'd always seen tenacity as a valuable trait for an agent to possess, personal experience had shown him that the reckless variety ended in either death or a commendation.

If he'd been alone, he might have been tempted to continue on, to put himself at risk, but he had no intention of putting her life on the line. Not when they were without protective vests and carried weapons that, while accurate and more powerful than a rifle at close range, became less so at greater distances.

And not when he suspected that they were being manipulated right into an ambush.

"To go after him we need to be better equipped. Warmer clothes, camouflage, body armor and assault weapons for starters."

When her mouth tightened, he knew she wasn't happy about the decision.

The cell phone in his pocket vibrated.

"Yeah."

It was Larson. "Unless you're on to something up there, you might want to come back and take a look at this."

"What is it?"

"I can tell you what it is. I just can't tell you what it means exactly."

Chapter Twelve

Larson met them at the bottom of the utility easement with
their coats. "I thought you two might want these."

Beth didn't miss the look of speculation in Larson's
gaze as he passed her jacket. Maybe he was beginning to
recognize that he'd misjudged her.

"Thanks." Despite her soaked and muddy condition, she
dragged it on. She was cold and tired and still frustrated by
Mark's decision to break off the pursuit, but was determined
to keep all those things to herself. She couldn't afford to
reveal any sign of weakness. Nor did she plan to do anything
that might seem to substantiate the lies in her personnel file.

"So what did you find?" Mark adjusted the collar on
his suit coat.

"Come see." Larson headed for the bluff and the huge
flat area of rock resembling a four-foot-high raised stage.
Reaching it, he bound up easily, followed by Mark.

Once on top, Mark turned back, extending a hand down
to her. They were both covered in mud and wet.

When she didn't reach up right away, he smiled. "I
know it's not thirty vertical feet, but place your foot on that
lip of rock, and I'll help you."

His fingers were strong and firm and not nearly as chilled as her own were. And as they closed around hers, a warmth flooded her veins. It wasn't as if they hadn't touched numerous times during the past half hour, but somehow it felt different this time. It felt more personal. More invasive.

He moved backward as he pulled her up, giving her room to land. But even when she was standing in front of him, with only inches separating them, he didn't let her go.

Perhaps because he thought she was too close to the edge and if he did, she'd lose her balance and slip backward. But the truth was she'd lost her balance around him three years ago. And even now when she was supposed to be this trained special agent, this professional law enforcement machine, he reminded her that beneath all that, she was still very much a woman.

"Thanks." When she made a move to step past him, he let go of her. In the next instant, though, she wished he hadn't. With the rock being so narrow, the movement had brought her uncomfortably close to the edge.

Even though she'd never particularly cared for extreme heights—especially the straight down and without railings variety like this one—they drew her in. Like a pretty picture compelling her to move closer.

She looked over and down onto the top of the trees below, her heart rate climbing again. Her gaze backtracked until it reached the miniaturized white clapboard farmhouse below. Lookouts didn't come any better than this one.

Turning, she got her first glimpse of what Larson had brought them to see—a lawn chair draped in a dark blanket. With a leaden sky as a backdrop and sitting on rock nearly the same shade of gray, the chair almost seemed to float in midair.

She managed to catch up to Mark before he reached Larson.

"I found the Ravenel name written on the chair and in the sleeping bag," Larson said.

Mark frowned. "See if we can determine from where on the property they were taken and if there's any way to narrow the time frame of when they were removed. I want to know if he's been sitting up here for days, watching, waiting for us to find the bodies? Or if he set this all up a few hours ago?"

Beth turned her face into the wind, using it to push the hair away from her cheeks. "Why would the timing matter?"

"Because, if the 911 call was his way of getting you out in the open, it suggests that he's becoming fixated on you. It explains his sloppiness this morning."

"And what if he is obsessed with me?"

"Then we'll use it to our advantage. See if we can force him into being sloppy again."

Fixated. Obsessed. She'd never considered those words particularly scary, but in the present context they certainly carried some menacing undertones.

She didn't bother to ask why she'd been singled out. The only person who could answer that question with any authority was their unsub. And maybe he didn't fully understand the reasons behind his own behavior. Obsessions rarely had any foundation in reality, were instead based on skewed perceptions.

Squatting next to the chair, Mark reached under, nudging a section of orange peel out into the open. "Seems our guy likes fresh fruit."

Beth dropped down next to him. "Looks like there's enough here for more than one orange."

Now Larson joined them, peering under the chair. "There was a bowl of them on Ravenel's kitchen table."

"See if they're the same kind. And find out if the Ravenels had a .22 caliber rifle."

She shifted her gaze toward the farm nearly a thousand feet below.

Is that what the shooter had been doing as he watched the bodies of his victims carted out? Had he sat here calmly peeling and eating stolen oranges? Treating what was happening below as entertainment?

Her chest tightened at the idea. Somehow she knew she was right, though. And for the first time she acknowledged her apprehension. The phone call last night had initially unsettled her, but by this morning she'd felt mostly empowered by it. Because it seemed to guarantee that she'd get what she'd been wanting most. The opportunity to prove herself.

But at what cost?

Because it was bound to be less unsettling than her current thoughts, she forced herself to refocus on what Mark and Larson were discussing.

"There'll be fifty agents here in the next hour and an additional thirty by nightfall," Larson said. "The forest service has been alerted and all roads in or out of the area are being closely monitored. But I've got to tell you, Gerritsen, even with all that... These are the same mountains that Abe Rutherford disappeared into after bombing those three clinics six years ago. There were two hundred agents swarming all over the Nantahala Forest for months with no results."

Mark straightened. "This guy isn't Rutherford. He's not looking to disappear. He's looking to make a name for himself. I just want to make sure he doesn't do it by piling up bodies."

ELEVEN HOURS LATER, the sun having sunk hours ago behind the towering pines and the mountains, Mark and Beth, along with a large task force of both local and federal law enforcement officers walked out of the Nantahala Forest cold, tired and hungry.

And with nothing to show for their efforts.

With eighty-two additional FBI agents having joined the investigation in the past eight hours, there weren't enough hotel rooms in Bellingham. So many of them would be driving treacherous mountain roads for nearly an hour to find a bed. And at daybreak they'd be back. A pattern that would continue until either the killer was captured, or there was definitive proof that he was no longer hiding in the forest.

The most likely *proof* of his defection would come with an extremely high price tag—more victims.

Beth left Mark talking to a forest ranger at the picnic pavilion. With the vehicles in the parking lot rapidly thinning out, the restrooms would be locked up shortly.

She passed a couple of local deputies and several FBI agents on the trail, but there were fewer of them than earlier.

As she walked into the ladies' room, Special Agent Jenny Springer was standing at the closest sink. Like the rest of them, she was dressed in jeans, boots and a black baseball cap with FBI across the front of it.

Glancing over as the door dropped closed behind Beth, Jenny shook the water off her hands. "This is the first time in years I've been involved in the actual manhunt, and today was my wake-up call. I need to get back in the gym on a regular basis." She grabbed a handful of toilet paper to dry her hands on. "But I heard you scored one for our gender."

At Beth's perplexed expression, Jenny said, "Thirty-foot free climb and keeping up with Mark Gerritsen. Not many women can do that." She removed her cap, ran a hand across the top of her head as if trying to fluff her flattened hair. "Must have been unsettling. Getting that call last night. Talking to our guy."

"Sure." Beth started to fold her arms in front of her, but then didn't, aware that Jenny would recognize the body language. Would know that the current topic made her anxious.

"But you're having second thoughts about it now? Wondering if you're up to the challenge?"

Beth didn't say anything for several seconds, slightly shaken by Jenny's analysis. Mostly because it was dead-on. For most of the afternoon, she'd been thinking about the next phone call, trying to prepare herself emotionally for it. And had been worried that when the time came, she'd fail. And because she did, more people would die.

She would die.

Jenny studied her briefly. "You're wondering if you have what it takes?"

"I suppose I am."

"I'm just going to be blunt here. I've heard some of the rumors that have been circulating about your recent troubles with Monroe. That kind of thing can really undercut an agent's confidence. Make her question every move she makes. Every decision. And when cases are discussed, she starts holding back, afraid if she opens her mouth, she'll look incompetent." Jenny paused. "I haven't seen anything to suggest there's any truth to those rumors."

She pulled the hat back on. "I've worked with Gerritsen a number of times. He's no fool. If he didn't think you could handle it, you wouldn't be here."

Jenny opened the outside door. "Want me to wait for you?"

Beth shook her head. "No. I'll be fine. I'll be right behind you."

Several minutes later Beth removed the baseball cap, leaving it on the edge of the sink while she splashed water on her face. Jenny's vote of confidence had taken her by surprise and, more important, made her reexamine her actions over the past four months. Beth realized she'd been holding back. She'd been analyzing and questioning herself endlessly. Monroe had taken lies and nearly made them truths. But only because she'd let him.

Since her arrival in Bellingham, though, she'd begun to trust herself again.

Tossing the wad of tissue she'd used to wipe her face into the trash, she stepped back outside. Perhaps it was only that she'd just left a lighted space, but the trail seemed darker.

Unzipping her jacket to make her weapon more accessible, she hesitated, making excuses for her sudden and unwarranted jumpiness. She was tired. Kind words had lowered her defenses. A faceless monster planned to kill her. Only the last of those could actually harm her, and she didn't for a minute believe the monster was anywhere near by.

He was too smart for that.

Almost as soon as Beth stepped from beneath the overhang and headed toward the pavilion, the night went from dark to bathed in soft light. Glancing up, she realized a full moon had just breached the mountain to the east and seemed to teeter atop the saw tooth silhouettes of towering pines.

The sight made her slow and then come to a complete stop.

In the relative stillness, she could hear the Nantahala Falls crashing through the gorge a mile away. Nantahala. The Cherokee word for *land of the noon-day sun*. She'd been in North Carolina for a day and a half now, but the vastness of the forest, the deep, deep gorges that saw only fleeting sunlight when the sun was straight overhead, had completely awed her. And now this moon.

She couldn't recall the last time she'd seen one quite so huge.

The hairs at the back of her neck came to attention, but it happened so slowly that she thought a breeze was responsible. Until she heard the first real rustle that couldn't be attributed to the wind.

She searched the deeper shadows beneath the trees in front of her. Her heart slammed hard behind her ribs, its rate climbing even as she tried to rein it in. Even as she told herself that it was just a foraging animal. A raccoon looking to check out the trash cans.

Slipping her hand inside her jacket, she reached for her gun just as a man's shape separated itself from the trees. Her chest tightened, but not nearly as hard as her fingers did on her weapon. She left it holstered, waiting for some sign of his intentions.

He took an additional step toward her. "Sorry. I didn't mean to frighten you."

"You didn't," she lied. The only thing she could really make out was his rangy build. Who was he? What was he doing out here?

He motioned up. "It's an exquisite sight, isn't it? Some in these parts call it a hunter's moon."

As he walked toward her, she left her hand resting on her weapon. Because he never completely moved out from beneath the trees, even when he got to within seven or eight feet of her, she still couldn't see his face clearly. But she recognized his forest ranger jacket. She'd probably met him at some point during the day, but there was nothing particularly familiar about him.

Exhaling, she let go of her weapon and forced her lips into a welcoming smile. "Come to lock up the restrooms?" she asked, still unable to completely shake her nervousness.

"Yes. And your boss asked me to check on you. To see if you were okay."

For the first time in several minutes, she was able to take a deep breath. She had nothing to be uneasy about. Mark had sent the ranger.

"I'm okay." She almost felt foolish now. "Thanks. I was just heading back." She rezipped her coat and shoved her bare hands into the deep pockets.

"Good night, then," he offered as he started toward the restrooms.

"I've heard of a harvest moon and a blue one, but why a hunter's moon?"

He turned back at the question. "They call it that because it's so big and bright that even nocturnal animals become easy prey."

"Makes sense, I guess." She walked backward a step or two. "Well. Have a good night."

"You, too."

She was nearly to the pavilion when she remembered leaving her hat in the restroom and went back to get it.

Chapter Thirteen

"So this sector is the least accessible region of the forest?" Mark asked, pointing to an area dead center of the large map. Lifting his gaze, he waited for the ranger on the opposite side of the picnic table to respond.

Because of the breeze and the poor lighting under the pavilion, two battery lanterns not only provided the needed light but also held down the edges of the map.

A propane heater had been brought in earlier to warm the space—an impossible task, given that it was an open structure. Several minutes ago, though, it had run out of fuel.

Straightening, the ranger folded his arms across his chest and tucked his hands into his armpits. "That's certainly the worst terrain, but there are others that are darn near as bad."

"But if our guy is familiar with the Nantahala and is looking to dig in for a few weeks, is this where he's likely to head?"

"Abe Rutherford was out there for sixteen months. But we're talking someone who was an army ranger and had survival skills."

"I think it's a fairly safe bet our guy has similar training."

Mark already had several agents working that angle,

pulling records of anyone from the area who had been in the armed services, focusing especially on those dishonorably discharged.

The ranger offered a tight nod. "Rutherford had two safe houses set up before he ever bombed the first clinic. If he hadn't, there's no way he could have survived a winter out there."

Was that what their guy had been doing the past few months? Establishing a base camp to operate out of? A place to return to after each strike? If that was the case, he would have begun stockpiling supplies sometime after early July. In a large city, a change of buying habits would go unnoticed, but here in Bellingham, they might not.

The ranger motioned toward the large thermos of coffee sitting on a nearby table. "I'm going to grab some. Can I bring you another cup?"

Mark shook his head. "It's late and I'm sure you're beat. For now, I think you've answered most of my questions."

"If you have more, I'll be here in the morning."

As the ranger walked off, Mark glanced at the map once more, focusing on the red dot marking the Ravenel home. If the killer was local, why start in Bellingham? Why not leave those targets closest to his base until last? He'd have to know that once he revealed himself, the manhunt would be unrelenting.

But then, nothing about this guy really seemed to add up. He wasn't acting like an extremist. His only targets so far appeared to be personal ones. He possessed a weapon capable of killing thousands at a time, but killed only a few, even if he'd aimed to kill the whole boys' basketball team, that was only twelve people. And now he wanted to make a game out of it.

Mark rubbed his lower face. It was like trying to build a house of cards from the top down. Unless you were a magician, it couldn't be done.

Maybe what he needed to do was give it a rest for an hour. Think about something else. Checking his watch, he discovered it was after nine already.

He still hadn't heard back from his attorney. Should he try phoning Traci? If she'd cooled down some, maybe he could convince her to work things out without getting any lawyers involved. She'd come around in the past, perhaps this time wouldn't be any different.

It was too late now, though. He'd have better luck calling in the morning when Addison and Gracie were busy with their video games. An unexpected and raw sense of nostalgia rolled over him as he thought about long-ago winter mornings when they'd watched cartoons in the family room while he fixed their breakfast. The way they'd giggled at the bunny-shaped pancakes. The way the scent of syrup had lingered in the kitchen for most of the day.

He loved his daughters more than anything in the world. But the truth was, he'd let them down. He'd been putting his job before them. Not for just the past four months, but for nearly a year now. Pretending that making the world a better place, a safer place, was more important than being there for them.

He obviously needed to make some changes in his life.

Lifting a lantern, he released one edge of the map, letting it roll up on its own.

It was time to pack it in, to head back to the hotel with Beth and wait for a phone call.

He glanced toward the picnic table where she'd headed after she'd grabbed the last cup of coffee. A group of searchers had come back late, and she'd gone over to talk to them. Not seeing her there, he shifted his gaze to the people near the walkway, his heart rate still normal but already beginning to climb.

Even with the poor lighting, as they parted and headed for the cars, he knew she wasn't among them.

The fatigue he'd been feeling seconds earlier vanished.

Where the hell was she? She wasn't to leave the pavilion for any reason without checking with him. He'd been very clear about it.

Hearing footsteps behind him, he turned. She'd just entered the pavilion and strolled toward him in that somewhat aggressive stride of hers. Even if he hadn't been able to see her face, he would have known her just by the way she moved. She stopped by the picnic table where the last three searchers had climbed to their feet, preparing to leave.

Trying to restrain his temper, Mark rolled up the map the rest of the way. By the time she reached him, he'd tamped down some of his anger, but not all of it.

"Looking for me?" she asked.

"You weren't to leave this pavilion without me. When I give an order, I expect it to be followed." He wrapped the rubber band around the map. "Without question." He nailed her with his gaze. "You understand?"

She didn't say anything for several seconds. He'd obviously blindsided her. He didn't know why, though. She should have known he'd be upset when she ignored a command.

"I went to the bathroom, not wandering out into the woods." Her mouth flattened. "I'm in no more danger now than I was in the parking garage two nights ago. I handled that situation. And I'll handle the next one."

"You damned well weren't my responsibility then."

The words hung between them for several seconds, long enough for Mark to realize just how loudly he'd said them. And that he was thankful that it was only the two of them in the pavilion now.

Beth ducked her head, running her hand through her hair. Meeting his gaze, she spoke in a tone that may not have been calm, but was certainly controlled. "And your only responsibility now is as my senior officer."

Faced with her composure, Mark managed to get a foothold into his own. "We both know my culpability goes beyond that. That I hold at least partial blame. If I hadn't shoved you out there in front of him, he wouldn't even know you exist."

"And if he didn't, where would this investigation be?" She folded her arms. "Let's get one thing straight here. You may have requested the transfer, but I consider it an opportunity. One that I was lucky to get."

Frowning, he stepped in closer. "The chance to be bait?"

"No." Her gray eyes narrowed slightly as she lifted her chin to meet his gaze. "The chance to do my job. The opportunity to pursue a career that I happen to love."

He scanned her face. How in the hell could he argue with any of it? Hadn't she proven herself more than once today?

Hell. Maybe he was overreacting here. She was a trained FBI agent. One who hadn't hesitated to use lethal force when it was necessary. And he really had no reason to believe the man they hunted would come after her. Not this early in the game.

But when he'd looked up and been unable to find her...

He glanced away, troubled by the direction of his thoughts. But when he looked back, she was running a hand through her hair again, briefly exposing her right temple and the bullet graze just above it.

His gut tightened. She didn't seem to recognize just how damn close she'd come two nights ago.

He reached out, resting his fingers against her cheek. She seemed startled by the contact, her eyes first widening as they met his and then almost immediately narrowing, becoming guarded again.

Her skin was unbelievably soft beneath his fingertips and cool. He'd wanted to touch her a dozen times in the past forty-eight hours, but something had always stopped him—maybe only the desire to do the right thing.

So what in the hell was he doing now?

"I know you believe the reason it was Leon Tyber dead on that garage floor and not you was all the drills you ran in Hogan's Alley and the hours you spent on the shooting range."

He brushed his thumb along her right cheekbone, just missing the injury. "But the truth is…you came within an inch of losing your life. It could just as easily have been you on that floor."

His chest tightened as he imagined what it would have been like to find her body sprawled on the cold concrete instead of Tyber's.

She angled her chin up a bit more. Since it was her usual MO, he assumed it was with the intention of refuting his words, but she didn't. Instead she stood there mutely. He liked her chin, the way it popped up when she was challenged, like a fighter daring you to take your best shot. And even sexier, the soft, feminine cleft at its end.

When her bare lips softened and then parted, he realized the tightness in his chest no longer had anything to do with anger or concern.

He shifted his gaze to where he was touching her. He shouldn't be. Not like this. Nor should he be thinking about sleeping with her, but God help him, he was. And there was nothing abstract about it. He was imagining her firm thighs locked around him. Her tight abdomen rising up to meet him. Her harsh breathing in his ear as she came beneath him.

And from what he saw in her dark eyes, she was, too.

As if she'd been holding her breath, she suddenly exhaled, the warmth of it brushing the underside of his wrist. The sensation climbed his arm and shot deep into his body where the fantasies of seconds earlier already had him half-hard.

Unable to stop himself, he brushed his thumb over her bare lips and then slowly dipped his mouth toward hers. As their lips met, hers softened beneath his. She tasted like coffee.

Reaching out, his hand closed over her right hip, his fingertips flexing against denim as he tugged her nearer, deepening the kiss.

Wrapping her arms around his neck, she shifted in even closer, her breathing as ragged as his own. Her mouth opened beneath his as her abdomen brushed against his arousal. He felt control skating beyond his grasp. She was so damned sexy.

Pulling back, he looked into her eyes. They were as dark and as desperate as his own. Sliding his fingers through her hair, he lowered his lips to hers again and kissed her deeply, fiercely.

Her cell phone went off, the ring tone surprisingly loud. He felt her flinch with the second ring, and before it rang a third time, she was pulling away. He didn't hesitate to let her go.

And by the time it rang a fourth time, his regret had already set in. Backing away, she answered it.

"Yes, Father." Turning, she took several more steps, casting an uncomfortable glance over her shoulder as she moved away. "I got the message and I was planning to call."

She rubbed her forehead. "When?" Her voice dropped, the strain coming through for the first time. "Later, I guess. When I got back to the hotel."

As she listened, she paced several more feet, and because she still had her back to him, he watched her.

"Is that what Monroe told you? That the reassignment was temporary?"

Mark grabbed the map, wondering about not only the relationship between Beth and her father, but the one between her father and Bill Monroe, too. Why was Bill Monroe talking to Beth's father about things he clearly had no right to?

"Are you suggesting that you've been in contact with my doctor? That would be a clear violation of HIPPA."

Her shoulders stiffened. "But I didn't ask you to call their office, did I?"

She went silent for several seconds, and then said in an angry tone, "This conversation is over."

Even after she ended the call, she didn't face him right away, and he assumed that she was trying to collect herself.

Something inside him wanted to reach out to her, but he held it in check. He'd known that touching her would be a mistake and that kissing her would be an even bigger one.

Because now that he had, there was no way to go back, to pretend it hadn't happened.

Or to pretend that he didn't want it to happen again.

MARK HELD OPEN the door to the pizza joint. After the long day outside, when Beth stepped into the unexpected warmth, the aromas were welcoming. She scanned the interior. Quite a few tables were covered in the remnants of recent meals, but there were no other actual diners. Country music played on what sounded like a cheap radio in the kitchen. The sign outside had said they closed at ten and it was already nine-forty.

Before they'd entered the restaurant, she hadn't been all that hungry, but now her stomach growled.

A waitress stuck her head out the kitchen door. "Seat yourselves."

Mark motioned toward a back corner booth. "Why don't we try that one?"

Beth offered a silent nod and headed for it, aware of him just behind her as she wound her way through the tables in the center of the room. She dug her hands a little deeper into her pockets as she walked.

He'd spent most of the drive back to town on his cell phone, checking in with agents who hadn't been involved in the manhunt today, who'd been given other assignments instead. And she'd been extremely thankful that he'd been otherwise engaged because it had given her some time to pull herself together.

She'd known from the beginning that she was attracted to him and known that it wasn't completely one sided. And that getting involved with him on anything but a professional level would be stupid.

If you want something badly enough, you'll go against your best judgment.

Which is exactly what she'd done. And what she couldn't let happen again.

From the vibes he was giving off and the way he so carefully avoided any type of physical contact with her, she assumed he regretted the kiss every bit as much as she did.

Regretting and forgetting were two entirely different things, though.

Before sliding into the booth, she peeled off the heavy coat. The waitress had trailed behind and after explaining that the oven would be shut down soon, took their order.

Beth waited for the mugs of beer to be delivered before asking, "Has anything turned up yet connecting Thesing to the Ravenels?"

"No." He took a long sip. "And the list of ex-military with connections to this area is a long one. It will probably take twenty-four hours to check out everyone on it."

"What about you? Did you do any time in the military?"

"I did four years before going to college. Even after we moved away from the farm, money was always tight."

He rubbed his jaw, the action drawing attention to the five-o'clock shadow, reminding her how the slight stubble had felt against her skin.

"How'd you end up in counterterrorism?"

"I was three blocks from ground zero when 9/11 happened. I requested a transfer the next morning."

Having finished his beer, he relaxed back and folded his hands on the table between them. "What is the relationship between your father and Bill Monroe?"

The question caught her so completely off guard that the bottom of the mug clacked against the table top as she set it down. She knew he was scrutinizing her, so avoided looking up.

She debated not responding, but in all fairness, he had put a lot on the line when he'd requested her transfer, so maybe she owed him an answer.

Inhaling sharply, she fought the growing tightness in her lungs, worried that when she'd finished with this question, he'd ask her about the reason behind Bill Monroe's vendetta.

"There is no relationship between my father and Monroe beyond the occasional phone call," she answered cautiously. "And I need to start by explaining that my mother wasn't American and had grown up in a society where women deferred without question to their men." Her mouth tightened, recalling her mother's courage when it came to her daughter, to seeing that Beth was raised differently. "She was the kind of wife my father wanted. She was never a true partner, but more a facilitator. She made his life easy. Was a beautiful and consummate hostess. All of which were desirable qualities in a diplomat's wife."

She took a sip of beer. "Some people think it was my father's decision that I be raised in the States, spending only summers overseas with them."

Mark leaned forward. "But it wasn't?"

"No. It was my mother." She inhaled softly. "She sent me to live with my father's parents, allowed them to raise her daughter because she wanted me to be completely American. She always used to say that freedom wasn't just a state of being it was a state of mind. Even when he retired and they were living full-time in the States, she never could make that transition. In her mind she always had to defer to him."

She looked away. Had she really needed to tell him all that? To go into quite that much detail?

"When I was released from the hospital four months ago, I spent fourteen days pretending I was okay and fourteen nights waiting for Rabbit Rheaume to send someone to kill me. I decided to take vacation time, go home for a few weeks. The security at my father's place is the best money can buy. I was hoping a different environment and a feeling of safety might help me turn the corner. And I guess because I'd only seen him twice during the time I was working the Rheaume case, I was hoping to spend some time with my father. To reconnect. We had several long talks, in some of them I revealed too much. He ordered me to resign from the FBI. When I refused, he went behind my back and called Bill Monroe."

"And said what?"

"That I was having nightmares. That I'd told him that I was concerned about my ability to function. It wasn't that my father lied, it was just the idea that when my back was against the wall, he turned his on me, too." She nudged the mug to one side. "We'll get beyond it eventually."

Even as she said those words, she realized just how foolish they were. Tomorrow was guaranteed to no one.

Her least of all.

IT WAS AFTER 3:00 a.m. when Beth scrambled out of bed, dragging half the covers onto the floor in the process.

For the past hour she'd been staring at the black void overhead, unable to shake the feeling the ceiling was slowly pressing down on her like a junkyard crusher. And that the reason she couldn't breathe was because the room had become so small it no longer held enough oxygen.

Logically she knew the ceiling hadn't moved and that there was plenty of air, but somehow all the logic in the world wasn't enough right now. She needed fresh air.

With desperate, unsteady hands, she jerked an oversize sweatshirt over her T-shirt and running shorts. She couldn't seem to get warm. It was as if there was this big block of ice somewhere deep inside her that just kept radiating cold.

Why in the hell did she have to have a panic attack tonight? With Mark in the adjoining room? With only an unlocked door between them?

Trying to hold on to the last edges of her self-control, she pulled on the sliding glass door, letting it creep soundlessly along the metal track. She couldn't let him see her. Not like this. She knew what she looked like right now. Frantic. Out of control.

Even when she had the door open, she didn't step outside. Instead, she sagged just inside. The first frigid blast of air on her bare legs was brutal, but the first cauterizing lungful was pure heaven. And after several minutes, the raw panic began to fade. Enough that she finally could concentrate on the landscape. It was a serene scene, the rolling lawn stretching uphill until it reached a line of hemlocks above. The light frost on the grass looked silvery in the moonlight.

She breathed deeply and evenly. Nights were always the worst. Without the distractions of duties to be fulfilled, of immediate challenges to be met, there was too much time to think. And worse still, to remember the terror of being locked inside a car trunk, the odor of burning leather seats, of animal skin, reaching her…knowing that she would be next.

But tonight her subconscious had served up new images, those of the two plumbers and of the Ravenels. Maybe it was because she'd come so close to dying that she could almost physically feel the emotional anguish and terror of their last moments on earth.

And now she was waiting for a call from the man who had so callously orchestrated those deaths. He'd said he might spare her, but she knew better.

Only one of them would survive.

Why her, though? Why had he chosen her?

Her chest had already started to tighten again when the door between the two adjoining rooms slowly opened. Glancing over, she saw Mark's silhouette. When he'd heard her moving around, had he assumed she'd received another call from the killer?

"Can't sleep?" he asked quietly.

"No." Turning to face him, she was surprised to see that he wore sweat bottoms that rode low at his lean hips and nothing else. The milky-blue light of the moon coming through the glass revealed every well-defined muscle of his chest and abdomen. She hurriedly glanced away, snugging her arms in front of her. Any other time, just looking at him might have made it possible to at least briefly push more lethal thoughts to the side, but not tonight.

"Want company?"

"Sure." She would have preferred to turn down the offer. To roll up into herself to hide. But she suspected refusing would only make him curious.

Stepping past her, he leaned against the wall on the opposite side of the slider, facing her. She glanced at him quickly, but then turned her attention back outside again, pretending there was something out there that intrigued her.

After several seconds he leaned toward her, the action probably meant to capture her attention. "You know there's a possibility that he won't call tonight, that we've thrown him off his game. At least temporarily."

"I know," she said, still staring outside. "Rutherford went to ground for sixteen months before he was captured. Hid out in these mountains. Survived on salamanders and acorns. I hope this time is different."

Out of the corner of her eye, she saw him frown. "Sixteen months without a bombing? Without innocent people losing their lives? I'll take that any day."

She knew he was right.

But if this killer disappeared for months and months, or even years…She forced air a little deeper into her lungs. She'd given nearly two years of her life to the Rheaume investigation, dealing with the stress and the knowledge that if her cover was blown Rabbit would kill her. She didn't want to spend a similar amount of time waiting for this killer to resurface, always looking over her shoulder, wondering if he was right behind her, wondering if in the next instant she was going to wind up like his other victims.

She'd been isolated for so long, first because of an investigation that made it a necessity and then because of the fallout from that same investigation. For the past four months, previous friends had been reaching out to her, but she'd turned them away. Afraid for their safety. Afraid that if Rheaume tried again, someone she cared about might get hurt.

What if she hadn't been alone in that garage two nights ago?

She didn't even realize there were tears on her cheeks until he was pulling her into his arms, against his lean body. Despite the way he radiated the warmth, the strength she so desperately needed, her arms remained limp at her sides. After months and years of relying on only her own stores of strength, she didn't know how to accept it from him.

"Shush," he said, his voice pitched low and slightly rough. "It's going to be okay."

She tried to smother the first harsh sob against his chest, tried to push the next one back down her throat, but it was no good. Now that one of them had escaped, there was no stopping the rest. Her hands crept up to his waist, rested there for several seconds with curled fingers before she finally wrapped her arms around him and held on tight.

She didn't try to lie to herself. The tears weren't for other people. They were selfish ones. She was just so damned tired of it all. Of fighting for her job, her life.

"Shush. Nothing's going to happen to you. I won't let it."

She wanted to believe him. Wanted to be able to trust that somehow he could protect her. But the truth was, even he wasn't safe.

Especially when he stood between her and the man they hunted.

His arms stayed locked around her until her sobs faded. Until her muscles loosened. Until she became aware that his hands ran slowly up and down her back.

Embarrassed, she attempted to back away. "I'm sorry. I don't…"

"There's nothing for you to be sorry about." Opening his arms, he still didn't let her go, his right hand closing on her left shoulder.

"Come on." He turned her toward the bed. "Let's get you warm."

Chapter Fourteen

After tucking her in, pulling the sheet and blanket up around her chin, Mark crossed to the sliding glass door, intending to close the curtains.

"Please don't," she said.

"Okay." He turned toward the door connecting their rooms.

"I meant please don't leave. I want you to stay."

He glanced over his shoulder, his gaze connecting with hers. The moonlight coming through the slider didn't quite reach the bed, so he couldn't really see her face. But then, he didn't have to. Everything he needed to know had been in her voice. She didn't want to be alone. She was still dealing with demons. And after the kiss earlier, he was dealing with a few of his own.

As he approached the bed, she shifted, making room. But as soon as she had, she lay back and closed her eyes.

It was only then that he realized what asking him had probably cost her.

Stretching out next to her, he pulled the covers over them both.

She was scared. He understood that. Anyone in her situation would be frightened. What he didn't fully understand was why she believed she shouldn't be afraid. Why she thought that justified fear made her weak.

"Talk to me," she said in the silence. "About anything."

It sounded like such a simple request, but it wasn't. Plenty of things came to mind. Like how he'd been awake for hours before he'd heard her get out of bed. Only, it hadn't been the anticipation of a killer's phone call robbing him of sleep. It had been the knowledge that she was only steps away. That there wasn't even a locked door between them. And that after the kiss earlier, odds were she wouldn't refuse him.

Even though her invitation had nothing to do with sex, his body had still gone hard. God. He should never have kissed her. Because now that he had, he couldn't get her out of his mind. Couldn't stop thinking about not just how sexy she was, but also how competent and resilient and…interesting. He'd noticed that trait when she'd been his student.

She stirred beside him, the mattress bouncing lightly as she turned to face him. "Tell me about your daughters."

"What do you want to know?"

"Do you get to see them much?"

"No. Not as much as I should. It's been seven weeks this time." And he didn't know how many more would go by before he'd get back to Virginia. So much depended on what happened with the investigation.

"Is that what your ex-wife was upset about? Your not seeing them enough?"

He'd known Beth had overheard part of the phone call, so her question didn't surprise him. What did was that he was telling her any of this.

"I was supposed to have the girls this weekend, should

have picked them up today after school. It was the third time that I canceled like that. Traci was worried how the girls were going to take it." He looked over at Beth. "When I wasn't able to make it the last time, Gracie became convinced that something had happened to me. That I wasn't ever coming home again." He ran a hand roughly over his face. "Traci had to deal with the fallout. It's hard on her." He paused.

"It's obviously hard on you, too," Beth said.

Mark reached out, brushing his fingers along Beth's cheekbone. "You and me, we see some pretty tough things. But I've discovered one of the hardest of all is seeing my daughter scared. Seeing anyone you care about scared is hard," he corrected. "Especially when they believe it means they're less than they should be."

His thumb brushed across her lips. "You're a very courageous woman, Beth. Don't let anyone convince you otherwise."

She started to turn away, but he wouldn't let her. "Being brave doesn't mean being without fear and never asking for help. We all have to sometimes." He smoothed her hair away from her face. "Why did Monroe assign you to the Rheaume case? You were less than thirteen months out of the academy."

She stiffened immediately. "You should ask him," she answered evasively.

"I'm asking you to trust me."

She rolled onto her back again and seemed to stare at the ceiling for more than a minute. "You remember that harbor bombing two years ago?"

"Sure."

"While working another case, I received a tip about a possible problem. I presented it to Bill Monroe. He said I wasn't to follow up on it, that he'd assign the lead to someone else. Someone with more experience. But he didn't. And I didn't find out until it was too late." She paused, this time glancing over at him. "I confronted him. He denied everything. And when I tried to take it to his boss, he made sure I couldn't. Made sure that it looked as if I had never given him the information in the first place. That I was the one who'd screwed up."

Mark had never liked the prick. "So he sent you undercover?"

She had looked away, but now glanced over at him again. "Yeah. I think he was hoping that Rabbit Rheaume would make me go away."

The anger that had been slowly building exploded inside him. Before he was through with Monroe, the man would wish he'd never met Beth.

Mark rolled onto his side and pulled her close. "I think it's time we both tried to get some sleep."

When the alarm on his phone went off in the next room hours later, he'd been awake for several minutes, but Beth was still sleeping peacefully. He couldn't recall the last time he'd shared a bed with a woman when it hadn't included sex. But then, what they'd managed to share fully dressed was more intimate than any sex act.

Beth stirred slightly as the alarm fell silent. It would go off again in five minutes. He'd let her sleep a few minutes more.

What was it about her that made him want to share parts of himself that he normally didn't?

When he and Traci had been first married, he'd brought aspects of his job home. He'd needed someone to talk to and she was the obvious choice. But he'd soon discovered his mistake. All the sharing may have been helping him, but not Traci. He'd wake up in the middle of the night and find her silently crying, worried that something would happen to him. That one night he wouldn't come home. It was easy to draw the parallel with what Gracie was going through right now.

Within months of entering the FBI, he stopped talking about his work and began to pretend that the investigations he'd been assigned were easier and safer. He and Traci had settled into a routine that in the end was at least partially responsible for their marriage falling apart.

Still mostly asleep, Beth groaned softly. She was flat on her stomach, her face half-buried in her pillow. As she opened her eyes, blinking even though the room was still mostly shadows, she met his gaze and smiled sleepily. "I can't believe I slept." She pushed up on her elbows. "What time is it?"

"About six-thirty." He traced the crease that sleep had left on her cheek. "You're beautiful in the morning, you know that?" Her eyes went dark as he leaned over and covered her mouth with his own. He had meant to give her just a quick wake-up kiss—all they had time for. But as soon as his lips brushed hers, her mouth opened under his, wet and welcoming. Jesus. She was sexy. Especially as she was now. Warm. Still muzzy with sleep. Not as guarded as she was when wide awake.

But unfortunately he was wide-awake. He knew that he was playing with fire. And that he wouldn't be the one who ended up burned. He couldn't do that to her. She had enough to contend with. She needed the other members of the unit to see her as the capable agent that she was, not as the woman in his bed.

She'd been hurt enough by jerks like Monroe. And even by her father. Mark had no intention of being the next in line.

It took everything inside him to pull back, to roll away from her soft body. From the raging need in his own.

When he glanced over his shoulder, she was already sitting on the opposite edge of the bed, her stiffly held back to him. He left without saying a word, pulling the connecting door closed as he went.

BETH JERKED THE BRUSH through her damp hair. She usually spent more than fifteen minutes drying it, torturing it smooth, but this morning she didn't have the patience for it. And the baseball cap would destroy her efforts, anyway.

When she'd gone back for her hat last night, she'd found the restroom door still unlocked but the cap gone. And no sign of the ranger.

She grabbed a spare cap. Gathering her hair in a rough ponytail, she slipped the back opening over it, settling the hat in place before knocking on the connecting door.

"Come in," Mark said.

When she entered, Larson was standing next to the door leading out into the hallway, and Mark was sliding his gun into the holster clipped at his waist. Both men wore jeans, sweatshirts marked with FBI on both the front and the back and hiking boots.

Mark's glance connected with hers in the mirror, but then he turned toward Larson, continuing their previous conversation. "Abe Rutherford's first two targets were small, only one or two casualties. It wasn't until he mastered his technique that he went after larger ones. Maybe our killer is doing the same thing. He could be a Rutherford fan."

Larson folded his arms in front of him. "So you think we should be looking for a connection between our killer and Rutherford?"

"And any environmentalist that Thesing was in contact with," Mark said. "I think we need to continue looking in all directions for the moment, until we have something that tells us otherwise."

As Mark grabbed the autoinjectors off the dresser and slid them into a case attached to his belt, Larson's speculative gaze settled on Beth. To avoid it, she checked her own weapon.

Eventually Larson gave up and shifted his attention to Mark again. "Command center is up and running over at the National Guard Armory now," Larson said as he opened the room door. Mark had ordered the change when it became apparent that the investigation not only needed more space, but also more security.

Five hours later the search party she'd been assigned to had walked nearly three miles into the forest, spaced ten feet apart and climbing steadily. Mark had divided the area to be searched into grids, assigning one to each of the seven teams. At that rate it would still take them a month to cover every square mile and didn't address the probability that, like Rutherford, their killer would continue to move around at night.

Beth paused to take a swig of water and to catch her breath. Despite the cold temperatures, she was beginning to perspire beneath the soft body armor and heavy sweatshirt. Starting out this morning, her leg muscles had been stiff. Once they'd loosened up some, though, she'd been fine. But within the last half mile or so, they'd started to cramp up on her. A condition that would become increasingly difficult to cope with and to hide.

Feeling Mark's gaze on her, she glanced over. He'd been keeping a close eye on her without ever getting too close.

And maybe it was better that way since she didn't know what she'd say to him, anyway. She was feeling overexposed at the moment. Wishing he'd never walked into her room last night. Wishing he hadn't seen her fall apart the way she did. And most of all, wishing that she could forget how when he'd kissed her this morning, she'd wanted him to stay.

But considering they were in the midst of what was quickly becoming one of the largest manhunts of all time, thinking about anything personal seemed wrong somehow.

She screwed on the cap to the water bottle. At least she didn't have to put up with Larson's scrutiny. Mark had assigned Larson the grid containing the roughest terrain, accessible only with the use of climbing gear and guts. The same twelve-square-mile area where Rutherford had disappeared for sixteen months.

It would take more than a day to hike in, and once there, the search party of nine agents and three local trackers would stay until they'd covered every square inch. And when they left, they'd leave behind surveillance equipment so the area could be remotely monitored.

As she was about to put away the water bottle, her cell phone went off. She recognized the Maryland area code, but not the number.

"Sleep well?"

At the familiar voice, her chest tightened with apprehension and her suddenly nerveless fingers dropped the bottle.

She looked for Mark, but didn't see him. Only a short distance from where he'd last been standing, though, were what the locals called rhododendron hells, an area where the bush was so thick it was nearly impenetrable. Making the assumption that he'd gone in to search it, she started walking toward the area.

"How did you get this number?"

"I'm not without resources."

He was mocking her. "That goes without saying. If you were, you wouldn't have the MX141."

"You did well yesterday. You're quite the jock."

"Not really. But still enough of one to nearly catch you." She was to challenge him at every opportunity. Not openly, but in a cautious, oblique manner that undermined his ego and put him on the defensive. The hope was that he'd reveal details about himself or about his plans.

He chuckled. "There's always next time."

She was nearly to the dense brush when Mark pushed his way out into the open again. Something in her face must have told him who the caller was.

"How did you know Harvey Thesing?"

Another soft chuckle. "We haven't even started playing yet, and you're already breaking the first rule of our little game."

"Then maybe you should fill me in. Let me know how it works."

"Rule number one. You ask too many questions, I hang up."

It was the one thing she couldn't allow to happen. Beth felt dread pool in her gut. "Agreed."

"What the hell do you think this is—a democracy?"

Because she didn't think he expected her to answer and she was afraid saying anything might piss him off, she remained silent.

"You've got this phone number in your caller ID. As soon as we're done talking, I'm going to take the battery out of this cell phone. But every few hours I'll put it back in for one minute. Just long enough for you to locate me. Do you understand?"

"Yes."

"Ever done any deer hunting?"

"No." Beth's gaze connected with Mark's. "I don't kill for the fun of it."

"Neither do I."

"Why do you kill, then?" She asked the question before she could stop herself and then waited the tensest split second of her life to see if he'd hang up.

"Because I can," he said, and she could hear the amusement in his voice. "Ever play connect the dots as a kid?"

"Yes."

"Well, that's what we're playing here. You connect them fast enough, you just might be able to stop me. If you don't, people die."

Chapter Fifteen

Mark already had the command center on the line when the killer disconnected. Grabbing her phone, he went to the incoming log. "I need to know the GPS coordinates of this cell phone number during the past few minutes, and I want it yesterday." As he read the number he realized that the area code was a familiar one. A Fredricks, Maryland, one.

Disconnecting and seeing just how pale Beth was, his inclination was to pull her into his arms. Instead, aware that they had an audience, he helped her to the closest tree.

"Sit with your back against the trunk."

After she slid down, he squatted in front of her, passed his own water bottle to her and waited while she took several sips.

"Okay. I need you to tell me everything he said."

They spent several minutes going over the conversation, the instructions she'd been given.

When his cell rang, he answered it. "What do you have?"

Mark knew the name of the agent on the end, but wouldn't have been able to put a face with it.

"He's at a truck stop just outside Atlanta, Georgia. The field office there is being contacted right now."

"And who is the phone registered to?"

"Harvey Thesing." The name didn't come as a surprise to Mark. When he'd seen the area code, he'd guessed as much.

"As soon as the local agents reach the truck stop, have them contact me."

While he'd been talking, Beth had climbed to her feet.

His gaze connected with hers as he closed his cell. He couldn't seem to stop himself from reaching out, but as soon as his fingers touched her cheek, she pulled back and turned her head slightly. With no other choice, he allowed his hand to drop again, recognizing that he owed her an explanation for his hasty retreat this morning.

He didn't know how he was going to provide one, though, since he couldn't fully explain it to himself.

At the time, he'd told himself it was because he wanted to protect her. Now he suspected there had been more to it. That, even more than protecting her, he'd been trying to protect himself. Not from any type of career fallout, but from something much more personal.

He'd been alone, a bachelor, for four years now, but had never felt particularly lonely. Until this morning. Until he'd pulled that door closed behind him.

"Come on, Benedict. It looks as if we're headed to Atlanta to start with."

It would take two and a half hours by car, but did they have that much time? How soon before the next *dot* was provided?

And how in the hell were they suppose to beat him there if they were always one step behind?

THE HIKE BACK took considerably less time because they were no longer looking for signs of the killer and because they were headed downhill. By the time they reached the staging area, a helicopter was waiting to take them to Atlanta.

Beth was pleased but surprised to see that Jenny Springer had been chosen to accompany them. The fourth agent riding with them was a member of the counterterrorism unit, Special Agent Dan Sturbridge. He was close to fifty and looked more like a marine than a special agent. She'd met him the first day, but she'd had little contact with him since.

As the pilot pulled open the door and motioned for them to climb in, Beth felt the first twinges of uncertainty. But it was nothing like what it usually was. The claustrophobia was getting better. Only a few weeks ago, she would have freaked just thinking about climbing into an elevator, let alone a helicopter.

Deep, slow breaths, Benedict.

She'd managed to survive the plane ride two days ago, hadn't she? But there had been a moment or two when if someone had handed her a parachute, she would have made use of it.

She felt a hand rest against her lower back. She looked up, her gaze meeting Mark's somber one. "You'll be fine."

She'd lost count of the times he'd said those words over the past few days.

With no other choice, she stepped aboard and, taking a seat, slipped on the headset that would allow them to communicate with one another during the flight.

As they lifted off, she looked down at the receding forest, recalling Mark telling her that he would take sixteen months without innocent lives being lost. Suddenly she wished the same and felt ashamed that she'd ever felt any differently.

Shifting her gaze, she caught sight of a news crew below, their camera aimed up at the helicopter.

Elvis has left the building.

Maybe now that the focus of the manhunt was elsewhere, the media would follow, leaving the people of Bellingham to begin the healing process. The helicopter gently swayed as the pilot turned it southwest.

Her heart might have missed half a beat and her breathing was on the quick side, but all in all, she was doing much better than she'd anticipated. Taking a deep breath, she held it for half a minute before letting it go.

"You know," Beth said, turning away from the view and focusing on Mark who sat across from her, "there's nothing to say that the unsub isn't in a helicopter right now or on a commercial flight to the West Coast."

Mark adjusted his mike. "If he's flying, it's not commercial. He needs to keep the chemical with him. Under current guidelines, it would have to go into checked luggage. He can't risk the airline losing his bag and putting him out of business. And as far as distance, he can't go too far. His game only works if we're close enough that we could conceivably catch him."

"Why the game, though?" Beth asked. "Why risk letting us get too close? Unless he wants us to stop him."

"I don't think that's what he wants. But we're not really going to know until we figure out why the Ravenels and why the school. Even if they were practice runs for him, they were still chosen for a reason. We figure that out and we start to figure him out." Mark glanced over at Jenny. "Did you turn up anything that connects Harvey Thesing and Abe Rutherford?"

"Several names came up, but I don't think they're going to be the break we're looking for. At least, not immediately. They're long-time activists. They donate heavily and they keep their governors and senators buried in letters. However, there's nothing that suggests any connection to a more extremist group. But to be on the thorough side, I contacted the field offices in their areas to do a more complete check of recent activities."

Dan Sturbridge flipped the mike into place. "One or two names on the dishonorably discharged military list also turned up on an antigovernment list. And a few were students of Richard Ravenel. Scott Duzenberry is tracking them down."

Beth retrieved her cell phone and upped the ring volume so she'd be able to hear it above the noise of the rotors. She'd given both her father and the unsub special ring tones.

The killer hadn't said he'd call. Only that he'd restore the battery in the phone so they could *see* him.

Stretching his feet out in front of him, Mark settled back in the seat. When their gazes met, she saw frustration in his eyes.

Having worked next to him for days now, she'd witnessed firsthand what it took to run this type of investigation. Not only great investigative skills, but management ones, too. And the ability to thrive under pressure.

But even Mark was feeling the strain of the past few days.

It hadn't been just days for him, though. He'd been working the case 24/7 for the past four months, ignoring his personal life.

Last night in the quiet darkness, he'd talked about his daughters. It was obvious that he loved them. And that he felt he'd let them down. Somewhere, laced within his words, had been an unspoken question. Should he leave the FBI? Shouldn't family come first? Before the country he'd taken an oath to protect and defend?

The fact that he grappled with those questions said a lot about the kind of man he was. The kind any woman would want beside her.

Beth turned and stared out the window.

THE HELICOPTER LANDED in Atlanta, Georgia, just over an hour and fifteen minutes later. A steady rain was already falling, but with the lower elevation, the temperature was ten degrees warmer than what they'd left behind in Bellingham.

Two SUVs were already waiting. Grabbing their luggage, they made the transfer in seconds.

Beth slammed the back gate closed. "I have the directions to the truck stop. Want me to drive?"

Mark had already pulled open the driver's door but now moved aside. Because he was on his cell phone, he gave a thumbs-up before walking around to the passenger side.

Saturday traffic was relatively light, so even with the wet road conditions they were making good time until they got to within several blocks of the truck stop.

Nothing looked very good beneath somber gray sky and drizzling rain, but the area they were in was obviously one of those in the early stages of flux.

The tightly packed, brick buildings lining both sides of the street looked old enough to be called historic. Some had For Sale signs out front, others had the trendy neon variety. Most of the businesses seemed to be the kind favored by first-time entrepreneurs: antique shops, an Internet coffee bar, an upholstery shop.

It definitely seemed like an unusual area for a truck stop.

Seeing the road block ahead, Beth started looking for a parking place. It was only then that she gave any thought to the second SUV and that it was no longer behind them.

But maybe Dan had known what kind of mess there was likely to be and had grabbed the first spot he'd found.

Mark was handling his ninth or tenth call now, this one about the ex-military angle. "Keep me posted." Disconnecting one call, he started to dial another. "You're a good driver, Benedict."

It was the second time today that he'd called her Benedict. First he'd left this morning without saying anything and now he was back to calling her Benedict. Seemed like a pretty clear indication of where things stood between them. She tried to tell herself that it was for the best, but couldn't quite ignore the sense of disappointment that settled in her chest.

Finally realizing that she wasn't going to find a space and that with vehicles crammed on both sides of the street, turning around was going to be difficult, she slammed the Explorer in Reverse, intending to back down the street until she found a spot. But as she shifted her foot off the brake and onto the gas, a fire truck came barreling in behind, siren going full blast.

With no other options, she jumped the curb in front of a coffee shop, forcing people to back out of her way.

As soon as the truck passed, she shifted the vehicle into Reverse.

Mark reached over and turned off the ignition. "No time for that. They're not going to be handing out any tickets today." Grabbing his baseball cap, he tugged it on.

Despite the worsening rain, people from nearby businesses continued to crowd the sidewalk. Mark and Beth hurriedly pushed their way through, ignoring the questions that flew at them from all sides. The sound of another siren could be heard above that of nearby interstate traffic.

Just before they reached the barricade, Mark's phone rang again. Answering it, he listened and then hung up without ever speaking. "Hazmat's on the scene. No fatalities and no indication yet that our guy used MX141. And Jenny and Dan are stuck out on the interstate, caught behind an accident. I told them to steer clear of here for the moment."

Holding his badge up for the patrol officer manning the barrier to see, Mark moved through the opening ahead of Beth.

The rain was coming down a bit more steadily now, and she could feel the dampness finally penetrating the sweatshirt and the T-shirt she wore beneath.

Crossing the street, they headed for Pete's Truck Stop. A semi had been backed up to the building, and men in full hazmat gear were carrying box after box of merchandise out of the store and loading it onto the truck. Every shelf would be cleared, each food item tested before being incinerated.

As they negotiated past the last set of barricades, the patrol officer pointed toward the front entrance of the building. "You'll find Special Agent Sheffield just around the other side."

Though Sheffield looked to be only in his late forties, his blond hair already showed silver streaks at the temples. After introductions, he gave them a rundown. "We've pulled the surveillance footage and collected the charge slips, but it'll take some time to obtain driver's license photos and do the eliminations."

Beth knew that even with a dozen agents working the eliminations, it would take at least five or six hours. And when they were done, they'd be left with the pictures of everyone who'd paid cash and maybe if they were extremely lucky, the killer's, too.

"After we evacuated, we interviewed the employees and any customers still on the lot, but nobody saw anything."

"Doesn't surprise me," Mark said, and Beth silently agreed.

"All I can say is your unsub either got lucky or he did his homework. This is the busiest stop in the area."

Mark's mouth flattened. "It wasn't luck."

Unfortunately, it appeared as if their guy may have gotten his act back together. If so, they couldn't count on any more slip-ups like yesterday morning.

"If you come up with anything, give me a call," Mark said.

"Will do."

Mark adjusted the baseball cap, pulling it even closer down over his eyes as they headed back to the SUV. "It's unlikely that our guy was stupid enough to get caught on surveillance tape or using a credit card. I think he's back in control."

Stopping, he glanced toward the interstate. "He didn't choose Atlanta just because of its size, he also chose it because within minutes of here, there are major highways going in every direction."

"So we can't even make an educated guess if he's heading north, south, east or west," Beth said.

Mark's mouth thinned as he glanced at his watch. "It's been over two hours. Assuming he's been moving the whole time, he has a two-hour lead on us right now.

"Two hours and growing."

Chapter Sixteen

Sitting on the sidelines waiting for the fight to be brought to him wasn't Mark's style.

One way or another they were going to have to find a way to throw the unsub off his game again.

Beth opened the back end of the SUV and then her suitcase, grabbing some clothes. "Give me a sec, I'm going to get out of this wet stuff." She tossed down her cap and started to peel off the sweatshirt.

Climbing behind the wheel, Mark retrieved the road map and spread it out in his lap. He tried to ignore what was going on behind the vehicle, but he couldn't quite keep his gaze from shifting to the rearview mirror.

The sweatshirt was already gone and she was tugging off her T-shirt. The bra beneath was the athletic type. When her gaze suddenly connected with his in the mirror, he didn't look away. She jerked on a dry T-shirt and then the sweatshirt. Grabbing her cap, she slammed the back gate and climbed into the passenger side.

Her mouth was set in a stiff line, and she had deep shadows under her eyes. And he couldn't quite forget the way she'd looked this morning asleep next to him. Or the way he'd left her so abruptly.

He started the car. "Let's grab some coffee and come up with a game plan of our own."

Mark's phone rang as he was putting the car in gear.

"We just got another coordinate for you, but this time the phone is staying active. And it doesn't appear to be moving."

He could think of only one reason why the killer would leave the battery in. Because time was up. And he wanted them to know it.

"Where," Mark asked.

"VerMar Beach. Florida's east coast. Just north of Palm Beach."

"He was just here in Atlanta two and a half hours ago. Start checking charter flights between Atlanta and South Florida. And book us seats on the next one out of Atlanta and headed anywhere close to VerMar Beach."

WITH THE ATLANTIC OCEAN on one side and the inner-coastal on the other side, the town of VerMar was a well-kept secret. A community of large estates hidden from public view behind tall, ornate fences and lush tropical plantings. It wasn't Palm Beach. It was the new playground of the well-heeled and indolent rich.

As soon as they turned onto Ocean Drive, the north-south boulevard that bisected VerMar, a local patrol officer stopped them.

Rolling down his window, Mark passed their badges. After scanning them, the officer handed them back. "It's Oceanside three miles down. You can't miss it."

Bellingham as a target had surprised Mark, but so, too, did VerMar. Mostly because they were at the opposite end of the socio-economic scale.

He glanced over at Beth. She didn't appear to be particularly wowed by the estates they passed, but then she'd been raised with money, so maybe they didn't seem quite so special to her.

"Do you like the beach?" he asked.

"Yes. And I like the water. Or at least I did before all this started. I haven't been able to take a shower without checking out the showerhead first. I suppose that makes me paranoid."

"No. That makes you normal."

He realized there were so many things that he didn't know about her. Things he wanted to find out when this was all through.

Turning into the elaborate entrance to Ocean Club, they were stopped again, their IDs checked before they were allowed to proceed.

The drive was long and winding. Royal palms lined the wide boulevard and were lit from beneath. The stiff breeze off the Atlantic shoved their fronds about.

Even before the SUV swept around the last graceful curve, he could see the flashing emergency lights ahead.

Fire trucks and ambulances and patrol cars were everywhere. And when every available square inch of pavement had been utilized, they'd resorted to using the St. Augustine grass. Mark followed suit. Getting out, he reached into the back seat and grabbed his hazmat gear.

"There's no reason for both of us to suit up." He sensed her relief. "Why don't you get a list of the guests? As soon as I check out the scene, we'll get started interviewing."

THIRTY MINUTES LATER Beth hit the play button, the screen on her laptop coming to life again.

Since she'd set up in a small meeting room where the

women members of the exclusive Ocean Club played bridge on Wednesdays and Fridays, she'd been systematically downloading and reviewing the videos taken by wedding guests. Until each of them could be interviewed, they'd been evacuated to the marina clubhouse.

Unlike some of the other recordings she'd viewed, the current one had been filmed by a more experienced hand. There was no jumping about, no shots of marble floors and feet or oversize crystal chandeliers.

She edged up the volume, but for the moment the only sound being picked up as the camera slowly panned around the main dining room was from the numerous conversations going on at nearby tables.

As a diplomat's daughter, Beth had seen plenty of beautiful rooms, but none had been any more elegant or refined than this one. It looked like something out of a Fitzgerald novel.

Dressed in gowns and tuxes, the guests were equally stylish and included several congressmen and the owner of a broadcasting network. Influential friends for an influential man. Senator Robert Wilkes, father of the bride, was well-known in Washington circles.

The scene suddenly changed, the lens now aimed at a pair of oversize French doors. Background noise faded as conversations dwindled to silence and people turned to face the opening.

Her chest tightened as she waited for what came next.

The doors were thrown wide, and the man holding the camera spoke for the first time. "And here comes the couple of the hour."

Beth's heart squeezed as Amanda and Nelson Peterson rushed into the room, smiling as if they'd just hit the lottery.

And from all appearances they had. They had it all, beauty, wealth and love.

Amanda was beautiful, a petite blonde with a large smile. Nelson was tall and dark and extremely handsome. They'd been holding hands the whole time, but now Nelson raised their clasped hands into the air. "Give it up for the most beautiful bride in the world." His smile was wide and as the camera came in for a close up, his eyes were filled with love and pride.

Today was to have been a beginning…

Pausing the film, Beth took a deep breath, preparing herself not to just watch the rest, but to study it closely, looking for additional clues.

She blinked away the tears that had collected despite her best attempts.

She'd come to know the other victims through crime-scene photos and from detailed but dry reports gathered by other agents. For the most part she'd been able to distance herself emotionally. But not this time. This time there was no isolating herself from any of the images caught by the camcorder—the joyful ones or the horrific ones.

Reading about what happened when MX141 came in contact with the human body was one thing, but watching it…

Nothing had prepared her for that. Or for the possibility that she was seeing her own death.

Her hands had been resting on the edge of the table, but looking down, she realized they had now curled into tight fists. How in the hell were they going to stop this guy? How many more people were going to have to die? And would she be one of them?

She looked up as Mark opened the door. Just seeing him made it easier for her to breathe, for her briefly to hide her fear.

Instead of entering, he lingered in the doorway, one hand on the doorknob, his broad shoulders filling the opening.

"How'd it go?" she asked. "Did you find the cell phone?"

"Yeah. As he was leaving, he tossed it in the bushes just outside the front doors. A local deputy found it."

"Why throw it away?"

"I don't know." His mouth thinned. "We'll be using the room across the hall to conduct interviews. I was going to get started with the senator, and have you talk to his wife in here. Miami is sending more agents to help with the interviewing. They should be here within the hour."

She nodded. "If you're going to be talking to the senator, I think you need to see this first."

He walked around the table and stopped next to her. "Then you found something?"

"Yeah. The other films I've reviewed stopped before this point."

Instead of sitting, Mark leaned down to watch, bracing one hand on the edge of the table and the other on the back of her chair. His nearness was enough of a distraction that she didn't hit Play immediately.

She felt his puzzled gaze on her, and then he reached past her and started the film from where she'd stopped it.

Instead of watching the screen, she studied him out of the corner of her eye. Even after everything they'd been through today, he still projected an amazing amount of energy and at the same time a level of competence that made it possible for her to believe they could actually win. That this killer could be caught.

That she might not meet the same end as the killer's most recent victim.

She found herself wanting to reach up, to run her hand

along his jawline, to feel the roughness and the warmth of his skin against her chilled hands. She recalled the way he'd held her last night, the way he'd made her feel safe and knew more than anything that was what she wanted to feel right now.

Forcing her thoughts away from him and back on the screen again, she watched as the camera followed the bride and the groom to the table of honor where the parents of both waited.

The groom's mother wasn't particularly beautiful and was nearly half a head taller than her narrow-shouldered husband, but they were old-moneyed Palm Beach.

The bride's parents were their polar opposites. Senator Robert Wilkes had come from a middle-class family and was tall, broad shouldered and darkly handsome. Mrs. Cindy Wilkes had been the reigning Miss Florida twenty-five years ago and looked as if she could still give this year's contestants a run for their money.

Despite their differences, both families seemed genuinely thrilled with the union of their children.

Mark shifted his stance as if impatient.

She tried to ignore the way her respirations had quickened. "It's coming up here soon. Watch the champagne glass."

It was only when the senator came to his feet somewhat unsteadily that it became apparent he'd already done too much celebrating and was well on his way to being drunk. And when he picked up a fork and loudly tapped it against the side of his water glass, disapproval blossomed on the faces of Cindy Wilkes and Gloria Peterson.

He smiled loosely as he reached for the champagne glass in front of him. "It's time for a toast—"

Amanda got to the glass first, though, and wrapping her

fingers around it, picked it up. "It's my turn to make a toast." She raised the glass. "To my new in-laws. Thank you for allowing me to be part of your family." She tipped the glass to her lips and sipped.

A stunned expression blossomed on her face. As she collapsed and started to convulse, Mark hit the stop button, his face grim. "The glass wasn't meant for her. The target was Senator Wilkes."

Chapter Seventeen

Beth could hear Cindy Wilkes screaming at her husband even before Mark opened the door to the room across the hall.

Robert Wilkes sat with his elbows propped on the table, head bowed, hands resting on either side of his head. To the untrained eye, he looked dejected, but the tension in his shoulders said otherwise.

Cindy Wilkes had her back to the door and was leaning across the table, her face only inches from her husband's. "It was our daughter's wedding day, for God's sake. Couldn't you stay sober for one goddamn day?"

Robert Wilkes' fingers slowly dug into his scalp like a man trying to claw something out of his brain. "What the friggin' hell are you saying?" His fists suddenly slammed onto the table in front of him, almost striking his wife's face. "That if I'd knocked back a few less bourbons, she'd be alive? That is friggin' bullshit!"

Seeing them, Robert Wilkes broke off and straightened.

Beth was amazed at how he managed to pull himself together. One second the politician was a man ready for a fight and the next he looked as if he was ready for Meet the Press. Cindy Wilkes was the exact opposite, once robbed of anger she seemed to shrink. As if that had been the only thing keeping her erect.

Mark motioned Beth into the room and then closed the door. "Actually, Senator, she would be alive. We have reason to believe that you were the intended target."

"What are you talking about? My daughter had a seizure. A heart attack. Something. I don't know." Suddenly he looked totally lost and completely alone.

"No, sir. Your daughter was poisoned. She came in contact with a chemical, a toxin."

"What in the hell are you talking about?" Throwing his shoulders back, the senator looked incredulous. "Why would anyone…"

"Maybe you both should sit down," Beth suggested and helped Cindy Wilkes into the chair next to her husband. After pouring and delivering a glass of water to the crying woman, Beth took a seat next to Mark.

Mark unzipped the soft-sided legal binder and pulled out a photo of Harvey Thesing. "Have you ever seen this man?" He placed it on the table.

Wilkes picked up the enlargement of Thesing's driver's license photo and studied it for several seconds. "Yeah. He was with Gil Carson at a charity event." Wilkes put down the picture.

"Do you mean lobbyist Gil Carson?" Mark asked. "The man who is currently under investigation?"

"Yes." Wilkes tapped at the center of the picture. "Gil Carson came up and pointed to this guy across the room and said this guy wanted to meet with me. I told him…I told Carson to get the hell away from me." Wilkes looked away. When he looked back, his jaw was set. "Tell me what in the hell is going on here?" He stabbed at the photo.

"Who in the hell is this man? What does he have to do with my daughter's…?" Looking away, he took a deep breath.

"He was a chemist," Mark said. "Employed by the lab where the chemical was developed."

"Developed for what?"

When Mark ignored the question, Wilkes wrapped his fingers around Mark's closest wrist. "I asked you a damn question!"

"And I'm asking you to remove your hand, sir."

After several seconds Wilkes let go and leaned back. "I have friends in high places."

"I'm sure you do, sir." Mark folded his hands over the portfolio. "What can you tell me about Carson? About his politics? And do you have any reason to believe he might want to harm you?"

"Seven or eight years ago he was one of the best lobbyists in Washington. Until he started seeing himself as a power broker and got greedy. When he did, doors started closing in his face."

"Yours included?" Beth asked. She hadn't been following the investigation closely, but knew that several members of congress were also under investigation.

Wilkes scraped his hands through his hair. "No. Not right away. Carson knew his stuff. Could present both sides. I continued to meet with him long after others on the Hill stopped. I figured that was my job. To listen to all sides before making a final decision. I always made it very clear that I vote my conscience."

Wilkes exhaled sharply. "Then around the middle of June I learned that Carson had approached a certain lawmaker, a close friend of mine and tried to buy his vote. This lawmaker's granddaughter had some major medical problems that insurance wouldn't cover. Carson was taking advantage of my friend's desperation. Long story short, my friend took the money. A week later, when he came to me, I counseled him to give it back. That if he didn't, Carson would own him. When this friend returned the money, Carson threatened him. Either he voted in favor of the environmental group or he'd be sorry."

Wilkes rubbed his bloodshot eyes. "I took what I knew to the authorities. A month ago Carson found out I was the one who blew the whistle on him."

"Did you ever socialize with him? Do you know anything about his background? Where he was from?"

"I used him for information and that was it. But I do remember his talking about being a military brat. That would have been when he was lobbying for a tank manufacture. Carson was a real apolitical chameleon. He'd represent anything as long as it paid well."

"So you don't think he's necessarily concerned about the environment?"

"No."

Could Carson be their man? Everything was strictly circumstantial, but there was enough of it to be fairly compelling.

Cindy Wilkes had been crying quietly, but now broke down in heaving sobs, her hands covering her mouth. She got to her feet. "You'll have to excuse me," she said, and headed for the door.

Concerned, Beth got up and followed her out, catching up to her in the hallway. "Mrs. Wilkes?" Beth said, touching the woman on her shoulder.

Turning, Mrs. Wilkes reached out. She wrapped her arms around Beth and held on tight, sobbing. Beth hugged her back, unsuccessfully trying to block out what she'd seen on the video tape. It had been difficult for her to watch. She couldn't imagine how terrifying it had been for this woman to actually be in the same room as it was happening. To watch her only daughter go into convulsions. To look into her daughter's frightened eyes and be able to do nothing.

Two special agents from the Palm Beach field office stood close by in the quiet hallway. They briefly looked at her but then turned away.

It was only a matter of a few minutes later that Robert Wilkes walked out, his expression grim, his posture slightly stooped. Looking up and seeing him, Cindy Wilkes backed away from Beth.

Beth would have liked to find the right words, but there really didn't seem to be any, so she settled for, "I'm so sorry about your loss."

Robert and Cindy Wilkes held on to each other as they walked toward the rear entrance. The couple only made it halfway to the doors before Cindy Wilkes suddenly crumbled at her husband's side. One moment he was trying to support her, to keep her on her feet, and the next they were both on their knees, holding on to each other, their shoulders heaving, their sobs filling the corridor.

Beth started toward them, uncertain what she'd do when she reached them, but unable to stand by and just watch.

Mark's hand on her shoulder stopped her.

Turning, he guided her away from them. He motioned to the closest special agent. "Give them some privacy, but stay with them at all times."

As she and Mark continued down the hallway, Beth looked over at him. "Did the Senator tell you anything else after I left?"

"When I mentioned the possibility that his friend might be the next target, he gave me his name. I'll make a call. Have him and his family picked up as a precaution."

"So you think it's Carson?"

Mark shrugged. "Maybe by morning we'll know more."

As THEY WERE NEARING the lobby door, her cell phone rang. Hearing the ring tone—an old, nostalgic tune that she knew was her father's, she let it go to voice mail.

But almost immediately she regretted the decision. As Mark stopped to talk to the club manager, she excused herself and stepped just outside the nearest door. The night air was balmy, carried the scent of the nearby Atlantic.

Listening to Cindy Wilkes pour out her heart and her grief had made Beth realize that even if her father was in the wrong, even if he wasn't always an easy man, he was still her father. As she'd told Mark the other night, she and her father would eventually get past everything.

But at what cost? How much time would they have lost? And what if something did happen to her…?

Beth dialed her father's number. When he answered, she said, "I couldn't get to my phone. I'm sorry."

"No. I'm the one who is sorry. About the way I've been interfering. I know how much your career means to you, but…"

"You were worried. I know." It was the first time in her memory that her father had apologized. Usually they somehow managed to make up without either of them taking blame.

"You okay?" he asked, and she could hear the concern in his voice.

"I'm fine."

"How's the new assignment going?"

She rubbed her eyes. "Is it okay if we don't talk about work right now?"

"Sure."

Beth wandered a few steps from the door. "You remember how much Mom liked the beach? How we'd take flashlights after dark and walk along it? Looking for those little crabs that scurry around at night?"

"And the way she would collect shells? I just came across a box of them the other day." Beth could hear the emotion piling up in his voice and felt her own chest tighten.

"Were you searching for something?"

"No. I was looking… I was…" There a sense of loneliness not just in his voice but in the statement, too.

Had he been digging through cabinets and closets, hoping to stumble on something that would remind him of her mother?

Turning back, she saw Mark still talking to the manager. He lifted his chin, indicating that he knew where she'd gone.

Her father cleared his throat. "Beth?"

He'd obviously thought they'd been disconnected. "I was thinking. Maybe we could go someplace warm this Christmas. A beach somewhere."

There was a pause where it was her turn to wonder if they'd been disconnected.

"I'd like that," he said simply, but she could hear the emotion in his voice. Why hadn't she understood just how hard the past two years had been on him, too? To lose her mother to cancer and then almost immediately to lose Beth when she'd gone undercover.

"I'll call you soon and we'll talk about it, okay?"

"That sounds fine."

"I need to go." She glanced over her shoulder, checking on Mark again.

"Okay," her father said. "But do me a favor."

"Sure. What?"

"Save the world if you have to, but take care of yourself at the same time."

"I will. And I love you," she said as she ended the call, but she wondered if he'd heard her.

When her phone rang almost immediately, she knew it wasn't her father calling back, but assumed it would be one of the other agents.

"We've both had a very busy day, haven't we?"

At the sound of his voice, her fingers tightened on the phone and adrenaline surged through her. She wasn't ready to handle this bastard. Not so soon after watching a woman die on her wedding day. Not after witnessing the grieving parents deal with the horror of their daughter's senseless death and watching a strong man brought to his knees as he realized that he had been a target. That the daughter he so obviously loved had lost her life because of him.

"Go to hell!" She hung up on the bastard. Almost immediately, the phone rang. She let it go to voice mail, but it wasn't more then five seconds before it was ringing again. This time she answered it. "I'm flattered. You obviously have me on speed dial."

"Bitch. Don't do that again. No one hangs up on—"

She disconnected, expecting him to call right back. When he didn't she started to worry that she'd screwed up, that her decision to shake up the power dynamic between them had been a wrong one. But she'd had to do something. Acting like a lamb being led to slaughter, meekly accepting his rules and cautiously challenging him hadn't really gotten them any closer to catching him.

Beth glanced back inside to where Mark was still talking to the local police chief and several security officers for the resort. What was she going to tell him if the bastard didn't call back? There was no way that she could whitewash what she'd just done. She had disobeyed a direct order not to openly challenge the bastard.

Then she realized that she was worrying about the wrong thing. That for the moment at least she needed to consider how she was going to handle things if the bastard did call back. Turning her back to the glass wall again, she stared down at the cell-phone screen. Apologizing was out of the question. It would show too much desperation on her part. Was the man on the other end Carson? And if it was, how would he react if she used his name? She decided against it, though, almost immediately. For the moment, if this was Carson, he had no idea that they were on to him.

Maybe she should just treat him like any other man who had called her a bitch. There would be nothing challenging in the stance, and at the same time, she wouldn't really be backing down.

She was still working out her strategy when the call came in. On the second ring she answered it. "No one calls me a bitch." She was careful to keep her voice neutral. There was a fairly long pause while she waited. Had she just made yet another miscalculation? If he hung up now…

"I bet the videos made for some interesting viewing. Think maybe I could get a copy?"

She exhaled, the tightness in her chest easing despite his request. "Sure. Just stop on by, and I'll have one ready for you. And a pair of handcuffs to go with it."

"The spoiler of fun."

As it had in all the previous calls, his voice carried an edge of amusement. This time she didn't find it quite so unsettling. "What is it that you want?"

"Conversation. Someone to share all the highlights of the trip with." He chuckled softly. "Solitary vacations are such a bitch, don't you think?"

A vacation? "Perhaps you shouldn't have killed your partner, then."

He ignored her observation, instead returned to an earlier thread. "Think I could get a copy of the photos you guys took at the farmhouse for my vacation scrapbook?"

"Tell me why you chose that family, and I'll think about it."

"That's okay. I took my own. If you're not in any hurry for them, I could e-mail a set when my itinerary isn't quite so full." He chuckled. "For now, though, you better rest up."

The idea that he'd gone back in to take photos sickened her, but she couldn't let it show. "Why's that?"

"Because tomorrow starts a new game. New stakes. New rules." As he paused, she could hear the piano in the background. "So good night, Beth, and pleasant dreams."

The line went dead.

New game. New rules. New stakes. As she started to lower the phone, she felt someone standing right behind her.

"I assume that was our guy again?" Mark took the phone from her. As she started to fill him in, he checked the number.

She could have lied to protect herself, not fully disclosing how she'd handled the call, but this wasn't really about her, about keeping her job. It was about stopping a killer.

Mark's expression turned troubled as he listened. He'd

trusted her. She'd let him down. And in the process had possibly put countless lives at risk.

"I'm sorry. I know I shouldn't have but—"

"Don't apologize for making the right decision. You've got him talking now, seeing you as a confidante of sorts."

His hands closed over her shoulders, his thumbs brushing across her collarbone. "What you need is to get some rest. Which is what you're going to do right now. I arranged for a bungalow. There was only one available, but it has a separate bedroom. You can have the bed. I'll take the couch."

If she hadn't been so damn scared, she might have seen the irony in his worrying about where they'd sleep. They'd already shared a bed. And she doubted either of them would be getting much sleep tonight no matter where they laid their bodies.

LIKE THE REST of the property, the bungalow was beautiful, but much more casual than the main building. The floors and ceilings were heart pine, the furniture covered in white duck slip covers. Large shells and nautical items filled the bookshelves in the living room. A small morning kitchen outfitted with a coffeemaker and a small stainless steel refrigerator was tucked just outside the bedroom.

The wall facing the ocean was floor-to-ceiling glass, and because it was dark outside, she saw her reflection. Beth tightened her arms in front of her and turned away. The wild-haired woman with the too-big eyes didn't even look like her.

Walking into the bedroom and seeing more large windows, she immediately closed the drapes.

When she returned from the bedroom door, Mark was

setting up his laptop on the desk in front of the living room window.

"If you don't mind, I think I'll catch a shower," she said and grabbed her suitcase.

Thirty minutes later when she walked out of the bedroom, he was reviewing another of the wedding videos. Not on the laptop, but on the large plasma television. Seeing her, he turned it off.

His feet were propped on the ottoman in the center of the seating area, and he looked oddly at ease. Or maybe it was that she was anything but relaxed.

He lifted a wineglass. "I opened some wine. It's there on the counter."

Any other time she would have had a glass or two to calm her nerves, but when he'd lifted the glass it had reminded her too much of Amanda proposing a toast.

Chapter Eighteen

Less than an hour later, Beth climbed into the kingsize bed, but within ten minutes she was up again, standing at the large window, staring out at the beach. Even with the thick glass, she could hear the harsh surf as it crashed against the sand. The clouds riding the horizon flirted with the rising moon. Last night she'd watched it breach a mountain, tonight it was the ocean that it rose above.

She glanced at the bed with longing. She was so tired, so desperate for sleep, but every time she'd closed her eyes, her mind replayed in panoramic detail the last moments of Amanda's life. The horror, the incomprehension in her eyes and in the eyes of everyone around her.

A new game, with new stakes and new rules.

She couldn't quite block out the fear that she could be next. That no matter how strong she was or how determined Mark was, it wouldn't be enough. Just before she'd retreated to the dark bedroom, he'd received a preliminary report on Carson as well as a photo. She'd read the report, but refused to look at the picture, afraid that his face, too, would rob her of sleep.

Her shoulders jerked as a razor-sharp shiver climbed

through her body. She wasn't chilled, though, she was frightened. If only she could shut it out for one whole night. If only she could find a dreamless sleep.

It had been over two years since she'd felt safe. Since she'd felt naively invincible. She wondered if she'd ever feel either of those things again.

Hearing the bedroom door open behind her, she turned. Mark stood in the doorway. Seeing her there, he walked toward her.

"I thought I heard you up."

"Just restless." They both knew she was lying.

As he wrapped his arms around from behind, pulling her back against his lean body, the moon suddenly broke free of the distant cloud cover. Whitecaps that had been barely visible before turned almost iridescent.

"Beautiful moon, isn't it?" Mark murmured next to her ear, his warm breath stirring her hair.

"A hunter's moon. That's what the ranger you sent to get me last night called it."

Mark's body tensed behind her. Even before he turned her to face him, she knew something was wrong but couldn't understand what.

His fingers tightened on her shoulders. "When was this?"

"When I walked over to the restroom—"

"I didn't send anyone looking for you."

She swallowed against the lump of fear that grew in her throat. It wasn't possible. Was it? She looked up into his face. "I need to see Carson's photo."

She followed him back into the living room. As soon as he ran his finger over the touch pad, the face came into focus.

He'd stayed mostly in the shadows, but she still recognized the face.

"Beth?"

Her fingers curled at her side.

"That's him. That's the man. I stopped to look at the moon, and he stepped out of the trees. He was wearing a forest ranger's jacket." Last night she'd stood within five feet of the man they hunted. She rubbed her forehead. How could she have been so stupid? "I sensed something wasn't right, but I kept telling myself that I was imagining it."

Carson could have taken her then. When she'd turned her back to walk away. Why hadn't he? Why had he let her go? Why had he let her believe that she was clever?

With a grim expression, Mark pulled her into his arms. This time she wrapped hers around him and held on tight, as if as long as she did, she'd be safe.

She didn't cry. It was as if she was so numb that she couldn't anymore. As if she'd been frightened for so long that it no longer registered.

"Come morning, you're going somewhere safe." His arms tightened around her. "Until this is over. Somewhere I won't have to worry about him finding you. He's no longer a ghost. We have a name now. Agents are already on their way to his home. In another few hours we'll be able to track his credit card use."

He wanted to send her someplace safe. Because he cared about her. Come morning, she'd argue with him, make him see that she'd be safer with him than she would be anywhere else. But for tonight she wanted to forget everything. Needed to feel something besides the aching cold inside her.

As she reached up and ran her fingertips over his lips, he went stock-still. His eyes narrowed slightly and his breathing turned slightly irregular. She could feel the tension radiating from his body. Felt her pulse kick a little harder in response. She'd never tried to seduce a man. At least not one like Mark.

His firm chest was only inches from her. She lowered her lips kissing him there, trailing her lips upward to press yet another kiss at the hollow of his throat. As she looked up at him this time, his hand slid from her shoulder upward, his thumb tracing the side of her neck and then her jawline. When he reached the back of her neck, he drew her to him, angling her lips up to his.

He kissed her slowly at first, taking his time, tasting the corners of her mouth. And then suddenly, as if he couldn't stop himself, he deepened the kiss. Her lips opened beneath his, wanting more.

His hand had been resting at her hip for nearly a minute, but now moved upward, taking the hem of her T-shirt with it. Cool air reached her exposed skin, but it was the warmth of his hand that made her shiver. Made her want more. And when he finally reached a breast, she arched into the caress. Her breath caught and then escaped in a rush as he gently teased the tip, the sensation settling at her very core.

He lifted his lips from hers but didn't pull away, his warm breath brushing across them still. "Are you sure?" His voice was tight and slightly raspy.

"I'm sure."

He turned and led her into the bedroom where moonlight pooled down onto the floor but didn't quite reach the bed.

She sat on the edge, expecting him to follow her down, but he didn't. Instead, he dropped to his knees in front of her, leaning in to slowly kiss her again. Easing back slightly, he pushed her T-shirt up slowly, exposing her. She tugged it the rest of the way, dropping it among the sheets as his warm mouth closed over the tip of one breast.

Her muscles seemed to melt, and as his lips and tongue and teeth moved over her, her hands ran through his short dark hair.

When she didn't think she could stand anymore, he pushed her gently backward. As he did, she reached for him, wanting to bring him with her, wanting to feel the weight of his body covering hers.

But he didn't. Instead, he teased down her boxer shorts, his lips and tongue exploring each exposed inch. As the light stubble along his jaw rasped her inner thigh, she couldn't bite back the soft moan that built at the back of her throat. And when, a second later, his warm breath brushed against her very core, her body arched. There was magic in those movements. Delicious magic.

And then he was on the bed with her, stretched out beside her, no longer wearing the sweatpants. Turning her face to his, he kissed her softly as one hand followed the line of her hip. As his fingers touched her between the thighs, they parted. He continued to kiss her as his fingers stroked, then circled slowly and then probed, dragging sensations out of her that she'd never felt before.

Reaching down, she stilled his hand, stopping the magic. "I don't want to be the only one," she said, her breath unsteady, her skin slick and on fire. She reached for him and ran her hand upward along his length, feeling the heat and the power.

He pulled her lips to his again, his mouth moving over hers with desperation now, his breathing just as uneven as her own.

He shifted over her, his gaze connecting with hers as he pushed slowly into her, the stretching heat as he filled her briefly robbing her of breath.

He looked down at her, his gaze intense, and then lowered his lips until they were all but touching hers. "You're beautiful," he murmured.

He began to move. Slowly at first, with firm but gentle strokes that she rose up to meet. Then he thrust harder and harder still, filling her with a maddening mixture of pleasure and need.

Within minutes his breathing tightened as he fought to postpone his surrender. And she could feel her own building deep inside her. Could feel her body reaching for the ultimate release. She wrapped her legs around him, dragging him into her, wanting all of him. Needing all of him.

Starting deep inside her, hot pleasure shot through her body. She arched up, a harsh moan being torn from deep inside her as she started to come.

His rhythm changed and he thrust hard and deep, his breathing as ragged as her own now as he pushed her over the edge. As soon as he had, his thrusts slowed. And then she felt the subtle jerk of his body, the heavy throbbing deep inside her.

Leaning over her, breathing hard, Mark's lips and teeth teased her chin. "There isn't anything about you that isn't sexy as hell."

He seemed to study her face intently for several seconds before his eyes narrowed. Suddenly lowering his head, he pressed his forehead to hers.

For several minutes, because they were so busy catching their breaths, neither one of them spoke or moved again. And then suddenly he rolled to the side, taking her with him. He dragged the sheet up over them and pulled her in tight.

And for the first time in years she felt safe.

Chapter Nineteen

It was still the middle of the night when Mark slipped out of bed and pulled on sweats.

Crossing to the window, he looked out at the night. The moon was high now. A hunter's moon. A cold sense of unease settled in his gut just thinking about what could have happened last night. How close Carson had been able to get to her.

Why risk it, though? Because he felt empowered? Because he believed himself unstoppable? Or because he hadn't been able to stop himself? Because even stronger than the desire to kill was the need to be near Beth?

If the latter was true, no place was going to be safe until Carson was in custody.

Hearing her stir, he was tempted to strip and join her once more beneath the covers. To make love one more time before letting reality intrude.

He slowly rubbed the back of his neck. What in the hell was he going to do? There was no going back, pretending that tonight had never happened. But was there any way for them to move forward? He'd been a loner for four years now. The thought no sooner flowed through his mind than he recognized the underlying fallacy. It hadn't been just four years, it had been a lifetime. Even during eight years of marriage, he'd always held something back.

So what made him think he could change now? That he could open up with even Beth. Because she made him want that level of intimacy more?

He stared down at her. What made him think that he could give her what she needed? He tugged the sheet over her bare shoulder. His fingers curled as his hand dropped away.

Leaving her, knowing that he wouldn't be able to sleep, he turned on the computer out in the living room and opened the report that had been e-mailed to him during the past few hours.

While he'd been making love to a woman under his command. It wasn't a hanging offense maybe, but it was a punishable one.

Closing his mind to that line of thought, he started reading the report.

Carson had already been under investigation for tax evasion, fraud and conspiracy to bribe a public official, so there had been quite a bit of background information going in. The late-night search and several key interviews had turned up some additional insights into the man.

Just over four months ago, Carson had learned he had terminal cancer. And recently he'd been prescribed some heavy duty pain medication.

First legal problems, then the medical kind and finally financial ones. All of Carson's recent troubles had added up to a drained bank account. Which led to the most promising break for them. Unable to access any cash, he'd been forced to use credit cards that could be easily tracked. And that wasn't the only good news. Even though it wasn't turned on at the moment, there was a cell phone registered to Carson. Over the past few weeks, three calls had been logged to a Maryland oncologist, suggesting that Carson kept the phone with him.

Between the credit cards and the cell phone, they should be able to take him down—unless he found out they were on to him. If he did, they'd be worse than screwed. For the moment Carson felt invisible. Once he realized he wasn't, there was no way to predict how he would react. Especially considering that he wasn't just a military brat, he'd also spent several years in Special Forces. He'd received an honorable discharge shortly after the Gulf War, but some of the wording in the transcripts suggested that may have been because his father, a thirty-year decorated veteran, had called in some favors.

The next area ran through Carson's life chronologically, much of the information compiled using information on the father's military career. Gil Carson had been born in Arizona. The first move had taken him to Fort Hood in Texas. The location rang a bell with Mark. Harvey Thesing had never joined the military, but his mother had been an army mechanic. Mark grabbed the Thesing file, locating the section that dealt with the chemist's early background. Twenty-two years ago, Thesing's mother and Carson's father had been stationed at the same base. Was it possible that they had met there?

But why hadn't Carson's name come up on the list of known associates for Thesing? Because they hadn't had contact during the interim? Come morning, Mark would have agents from the closest field office check it out more thoroughly.

Mark refocused on the Carson report. When Carson had

been seventeen, he'd been sent to live with an aunt just outside Bellingham. He'd attended the high school for less than a month before withdrawing to be home schooled. Mark rubbed his forehead. Richard Ravenel would have been the basketball coach during that time. But it seemed unlikely that the problem between them could have had anything to do with basketball or school.

Which left what?

Mark retrieved the soft-sided briefcase propped against the desk and grabbed out the Ravenel file. Livengood had said the daughter had died from some type of hunting accident. Believing it unrelated to the current situation, Mark had only scanned the report. He now read it much more closely. Because the shooting had taken place during deer season and in an area frequented by hunters, it had been ruled a hunting accident, but no one had ever been charged. A .306 round had obliterated the young woman's chest. There'd been nothing left of Kim Ravenel's heart.

He checked the date. Carson had still been in Bellingham at the time. Mark scanned back through the Carson report again, locating the date he'd joined the army. It was less than a week after the girl's death. Coincidence? Or was it possible that Kim Ravenel had been Gil Carson's first victim?

Had Kim spurned Carson's advances? Or considering that Carson had returned years later to kill the rest of the family, maybe Richard Ravenel had forbidden his daughter from seeing Carson? Or maybe, like the rabbit that Carson had left behind that day, maybe even at seventeen he liked to kill.

As Mark read the next paragraph, a sense of extreme

unease set in. Three weeks after Gil Carson's discharge from
the military, his father had been killed in a hunting accident.

Mark was no longer wondering if Gil Carson was responsible for two murders, he was now wondering just
how many others Carson had killed.

Flipping to the last page of the Ravenal report, Mark felt
his lungs shut down. The young woman's face staring back
at him bore a striking resemblance to Beth.

If he'd been having second thoughts about sending Beth
away, he no longer did.

As he had pointed out earlier, they had a name now.
Ways to track this killer. She'd risked enough already. Deep
down inside, he knew none of those was the real reason he
was pulling her off this investigation, though. It was because
he didn't want to see anything happen to her, and realizing
that brought into focus just how much she meant to him.

Booting down the computer, he headed back to bed. For
a few more hours he could hold her in his arms. Could hold
tomorrow at bay.

JUST AFTER 6:00 A.M. he sat in the living room with his cup
of coffee.

The sun was a peachy-orange spill of light at the
horizon, the ocean calmer than it had been last night. And
in many ways, he felt calmer, too. More focused.

He'd found an extra blanket and pillow and had made
up the couch to look as if he'd slept there and not with Beth.
Better to maintain the illusion at least.

He picked up his cell phone and dialed Traci's number.
Maybe it was a bit early, but he was afraid if he didn't make
the call now, things would get crazy again, and he wouldn't
get the chance.

She answered on the fourth ring, her voice husky with sleep.

"Hi," he said simply. "I know it's early, but I was hoping we might be able to talk."

"Okay," she said, her voice soft and somewhat indistinct. "Let me just wake up a bit here."

"Maybe while you do, I could just talk. Spill my guts a little bit."

"Sure."

"I've been thinking a lot about Gracie, about what she's going through. And thinking about what I put you through those last few years. You're right. I was never there. It wasn't because I didn't want to be. But I know that needs to change. When I put this current investigation to bed, I'm going to make some changes."

"Is the investigation you're working on right now more important than your daughter crying herself to sleep at night?"

That was such a tough question. One that there was no real answer for. "Nothing is more important to me than Gracie and Addison. But we all have to make sacrifices."

"They're children, Mark, they shouldn't have to make too many of them. They only get one childhood. You only get one opportunity to see them grow up."

He wiped a hand down his face. "I'm just asking you to hold off talking to the lawyers for a few more days. Until this is behind me. Can you do that for me?"

There was a long pause, sounds of covers being kicked aside.

"Can you do that for me?" he asked again.

"Yeah. We don't have to make any decisions right now."

He heard the old four-poster bed squeak. "We need to

talk about something else, too. I've been dating this man for about six months now, and…"

He was about to ask why he hadn't been told but then realized that if he'd been around more, he would have known. "Is it serious?"

"Yes. We haven't set a date yet."

"Is he a good guy?"

"Yeah. You're going to like him."

BETH SPENT MORE TIME blow drying her hair and getting dressed this morning than she had the previous one. Partly because she wouldn't be tramping around a forest and partly to give herself time to think about what had happened last night. To sort out her feelings some. She was in love with Mark Gerritsen. There was no longer any way she could deny it. Three years ago when she'd been his student, she'd fallen in love with the bigger-than-life idea of Mark Gerritsen, but over the past few days she'd fallen in love with the man himself.

But was there any reason to believe he felt anything?

And if he didn't… What would she do then?

When she stepped out into the living room, Mark was just getting off the phone. Looking up, he smiled.

"You look beautiful."

"Thanks." She poured herself a cup of coffee. When she stopped next to where he was sitting in the desk chair, he took the cup from her and placed it next to his before pulling her onto his lap. He gave her a very leisurely kiss.

Pulling back slightly, he smiled. "Good morning."

She was smiling, too, now. But then, out of the corner of her eye, she noticed the blanket and pillow on the couch.

Why go to the trouble to make it appear as if he'd slept out here? Unless he was expecting company…

He started to kiss her again, but this time she moved backward slightly, withholding her lips. Her eyes narrowed. "What's going on?"

His hold briefly tightened, but then, possibly feeling her stiffen in his arms, he released her. "We need to talk."

She moved away nervously, taking her coffee with her. When she'd put enough distance between them, she faced him. "Talk about what?"

Mark's mouth thinned and his expression became shuttered again. The way it was most of the time. Except when he gave good-morning kisses and when he was deep inside her. Beth put down the cup and folded her arms in front of her.

"Larson's on his way over," Mark said. "He's going to be putting you on a plane this morning."

"Why are you doing this?"

Clasping his hands in front of him, he looked up at her, his mouth set in a hard line. "Why do you think?"

"Because you're putting my safety in front of this country's?"

He didn't argue. Maybe she should have taken some comfort in the idea that he did care about her. That maybe he'd been feeling some of the same things this morning that she had been. But she didn't. Because she knew in the end, if another person died because of the decision, he would find it difficult to live with himself.

He'd briefly looked away, but his gaze now met hers. "We have a name now and a credit card trail to follow. With other ways to track him, there's no longer any reason for you to continue putting yourself in that kind of risk. And as your supervisor, doing anything that puts you needlessly in danger…" He rubbed his mouth.

She could tell that even he wasn't buying what he was trying to sell her. "But you still need me."

He remained mute. A knock sounded at the front door. "That'll be your ride."

"So that's it?"

"Yes."

As Mark let Larson in, she shoved her clothes into the suitcase and gathered up the toiletries she'd left in the bathroom.

She offered a tight nod to her escort. "When did you arrive?"

"Couple of hours ago." Larson gave Mark a quizzical look, his gaze briefly scanning the couch and then the two of them. It was obvious that he knew that Mark hadn't slept out here, but he didn't say anything. Instead, he picked up her suitcase.

As she was about to follow him out, Mark grabbed her by the upper arm, tugged her away from the opening. He kissed her fast and hard and thoroughly. Pulling back, he studied her face. "Keep yourself safe."

She was afraid to speak, afraid of what might spill out of her mouth, so offered a slight nod.

When she stepped outside, Larson was just tossing her suitcase in the backseat. Instead of pulling the dark sedan in, he'd backed it in.

The morning was cooler than she'd expected, the air heavy with moisture and a briny scent. Not even a foot from the bungalow's door and she already felt sticky. As if she'd spent an hour walking the beach.

Larson's cell phone rang. Backing away from the car,

he answered it as she slid into the passenger side. She was clicking her seat belt across her when she heard the choked-off grunt and the sound of a body dropping.

Before she could react, a man wearing an FBI hat…Carson…slid into the driver's seat and reached for the ignition. She wondered if the hat was hers. If he'd found it in the restroom.

The seat belt blocked easy access to her weapon. She went for the SIG-Sauer anyway. But before her fingers reached it, she felt the icy-cold contact of a gun barrel at her temple.

"If you move, I'll put a bullet in your head right here and now."

She studied his face out of the corner of her eye. He looked like a man who was barely holding on. She couldn't see the weapon he held to her head, or even the finger resting against its trigger, but she saw the way his arm shook slightly.

She slowly lifted her hands, indicating she'd do as he asked.

As soon as she did, Carson punched the accelerator, the rear tires of the sedan flinging gravel everywhere.

Chapter Twenty

As soon as she walked out the door, as soon as Mark heard it close behind her, he started second-guessing himself. Had he made the right decision? Was sending her away the right thing to do?

Reaching the window overlooking the beach, he stared out at the deserted stretch of sand, admitting that what he really wanted to do was take her away himself.

That hadn't been an option, though. He had a job to finish.

And then something hard rained against the front door. Not even taking the time to identify what had caused it, he ripped open the door just in time to see the shadow of the dark Taurus disappear down the heavily landscaped lane.

He brought up the automatic, but never got a chance to get off the first shot.

Cursing, he lowered his weapon. He was just as likely to hit Beth as Carson.

Dropping down next to Larson, he checked for a pulse, thought that maybe he felt one. Leaving the bungalow's door standing wide open, he jumped into the SUV. As he negotiated the drive, he called for an ambulance. There was nothing he could do for his friend right now.

He sped past the guard gate, nearly running down the security guard who'd been foolish enough to try to stop him. How in the hell had Carson managed to get by security? Since last night, the Ocean Club had been crawling with both private security and public law enforcement.

Hitting the main road, he paused. Which way? Knowing that any hesitation ate up important seconds, he turned right, praying that he was right.

Mark placed a call, requesting GPS coordinates for Beth's cell, and then waited tense minutes for a response.

The agent on the other end gave him the coordinates, and he set the navigation system. His fingers tightened on the steering wheel. "Now I need someone to check recent activities on Gil Carson's charge cards. And Special Agent Beth Benedict's, too."

Accessing credit card activity would take time, maybe more than they had.

Up until now Carson had seemed to prefer areas with enough traffic that he could get himself lost among it. To the right was VerMar's small downtown area with quaint shops. But nothing would be open at this time of morning. But Carson's behavior suggested that he was beginning to unravel. Wasn't thinking as clearly as he had been in the beginning.

This morning's kidnapping was a good indication of just how far he'd gone in the downward spiral. For months he'd managed to avoid detection. He'd pulled off the school killings without anyone ever seeing him. And it would have been the same at the Ravenel place if he hadn't made the 911 call.

But he hadn't been able to stop himself.

Just as he hadn't been able to stop the blitzkrieg-style attack this morning. An organized offender would never have attempted it. Too many variables. No way to control any aspect of the situation.

Mark's gut instincts had told him that Carson was falling apart. That Carson was about to make his big move. Mark just hadn't expected it quite so soon. But he should have.

A new game with new stakes and new rules.

Because Mark had gotten sloppy, Beth was very possibly going to die. With Carson's current legal and medical problems and his ex-military background, it was unlikely that he'd allow himself to be taken alive.

Maybe the only ace they held at the moment was that Gil Carson had no idea they now knew his identity.

BETH GLANCED OVER at Carson. He'd shaved within the past forty-eight hours maybe, but not within the past twenty-four, and it looked as if he'd slept in his clothing.

Shifting her gaze downward without moving her chin, she saw the sand covering the floor mat. Was that how he'd gotten by security? By using the beach?

The gun he held on her was a nickel-plated .357.

He was being forced to split his attention between her and the road. She recalled the driver's license photo. The well-groomed appearance. The clean-shaven face. The neatly combed blond hair. This man looked as if he'd spent the night drunk on the beach, sleeping among the crabs and seaweed. And he didn't smell much better, either.

What about Larson? Was he hurt, or was he dead? And did anyone, did Mark know that Carson had her? If not...

"I said, undo your safety belt, Beth."

As she started to reach down with her left hand, she realized it was shaking uncontrollably. It wasn't just adrenaline this time. She was damned scared. Her fingers curled hesitantly as she tried to get control of her fear. She needed to stay calm.

"Now, Beth!"

She pushed on the release button. Pulled her hand out of the way as the belt retracted across her. Her weapon would be next. When it came to holding a gun, she was ambidextrous, could use either hand. He wouldn't know that. Could she use it to her advantage?

"Now the gun! I want you to reach across with your right hand and very slowly, using only two fingers, I want you to remove it. No sudden moves."

Fear pooled in her chest again, her breathing going shallow as she considered what her next move should be. And then she remembered that the weapon in her holster wasn't her usual one, didn't have an ambidextrous safety. That she'd had to turn over the weapon she normally carried after the garage shooting. And there was no way she'd be able to get a left-handed safety off with her right hand quickly enough.

With no choice, using the thumb and index finger of her right hand, she carefully lifted her weapon free of the holster. Once it was gone, there would only be her cell phone left.

The window beside her slid down silently, the wind screaming inside. Carson had originally taken the same road as she and Mark had used last night, but had since made a number of turns. They were now on a straight stretch of roadway with some type of crop field on either side and no signs of development.

"Toss it, Beth!"

She complied.

"Now your phone."

She unclipped it from her belt, but then fumbled it. It dropped down between the door and the seat. The butt of Carson's weapon slammed into the side of her head with enough force that she was momentarily disoriented. Pain radiated through her skull.

"That was very stupid. Either you find the cell phone now, Beth, or you get a bullet in the head!"

Having seen Amanda Wilkes's death, getting shot didn't sound so bad. But she shoved her hand into the space repeatedly to buy time to sort out her options. The phone might be the only way that Mark would be able to find her. And more importantly stop Carson.

"I'm not bluffing here, Beth. If I have to stop this car to get that phone, they'll find you in a ditch with six rounds in your skull."

His constant use of her name was beginning to bother her. As he took a curve too fast, the momentum shifted the phone enough that it bumped into her fingers.

Should she pick it up?

She didn't doubt that if she didn't come up with it fairly soon, he'd kill her. But would he do it in the car? While they were still moving? Or would he pull over first? If he did, she might have some kind of chance at survival.

She still felt dazed from the blow and at the same time terrified. She wondered how clearly she was actually thinking.

Carson lifted the gun and grinned. "Time's up, Beth!"

Her fingers scrambled to grab the cell phone. She tossed it out the window.

As he closed the window, she glanced over at Carson. She didn't know where he'd gotten the flexi cuffs from but as they landed in her lap, she reached for them.

"Put them on."

She put one side on and tightened it around her wrist. When she went to slide her other wrist through the other side, he stopped her.

"Not in front. In back."

Shifting forward, she put her hands behind her back and even managed to get her second wrist through the plastic loop. As soon as she did, Carson reached over and tightened it. He checked both twice before seeming satisfied.

She leaned back, her hands now trapped behind her. She'd been frightened up to this point, but now the sense of inevitability took her by the throat. She felt the sharp pressure of her full bladder and for the first time understood how frightened people could lose control.

When her gaze met Carson's this time, he grinned.

She realized he also suddenly looked less edgy. Was that because after disarming her, after getting rid of her phone, after binding her, he finally felt back in control?

Should she try to shake him up somehow? Maybe let him know that they'd been aware of his identity since last night? Or would that only serve to tip him off and make him more cautious? And more likely to panic?

Maybe what she needed to do was start with what he would see as a nonthreatening line of questioning.

"Why me?" she asked.

"What do you mean?"

"Of all the people out there, why call me?"

"It was the way you looked at the camera. As if you weren't afraid of anything. As if your confidence was unshakable."

"And you found that appealing?"

"That and the way you looked. I've had some good times just thinking about you, Beth. About what I was going to do to you. All those things I've wanted to do to other women but couldn't because I had a reputation, a life to protect."

Beth swallowed against the expanding lump of fear in her throat. She was breathing shallow and fast almost before she realized it. Catching herself, she tried to slow it down, tried to force more air into her lungs each time.

Now more than ever, she needed to stay calm. Raping her would take time. Would buy time for her to be found.

And as long as he was raping her, maybe people wouldn't be dying.

How much time did she have? How long before they reached the spot he'd chosen for the rape?

Dwelling on the coming attack wasn't going to help her any. Maybe if she kept him talking, she could learn more things about him... Maybe she'd find something that could help her in some way.

"How did you get Thesing to steal the chemical?"

Carson took his eyes off the road. "I didn't. He came to me. He'd gotten cold feet about the chemical and thought the lab should be forced to destroy what they'd stockpiled. He figured that if he stole some, they'd panic at the very least. But they didn't. He contacted me hoping I'd put him in touch with someone who could bring it to the public attention. He figured once people knew, the lab's hand would be forced."

"So how did Thesing wind up dead?"

"I suggested I had a better way to handle things. I'd sell it to the highest bidder."

"And he wasn't about to go along."

"Harvey?" He snorted. "Hell, no. He was a real Boy Scout."

"So why haven't you sold it? I would think it would be worth a large fortune to the right people."

He looked over at her. "You can't spend money where we're both headed."

Chapter Twenty-One

Mark was ankle deep in mud by the time he could grab Beth's cell phone out of the ditch bordering the Florida Turnpike.

After negotiating the slick incline, he flung the phone into the backseat of the SUV and then turned as a semi rig roared past.

Carson seemed to be headed north, but he would have had numerous opportunities to switch cars so there was no way to be even certain what type of vehicle he was driving now. It wasn't the BMW registered to him, though. That one was still safely parked in Carson's garage.

And what about the MX141? Had Carson had it with him when he'd taken Beth this morning? Or was that where he was headed now? To retrieve the chemical?

And once he did, what then? Where was he planning to use it? And what were his plans for Beth?

As he jumped back into the SUV, his cell phone rang. This time the voice belonged to Jenny Springer. "Beth's credit card is being used at a gas station just north of YeeHaw Junction. Highway patrol has been alerted and they're on the way."

Tires spun, the back end of the SUV fishtailing as it

lunged back onto the roadway. YeeHaw Junction was only a few miles ahead. Five or seven at most.

Mark watched in the rearview mirror as the white pickup changed lanes to avoid hitting him. "Are they aware of what Carson may have onboard?"

"They've been told about the chemical."

"How far is the nearest Hazmat Response Unit?" Mark asked.

"Miami," Jenny said. "I'll contact them now."

"Any idea what kind of car they're in?"

"A black Taurus."

"Tell Highway Patrol to stay back. We need to find a way to limit casualties here."

He had to find a way to save Beth.

But what if she was already dead? What if after throwing away her phone, Carson had already killed her, thrown her away, too?

Mark jerked a hand through his hair. He couldn't start thinking like that. She was smart. Resourceful. Tenacious. If any woman could survive Carson, she could.

Mark glanced down at the assault rifle on the passenger seat. And she would know that he was coming for her.

Or would she?

Maybe she hadn't understood what sending her to safety had meant. That he couldn't handle the idea of anything happening to her. That he had put her safety so far above everyone else's that it made a mockery of the oath he'd taken.

Catching sight of the black Taurus just ahead, Mark closed in cautiously, getting only close enough to see that there was a passenger in the car before backing off. The Taurus was sticking to the speed limit and to the right-hand lane. Carson was trying to play it safe. He couldn't afford to be stopped. Not with Beth in the car.

As Mark followed just far enough behind that Carson wouldn't spot him, he tried to determine the best way to take down Carson. The safest way to rescue Beth while putting as few people as possible at risk.

As they continued to travel north, other agents joined the procession, some ahead of Carson and others behind Mark. So far Carson still hadn't done anything that would indicate he knew he was being followed.

He'd moved into the center lane now, but still stayed reasonably close to the posted speed.

And then suddenly, just south of Orlando, Carson swerved across the right lane, nearly colliding with a delivery truck as he took the exit ramp at the last second, forcing Mark and the others to do the same.

Now that they'd been made, it was time to end things. They couldn't afford to hold off any longer. They had to take down Carson fast and hard. Before he had a chance to use the MX141.

But Mark couldn't block out that it was Beth sitting beside Carson right now.

Acceptable casualties.

For every other officer involved in the takedown, she was just that. They couldn't worry about one life when there was a far greater number hanging in the balance.

But if you loved that one person…

Mark shot around the black Taurus, cutting him off as other agents raced to box him in on all sides. The road was a rural two-lane.

As the cars in front of Carson slowed, he was forced to, as well. He tried to muscle the car to his left out of the way, but the midsize vehicle he was in didn't have enough mass to accomplish it.

As soon as the Taurus came to a stop, the passenger door was pushed open and Carson shoved Beth out first, keeping her in front of him and the open door still at his back. He was wearing body armor over his clothing. He tossed a small navy-blue duffel on the ground at their feet.

Beth's hands appeared to be bound behind her, otherwise she seemed to be in reasonably good shape.

Carson reached back and grabbed something that had been on the passenger seat. It wasn't the assault rifle that Mark expected, it was a shotgun.

Instead of pointing it toward them, Carson seemed to aim it at the duffel. Why? Because the bag held the chemical? Because he'd developed a new method of dispersal that he was about to try out?

"If you want to live, you'll back off," Carson yelled.

Mark couldn't take his eyes off Beth's face. She'd survived this long because she was smart. She'd known how to handle Carson.

"Do what you have to, Mark," she yelled. "Kill him here and now."

Mark couldn't though.

Everything seemed to go briefly silent. Even the breeze that sifted by. The grasses along the road swayed gracefully beneath a painfully blue sky. Sunlight reflected off the road sign just visible behind Carson and Beth. Seeing it, Mark knew what Carson's target had been. One of the area's many theme parks.

"Do the right thing," Beth yelled, "before more people get hurt."

She suddenly threw her body backward, slamming the

back of her skull into Carson's chin and then dropping to the ground in one fluid motion. Trusting him with her life.

Mark took the shot, delivering a quick double-tap. Everything was still moving in slow motion, allowing him to really see, to dissect each second. To live in it. To feel the relief as Beth looked up and smiled at him. And then to feel the terror as Carson's shotgun went off. The duffel bag exploded, a geyser of fluid spraying anything within range. Carson staggered a few feet before going down.

Beth went into convulsions, her body jerking as if she was hooked up to a thousand volts.

Throwing down the assault rifle, Mark rushed forward.

Several agents tried to stop him, but he broke free.

Grabbing her with his bare hands, he dragged her away from the debris.

He barely had time to uncap the autoinjector and to plunge it into her thigh muscle before his own body started to feel the effects of the nerve agent.

Pulling the cap off the second injector, he plunged it into his own thigh.

Chapter Twenty-Two

Hours later when he first started coming around, Mark didn't know where he was or what had happened to him. Why his head hurt and why his muscles continued to contract painfully.

He tried to move, but he couldn't, and because it was easier, he allowed himself to sink into the warm nothingness again.

The next time he floated to consciousness, he realized that he was in a darkened hospital room. He could hear the rhythmic beep of a monitor somewhere behind him, the soft hiss of the oxygen mask. The sounds beyond the closed doors that suggested, despite the gloom in the room, that it was daytime.

As he came around a bit more, he finally remembered what had happened. The reason he was in a hospital bed. His gut twisted as memories flooded his brain.

Beth collapsing onto the pavement.

Hands holding him back as he tried to reach her.

The moment he'd broken free.

Her body convulsing as he dragged her away.

And then…and then nothing.

He clenched his eyes shut at the sudden pain of realization ripping through him.

Beth?

The door opened, harsh light stabbing his eyes briefly before it dropped closed behind whoever had entered. He tried to turn his head but couldn't seem to make his body work.

The nurse leaned over him. "They've given you medications to slow muscle contractions. You'll be able to move normally by tomorrow."

"Beth?" he managed to get out but even to his own ears it sounded more like a soft exhale than a name.

The nurse pulled the blanket up, adjusted the position of the oxygen line and checked the IVs.

As she was preparing to leave, her hand brushed across his and he managed to close his fingers on hers.

She looked down, her expression startled but kind.

"Beth?" He knew he was crying but didn't care.

Her expression softened. Because he couldn't, she slowly turned his head for him.

"She's right there."

"How?"

"She'll be fine."

Epilogue

Six Weeks Later

Beth took the last turn up the steep gravel drive, pulling in behind the silver Explorer. Because of the Christmas trip to Sanibel, Florida, and the fitness evaluation she'd had to undergo as a formality, it had been nearly three weeks since she'd seen Mark at Larson's funeral. Even though they'd talked often on the phone, she'd missed him even more than she'd expected.

But had he missed her?

Stalling now, she took a few moments to check out the quaint two-story cabin surrounded by tall pine trees. The snow that had fallen overnight clung not just to the front of the structure but to the branches of the trees, too. With no other homes in sight, the idyllic scene almost resembled a Christmas card.

Still fighting a mixture of excitement and apprehension, she climbed out. The air was unbelievably frigid, the kind of dry cold that seemed to burn the lungs. For several seconds, she absorbed the utter silence, and then closed the door behind her.

She started to retrieve her suitcase from the backseat, but then didn't. This wasn't just the first time she'd been invited up here, it was also the first time she was to meet Gracie and Addison.

What if they didn't like her?

Mark opened the front door even before she reached it. Her heart turned over and then raced as he smiled at her.

"Sorry I couldn't get here sooner," she said nervously. "I had to wait on the carpenter. He's going to start the remodeling in the morning." Once she'd taken down the wall between the kitchen and the breakfast room, she'd decided to indulge in a new kitchen.

"You're right on time. I was just putting the spaghetti on." He closed the door behind her. "How are you in the kitchen?"

"Spaghetti I can handle."

Grinning, he pulled her into his arms. "What about me? Can you handle me?"

She twisted her fingers into his shirt collar and dragged his mouth down until it was a whisper from hers. "Depends on what kind of handling you're interested in."

Sensing that they were no longer alone, she pulled back awkwardly. Mark's two daughters stood near the hall entrance. As Beth smiled, the one she assumed because of her size was Addison, reached for her sister's hand. Evidently, Beth wasn't the only one who was nervous.

"Gracie, Addison. I'd like you to meet Beth."

They both approached, offering their small hands for her to shake, but neither of them said anything.

Reaching into her coat pocket, Beth produced two wrapped jewelry boxes. She was still uncomfortably aware that they might see the gifts as an attempt to bribe them into liking her. And maybe it was just a little bit.

She knelt down. "I went to Florida over the holidays," she said uncertainly as she handed out the presents.

Even as Addison ripped away the paper, Gracie stood unmoving.

Addison's small fingers picked up the delicate silver bracelet with a dolphin charm.

"Your dad told me that last summer when you went to Florida, you and Gracie and your mom got to swim with the dolphins."

Perhaps only because she knew she had to, Gracie slowly peeled open her gift and, like Addison, picked up the bracelet.

"What do you say, girls?" Mark asked.

Both Gracie and Addison chimed in with a thank-you, but Addison stepped forward, offering a brief hug that Beth hadn't been prepared for.

"You're both welcome."

Mark motioned with his head. "Why don't you girls go play another game of checkers while Beth and I finish dinner?"

Watching them leave, Beth knew she'd been expecting too much. She'd been eager to meet Mark's daughters and had been anxious that they like her, but she couldn't expect them to share those sentiments.

Mark wrapped her hand in his. "Come on. You can tell me all the news while I boil pasta."

The kitchen smelled divine. Homey. Mark turned up the burner beneath the pot and then handed her a glass of red wine, steering her to a bar stool. "Sit. Relax."

"I thought you wanted help."

"No. I just wanted to know if you can cook. For future reference." He picked up a carrot, scraping it clean and then slicing it expertly. "So how's your new boss?"

"Tom? He's doing fine." When Bill Monroe was suddenly transferred to Idaho, Tom Weston had been promoted to supervisory special agent.

She took a quick sip. "In fact on the way up here today, I learned that I've been completely cleared, that I'll be returning to full duties after the holidays." She'd thought it would bother her that after everything Monroe had done to her, the only punishment he'd received was a transfer. But it didn't.

He dumped the noodles into the strainer. "Where's your luggage?"

"I left it in the car for now."

"In case you have to make a fast escape?"

"I just wasn't sure… You have the girls this weekend. I thought maybe it wouldn't be wise…"

He crossed to where she sat and pulled her into his arms. "You're the first woman I've invited up here since the divorce. And the first one I've introduced to them. And there's a reason that both of those things are true, Beth."

She knew what he was trying to say. That what he felt for her wasn't casual. She'd known for weeks now that she was in love with him, but it was scary being that way alone.

Cradling her face between his warm hands, he lowered his lips. "What I'm trying to say is I love you." He kissed her slowly and completely. "And I'm hoping that you feel the same way about me."

Emotion welled up inside her as she met his gaze. "I do."

"Enough to say those same two words in front of a minister?"

She wanted to throw herself into his arms, but something kept her from doing it.

"Marry me, Beth."

"What about the girls? What if they don't like me?"

"Maybe they won't. Maybe they'll love you instead." He straightened. "I know it's a package deal. And I know we've never talked about how you feel about children, or about babies. If you don't want to have children of your own, I understand—"

"But I do. And I want to have them with you."

TERMS OF
ATTRACTION

BY
KYLIE BRANT

Kylie Brant is a bestselling, award-winning author of twenty-five novels. When she's not dreaming up stories of romance and suspense, she works as a teacher for learning-disabled children.

Kylie invites readers to check out her website at www. kyliebrant.com for news, backlist and information about upcoming releases. She can be contacted by e-mail at kyliebrant@hotmail.com.

For Keaden, my newest grandson,
who already owns a piece of my heart.

Acknowledgements

As always, a huge thank-you to Kyle Hiller,
Captain, Special Response Team, for your generous
assistance. I'm awed by both your knowledge
and your dedication to duty!

Chapter 1

Ava Carter lay motionless atop the gravel and tar flat roof squinting through the Nightforce scope of the Remington 700 rifle. She'd been in position for nearly four hours; under a "weapons tight" command for two. If all went according to plan, the subject would be on his way—in one piece—in less than fifteen minutes.

The rheumy late February sun labored to pierce the light cloud cover, and there was small blessing in that. Temperatures still hovered in the high sixties. And even without direct sunlight she could feel a thin trickle of perspiration snaking down her back beneath the LBV vest.

The breeze kissing her cheek seemed to have gotten a little stronger. "Check the wind meter again."

Her spotter, Steve Banes, held up the pocket calibrator. "Six point two four miles per hour."

Ava adjusted the dope of her rifle slightly. Steve picked

up his high-powered binoculars again and spoke into the Motorola radio. "Side three, opening three. No movement."

She reached for her own set of binoculars. Through them she could clearly see the black RV that served as the SWAT command center parked a hundred yards from the civic center. She could make out the figure of a man through one of the windows, hunched over a computer.

Her gaze passed over the RV to scan the area. She and Steve were positioned on top of a building across the road about eight hundred yards from the civic center. The building they were observing was circular, with an oddly pitched roof that was supposed to enhance the acoustics inside. Beneath the overhang were narrow windows encircling the building.

The inner perimeter seemed secure. The interested public was still inside listening to Antonio de la Reyes. But it was his detractors that were cause for concern.

From this angle she could only see a corner of the group of protesters and media vans secured behind the outer perimeter in front of the civic center. There were still a few signs waving, but a majority of the picketers had wisely decided to save their strength for when de la Reyes made his exit.

Hopefully once they figured out he wasn't coming out the front, de la Reyes would be on his way to the airport. Out of Metro City. Out of California and back to his small South American country of San Baltes.

Good riddance.

It wasn't his politics Ava objected to, though his eloquent arguments for opening the borders of America didn't resonate for her. It was the target he presented. In the last week alone, as he'd traveled the country, he'd received almost a dozen death threats. Pretty unpopular for a visiting dignitary. She'd heard there was a small rebel contingent in his own country that was just as anxious to see him dead.

She was only anxious to see him gone.

"What's he even doing here?" grumbled Banes. He was a

large man, heavily muscled. His shaved head was the color of her morning double mocha latte and glistened with sweat.

"He has relatives here, I think I heard. His mother lived in Metro City until the seventies."

Banes's droopy dark mustache twitched in what might have been a smirk. "Like you'd remember anything about the seventies."

"Just enough to know seventy-seven was a very good year." Ava continued to scan the area. They'd had this conversation often enough in the past that she could participate without thinking. Banes had a good fifteen years on her, and he liked to rib her about his experience. He'd been on SWAT ten years longer than she had. He was a damn good marksman, ranking second in the Metro City PD, fourth in the state.

Ava ranked first in both.

"Have you ever been inside?"

She nodded. "Took my son to a concert there once. It's pretty nice. All the seats have a good view of the stage." It must have been about three years ago, when Alex was twelve, before he became afflicted with that weird teenage parental anathema. At fifteen he could barely be convinced to be seen with her at the mall.

The radio crackled. "De la Reyes has left the stage. Subject will be exiting from side three, opening one in the next two minutes."

Ava kept the binoculars raised. De la Reyes's white limo approached slowly and rolled to a stop by the curb. It would have been checked thoroughly before being allowed through the inner perimeter. Security inside the building would be directing the public out the front. Officers would keep the people from circling around to the back entrance. Everything was working according to plan.

She was about to lower the binoculars when something caught her eye. A glint in one of the civic center's upper windows. In the next instant it had disappeared. "Do you see anything up there?"

Banes trained his binoculars in the area she was pointing to. "Nope."

"Must have been the sun," she muttered. But there was very little sunlight today. Which made it more likely she'd seen a reflection of some sort. But of what?

"Wait." She and Banes spoke simultaneously. She went on. "You see it, too, right? What is that?"

Both of them stared for long moments through their binoculars. A chill broke out over Ava's skin as comprehension slammed into her. "It's a scope."

Banes grabbed the radio. "We've got a reflection in side three, window seven. Looks like it could be from a rifle scope."

"Cold Shot in position?" came the answer.

"Affirmative."

"Weapons tight. We'll send someone inside to check it out."

Ava set down the binoculars and peered through the Nightforce scope of her Remington. She made the minute adjustments necessary to focus on the window in question. "I see the barrel," she reported quietly. A familiar deadly calm settled over her. "Can you get another angle and make it out?"

Steve belly-crawled several yards away and took another look through the binoculars. As an answer, he spoke through the radio. "We've got a weapon sighted and verified. Side three, window seven."

The radio crackled. "Keep target inside. We've got a sighting."

She heard the voice as if from a distance. Ava's entire system had slowed. Breathing. Nerves. Heart rate. Everything was focused on the individual on the other end of that rifle across the road. The best shot would be to shoot perpendicular from the window. But she didn't have time to change position. Shooting at an angle meant firing two shots. The first to break the glass and the second to hit the target.

"What the hell?" muttered Banes as the back door entrance opened. Ava recognized de la Reyes surrounded by his private contingent of security and three tactical officers hurrying toward the steps.

"Weapons loose. Engage, engage."

She was dimly aware of the group surrounding de la Reyes halting. Retreating toward the civic center. Her finger squeezed the trigger and fired twice in quick succession through the target window. Nearly simultaneously an answering shot sounded and one of the bodies on the steps crumpled.

Ava gave her watch a surreptitious look and sighed mentally. If this was going to drag on much longer she'd need to excuse herself and text Alex. He'd be getting out of basketball practice soon and might need to catch a different ride home.

The debriefing was going more slowly than usual. But then nothing about this incident had proven normal yet.

The door to the conference room opened and Chief of Police Carl Sanders entered, flanked by his deputy chief, Robert Grey. They were followed by Antonio de la Reyes and a few men she remembered from his security contingent.

There was a scraping of chairs as a few of the SWAT officers made room at the long table. Ava sat still as the newcomers stared her way, feeling like an insect on a pin.

"There she is, gentlemen. The officer of the hour."

There was little doubt about whom Sanders was referring to. Ava was the only woman in the room. Without looking away from her, de la Reyes circled the table to come to a halt before her.

"Ms. Carter," he said in melodic fluent English. "I am in your debt."

Since he'd taken her hand and looked to be in no hurry to free it, Ava rose, ill at ease. "I'm glad it worked out."

He looked more like a movie star than a politician. He was no taller than she, about five nine, with glossy dark hair and soulful brown eyes. But she recognized the tailor-fitted suit he wore and the designer shoes. His country's impoverishment didn't extend to this man.

"It worked out, as you say, for all but your fellow officer." Finally de la Reyes released her hand and glanced back at Sanders. "But I am told the man is well."

Sanders nodded, his craggy face grim. "Sergeant Talbot was saved by his vest. He'll be sore for a few days, but he's already been released from the hospital."

There was a collective murmur of relief from the room's occupants.

De la Reyes went to sit in a nearby free chair and Ava sank into her own with a sense of reprieve. She'd never learned to enjoy the spotlight.

Sanders pulled out a chair. "The would-be assassin has been identified."

"His name is Pedro Cabrerra." Ava recognized the man passing out sheets as head of the American company providing de la Reyes security while in the country. He was the sort of man who left an impression.

A shade under six feet, he had a commanding presence, even in a roomful of cops. His streaked blond hair bordered on shaggy, his pale green gaze hawklike. His face was tanned as a surfer's and his body looked broad and rock hewn beneath his suit. Unlike de la Reyes, whose expensive clothes gilded his sophisticated appearance, this man's suit only served to highlight what he was beneath it. A warrior. No amount of gloss or polish could ever mask his rough edges.

"I am sorry." De la Reyes lifted a hand to indicate the man passing out Cabrerra's likeness. "Cael McCabe. He owns the security company I hired shortly before I came to the States."

McCabe was the only one to remain standing. And he didn't so much pace the room as prowl. "Cabrerra was a trusted member of Senor de la Reyes's private security detail who traveled with him from San Baltes."

"He is…was," de la Reyes corrected himself, "my first cousin. Our fathers are brothers."

Ava saw the grief in the man's eyes and felt a moment of sympathy. Bad enough for complete strangers to want you dead. But when your own family went gunning for you…that transcended politics. It didn't get any more personal.

"Cabrerra was part of the security contingent to go through the civic center prior to Antonio's appearance there."

"But how the hell did he smuggle in a weapon?" Chief Sanders demanded. "Rifle, scope, tripod…he didn't carry all that equipment in when he was helping with the security sweep."

"He probably went in the night before," McCabe responded. There was the slightest hint of Georgia in his voice. He might have lost the drawl, but the rounded vowels gave him away. "The windows aren't wired to the alarm system. No reason to be. They're too narrow for a person to enter through. He must have rappelled up the side of the building with the equipment in a bag over his shoulder. We found a window with the lock drilled out. All he had to do then was open the window, drop the bag inside and close it again. He just had to make sure he was first in the building the next morning so he could choose the section he was going to 'secure.' Stash the equipment until he needed it."

"Those windows all open onto hallways that circle the top of the building," SWAT commander Harv Mendel observed.

McCabe nodded. "He probably locked the doors leading to the seating. Hard to blend in if he'd tried to take out Antonio during his speech. But leaving the building…he could have arrived on-scene moments later and no one would have suspected him. Better yet, everyone would have figured it was one of the nut jobs that have been issuing threats. Not one of his own countrymen."

The mood in the room went grim. "No offense, Senor de la Reyes…" The chief stumbled a bit over the pronunciation. "But he had five days and as many cities to act before you stopped in Metro City. What was he waiting for?"

"This I do not know."

"I can guess." McCabe shoved his hands in the pockets of his dark suit jacket, the motion pulling the fabric tight across his shoulders. "He figured this was his best chance to get away with it. He counted on a smaller police force. Less experienced security." He sent a slight smile at Ava. "He figured wrong."

The effect of that smile sent a frisson clear down her spine. Nerve endings quivered in response. Long-dormant hormones stirred. Ava straightened in her chair and stared back at McCabe, fighting for an impassive expression. There wasn't a man alive who could affect her with just a look. Few who could affect her *at all*. A man that potent wasn't just one to be wary of.

He was downright lethal.

"Ms. Carter."

She half turned, her posture wary. Cael quickened his stride to catch up with her and wondered, not for the first time, what it was about the woman that drew this visceral immediate response. She was attractive, with hair and eyes so dark she could pass for a countrywoman of de la Reyes, if it weren't for her pale skin. But he didn't react to every attractive female he saw, especially on a job.

"What is it, McCabe?"

One corner of his mouth kicked up at the impatience in her tone. Her voice was a low alto, slightly raspy. Every time he heard it he thought of sex. Hot and sweaty and exhausting.

"If you've got a few minutes, I'd like to buy you a drink." He was close enough to see the mask slide over her expression, and found himself intrigued yet again. Maybe she was used to men hitting on her and had developed an instant defense. He wasn't hitting on her, but he'd be lying if he said the thought hadn't occurred to him.

"Sorry. I need to get home." There was no trace of regret in her voice. She pushed open the door of the Metro City Police Headquarters and jogged down the steps.

"I'll walk you to your car, then." And it satisfied something inside him to intercept her sidewise glance, half irritated and half questioning. But she made no effort at conversation, clearly leaving that up to him.

He shoved his hands in his suit pockets and fleetingly wondered how long it would be before he could change into something that didn't feel like a straitjacket. "So. Good shooting today. Were you lucky or are you that good?"

"I'm that good," she said without a hint of modesty. And because it was no more than he'd heard, he nodded.

"Cold Shot. That's your call sign, right? From what I hear, it's well earned." They stepped into the parking lot. "Who spotted the shooter first?"

"I work with a partner. He was in the conference room. Steve Banes."

And that, he noted, didn't answer the question. "Banes told your chief that you noticed it first." She didn't respond and he took that as an affirmative. So she wasn't quick to take credit, a team player. Both facts only cemented his earlier decision. "I'd like to offer you a job."

The hitch in her gait was the only sign he'd surprised her. "No." Then after a pause that made it clear it was an after-thought, she added, "Thanks."

"Haven't heard my offer yet." He figured which was her car before she stopped in front of it. A Pontiac, seven or eight years old, and showing its age. "My company, Global Security, spe-cializes in a full array of security solutions. I'm always looking to hire qualified individuals. Your performance today was im-pressive." Even more impressive had been what Chief Sanders had to say about Carter's experience. He was still trying to square her reputation with the tall, lithe woman beside him who'd look more at home on a runway than in SWAT gear.

She clicked the automatic opener on the car, then reached for the handle, offering him a polite smile. "Like I said, I'm not inter-ested. I've got a son and I have no intention of uprooting him."

Disappointment stabbed through him, surprising in its strength. He'd also heard about her son, so her refusal wasn't totally unexpected. What was unexpected was hearing himself offer, "I've got some employees that freelance for me. Work special jobs during their vacations. If you ever want to consider that, give me a call." He handed her a card, quoting the range of pay.

Her eyes widened, her first real reaction since they'd started the conversation. "A month?"

"A week. Of course, it depends on the job."

Looking bemused, she accepted the card and slipped it into the pocket of her jacket. "The bodyguard business must be lucrative."

"I prefer personal protection specialists, and yeah." He lifted a shoulder. "It's a dangerous world."

"Tell me about it." She opened the car door, got in. "Goodbye, McCabe."

He stepped away, watching her back out of the space. Leave the lot. And wondered why he was feeling so disappointed that a woman he barely knew was driving out of his life.

She might have made it in time to pick up Alex, Ava thought darkly, as she reparked her car in the half-empty police headquarters lot thirty minutes later. Probably would have, given that he always seemed to be the last one out of the locker room. But the terse phone call she'd received when she'd been halfway to the East High School gym had ended hopes of getting home any time soon.

Her mood grim, she jogged up the steps to the building and flashed her ID at the officer manning the front desk. She strode by with barely a pause in her step, heading toward the stairs leading to the administrative offices. Chief Sanders hadn't been particularly forthcoming on the phone. But it wasn't like she could turn down his "request" that she head back in for yet another meeting.

Questions tumbled through her mind like circus acrobats. Had a question arisen regarding Cabrerra's death? It had been a clean shoot, but she'd seen more than one SWAT sniper get caught up in bureaucratic bullshit after a public outcry.

She took the steps to the second floor two at a time. It was much too early for Sanders to be taking flak for the incident response. The nightly news had just aired. And the mayor, never her favorite person, wouldn't have a reaction until the results of his daily polls were weighed.

Since it was impossible to guess the agenda for the meeting, Ava tried to shove her questions aside. But that didn't dissipate the knot of nerves tightening in her stomach.

Knocking on the closed door of Sanders's office, she awaited the chief's growled invitation before entering. Immediately her gaze went to the strangers seated across the desk from the chief. She made them out as feds immediately. Their dark suits and arrogant expressions were more telling than badges.

"Detective Carter." Chief Sanders waved her toward a chair. Ava sat in one a couple feet from the strangers. She felt the two men's gazes on her, bold and appraising, so she returned their stares unflinchingly. With a few notable exceptions, she held feds in as low esteem as she did politicians, for much the same reasons.

"DHS Agents Samuelson and Paulus," Sanders continued, with what passed for an introduction. The men gave her slight nods, and Ava struggled to hide her jolt of shock. What would Homeland Security want with her? Because it was at their request that Sanders had ordered her back. That much was clear.

"I'm sure you're anxious to get home, Detective Carter," started Samuelson. He was a tall, spare man, with slicked-back thinning dark hair and a tan that didn't quite hide the old acne scars on his face. "I'll get right to the point. I understand from Chief Sanders that you've met Cael McCabe, the owner of Global Securities."

"Yes."

The agent seemed to be waiting for her to go on, but when she didn't, he pressed, "The two of you were seen together in the parking lot afterward."

"Yes." Seen by whom? Who had been the person of interest? McCabe or her?

A note of impatience crept into Samuelson's tone. "Did the two of you have a conversation?"

"Yes." She saw Sanders hide a smile at her less than enlightening responses. But she was damned if she was going to feed the feds any information before they extended her the same courtesy.

"We'd like to know what you discussed." It was the first time Agent Paulus had spoken, and Ava shifted her attention to him. He was a good foot shorter than Samuelson, stocky, with coarse gingery hair and nearly invisible eyebrows.

"Why?"

"Because we asked, Ms. Carter." Samuelson's omission of her title didn't escape her. Neither did his biting tone. She was familiar with the intimidation tactics feds could use to leverage information. She glanced again at Sanders and he gave her a small nod.

She leaned back in her chair, feigning nonchalance. "He offered me a job." The two agents exchanged a look. Clearly she'd startled them. But even more surprising was the suppressed excitement she sensed her words elicited from them.

"With Global Securities?" Samuelson barely waited for her nod before pressing, "And what was your answer?"

"I told him I wasn't interested." Her interest was piqued now, however.

"We'd like you to reconsider your answer to McCabe's job offer," Samuelson said. Though couched as a suggestion, it sounded more like a command. "There's a matter of national security you could assist with by doing so."

"Why would I do that?" She didn't understand Chief

Sanders's silence, but she was tiring of the subterfuge. And her diplomacy skills tended to thin when she was tired.

"Patriotism?" offered Paulus. "Duty to your country? Commitment to national freedom?"

Anger coursed through her, a hot rush of feeling. Although she knew she was being manipulated, she was helpless to stem her response. "I'm recently recovered from taking a bullet because of my line of work. Just got back on the job two weeks ago. Tread carefully, gentlemen. You might not want to question my sense of duty."

"She's right." As if Sanders could remain quiet no longer, he came forward in his chair, aimed a steely look at the agents. "Detective Carter is a valued member of our force, and of our incident response unit. Time to fish or cut bait, gentlemen. If you want interagency cooperation, you have to be open about the mission you're asking Detective Carter's help on."

"Of course." Samuelson smoothed his muted striped tie, his manner stiff. "We were getting to that. Our agency has an interest in Antonio de la Reyes's new government and of the political climate in San Baltes. McCabe is providing security for de la Reyes, and anyone on his team would have access to certain... intelligence...that would help us with our threat assessment of the newly formed government there. With your heroics today, we thought you'd be in the perfect position to impress McCabe. Petition him for a position on his team." He gave her a small smile devoid of sincerity. "Obviously you already accomplished that feat. He was impressed enough to offer you a job, which would make your task even more plausible."

It was amazing, Ava thought cynically, what passed for open communication with these guys. Or maybe they really underestimated her intelligence enough that they thought she'd buy their story unquestioningly. "Why do you need me? Why not approach McCabe directly for the information?" She read her answer from the pained expressions on the agents' faces.

"Mr. McCabe was disinterested in cooperating."

Ava's lips quirked. She could imagine McCabe's response had been somewhat less polite than Samuelson indicated. Her estimation of the security consultant kicked up a notch.

"Well, I'm confused." She gave the agents an easy shrug. "The situation you're outlining sounds like a matter for the CIA, not DHS. Your involvement means there's a terrorism component to your concern. I must have missed it when you mentioned that part."

"This is extremely sensitive." Agent Paulus cast a look at the other agent as he spoke. "Whatever your response, I hope we can count on your discretion." He waited expectantly, but when Ava said nothing, he went on. "Alberto Martinez, the former leader of San Baltes, was a corrupt dictator. We have reason to believe money from his government was supporting terrorist attacks throughout South America. Naturally we're eager for the opportunity to explore the degree to which that network still exists. Your placement on McCabe's team gives us such an opportunity."

"I'm sorry." Her voice was insincere. "As I told Mr. McCabe, I have a job here. A teenage son to care for. I'm not free to take the job even if I wanted to."

"Captain Sanders assures us that your job would be waiting for you during your absence, as would your spot on SWAT. And your ex-husband could care for your son while you're gone, couldn't he?"

Everything in Ava stilled. Her glance flicked to the chief and back to Samuelson. It was impossible to be sure whether they'd gotten the personal details of her life from Sanders or from their own digging, but she'd bet on the latter. DHS wasn't known for their regard for individuals' privacy.

The only question remaining was how deep they'd dug.

"The answer's still no." Inwardly seething, Ava made sure her emotions didn't show in her expression. A sense of duty had formed her desire to enter the police force, but this…they were asking her to deceive McCabe, if in fact she could convince him to put her on de la Reyes's detail. To act as a spy while she was in San Baltes.

She'd worked plenty of undercover cases, but there was nothing compelling about the agents' request. They could cite national security all they wanted, but they'd failed to convince her of the urgency of this particular task. And even she was surprised at the level of distaste she felt for it.

"So that's it, gentlemen." Sanders rose, indicating the meeting was at an end. Ava couldn't tell if he approved of her response or not. "I said I'd release Detective Carter if she agreed, but you have her answer. I'm afraid I have another meeting in a few minutes."

They all rose, and the tall agent reached into his pocket to withdraw a card. He handed it to her. "In case you reconsider."

When Ava went to take it, the man didn't release the card immediately. Her gaze met his.

"Think it over, Ms. Carter." His voice was pitched low enough to reach only her ears. "I happen to believe a single act of patriotism can erase years of disloyalty. Years that might prove embarrassing should they be made public."

The freshly healed scar on her shoulder throbbed at his thinly veiled warning. He finally released the card and she slipped it into her suit pocket. Turning without a word, she headed for the door, wondering frantically just how thorough their investigation of her had been.

Because she didn't think she was imagining the threat in Samuelson's parting words.

Chapter 2

Once back in her car, Ava checked her cell phone and found a text message from Alex assuring her he'd find another ride home. She slipped the key in the ignition, but then sat still for a few moments, her fingers clenching and unclenching on the steering wheel.

It was ridiculous to let Samuelson rattle her. She was accustomed to the strong-arm tactics feds used to get what they wanted, but surely his was an empty threat. Her occupation was a daily testament to her patriotism. She didn't have to fly to another country to prove it. Just as she didn't have to constantly strive to negate her radical upbringing. How many times had her ex-husband reminded her of that?

Apparently, not often enough.

Perhaps she'd misinterpreted his words. Ava had the thought, tried to believe it. The assignment the man had described didn't seem all that vital to national security. So he'd left something out, hardly surprising when dealing with feds.

Which made it impossible to decide whether he'd been bluffing about making trouble for her.

She headed out of the lot and turned on the busy Belleview Boulevard. They lived on the outskirts of the city, a fact her son had grown to hate as his social relationships had become the center of his life. But at the time she and Danny had bought the property, it was quite a bit cheaper to live farther out. That was before trendy developments had started popping up all over in what had previously been a spacious, peaceful area.

Things changed. Ava slowed as she came up on a blue-haired woman who could barely see over the top of the steering wheel. Her neighborhood wasn't the only evidence of that. Less than five years after they'd bought the house, she and Danny had separated. They'd been divorced for nearly three years.

Turning at her corner, she immediately recognized the blue Toyota parked at the curb in front of her house. Her stomach plummeted. It had been a long, stressful day. She and her ex-husband had an amiable relationship, but she wasn't in the mood to deal with him tonight. All she wanted was a hot meal and a cold beer. Maybe sitting down with Alex to catch the Lakers game on ESPN.

All of which would have to wait until Danny was gone.

Pulling to a stop under the carport, she got out of the vehicle, leaving her gear locked in the trunk. Normally she'd put her rifle in the gun safe, but that would mean carrying it into the house and Danny had never hidden his disapproval about her participation on Alpha Squad. It had been one of the things that had driven them apart.

Pushing open the front door, she saw her ex-husband and Alex sitting on the couch talking animatedly. If their sudden silence at her appearance wasn't a tip-off that they were up to something, their guilty expressions would have been.

Ava closed the door behind her and raised a quizzical brow. "So, what are you two hatching?"

"Nothing." Her son was a horrible liar. His eyes, as dark

as her own, were alight with excitement. His entire body practically quivered with it. "Dad called right after your text, and when I told him I needed a ride he said he'd pick me up."

"Uh-huh." She grabbed him playfully as she walked by the couch, dropping a kiss on his brown mop of hair before he could dodge away. "Did you also tell him we're going shopping tomorrow and you have to get all your homework done tonight?"

"Oh man." Alex slumped against the couch. "Can't you just go and bring some stuff home for me to look at?"

She cocked her head, pretended to consider it. "You mean bring home different sizes and fashions for you to try on and then take back whatever you don't want? Sort of like your own personal shopper?"

"Yeah."

"Nope." Ava dropped in a chair and fixed Alex with a steady look. "Go on and do your English while I talk to your dad. I'll order something for supper."

His excitement visibly dimmed, Alex got up and slouched out of the room, muttering, "Okay, but the next kid I see at the mall that calls you a MILF, I'm gonna punch him in the face."

"Violence is never the answer, Alex," Danny said reprovingly.

But Ava was less focused on her ex-husband's words than she was on her son's. "What is that? MILF? He's complained about that before." She swung her puzzled gaze to Danny's, but her ex looked just as mystified as she was. She'd have to remember to ask one of the other cops. Danny wasn't exactly up on teenage vernacular.

"Thanks for bringing him home."

Her ex-husband took off his rimless glasses and cleaned the lenses on his shirt, his fine white-blond hair falling in his eyes. "I wanted to come by and talk to you tonight anyway. It worked out."

"Must be big." She waited for him to put his glasses back on, blink at her owlishly. "I haven't seen Alex that excited since the baseball coach moved him up to play JV last year."

"Well." Danny gave her that boyish smile that once would have softened something inside her. "It is big. But how big depends on you."

For the second time in an hour Ava found herself wishing for a beer. "Danny. It's been a long day. Just spill it, okay?"

He fingered his white collar, a nervous habit he had. "I just told him about a mission trip I have planned. I booked some flights to Tanzania for this summer for myself and a few other church members. We're going to help build some schools. Train teachers. I'll be gone the entire summer."

"That's longer than usual." She reached for the lever to kick up the footrest on her recliner and smothered a purr of satisfaction when the chair responded. "Your church must have really done some major fund-raising for this trip."

His gaze skirted hers. "The church remains committed to our missionary work. But with the upcoming renovations to the building planned…well, money is tight. I funded it myself."

"You…" Ava gaped at him. "You don't have any money." The child support he sent her was modest. His salary as assistant pastor in a small church was less than what she made, and cops weren't exactly featured on *Lifestyles of the Rich and Famous*. "Where would you get…" Her stomach plummeted. "Oh, Danny. Tell me you didn't."

He folded his hands on his knees and leaned forward, his choirboy face earnest. "These people are among the poorest in the world, Ava. They live in mud huts. Some of the children walk ten miles a day to school. Try to put things in perspective. If some personal sacrifice means we can help hundreds of less fortunate…"

The last thing she needed right now was another lecture on *sacrifice*. She came upright and out of the chair in one smooth motion, her fists balled at her sides. "The sacrifice is hardly personal when it's your son paying the price. Did you tell Alex you financed this trip by selling the bonds you were saving for his college costs?"

His chin squared. He'd never once raised his voice in all the years she'd known him, but she recognized that expression. It meant he wouldn't budge from his position. "You still have your savings for him, right? And he doesn't have to go to MIT. There's a perfectly adequate college right here in Metro City."

Ava closed her eyes, gritting her teeth against the hot words that trembled on her tongue. "He's talked of nothing else for three years. He got a two thousand on the SAT as a freshman, Danny. He's not going to the local college." Her son's proficiency in academics, especially in math and science, had been noticed early in elementary school. She'd been saving what she could for his future since then. They both had. At least until now.

"MIT gives need-based scholarships anyway. And if he has to borrow some money, he'll appreciate his education more." Danny's voice turned indulgent. "The Lord will provide, Ava. You just have to believe."

She stared at him, her breathing strangled. Which of them had changed more since they'd first met at seventeen and twenty? No real puzzle there. Danny was still the dreamy-eyed idealist, with the biggest heart she'd ever met. So big sometimes that it blinded him to the needs of his own family. While she…after eleven years on the force, she'd learned that all people weren't inherently good. That evil was more than a concept. And if you didn't take care of your own, no one else would.

Turning her back on him, she fought to keep her voice steady. "You need to go."

"Ava—"

"Now." She could feel the temper heating her from the inside out. The tightness in her chest heralded an impending explosion. Alex didn't need to hear his parents arguing. He'd heard plenty of that before they'd split.

There was nothing to argue about at any rate. The bonds were gone. And nothing she could say would convince Danny he'd violated a trust by using them.

A thought struck her there, comprehension piercing anger. She whirled to see Danny halfway through the door. "Wait." He halted. "That's not what had Alex so excited. What'd you tell him?"

His sheepish look was its own answer. "I meant to run it by you first. Really. But we got to talking, and seeing how interested he was, it just came out. But I warned him that you were going to have the final say, Ava. I swear I did."

"No."

"It would be a wonderful experience for him." Her ex let go of the doorknob and moved closer to her. "He'll learn compassion for others...."

"My son doesn't need to travel ten thousand miles to learn compassion." Her voice shook with the effort it took to keep it steady. Odd how she could face down an armed robber. Take out a target at a thousand yards. But this...this had panic sprinting down her spine. Ice bumping through her veins. "And if you think I'm sending a fifteen-year-old boy halfway around the world with you this summer, you are seriously deranged."

"Pizza delivery."

Ava stood in her son's open doorway and waved the pizza box in front of her. Alex turned around in his desk chair and grinned in delight. "Meat lover's with mushrooms and green olives?"

"Yes, O Gluttonous One." When she entered his room, her son's eyes widened. "I get to eat in my room?" The practice had been banned after Ava had discovered why the house had such an ant infestation. Alex tended to forget the leftovers he shoved under his bed, but the ants never did.

"It's a onetime offer, and mealtime rules apply. Put a shirt on." He must have showered, because his hair was damp and he was clad only in baggy basketball shorts. He got up and pulled a T-shirt over his head, and she was struck anew by the definition in his back and shoulders. He already stood eye-to-eye with her at five nine. He'd surpass her by his next birthday. Girls had been calling the house for three years, but in the last twelve months or so Alex had been doing some calling of his own. Sometimes the years seemed to meld into nanoseconds. Another few blinks and he'd be off to college and she'd be alone for the first time in her life.

Shrugging off the bolt of emotion that twisted at the thought, she sat on his bed, cross-legged, with the box on her lap. She handed him a plate as he reached for the first slice of pizza, knowing he wasn't one to bother with such niceties on his own.

"This looks great. What are you going to eat?"

"Funny." But Ava withdrew two pieces just in case. Alex could work his way through the rest without a pause. His metabolism should rank as one of the Seven Wonders of the World.

They ate for a few minutes in companionable silence. After breaking all speed limits to wolf down three slices, he finally slowed enough to say, "Guess you're pretty pissed that Dad talked to me about going to Africa, huh?"

At her sharp glance he rolled his eyes and amended, "I mean 'mad.'"

She put her half-eaten slice down and reached for a napkin. "It's a big decision, Alex. And it's one we should have talked over before he mentioned it to you. So yeah, I'm not crazy about the idea."

"But you'll think about it, right? I mean, how cool would that be? I've never even been out of the country before."

"You've been to Mexico."

He waved off her correction. "Okay, I haven't been off the continent. When would I ever get a chance like this again?"

She wiped her fingers carefully, trying to hide her dismay. "It wouldn't be a pleasure trip. You'd be working. Living without indoor plumbing and electricity. No TV. No video games."

"I know that." He took another slice out of the box. "But I'd be doing some good, right? And think how that would look on my college application. You're always saying I need to list community service."

"I was thinking more like mentoring middle schoolers. Teaching Sunday school. And what about baseball?"

"Dad said I could fly out after the regular season is done. It's not like we're going to State this year. Not with Severin as the pitcher. Did you know his fastball is only clocked at sixty miles an hour?"

She had to smile at the disgusted expression on his face.

"So that would give me a good month there before I have to come back and get ready for school."

The bite Ava had just taken turned to ash in her mouth. She swallowed with effort. "What about our camping trip?" Each year she saved the majority of her vacation and they went to the mountains. Or the desert. Or the Southwest. They spent weeks poring over maps, planning their route and which campsites to stop at. Where to hike or kayak. They'd been talking about white-water rafting on the Snake River on their travels this summer.

Alex shrugged. "We camp every year. It's no big deal." Then he looked up, his face stricken. "I mean, we can go again next summer, right?"

He had a heart as soft as Danny's. Ava knew if she didn't reassure him, he'd beat himself up for hurting her feelings. "Right. But I still have to think about it."

"Okay." He reached for another slice, satisfied for the time being with her answer. But when he changed the topic to complain about a teacher who just happened to teach his least favorite subject—English—Ava's attention was only half on the conversation.

Her mind was reeling. First there'd been the unsettling meeting with DHS, then the double punch of the twin parental concerns she'd been handed tonight.

Experiencing a sinking certainty, Ava was beginning to believe that the solution to all three situations might be entwined.

"So, do you?"

Her attention jerked back to her son, who was regarding her impatiently. "Do I what?"

"Have some sort of genealogy information for me to use for this lame English paper."

Ava searched through the fragments of the last few moments of conversation that had registered, came up empty. "Why do you need that?"

Alex rolled his eyes. "Mo-om. I just told you about that family tree assignment Fulton gave us in English. I need something to put in the paper I have to write. Five pages. Five. Whole. Pages."

Ordinarily she would have commiserated with her son's dismay. She wasn't much of a writer herself. But for the second time that day she was reminded of her past, and it wasn't a recollection she cared for.

"I'm sorry, my family wasn't much for writing stuff like that down." That, at least, was the truth. She knew her grandparents' names but that was about it.

"No living relative you can get information from?"

She thought of her father then, the accompanying twist of pain familiar. "No." The lie didn't weigh heavily on her. She'd spent the first two years of Alex's life desperately trying to get her father to acknowledge her existence, and that of his grandson.

And then the next dozen years ignoring his.

"Great." Alex wadded up his napkin and slouched in his chair. "Now Fulton will make me take the information you do have and do a genealogy search on the Internet. Jonnie Winters had to do that last semester and it took him days. I was hoping just to write the report with what we already had."

Tiny shards of ice formed in Ava's blood. All sorts of information was available on the Internet. But one thing would not be found there: any trace of her father's death.

She considered for a moment having to explain to her son

why she'd lied to him all these years about their lack of relatives. Thought of how she'd tell him who and what his grandfather was. Who Ava used to be.

Her throat suddenly dry, she looked at Alex, who was regarding her expectantly. "How about you use your dad's genealogy for the paper? Grandpa Carter has notebooks full of their family history."

Hope glimmered in her son's eyes. "You think I could? It's not exactly my family since dad adopted me."

"Well, you share the same last name, so Mr. Fulton won't know that, will he?"

"Sweet," he said with satisfaction. "I thought of that earlier, but I thought…you know…maybe you'd think it was dishonest or something."

Ava caught Alex's eyes on her and it was all she could do not to squirm. Her hypocrisy weighted heavily on her. She'd endlessly preached truthfulness to her son while she'd spent his whole life lying to him about her family.

She smiled weakly, guilt slashing at her. There was little a parent wouldn't do to protect her child. But sometimes she wondered whom she was really protecting. Because in that moment she realized exactly how far she'd go to keep her past hidden, for both their sakes.

Cael stepped out of the shower and carelessly swiped a towel down his body as he reached for his ringing cell. It was after eleven, West Coast time. But he had operatives across the nation and in several countries with various time zones. And in accordance with Murphy's Law, it seemed like at least half of them had called with some sort of problem today.

He looked at the screen, didn't recognize the number. "Global Security." As he answered the call he fastened the towel around his waist, raking his fingers through his hair. Maybe he could manage a haircut before leaving the States again.

"McCabe."

That low smoky tone was immediately recognizable. So was the heat it elicited low in his belly. "Ava Carter."

There was a hesitation. Then, "I just noticed the time. I didn't realize it was so late."

"Not a problem. All hell's been breaking loose this evening and I haven't even thought about sleep yet." He headed out to the sitting area of his suite, perched on the arm of the couch, intrigued and wary. When they'd parted this afternoon he'd never expected to see her again. And he still had trouble understanding the source of the regret that thought had elicited.

But then later, when Benton had reported following Samuelson to police headquarters, where Carter had reappeared, too, his interest in her had taken on a whole different facet.

She didn't beat around the bush. "I've been thinking of your offer this afternoon. About short-term employment. Were you serious?"

His stomach twisted, a quick vicious lurch. It took more effort than it should have to respond evenly. "Yeah. How much time do you have available?"

"I have several weeks' leave accumulated."

"Then you could take some now, right?" With the words he baited the trap, prayed she wouldn't walk in. Heard it snap closed when she did.

"I could probably get approval for immediate leave."

"If you're serious about this I'd like to meet with you as soon as possible." Needed to, to find out what had caused her sudden about-face.

But he was very much afraid he already knew.

"All right. My shift tomorrow gets done at—"

"Tomorrow I'm flying to L.A. It'll have to be tonight." He crossed to the desk, found a pad and pen. "Give me directions to your place. I'll be there in thirty minutes." The reluctance in her voice as she recited the directions did nothing to dispel the determination spiking in his gut. As he disconnected the phone he clenched the instrument tightly in his hand, to avoid hurling it across the room. He didn't want to believe that DHS had drawn her into this. It would be a stretch, even for Samuelson.

But the possibility had to be explored. He crossed to his suitcase, pulled out some clothes. Dropping the towel, he began to dress swiftly. The fact that he was reluctant to credit the suspicions forming in his mind meant Ava Carter had already gotten under his skin.

Which made her dangerous in more ways than one.

The expression on Ava's face was wary as she pulled open the door before Cael had a chance to knock. Stepping aside to let him in, she said, "You move fast."

"I have to." Stepping inside, he shot a quick look around the place as she closed the door behind him. "I've got a killer schedule and we're spread a little thinner than I'd like."

He followed her to the leather couch and sat down, while she seated herself in the recliner facing him. On the way over he'd convinced himself that his earlier reaction to her was a combination of adrenaline and respect. That shot of hers today had been an impressive depiction of her talent.

But looking at hcr now, he realized he'd been kidding himself. Adrenaline had long faded, and it wasn't exactly respect that had him noticing her long, slim legs. Or the very female curves beneath the T-shirt she wore.

"So being shorthanded is the reason you wanted me to take vacation immediately?"

Her question yanked his attention back to business, where it would need to stay. If she was linked to Samuelson he'd have to tread carefully.

"Partially. But I've accepted an extension to my contract with de la Reyes. And your skills would come in useful during the course of that case."

Cael leaned back and propped one foot over the opposite knee, settling deeper into the couch. "De la Reyes needs personal protection more than ever. There's a rebel faction in his country working for a man who wants him out of power. With Cabrerra's betrayal, he can't afford to trust anyone. If his security detail has been infiltrated, why not his government? His household help? He needs outsiders to spearhead a safety regimen for him, until he can weed out those whose loyalty can be bought."

"And what happens to those people?"

He recognized the concern in her question. "Don't worry. Whatever you think of de la Reyes's politics, he came to power through a democratic election. He's lobbying our government for increased aid. He's hardly going to jeopardize that with civil rights violations. Those disloyal to him would be expelled from the country or jailed, but he wouldn't order them killed. He says he's committed to having his country recognized by the U.N. after decades of dictator rule. I believe him."

Ava looked less certain. "And the immediacy you spoke of earlier?"

"I need to accompany de la Reyes to L.A., which will be his last stop in the States. In two days we fly back to San Baltes. It'll take ten operatives to provide full security for him there once he resumes his full schedule. I can't have them all in place for at least a week."

"So I'd be providing protection until you can put a team together."

"*We'd* be providing protection," Cael corrected. "At least until the full detail is positioned. Are you as skilled with a handgun as you are with a rifle?"

She regarded him coolly. "Yes."

"Good. You'll be provided with both. I can expedite a passport if you don't have one."

"I do."

Giving a satisfied nod, he said, "So it's just a matter of getting the time off on short notice."

She raised her brows. "There's a matter of me agreeing first."

He didn't smile but something inside him lightened. Dead

tired, he shouldn't find it so damn stimulating to spar with her. Especially given what she might be hiding from him. "Ava, if you weren't interested you wouldn't have contacted me. Something changed between the time I spoke to you this afternoon and when you called earlier. Something that made you overlook your earlier objections."

She'd gone still, but not a flicker of expression crossed her face. "I'm not a cop, but I do have some deductive powers. That's how I keep my clients alive." He sat, barely breathing, waiting for her reply. Wanting desperately for her to prove those persistent little doubts swirling inside him wrong.

For a moment he thought she wouldn't answer. Was prepared to probe further. But then she said, her gaze skirting his, "After a visit from my ex-husband this afternoon I find myself in need of money." Her eyes came back to fix on his then, held steady. "If I decide to do this, regardless of my reasons, I'll put everything I've got into the assignment. I won't take it if I don't believe I can be of help to you."

He almost lost his train of thought for a moment, under her liquid chocolate gaze, before his resolve hardened. Nodding, he got to his feet, headed toward the door. "You check on that vacation time in the morning. I'll need your answer in twenty-four hours."

Closing the door behind him, he jogged down the steps toward his car. He could ill-afford to turn down her help if she did sign on. He hadn't been lying about needing her on de la Reyes's protection team.

But had *she* been lying to *him*?

He opened the door of the dark rental sedan, slid inside. Her story about a sudden need for money was plausible. It was also completely impossible to check out. Starting the ignition, he pulled away from the curb. Useless to wonder if it was a story cooked up between her and Samuelson. Or to speculate what her motivation would be for agreeing to join forces with the man.

He wanted—needed—to take her word at face value. But

Cael McCabe believed in being prepared. As much as he believed in revenge.

He glanced in his rearview mirror before switching lanes. If Ava Carter turned out to be working with Samuelson, he'd have no compunction about using her to destroy the man. And if that destroyed her in the process, well…

She would have gotten exactly what she deserved.

Chapter 3

Two days later Ava was jogging across the tarmac at LAX to the private jet waiting for her. A man she remembered from Cael's security detail at the civic center stood at the base of the steps leading into the plane. She flipped through her mental Rolodex. Bailey. Balsem. Benton. That was it. He'd been flanking de la Reyes's other side when Cabrerra fired at the man, hitting the officer instead. He was around her age, with wavy brown hair and a friendly puppy dog face that belied the seriousness of his occupation.

When she would have hurried up the steps by him, he reached for her bag. "I'll take care of this."

"I can handle it."

"Sorry." He didn't relinquish his grip on the suitcase. "Boss's orders."

Ava released the bag, hoping her uneasiness didn't show. She'd refused most of the high-tech tools Samuelson had tried to press on her, but she had accepted the minicamera hidden inside what looked like a normal pen. All parts were plastic or ceramic to pass undetected through security.

Heading into the jet, she reassured herself it was unlikely the item would raise any concerns. She was a cop, and she wouldn't have found the tiny camera if it hadn't been shown to her. It certainly looked harmless enough, clipped to a slim notepad in a zippered side compartment.

She paused before heading down the aisle. The surroundings were considerably more opulent than any she'd flown in before. There were six rows with two wide, comfortable-looking leather seats on either side of the aisle. Through an open door in the back she noted another compartment complete with wet bar and couches.

McCabe was seated midway back next to de la Reyes, and the two discontinued their conversation when she made an appearance. The president spoke first.

"Detective Carter." His face was wreathed in smiles. "It is a pleasure to see you again. Forgive me for not rising. My seat belt is fastened in preparation for departure."

Cael lifted a brow at her. "You cut it close," he noted.

Her nerves jittered. Considering the fact that she'd had to completely rearrange both her personal and private life in less than forty-eight hours, it was a miracle she'd made it on time.

And given her continued ambivalence about this task, it would have been a relief if the jet had taken off without her.

As the men resumed their conversation she took a free seat near the back behind an operative of Cael's she remembered from before. Sibbits, she thought his name was. He was exceedingly thin, as if all excess flesh had been carved away. His receding hairline was graying, and cropped short. The rest of the plane's occupants were part of de la Reyes's entourage.

Benton boarded the plane, minus her bag, and took a seat up front. It didn't take a rocket scientist to know that her luggage had been thoroughly searched before it had been stowed. The precaution only served to remind her of the precariousness of her situation. Until de la Reyes ascertained the level of infiltration, no one in his government was above suspicion.

And if Ava let her guard down in the slightest, a very different sort of suspicion would fall on her.

The jet's engines revved. Moments later it began rolling along the runway. She'd never been a nervous flier, but the anxiety from her situation had her remaining seated upright, muscles tight with tension. So it must have been sheer exhaustion that had her asleep before they'd been in the air a half hour.

Awareness prickled beneath her subconscious. In the dim recesses of her mind, an alarm shrilled. Ava struggled to surface from slumber, but it was like swimming against a powerful current. She couldn't manage to drag her eyes open.

She was floating in pale green seas, being tugged ashore by an unrelenting tide. The sensation might have been pleasant if she'd felt more in control. As it was, she fought against the inexorable force of nature, found herself betrayed by limbs that had turned weak and molten.

Opening her eyes, she was disoriented to see Cael's face close to hers, his gaze fixed and intense. It was with no little embarrassment that she realized his eyes were the exact shade of the sea she'd been lost in only moments ago. Sleep shredded defenses and dignity with equal ease. Exploited vulnerabilities usually kept guarded.

"We'll be landing in fifteen minutes."

Averting her gaze, she raised her seat forward. "You should have wakened me earlier."

"I figured you probably needed the sleep. It couldn't have been easy making all the arrangements you had to on such short notice."

The innocent words had remorse stabbing through her. She'd called him before she'd contacted DHS, half hoping he'd make the decision easy for her. If he hadn't invited her along on this particular mission, she would have been off the hook, having done her "duty."

But he hadn't made it easy for her. And neither had Samuelson, with his air of condescension, as if her eventual acquiescence had never been in question. She didn't know which made her feel worse, that she was deceiving a man who paid her salary for the duration of the job. Or that the money itself had played an undeniable part in her decision.

Turning back to McCabe, she said only, "What's in place so far?" Regardless of Samuelson's agenda for this trip, she was being paid to provide security protection, and that task would take precedence while she was in San Baltes.

His voice was pitched low. "I've got two men on the ground already. They'll have completed some preliminary work prior to our arrival. De la Reyes was originally scheduled to return to San Baltes tomorrow. His men, including the pilot, just found out this morning of the change of plans. I've tried to make sure none of them have had access to outside communication."

She asked shrewdly, "And the news of his early return has been leaked only to…?"

Cael gave her an approving look. "Rafael Gonzalez is de la Reyes's chief of Presidential Guard. It'd be like our Secret Service. Pedro Cabrerra was his most senior officer."

Ava's spine prickled as she grasped his meaning. "Even if Gonzalez shares Cabrerra's political leanings, he'd be crazy to try anything now. He has to realize his department will already be under suspicion."

"Which also makes it more urgent that he act. His entire branch is about to undergo intense scrutiny. If Gonzalez is affiliated with the rebels, he has one last chance to strike before his access to President de la Reyes becomes curtailed."

She nodded her understanding. "How do we know the rest of his security detail weren't in on Cabrerra's plan?"

Cael looked grim. "That's one of the questions my operatives are checking into. They're investigating all Cabrerra's associates, discreetly, of course. I have them meeting us at the airport to provide more security for the trip to the presidential palace."

"What will we have for weapons?"

"We'll have access to enough firepower to hold off a small rebel contingent." At her sharp glance, the corner of his mouth turned up. "Let's hope it's not needed. Our team will take over as the first security wave. The nationals will answer to us for now. You'll be in a rotation providing personal protection to de la Reyes at all times." His gaze raked her form. "I've got a vest for you. You'll wear it every minute you're on duty. And with the exception of the limited amount of time you'll spend sleeping, you'll always be on duty." He waited a moment before saying quietly, "Regrets?"

"I don't waste time on regrets." It was almost true. There was no way to make amends for her past. No reason why she should feel the need to. Most of the time she believed that. But Samuelson had unerringly pressed exactly the right button to have that old guilt rising to the surface again.

"Good to know."

There was something in his eyes, in his voice that had her glancing at him. Found him watching her, in much the same way he'd been when she'd first wakened. A slow heat suffused her body just recalling that moment. But she knew none of her inner embarrassment showed on her face. She'd learned long ago how to mask her emotions.

"You're completely still when you sleep." His voice had gone whisper soft. "Like a porcelain statue. Not even your expression changes. I imagine you're like that when you're in position for a shot."

There was something curiously intimate in knowing that he'd watched her while she slept. No one else had ever had the opportunity, with the exception of her ex. She'd never "slept" with Alex's birth father. Not in the literal sense.

She could feel heat crawling up her neck. Cael McCabe had a knack for catching her off guard, and that would have to change. She knew enough about him to realize he was a man to seize any vulnerability and turn it to his advantage.

She was already vulnerable enough. The deception she was engaged in made an undeniably dangerous situation even more explosive.

As the jet idled on the runway Ava donned her vest, then sat down to check the weapons she'd been assigned. Two men she didn't recognize had carried them aboard from one of the three black SUVs parked nearby. Both were beauties, the handgun a nine-millimeter Lugar semiautomatic and a Remington rifle and scope that could have been twins to her SWAT equipment. She strapped on her holster and clipped the pouch of extra ammunition around her waist. Looking around, she saw everyone else similarly equipping themselves, with the exception of de la Reyes, who was speaking on a cell phone. She had protective garb for him, too, before he exited the jet.

She waited patiently as McCabe spoke quietly to the newcomers. They must be the men he said he had on the ground already, gathering intelligence. Switching her attention to the dark waiting vehicles, she surmised McCabe's plan. The best way to arrange security would be to have the armored cars drive right up to the jet, load the bags and leave without ever entering the airport building. With a VIP like de la Reyes on board, she imagined, that wouldn't be difficult to arrange.

McCabe and the two strangers got up and headed toward the door. Cael turned back, caught her eye. "Be ready to move out in five minutes."

She nodded, rising to approach de la Reyes. He was speaking in rapid-fire Spanish, most of which she was able to follow. She was familiar enough with the language to converse with Hispanic victims on the job. She heard him tell whomever he was speaking to that he'd be arriving home tomorrow. So he was following Cael's orders, at least for now. And from his tone, she thought he was speaking to a woman. McCabe hadn't mentioned a wife, so maybe a girlfriend.

Glancing out the window, she saw McCabe walking close to the side of one of the SUVs, a long pole in his hand. Checking for bombs on the undercarriage of the vehicle, she noted with approval. He was leaving nothing to chance. The mirror on the other end of the pole would reveal anything hidden beneath. She had no doubt that the interior would be subjected to a similarly rigorous search.

Her spine prickled. His thoroughness was a chilling reminder that de la Reyes hadn't been delivered to safety once he'd reached his homeland. Just the opposite.

Once de la Reyes ended the conversation, Ava slid into the seat next to him. "You'll need to put this on before leaving the aircraft." She handed him his vest. "Just as a precaution."

The man eyed the garment for a moment before reaching for it. "Mr. McCabe leaves nothing to chance."

Ava helped him into the vest, expertly fastening it for him. "That quality of his will work in your favor. Your situation calls for caution."

His expression was rueful. "I am a man of action. But we must take care first that I live to take that action, true?"

"That's right."

De la Reyes peered out the window. "How much longer will it be? I have much to do now that I am back."

"This is all just routine, but as I said, McCabe is a stickler for precautions."

"So I see," he murmured, his gaze returning to the window. "He is, as we say in my country, *un hombre de la guerra*. A man of war, is he not?"

His words jolted her, they so closely resembled her own impression in the briefing just a few short days ago. A warrior. Ready for battle at a moment's notice.

For the first time she wondered about McCabe's background. Not his security business, which she'd thoroughly checked out before calling him. But whatever had prepared him for establishing the business. Military, certainly. Special forces, most likely. It would explain that tough edge he maintained that the most civilized of garments or surroundings couldn't quite mask.

One of the vehicles pulled up to the aircraft steps. Ava led de la Reyes to the doorway. She and Benton flanked the man as they hurried him to the waiting SUV.

McCabe was behind the wheel, Sibbits next to him. Ava had de la Reyes get in the middle with Benton, while she positioned herself in the third seat next to a large leather duffel bag. The president's men split up into the remaining vehicles. One of McCabe's operatives rode in each of them. When one SUV pulled out, they followed, and the third brought up the rear.

Cael turned around. He'd donned a pair of mirrored sunglasses. "The gear's on the seat next to you."

Ava leaned over to unzip the bag. Spreading it open, she blinked.

It was packed to launch a small war.

There were several grenades, extra weapons and what looked like a portable rocket launcher. There were rifle scopes, binoculars, night-vision goggles and extra ammunition. Ava looked up, caught McCabe's eyes on her in the rearview mirror. He'd prepared himself for anything.

She withdrew a pair of German-made high-powered binoculars and trained them out the back window. Cordoba was the capital city of San Baltes, surrounded by mountains on three sides and the Pacific Ocean on the other. The natural beauty of the surroundings was in stark contrast to the Third World squalor they traveled through on the highway heading toward the center of the city.

"I'm a big fan of one of your country's singers. Mirabel Estaban. Have you ever met her?" Benton asked de la Reyes.

"Ah, Senorita Estaban. She is very talented, yes? She sang at my inauguration celebration. Her music is very popular here."

"I saw her on YouTube. On the Internet? She was wearing this dress cut down to…" Ava glanced up in time to see Sibbits turn in his seat, directing a look at Benton, who spread his hands innocently. "What? It showed her talents, is all I'm saying. Plus she can really sing."

De la Reyes gave a deep-throated laugh. "You are a man to appreciate a gorgeous woman. I can assure you, my country has many such beauties. Perhaps you will have the opportunity to meet some of them in your stay here."

Ava returned to her vigil, tuning out the conversation. There were three lanes of traffic traveling in either direction, separated by a median filled with mud, weeds and debris. Their American-made SUVs stood out among the economy-sized vehicles zipping by them.

Something caught her eye and she stilled, peering hard through the binoculars. The late-model Jeep coming up fast in the next lane behind them looked familiar.

"Alert car 3, vehicle to their back and left. We saw that red Jeep when we left the airport. Again when we took the last exit. Three occupants. No, wait. Four."

A radio crackled, and then she heard Sibbit's voice. "Vehicle three, ready defensive tactics. Red Jeep with multiple occupants. Left lane, coming fast."

The Jeep drew nearer and Ava felt a familiar spike of adrenaline. "Weapons sighted. At least two rifles."

Sibbits repeated the information to the third vehicle, while she heard McCabe speaking into his own radio, ordering the first SUV to drop back and exchange places with them. Benton was urging de la Reyes onto the floor, while he grabbed his weapon.

Ava lowered the high-powered glasses long enough to duck out from under the rifle strap, and readied the weapon. Sliding off the safety, she steadied the rifle, sighted, waiting for the command. The third vehicle swerved behind them into the path of the red Jeep, to force it to decrease its speed.

Except it didn't slow down. The Jeep slammed into the SUV, and there was a screech of metal on metal. Gunfire was exchanged between the two vehicles.

"Do you have a shot?"

Ava peered through the rifle's site, readjusted position to make up for the trajectory through two windows. "Yes."

"Take it."

The Jeep rammed the third SUV again, sending it spinning into the side rail. Ava saw the man in the Jeep's front passenger seat swing his rifle toward their vehicle as it raced toward them. Ignoring him for the moment, she concentrated on the driver, and squeezed the trigger once. Twice.

The Jeep's windshield shattered and the vehicle jerked to the right as the driver slumped over the wheel. The shooter's shot went wild. Ava saw the passenger in the front seat lower his weapon to wrench at the wheel as it veered into the far lane of traffic in front of an open-bed truck hauling a load of caged chickens.

"Vehicle one dropping back."

The bullet hole through their back window sent out a spiderweb of cracks, ruining her visual. She reengaged the safety and swung a leg over the seat to kick the window out with one booted foot. Their SUV picked up speed, lengthening the distance away from the Jeep. She saw the other SUV's occupants returning fire with the shooters in the Jeep before it careened into the median, flipping over on its top.

Ava could hear Cael snapping orders, Sibbits trying to raise vehicle three's occupants on the radio. De la Reyes was on the phone commanding a police helicopter to contain the scene. But then the Jeep burst into flames.

There would be very little for the police to investigate once they finally arrived.

* * *

"I owe you thanks once again, Senorita Carter."

Ava shifted uncomfortably, sliding a sidelong glance toward Cael. "It was a team effort, sir."

They stood in the sitting room of de la Reyes's opulent personal quarters on the third level of the presidential palace. Antonio stood at a wet bar tucked in a corner, pouring himself a glass of wine. For the first time since she'd met the man she could read weariness on his face.

"It was, yes." He gave her a small smile as he offered her a glass of wine. Because she could think of no polite way to refuse, Ava took it. "And I have already conveyed my gratitude to Senor McCabe."

"Have you compiled the list I asked for?" Cael accepted the wine Antonio held toward him.

"I have. It is there for you, on top of the desk." De la Reyes raised his own glass and drank deeply as he turned to face them. Lowering the glass, he added, "It includes every person in my government, along with their position. I do not like to suspect any of the names on it." He gave them a grim smile. "Only one of them learned the date of my arrival from me."

Cael crossed to the desk and picked up the paper, scanning it quickly before lifting his gaze to meet the other man's. "The men you had in the States with you...I collected their cell phones prior to them boarding. It would have been nearly impossible for them to communicate our plans prior to boarding the plane."

"So that means Rafael Gonzalez has betrayed me?" De la Reyes dropped heavily into an ornately carved chair that looked to be centuries old. "He has been with me since before I won the presidency. I would have trusted him with my life. I have done so, on countless occasions."

Lifting a shoulder, Cael said, "We have to take precautions. I'll want to interrogate him, of course. We've already got him placed under house arrest. He'll be detained until we can be certain."

Antonio's head jerked up, the hopeful expression on his face impossible to miss. "You think he could be innocent? How can that be?"

"The pilot had to file a flight plan. It could be someone in the airport. Hell, someone in the tower might have been paid to tip off your enemies whenever your flight plan was received."

"Then we still have no way to be certain who has been disloyal, or whom they alerted. I do not see that we are any further ahead then we were in Metro City."

Cael gave a feral smile. "Leave it to me. Our investigation is already under way. I'll need access to the bank accounts of every name on that paper you compiled for me, as soon as possible."

De la Reyes nodded. "You shall have it. I'll make the calls first thing in the morning."

"Then I'll have some answers for you in a matter of days."

Antonio raised his glass in a silent salute. "I will wish you luck, then, Mr. McCabe, since your success may mean my survival."

Sibbits drew duty outside de la Reyes's quarters that night, so the rest of the crew gathered in a conference room on the first floor of the palace. While Benton and Cael swept it for electronic bugs, Ava mentally calculated the last time she'd gotten a full night's sleep. Since the answer was too dismal to contemplate, she dismissed it. It didn't appear to be changing any time in the near future.

Finally, everyone settled into a chair around the table. She was reminded of the briefing that had taken place after the shooting…was it only two days ago? Two and a half?

Cael made introductions. "Mike Reynolds and Luis Perez have made some inroads since they got here two days ago. I'll let them bring you up to date."

Ava turned her attention to the two men he indicated, the ones who'd had the vehicles and weapons waiting for them at the airport.

Both were swarthy and dark complexioned, although Reynolds was taller and leaner than the stocky Perez. She knew instinctively that McCabe had chosen them for their ability to blend in with the San Baltes residents. If they were fluent in Spanish, they wouldn't raise suspicion mingling in the markets and cantinas ferreting out information.

Reynolds lost no time. "De la Reyes is highly unpopular with some factions." He stood, handing out thick files to each of them. "Especially by those who support the deposed dictator, Alberto Martinez. But we don't think Martinez is the threat. For one thing, he's been in exile in Brazil for three years. His supporters don't look good for the assassination attempt. We couldn't find any indication that they have the organization to move in once de la Reyes is out of the way."

He stopped, and Perez took over. "It's more likely that the attempt was financed by this man." He held up a picture. "Enrico Ramirez. He's the leader of a very powerful drug cartel that operated out of San Baltes for two decades, apparently with Martinez's knowledge and approval. Like most of the drug lords in the South American countries, he runs his drugs down the river systems in the jungle. De la Reyes has been cracking down on criminal elements in the country, and although he hasn't managed to catch Ramirez, his efforts have seriously curtailed the man's activities, and profits. He's had forensic accountants secretly going through the banks' records for months, hoping to find those Ramirez is funneling his money through."

Ava studied the man in the picture. Plump and avuncular, he looked more like a favorite uncle than a ruthless drug dealer.

"Ramirez went into hiding two years ago, but it's believed that he's financing the rebel contingent that has been causing such unrest in the country for the last eighteen months."

"He's using them to get rid of de la Reyes so he can go back to business as usual," Cael surmised aloud. "Does he want Martinez back in control?"

"We don't think so." Reynolds spoke for the two of them.

"Apparently Martinez got too greedy. It's more likely that Ramirez will just install a puppet president that will do his bidding while he gets his drug trade moving freely again."

"So if this attempt wasn't politically motivated," Ava said, "that means Cabrerra's betrayal was bought and paid for by Ramirez. That doesn't help us protect de la Reyes, but it might make it easier to determine if anyone else in his government is prepared to turn on him."

Cael nodded. "We follow the money. Did anything come up on the rest of de la Reyes's security contingent he brought with him to the States?"

Perez shook his head. "No. But that doesn't mean they're in the clear yet."

"Follow up on them, then. Also the pilot of the presidential jet." Cael gave them the man's name and Reynolds jotted it down. "Find out who was working the control tower today. Any one of them could have accessed the flight plan and alerted a third party."

Sibbits spoke up. "Did you get any information from the occupants in the Jeep today?"

McCabe shook his head grimly. "Ava took out the driver and Perez got the passenger in the front seat. The two in the back were trapped inside the vehicle. Identification of the bodies will be difficult."

Remembering the flames that had engulfed the Jeep, Ava felt a quick shudder. It would have been a grisly death. But she wasn't going to waste sympathy on the unknown assailants. Not when she knew their intent.

"De la Reyes will elicit the cooperation of the banks in the country. A little forensic accounting will tell us if anyone working in his government is sitting on some unexplained piles of cash. That will help us eliminate people quickly."

He slid a gaze around the table. "Sibbits, Carter and Benton will take turns protecting de la Reyes, in eight-hour shifts. You'll be backed up by his guard detail, but don't trust any of them until they've been cleared. When you're not on duty, you'll be at my side assisting in the investigation. De la Reyes will be changing his schedule of public appearances and conducting business out of the palace until further notice.

"Reynolds and Perez will follow up on the pilot and the airport tower personnel. Stay on top of the local police. We need IDs on the occupants in that Jeep."

"There's one more thing."

All eyes turned to Reynolds. "Perez and I have both heard talk about the rebels' jungle camp. I think if enough money changed hands, we might be able to get its location."

Cael thought for a moment. "How reliable is this information?"

The two operatives looked at each other. "We both heard the same rumors," Reynolds said. "The guy who claims he's been there…" The man lifted one shoulder. "I'd make sure he showed me sort of proof before I gave him any cash."

"How much?"

He named a price that seemed ridiculously low to Ava. But, she reminded herself, she was in a country with a per capita income of three thousand American dollars a year. Where allegiance could be bought if pockets were deep enough.

And where lives could be snuffed out for the price of a week's groceries.

"If you can verify the location and the function of the camp, go for it. These places tend to be portable, though. Find out if he knows other sites they've maintained." Seemingly finished, Cael looked at each of them in turn. "I don't have to remind you to be careful. Our mission is to keep de la Reyes alive long enough to find out who he can trust. After that he can better protect himself. But if we can point him in Ramirez's direction before we leave…" He gave a ruthless smile. "That will be gravy. Maybe he'll be able to clean up the country for good."

* * *

Cael had insisted on accompanying Ava to her room. And after her initial protest—one that had done very little good—she gave in. She still hadn't gotten her bearings. The place looked more like an estate than a palace, but the interior was certainly lavish enough to qualify as palatial.

"We're on the second floor, in the back of the building," he told her. She heard weariness in his voice, although there were no visible signs of it. His shoulders were still straight, his gaze alert as he assessed their surroundings. "Our quarters are directly above the kitchen area."

"Where are we located from the president's quarters?"

"He has the entire floor above us. Not ideal, but at least we don't have to fear infiltration through the windows. If someone wants to get to him at night, they'd have to get through several layers of security."

"Security that we can't trust," she reminded him. The precariousness of their situation was disquieting. If Cabrerra had been acting alone, de la Reyes was as safe in his palace as he could be anywhere. But if his superior was involved… "If Gonzalez turns out to be dirty, the entire presidential guard is suspect." And if the drug dealer Ramirez had gotten to two individuals so close to the San Baltes president, it was a wonder de la Reyes had survived this long.

She made a mental note to mention the drug dealer's name to Samuelson when she returned. If Ramirez was intent in keeping the region unstable, he might not be above financing terrorists acts toward that end. Not for the first time, she wondered how much the DHS agent already knew. He hadn't told her all the details in his possession. She could figure that much.

"We assume nothing," Cael agreed. He stopped before a door and reached to open it for her. "But I thought the attempt today by the men in the Jeep was encouraging."

Ignoring the opulent bedroom before her, she stared hard

at him. "Encouraging. The way an earthquake is encouraging? A train wreck?"

He didn't smile, but his face lightened a fraction. Leaning a shoulder against the doorjamb, he folded his arms. "Poor choice of words, maybe. But the fact that another attempt was made before de la Reyes made it to the palace makes me think this place isn't seen as vulnerable. Either Ramirez doesn't have anyone else with easy access to de la Reyes, or the president's security makes an attempt here seem high risk. Either would be good news for us. Even if Gonzalez is involved, perhaps Cabrerra was his only accomplice."

Although she didn't share his optimism, she didn't contradict him. "I'm assuming you've taken precautions with the guard personnel since we haven't cleared any of them yet."

He stifled a yawn. The gesture made him seem a bit more human. Up until now, she'd been half convinced the man was part machine. "Gonzalez is bound and confined to quarters. One of us will have to be posted outside until the evidence condemns or clears him. We've got nationals at every entrance of the palace, stationed three deep every twelve feet. If someone got past the outer perimeter of security, he'd have to get past a slug of armed guards. The chances are minimal that every one of the guards stationed at a given entrance is corrupt. I feel good about our security for the short term."

She looked at him with renewed respect. "You've had some experience with this sort of thing."

Cael crossed one booted foot over the other. "Five years."

"And before that." She didn't know what made her continue to press. "Navy SEALs or Marine Recon?" There was a flicker in his eyes, his only reaction. "Could be Rangers, I suppose, although you don't strike me as the army type."

"Thank God for that," he said feelingly. "I was navy for twelve years. A SEAL for ten."

She nodded, ridiculously pleased that she'd guessed correctly. His training showed. And he looked far more at home in

the black khakis and matching polo shirt he wore than he had
in the suit he'd worn in Metro City. He'd look even more natural
in combat fatigues, face smeared with camo paint. There were
some men who never lost the edge acquired in active duty. On
Cael McCabe, she had a feeling that edge went bone deep.

When his look turned appraising she had to suppress the
urge to fidget like a schoolgirl. "So my background's an open
book. You're more difficult to read. You didn't acquire your
marksmanship in the military."

Wariness reared, an innate defense whenever conversation turned personal. "No." Moments passed and it was
apparent that her answer hadn't appeased his curiosity appreciably. So she gave him a carefully edited form of the truth.
"I learned from my dad. He had me shooting by the time I
was six. Competing at ten." Her skill had been the only thing
that had ever won his approval. An approval that had been just
as quickly withdrawn a few years later. Forever.

"Let me guess." A corner of his mouth curled. "He
wanted a son."

There was a kick in her chest at the accuracy of his words.
Funny how even a sliver of the truth could still sting, after all
these years. She hadn't seen her father since before Alex was
born, at his insistence. It was shaming to recall how long it
had taken her to realize that was for the best.

"He wanted someone other than me." The note of finality
in her tone was meant to close the subject. She'd already
shared far more than she had with most people. The past
could only trip her up. Slow her down. She lived her life in
the present. Alex. Her job. Her friends. Most of the time—
almost always—it was enough.

His half smile faded. "Yeah." There was a note of something unidentifiable in his tone. "I have a father like that
myself." Now he was the one who seemed eager to change the
subject. Pushing away from the doorjamb, he half turned to
view her bedroom through the open doorway and stilled.

Wondering at his reaction, she peered around his shoulder, scanned the room again.

It was unmistakably a woman's space. The marble floors were smudged with light rose, the walls blushed with the same color. The drapes had been pulled away from the windows so the sheers moved lazily in the air stirred by a trio of overhead fans. The furniture was feminine and fussy, with lots of dark wood and carving, all balanced on delicate legs.

There were more sheers surrounding the enormous four-poster bed. And once her attention turned to it, she, too, stared, nonplussed.

It was more like a lake than a bed, far larger than any standard size. It was covered in shimmering silk the color of the pale turquoise waters that edged the San Baltes shores. There were throw pillows the size of couch cushions arranged invitingly along its headboard. Gilted mirrors lined the ceiling above the bed, faithfully reflecting the surface beneath. Her bag sat on the rug beside the bed, looking utilitarian and out of place.

It was a room meant for a woman, but one used for entertaining a man. Ava wondered for the first time at the age of the building, and the occupants the room had been meant to house. It looked like the place the earlier dictator would have stashed his mistress, while he slept overhead with his wife and children. She turned to say as much to Cael, but found his gaze on her, alight with intensity. And the words slid down her throat, unuttered.

She'd seen his expression shrewd. Grim. But she'd never seen arousal there, though it was instantly recognizable now. The skin pulled tightly across his cheekbones and his mouth looked fuller somehow. More sensual. And the glint in his pale green eyes was predatory and intimate at once.

A silent moment stretched, a thrumming beat filled with a single unspoken thought. Images swarmed her mind, sexual and stimulating. Of bodies pressed against each other on the silk, limbs entwined, the reflection of flesh on flesh replicating the sensual scene. A visual echo of every touch. Each stroke and kiss. Enveloping the couple on the bed in a cocoon of intimacy.

She saw his gaze go past her, linger on that bed for a long instant before returning to her. She read his intent in his eyes. The slow descent of his mouth toward hers gave her plenty of time to move away. To say something to break the moment.

She did neither. Instead she closed that last small space between their lips and tasted him.

His hand snaked out to cup her nape, to urge her closer while his mouth twisted over hers. There was nothing tentative about his kiss. It was bold and compelling, much like the man himself. His tongue pressed her lips apart and swept into her mouth as if staking a claim. She pressed a bit closer and answered his unspoken demand with one of her own.

Her job often called for subterfuge. Hiding her past certainly did. Which was why she tried to be frankly honest in the rest of her life. So she didn't try to hide the heat that balled in the pit of her belly, rocketing through her system with tiny spirals of fire. She savored his flavor, rife with sexual promise. Even as she knew she'd never allow that promise to come to fruition.

His taste was darkly sensual, and it was all too easy to imagine the two of them moving just a few more yards to the bed a slight distance away, silent and beckoning. To unleash the desire sprinting through her veins and ride the passion until they were both spent and weak.

Just the glimmer of the idea was terrifying. Especially with this man. Under these circumstances. She was shocked at the totally inappropriateness of her reaction. She hadn't allowed her hormones to rule her common sense in over fifteen years. And there was too much at stake to do so now.

But there was a tiny part of her that was elated at the evidence that her sexuality wasn't dead after all. Just buried and dormant. And apparently just waiting to spring forth at the least suitable moment.

Appalled by the totally inappropriate direction of her thoughts, Ava broke the connection by stepping away. Taking a few paces into the room, she strove for steadiness, attempting to rein in her pulse that still rollicked like a runaway mare. "It's a little fussier than I'm used to, but I'm not inclined to be picky about where I sleep at this point. Even the boardroom was beginning to look good to me earlier."

There was a moment of silence, as if Cael was having difficulty deciding whether to follow her into normalcy or pull her back in his arms and convincing her to let passion rule.

And when his voice sounded normal behind her, she was contrary enough, female enough, to mourn, just a little. "You're on at seven a.m. Radio Benton and see where to meet them. I don't know how early a riser de la Reyes will be now that he's returned home. I'll hold briefings twice a day about the investigation, so you'll be updated sometime tomorrow evening. Wear a vest over your clothes. The vest and radio will be delivered to your room before you leave your shift."

She turned to look at him, and her lack of enthusiasm must have shown in her expression, because he said firmly, "Yeah, in this heat it's going to be uncomfortable, but wearing a vest is nonnegotiable when you're on duty. I'm going to make damn sure you make it safely back to Metro City."

His concern for her managed to strengthen the blade of guilt that refused to dissipate. A guilt that had no validity. She had every intention of earning every dollar of the outrageous salary he was paying her. She could do the job for him and still provide a full report to Samuelson. The two tasks weren't mutually exclusive.

When an inner voice jeered at the thought, she squelched it firmly. "I'll wear the vest, of course. But I'll make it safely home because I'm a professional. I know how to do my job."

"If you didn't you wouldn't be here." Cael reached for the knob. And she knew enough about men to recognize the source of the regret in his expression. "Lock your door, Ava."

He closed it behind him with a quiet *snick*. But for a moment she stood, transfixed. Surely it must be lack of sleep that had her senses so highly attuned. She was used to intercepting and deflecting male interest. She wasn't used to responding to it. Not in a very long time.

Jerkily, she moved to the door, secured it. It was merely a security precaution. Logically she knew that. They were in an unfamiliar country, surrounded by strangers, any one of whom might be willing to betray their client for the right price. There was no reason, none at all, to believe that Cael had had another meaning for the warning.

Like locking the door against *him*.

She quickly unpacked, neatly placing her meager belongings in drawers in the fancy bureau. Her toiletries sat atop a marbled vanity in the adjoining bathroom, looking functional and forlorn amidst the scroll and gilt that adorned the mirrors above the counter. Ava had never stayed in a room more destined to make her aware of her own femininity. It was fortunate she wouldn't be spending much time in it.

She brushed her teeth, then swiftly changed into a camisole and loose-fitting pajama shorts. It wouldn't do to recall just how much a woman she'd felt only moments earlier. When she'd read the desire on Cael McCabe's face. Felt a matching emotion. She'd barely dated since her divorce; hadn't even missed it. But McCabe called to all sorts of long-buried feelings in her, and none of them had anything remotely in common with "dating."

Padding back into the bedroom, she crossed to the bed and pulled back the silk comforter. Spying her empty luggage next to the dresser, she paused, recalling the camera pen she'd packed in it. It was probably as safe there as it would be anywhere in the room. But it would be safer still, not to mention more useful, if she concealed it on her person.

She went and picked up the bag and brought it back across the room. Not for the first time she wished she'd shunned the damn thing, along with all the other espionage gadgets Samuelson had tried to press on her. As if by doing so she could negate the vague feeling of disloyalty she felt to McCabe for her dual purpose here.

Unzipping the side compartment on the bag, she thrust her hand inside, brought out the notepad. With a hiss of frustration she tried again, her fingers searching the space. Ava's breathing hitched. Frantically, she pulled the luggage onto her lap so she could spread the pocket wide and peer inside.

It was empty.

The high-tech camera pen was missing. Her shoulders slumped as her mind raced. There were only a few plausible scenarios.

But she was betting on the one where it ended up in McCabe's hands.

Chapter 4

Cael leaned on the balcony railing as he stared out into the star-studded night, speaking on his cell to Reynolds. "Do it, then. But I'd feel better if you didn't go alone."

"This guy's greedy but not totally stupid. He'll show me the way to the jungle camp, but he's afraid of Ramirez. Most people around here are. I don't want to scare him off by bringing someone else along."

"Did you suggest a flyover?"

"He's okay with that, but from what he describes of the camp's whereabouts, I think it's unlikely we'd be able to see anything from the air."

Unsurprised, Cael nodded. That kind of camouflage would be exactly what would have led the rebels to hide the camps in the jungle to begin with. They'd carve out a space with machetes, leaving enough of the natural vegetation to still blend in with their surroundings, set up shop for a few weeks, and then move on to another spot. Within a few weeks, the jungle's encroachment would fill in the deserted camps, making them virtually undetectable again.

"Go ahead and set it up. I'll run it by de la Reyes in the morning, but I'm confident he'll be intrigued enough at the prospect that he'll authorize the payment. Just watch your back." It would take a tough individual to believe he could double-cross Reynolds, although Cael was more worried about the guy leading his man into an ambush. But he had enough confidence in Reynolds to know the man could take care of himself. The opportunity for intelligence gathering more than offset the danger.

When the conversation ended, Cael slipped the cell in his pants pocket and stripped his shirt over his head, laying it across the railing. He didn't move to reenter the bedroom. He wouldn't be able to sleep. Not when he was still feeling this restless.

He leaned his forearms on the railing, broodingly surveying the manicured grounds below. There were lots of details still to be ironed out. Variables to be examined and weighed as he sifted through options. But it wasn't the particulars of the job his mind was occupied with. It was the woman down the hall.

He hauled in a breath, caught the scent from the gardens below. And that, too, reminded him of Ava.

Touching her had been a mistake. A pleasurable one, to be sure, but a mistake all the same. He didn't mix business with pleasure. Not ever. Especially with a woman in his employ. One he wasn't even sure he could trust.

He'd never had a problem compartmentalizing before, adhering to that line that separated the professional from the personal. Granted, females were in a minority in his profession. Amelia Driscoll was the only woman he had on staff, but he trusted her instincts as much as he did any of his male operatives. Of course, Amelia had the voice and build of a drill sergeant, so his strictly business relationship with her wasn't exactly proof of his lack of bias.

He'd have to be dead not to notice Ava's looks, but it was

her skill that had led to his initial job offer. That had him setting aside paranoia and allowing her on the team, hedging his bets. If she had nothing to do with Samuelson, he was ahead one solid team member. If she was linked to the man, she was a valuable pawn to be used in the bitter game between Cael and the DHS agent.

He wouldn't hesitate to use any man who planned to double-cross him in just that way. So it was particularly discomfiting to identify the emotion swirling through him now.

Guilt. He moved his shoulders uncomfortably. He had no reason to feel guilty. If Ava was blameless, she'd never have to know the suspicion that he'd harbored even as he'd reached for her. Tasted her.

And if she wasn't blameless…he felt something inside him harden. Then God have mercy on her, because he'd show her none.

The slight breeze cooled his skin, which seemed heated and much too tight. It was time to quit kidding himself. His reaction to Ava Carter had nothing to do with the job. She was a woman he could admire physically and professionally, and that alone made her dangerous. Add in the fact that he actually *liked* her, liked her attitude, and her wariness and the intriguing hint of vulnerability she'd displayed earlier, and the caution flags were impossible to ignore.

It wasn't smart to take unnecessary risks in his line of work, where lives often hung in the balance. And it'd be hazardous indeed to get involved with Ava. How hazardous he didn't yet know.

Broodingly, he rested more of his weight against the railing, his gaze blind to the lights winking in the far-off distance. To the swoop of the bats as they pursued their evening meal.

The only image he saw was that of long dark hair and pale slender limbs against a turquoise pool of silk. Heat flooded his belly at the mental picture.

He wasn't a man ruled by his hormones. The folly of that path had been painfully learned his seventeenth year when Liza Watkin's father's descent into the basement had outpaced Cael's dexterity with his zipper. Patience and timing always paid off in the long run.

But he could know that, accept it and still stand here wishing he hadn't urged Ava Carter to lock her door.

A tiny sound pricked the deep cocoon of Ava's unconscious. She fought the binds of sleep sluggishly. It had been hours before she dropped off, and now slumber tugged at her with tiny anchors, slowing her return to awareness.

Then she felt heaviness settle over her, felt an all too human heat transfer to her skin, and instinct slugged through unconsciousness.

One hand shot out and up, made contact with flesh and cartilage. She heard a muffled grunt of pain even as she came fully awake, her other hand going unerringly for an eye gouge.

She was pinned more securely, a heavy weight distributed over her as the man above her battled to grip her hands. And when her eyes flew open, adjusted to the dim early morning light, her body went completely still.

Cael McCabe stared down at her, his expression menacing. His nose was already red and swelling.

"What are you doing in here?" she hissed, disbelief mingling with embarrassment. She heaved under him attempting, with a notable lack of success, to dislodge him.

"Getting the hell beat out of me, apparently."

She stared at him, struggling to shake off the sleep-induced cobwebs. He was already dressed, if you could call it that. A black ribbed undershirt clung to his well-defined torso and was tucked into army-green khakis. The shirt left his shoulders and arms bare, and she was supremely aware of the bulk of them, as he lay stretched out atop her. He was unshaven, his dark blond hair still mussed as if he'd been roused by a matter of some urgency.

"Is it de la Reyes?" she demanded. "Has there been a breach in the security?"

"You could say that."

She stilled, searching his face carefully for his meaning. His eye color was even more startling up close, their pale green a near match for her August birthstone, the name of which she could never recall. She had the belated observation that he'd managed to get a haircut before he'd left the States, although he didn't wear it military short, as some of his men did.

And that his position was far too intimate. Hers far too vulnerable. He had her arms stretched out above her head, caught in one hand so she couldn't follow through with instinct and blind him before she'd figured out who it was. Now that she had she was all too conscious that the sheet was bunched at her waist. And although the camisole covered her decently, she was still far too bare to appear before a man who was her employer.

Especially this man.

Ava tugged ineffectually at her wrists. "You can let me go," she said stiffly. Tiny needles of alarm were firing through her veins, but she fought against revealing the emotion. "Sorry about the punch earlier, but it would have been safer all around to just knock." Even as she had the thought, her gaze flew over his shoulder to the door behind him. The dead bolt was still engaged. So he hadn't come in through the door. And he'd yet to release her hands. "Mind telling me how you got in here?"

"Turns out we have adjoining balconies."

Her eyes narrowed. "No. We don't. The nearest balcony is a good five yards away." She knew because she'd checked before making the decision to leave one balcony door open to catch the fresh night breeze.

Although his lips curved, they didn't soften appreciably. "True. But it also turns out that I'm blessed with catlike dexterity and reflexes." His voice went lower as he bent his head closer to hers, close enough that she could feel the slight abrasion of whiskers against her jaw. "Some men might construe an open door as an invitation, Ava." His barely discernible drawl had grown thicker. "Were you issuing an invitation?"

A quick shiver shimmied down her spine and warmth flushed her system. She was certain he could feel it. "No. A man in your occupation knows there's always more than one way to read a situation."

His head lifted and the glint in his eye had tension shooting through her muscles. "I do." He gave a slow nod. "I surely do." Reaching down with one hand, he withdrew something from his pants pocket and held it up so she could see it. "So I'm real interested to hear your explanation for this."

A boulder lodged in her throat. He was holding the camera pen. The one Samuelson had pressed on her. The one she'd discovered missing from her luggage last night.

It took all her effort to manufacture a neutral tone. "You're here because you found a pen?"

He cocked his head. "It's all in the details, isn't it? I'm here because *this* pen was found in *your* luggage. Hell, I'm here because this is more than a pen, isn't it?" With a flip of his thumb he clicked the stem and held the pen perpendicular to her face. One more click had a tiny light winking at her as the camera engaged.

He shoved his face closer to hers, his expression forbidding. "I'm here because I'm real interested in how you happen to possess a costly little gadget that's a couple generations removed from what's available on the market right now. So start talking, Ava. Because my read of the situation is pretty ugly."

When she remained silent, his mouth twisted. "Although I haven't heard of it, I suppose it's possible this little item is available on the black market. Trouble with that theory is I can't see you buying anything that way. Too much a law-and-order kind of gal, aren't you, Ava?"

She swallowed hard, wondering what he'd think if he realized her embrace of the justice system came relatively late in her life.

He gave her a shake, the look in his eyes lethal. "Let's stop dicking around. Samuelson approached you?"

She tried again to wrench her hands free, temper spiking when his one-handed grip held. The accuracy of his guess was surprising, but there was no use lying to him, at this point. "Paulus and Samuelson."

A terrible stillness came over him at her affirmation. Seeing it, Ava was struck anew by the awful certainty that there was much much more to this assignment than DHS had bothered to reveal to her.

Because fury pumped off him in waves, the strength of which surrounded her. Squeezed her in an unforgiving vise. It was several moments before he spoke again. And she knew the effort it took for him to keep the judgment from his voice. "So what'd they offer you?"

Disconcerted, she shook her head. "Nothing."

"Threaten you with, then. That's Samuelson's game, anyway. What'd he have on you?"

Ava hesitated. Honesty only went so far. She was unwilling to dredge up her past in an effort to pacify McCabe. She doubted it would make a difference to him anyway.

"He appealed to my sense of patriotism," she said carefully. "He wanted information on the stability of this government and I agreed that I could supply it without compromising my assignment here. I still believe that."

His mouth twisted. "You still believe that, huh? You know what I believe?" He reached over to hook a finger in the thin strap of her camisole, and urge it slowly, inexorably over her shoulder. One tiny expanse of skin at a time. "I believe that you can tell a person's honor in what they do when they don't think anyone will find out." His meaning slipped neatly between her ribs, like a well-placed blade. With a crooked knuckle, he caressed the skin he bared, and she flinched, feeling cheap and humiliated.

"I believe," he continued, his voice going lower, rougher, "that a person who will betray me in one area will betray me in all. That little lesson came later in life but it left its mark."

His free hand slid up the column of her throat, cupped her chin, his grip just shy of cruel. "And I believe you made the biggest mistake in your life to throw in with Samuelson, Ava Carter. One that's going to cost you dearly."

A trickle of fear crept up her spine, though she refused to lower her gaze. Too late to worry that she didn't know this man; couldn't guess what experiences had forged him, or how far he'd go to achieve his ends.

But from the ruthless expression on his face, she knew she was going to find out.

"Aren't you being a little melodramatic?" She jerked her face away from his grasp, suddenly angry at her position. If the agent had allowed her to do this her way, de la Reyes would remain safe, Samuelson would have been provided with the information he wanted and McCabe would be none the wiser. She'd only be wrestling with her conscience, not with one hundred ninety pounds of mean, furious ex-SEAL.

"Your commitment to your client's privacy is commendable. And I don't blame you for being angry with me." Anger was too tame a word for the dangerous look in those pale green eyes. A look that was a decided contrast to the expression in them the last time they'd been together in this room. "But my providing Samuelson information about the political climate here is hardly going to endanger de la Reyes, or detract from the protection we're providing him."

The smile that curled one corner of his mouth then was derisive. "Is that what he told you? That he was concerned about the political climate in San Baltes? Either you're unbelievably gullible or you think I am. The U.S. has ignored San Baltes for decades. And now all of a sudden they're so concerned they require a covert spy operation consisting of one lone police officer from no-name, California?"

His words had the unease that had lingered in her belly since Samuelson's visit congealing into a hard knot of dread. Stubbornly, she refused to concede his point. "We're talking about DHS here. It's not beyond plausibility that they'd want to grab every opportunity to extract information, especially in a way that costs them nothing and doesn't lead back to them."

"It's not DHS, it's Samuelson," he corrected. "You remember him. Tall, humorless prick with a bad comb-over? Where he's concerned nothing is plausible, least of all his word. Face it, you were duped, Ava. He didn't urge you down here to get information on San Baltes, de la Reyes or the political climate. He sent you to get information on *me*."

Shocked, she regarded him with wide eyes, her mind racing furiously. But the more frantically it reached for answers, the less any of them made sense. "You're paranoid," she said finally.

"You know what they say." His voice had gone lower. Raspier. "Just because you're paranoid doesn't mean people aren't out to get you."

What the hell had she gotten herself entangled in? she wondered wildly. Some vendetta between a DHS agent and McCabe? Or was this man a raving lunatic?

She eyed him carefully. His face was all harsh angles in the early morning shadows, but his expression was determined. Whatever he was saying, he believed implicitly, even if he'd left out as much from his story as Samuelson had.

Silence stretched between them. He studied her from beneath lowered lids, and she became supremely conscious of the weight of him, the heat as she lay stretched out beneath him. Her lungs felt strangled. Last night she'd grappled with fragmented dreams, too similar to this moment for comfort.

But in the dreams their struggle on this bed ended much differently. And the memory of those unconscious snippets had her face burning.

"Get off me." She arched beneath him, the vulnerability of her position stinging. "I'm not having this conversation with a two-ton ex-military ape crushing me."

His fingers clasped her face and he sent a thumb skating across her lips. "Ava. Do you really think you're in the position to be giving orders here?"

"Perhaps not." She aimed a lethal stare at him. "But if I were you I'd start worrying about what I'll do when I'm no longer in this position."

"Threats." A thread of admiration entered his tone. "I was right about your guts at least, if nothing else."

She didn't respond. Because it was appearing all too clear that she'd been right about very little ever since meeting the man.

His heart thudded against hers, as if in an answering tattoo. He shifted infinitesimally and she went still. His shoulders blocked out the early morning light spilling into the room through the double doors he'd left open. His chest was broad and his biceps bulged with muscles. But it was the change in his expression that had the breath catching in her throat. That instant when temper and resolve were replaced by something much more primitive. Something that had flickers of heat igniting in her veins.

Their gazes melded and for one second all thought vanished. And that was perhaps the most dangerous moment of all.

In the next instant he rolled off her, with a suddenness that was disconcerting. "Get dressed," he rasped, rapidly crossing to the door. "We'll finish this in my office in ten minutes."

It was closer to a half hour before Ava stepped inside the boardroom turned command center. Cael felt her presence before he heard her enter. And that sensitivity, that awareness of her left him edgy.

"This is the president's final schedule for the day?" It took more effort than it should have to return his focus to Benton. It was his operative who had brought him the device found in Ava's bag. The device that had removed all doubt about the woman's reason for coming here.

Recalling it now had his stomach burning. Because even with the bitter sense of betrayal blooming fresh and raw inside him, he'd still reacted to her. His body had responded to the woman rather than the employee set to betray him. It wouldn't be the first time he'd given the benefit of the doubt to the wrong person.

But it would be the last time he made that mistake with Ava Carter.

He flicked a glance at Benton. "Thanks for bringing me this. As long as you've got Sibbits covering for you now, it's your turn to sleep."

The man looked at Ava, back again. "I can pull a double shift, Cael. Maybe between Sibbits and me—"

"That won't be necessary." He aimed a chilly smile at the woman in the doorway. "Ava is capable of pulling her weight here. As a matter of fact, she was quite convincing earlier today when she assured me of just that."

There was pleasure in watching her creamy skin flush, twin patches of color coming, then going in her cheeks. But her voice as she strolled into the room was maddenly nonchalant. "What happened to your face? Looks like someone slipped under your famed guard and clipped you a good one."

He touched his nose, which was more sore than he'd admit. He owed her for that. Owed her for far more, apparently. But her bravado sparked a sense of exhilaration. Damned if he didn't find it stimulating to spar with her. Unfortunately he found her stimulating in more ways than one.

He'd chosen the location of their prior skirmish poorly. He

could acknowledge that now, with the memory of her long, lean curves branded on his skin. Her scent emblazoned on his senses. But his body's reaction to her would have no bearing on the end result of their relationship. He'd make certain of that.

"You'll find that once my guard is breached I'm less trusting the next time." He was only half aware of Benton slipping out the door unnoticed, closing the door behind him.

She halted across the table from him, her hands resting lightly on the chair back. "It's encouraging to hear you tell Benton I'll be going on duty. We both know you can ill-afford to lose an operative right now. You need my skills and you need the extra manpower I provide. I'm not a threat to de le Reyes or to you. And whatever is going on between Agent Samuelson and you, I want no part of it."

Just the mention of the man's name shot Cael with a familiar bitter resolve. "Unfortunately, you've become central to what's between Samuelson and me." He gave a careless shrug. "Hard to work up much sympathy for you, in light of the circumstances. You came down here to gather information for the bastard, and you'll do just that. But I'll be the one to determine what information you deliver to him."

She gave a slight shake to her head. "What's your story? I can believe he left out a lot—a helluva lot—from the tale he wove for me, but he's a fed." Information was shared on a need-to-know basis, and according to most feds, there was damn little local law enforcement needed to know. "But if you believe he wanted me here because of you there must be a lot of history between the two of you. I deserve to know what that entails."

He tossed de la Reyes's schedule carelessly on the table. "Sure you want to get into what you *deserve*, Ava?" A moment passed and when she didn't rise to the bait, he lifted a shoulder. "We have a history, yeah. He hates my guts. I return the emotion, in spades. He'd like to see me dead. I'll settle for seeing him ruined." Flattening his palms on the table, he leaned forward, a measure of the satisfaction curling through him sounding in his voice.

"And you, Ava, are going to be the tool I use to make that happen."

Chapter 5

Their gazes clashed. Not a flicker of emotion crossed Ava's face, and Cael felt an unwilling tug of admiration. Sheer guts and skill wrapped up in a stunning package. It was too bad she'd had the damned poor judgment to throw in with Samuelson.

"I'm no one's *tool*," she said with heavy emphasis. "I don't know what's going on between the two of you, but I'm taking myself out of the equation."

He wondered if she realized the defiance in her tone was a dare. One that he was tempted, very tempted, to take her up on. "Oh, you're very much in the equation," he murmured. "Too much so for my peace of mind. You placed yourself right in the center of things." Fury looked good on her, he observed. Brought color to her cheeks and dangerous lights to those dark eyes.

"I'm not a pawn to be moved at will by you or your personal nemesis. So whatever game you're engaged in with Samuelson, you'll play it alone." Shoving away from the table, she walked to the door, spine straight.

And he let her go. There was nothing more to be discussed, at any rate. Ava Carter wasn't a woman who'd bend easily to a man's will. If she was telling the truth about her involvement with Samuelson, a big *if,* he reminded himself grimly, maybe she'd agreed out of a sense of duty to her country.

He considered that, his hands gripping and releasing the chair back as he regarded the door she'd closed behind her. He doubted the agent had offered her money. He was a shady son of a bitch, but he wouldn't dare leave a paper trail like that for his superiors to follow. No, he'd tried something else. Manipulative prick that he was, he'd try appealing to her patriotism or blackmail. He'd used similar methods with Cael over the years.

Moodily, he mulled over the possibilities. But the truth was staring him right in the face.

He'd never seen a woman more difficult to manipulate than Ava Carter. That left blackmail, or something like it. A woman like her would have few weaknesses, other than her son, of course.

Cael pulled his cell phone out of his pocket and pressed the number for the information broker he used on a regular basis. Something had to exist in Ava's life that he could use as leverage.

And whatever it was, he was going to discover it.

Then he was going to use it to acquire her cooperation to bring down Samuelson, once and for all.

Two things became very clear throughout the day Ava spent at de la Reyes's side. One was that he was an extremely busy man. He went from meeting to meeting, briefing to briefing, phone call to phone call with barely a moment to himself.

The second was that her presence, and that of the rest of McCabe's team, was fiercely resented by the palace guard. She imagined imprisoning their leader, Gonzalez, had been the first indignity. The next had been disarming some of them.

Ten national guardsmen were part of the president's protection contingent. And for the first time in her life, Ava wished she weren't bilingual. Because her language skills meant she could easily interpret the whispered grumbles of the men surrounding her. The asides that grew increasingly personal. Especially when she, on more than one occasion, inserted herself before a guardsman to maintain her position by the president's side at all times. Or when they were closed out of a private meeting with the president and one of his cabinet members, while she remained in the room.

She wondered why the nationals really expected that she'd be unable to understand their remarks. The term *puta* was, after all, pretty universally understood. So perhaps they didn't much care whether she spoke their language or not.

Because it would do no good to let on otherwise, she stood stoically through all the undertone conversations. Ignored the snippets of disparaging comments that drifted her way. And seethed silently when a couple of the guards discussed her physical attributes at length. And what they were better suited for.

The only positive note was that the frustration she felt was an admirable distraction from the earlier conversations with McCabe.

It would be more comfortable to regard the man as an oversuspicious zealot. But she shared his dim opinion of Samuelson. Had distrusted the man from the first. And could admit now how effortlessly the man had manipulated her. He'd discovered just enough about her to know what button to push; then he'd played her like a master.

And the bitterness accompanying that realization burned as much as McCabe's opinion of her did.

The problems with secrets was that they left one vulnerable. She shifted position and pretended not to hear the comments about the shape of her ass. She may well have decided to join McCabe's operatives anyway, given her sudden need of cash. But it had been her hunger to keep her past from crashing into her present that had cemented her decision, and it was easy to see what a mistake in judgment that had been.

One thing she was determined of—she wasn't going to let McCabe use her to deceive DHS Agent Samuelson. Whatever was going on between the two men would unfold without her. She'd failed to convince him of that earlier today, so she'd gone on duty with their argument unresolved. But she wasn't going to be the match that lit the fuse between them.

She shoved the troublesome thoughts away to concentrate on the three cabinet members currently meeting with de la Reyes. All had been searched, of course. But it was also her job to weigh and evaluate them for personal threat. Each had expressed horror at the president's near death in the States. Apparently the attempt on the man's life yesterday had been kept quiet. Probably McCabe's doing. None of the president's visitors today had mentioned it.

The conversation had turned to efforts to curb criminal elements in the country, and a familiar name was mentioned.

"We've intercepted and jailed a dozen more couriers we suspect work for Ramirez," Emanuel Ortega, head of Justicia, was reporting in Spanish. "We continue to strangle his ability to conduct his business."

"And what of his assets?" Antonio de la Reyes looked at a second man, his director of International Finance. "I want him stopped. To do so we must cripple him where it hurts him the most."

Ramon Jorge inclined his head. He was a wizened little man, the wrinkles in his face giving him a raisinlike appearance. "We've located the blind trusts he's using and put a stop to the offshore banking he was engaged in. His assets have been frozen."

De la Reyes slapped his palm on the polished teak table. "Excellent." Satisfaction laced his tone. "We can expect that to draw him out, if nothing else. Without ready cash, he'll become increasingly desperate."

The men exchanged glances, and Ava knew intuitively what they were thinking. A desperate man was increasingly dangerous. If Ramirez had anything to do with the attempts on the president's life, his survival had just gotten more precarious.

And their job here had become even more difficult.

It was later in the afternoon, during de la Reyes's meeting with the archbishop of his church, that the guardsmen on duty with her changed tactics, grew bolder.

The first brush of a body against hers had Ava shifting slightly. The second time it happened was harder to ignore. Especially when she turned to catch the smirk on the guardsman's face closest to her. She waited, teeth gritted, for his palm to move over her backside once more, then, eyes still straight ahead, snaked a hand behind to catch the marauding palm. With a quick practiced move she wrenched it up and back, surprising a muffled yelp from the guardsman.

The meeting room went silent. The archbishop sent an inquiring look their way and de la Reyes aimed a glare that encompassed the entire team. The man in back of Ava shuffled his feet and muttered an apology for the interruption. A moment later the president resumed the meeting. And the men surrounding her gave her plenty of room without crowding her for the duration.

The meetings lasted until well after five o'clock that evening, when the last visitor left and de la Reyes headed to his quarters to change prior to the evening meal. Sibbits was waiting outside the conference room with a new team of guardsmen. With a cursory nod toward Ava, he fell into step behind de la Reyes and strode out the door.

The National Guardsmen on her detail headed toward the door until her voice stopped them. *"Para a la derecha allí. Quiero una palabra con usted."*

Under any other circumstances, the men's reaction to her command, uttered in flawless Spanish, would have been comical. Ava's sense of humor, however, had vanished somewhere between *puta* and that hand on her ass.

She waited until she had their attention and continued on in their native tongue. "If today was an example of the way you do your job, I can guarantee that you will not remain employed much longer. I could round up a gang of ten-year-olds more professional than the bunch of you." Some of the men shot looks at each other, but all remained silent. Her voice grew more contemptuous. "Your antics were juvenile and distracting at a time where your caution should be at its highest point. You'd better report for shift tomorrow and impress me with your expertise or you'll all be looking for new jobs. Understand?"

Surprise had turned to sullenness on the men's faces after her spate of scathing Spanish. But there were enough muttered *"entendido"s* to satisfy her. She waited for the first of them to reach the door before adding, "Oh, and the next one who touches me? *I' rotura del ll su brazo maldito.*"

Her threat, delivered in as sunny a tone as she could manage, had a few of the guards exchanging glances, but all were silent as they trooped out.

Ava released a long hissed breath and worked her shoulders to release the tension of the day. Then felt that tension ratchet up again when Cael came striding into the room.

The long hours since their argument this morning vanished. Trepidation mingled with resolve. If he were here to start up where they left off this morning, he'd find her unswerved. Regardless of what he had in mind, there was no way he could force her into this unhealthy contention between him and the DHS agent.

But telling herself that didn't vanquish the trepidation curling in her stomach.

However, his words had nothing to do with their earlier

conversation. "I've got Perez and Reynolds in the field. I'll need you to take a shift at Gonzalez's quarters until Perez gets back in."

Shrugging off weariness, Ava agreed immediately. "All right. Where's he being held?"

"I'll show you." Cael waited for her to cross the room and closed the door behind her, before leading her through the halls toward an exit.

"I'll have a meal sent out, of course. Perez won't be back until late, so I'll spell you in a few hours."

"The head of Justicia told de la Reyes they've frozen Ramirez's assets."

Cael nodded. His stride was long, but she easily kept up with him as they made their way through the wending hallways. "I met with him after the meeting. His forensic analysts also have determined that a large unexplained deposit was made into both Cabrerra's and Gonzalez's account late last week."

Ava looked at him, adrenaline spiking. "While de la Reyes was in the States."

"That's right." Cael's frustration was apparent. "He's given us nothing so far, but I'm looking forward to hitting him with this new evidence and seeing if he gets more talkative. I don't want to trust any of his own men with the translation, though, so it'll have to wait until Perez or Reynolds gets back."

"I can translate." The offer was out of her mouth before she even took the time to consider it. But she found herself as eager as Cael to take the investigation to the next level and determine if Cabrerra's superior was as dirty as he'd been.

"You're bilingual?"

"As inconvenient as that turned out to be today," she said dryly, "I am. Fluent enough to translate if you want to interrogate the chief of the National Guard right now."

He'd stopped in his tracks and was studying her speculatively. "You seem to have all sorts of hidden talents, Ava." But his tone was anything but admiring.

Annoyed, she shrugged. "Or you can wait for Perez. It doesn't matter to me."

"I'd rather do it now." He still hadn't moved, but she knew his mind was racing. "I'm not fluent enough to be sure I'm making myself understood, especially to elicit the kind of details we're looking for." He was silent for a moment, regarding her with his piercing gaze. He'd pulled a shirt on over the ribbed undershirt he'd appeared in at dawn, and it matched the green fatigues he wore. The hue made his eye color more striking, and noticing that annoyed her.

She was here to do a job. Responding to McCabe on any level was a diversion she could ill-afford. The lecture she'd leveled at the guardsmen earlier could just as easily be applied to her. Distractions put lives at risk.

And that was only one of the many reasons it was a mistake to respond to this man. On any level.

As if coming to a sudden decision, he said, "Let's do it." He was moving again and she remained silent as they wound their way through the different levels of security he'd established inside and outside the palace walls.

Acres of well-tended grounds surrounded the palatial structure. Cael strode to a jeep parked nearby and once she got in, drove well beyond the palace, through yet another gate in a decorative stone wall.

Ava saw what amounted to a small village. It was here that the help would live.

Cael's next words underscored her impression. "Cooks, housekeepers and gardeners stay here." He gestured to rows of attached apartments, each slightly larger than an American double garage. "Their schedule is a fourteen-six rotation. Two straight weeks of work, then six days free. Most of them travel some distance to get home and see their families. But the leave and pay are regarded as quite generous in this country."

The jeep bumped along the brick drive, painted a dull red. The apartments and curb were whitewashed, and everything looked neat and well tended, if lacking the jaw dropping landscaping of the main grounds. But it was another half mile before Cael pointed to row upon row of single-story structures, much larger than the two-tiered apartments.

"These house the palace guard. Gonzalez is in the back one that sits in the center."

Ava recognized Benton standing outside the structure with an AR-15 rifle strapped across his chest. A thought occurred. "I would imagine that putting their senior officer under house arrest didn't go over too well with the guardsmen." She could attest to her team's antipathy, at least. "What's to stop them from overpowering the guard and releasing their superior?"

"If they're loyal to de la Reyes that allegiance will outweigh their fidelity to Gonzalez."

He seemed to be skirting the obvious. "And if they're not?"

"Then we hope the explosives we wired to Gonzalez's quarters, in full sight of the guardsmen, will serve as adequate detcrrent from any zealots intent on a rescue." Cael's grin was sharkish.

Remembering the weaponry and explosive devices in the back of the SUV they'd driven from the airport, Ava subsided. She had no doubt about his expertise with wiring and detonators. If he'd fitted Gonzalez's quarters with a combination of those, a rescue attempt would end up killing both the head of the palace guard, and the would-be rescuers.

It went without saying that whichever of Cael's operatives were standing guard would be dead first.

He pulled to a stop before the quarters and jumped out. Ava followed more slowly, as he engaged Benton in conversation. Walking up to the men, she saw the other operative flick her a glance and say, "Are you sure that's wise?"

Heat shot up her spine and she kept her expression carefully blank. He'd been the one to search her luggage, of course. The one to turn the camera over to his boss. And while McCabe had his own reasons for keeping her on here, it was clear that Benton didn't share them.

"I'm sure. Take the jeep and go get something to eat before grabbing some sleep. You'll be on de la Reyes again in a few hours."

The man wanted to argue. Ava could see that in his expression, which had suspicion flickering in it. But he was nothing if not well trained. Without another word he left them, climbed into the jeep and pulled away.

McCabe spent several moments keying in a code to the security keypad on the outside of the door. Then he took a bunch of keys from his pocket and inserted the proper one to unlock three different locks.

"Weapon ready."

Ava had her gun in her hand before the words even left his mouth. With a grim nod, he drew the sleek Luger from his shoulder holster and took up position at the other end of the doorway, swinging the door in.

When she followed him inside Ava saw a lone man, clad in undershirt, boxers and socks, seated in a leather recliner. If it weren't for the zip cord binding his ankles and wrists and the tether leading from them to a hook drilled into the plastered wall, he'd look like a middle-aged man relaxing on a weekend morning.

Of course, there was nothing relaxed about Rafael Gonzalez's expression. *"Hijo de Satan,"* the man spat. His look was venomous.

"Senor Gonzalez." Cael's voice was pleasant enough as he dragged a straight-backed chair out of the dining room to set it in front of the man. After gesturing Ava to it, he pulled another up for himself. "I understand you have been fed and given periodic restroom breaks, as per my instructions. Are there any medications you take regularly that we should be aware of?"

Ava repeated Cael's words in Spanish. The man's expression flickered a bit, but she thought it was in response to her command of his language rather than McCabe's inquiry about his well-being. He didn't appear to be a fan.

"Vaya al infierno."

Since the man's suggestion that Cael go to hell didn't appear to need a translation, Ava didn't offer one.

Gonzalez was barrel chested and thickly built, a powerful-looking man who should have appeared diminished by his position, but did not. He looked, she thought, pissed off and defiant. But not visibly frightened. He rattled off a spate of Spanish in a rush of angry words.

"He demands to know what you've done with President de la Reyes. He doesn't believe that the president ordered his imprisonment," Ava relayed.

"Maybe this will convince him." With his free hand, Cael extracted a folded sheet of paper with a seal on the back. He tossed it on the man's lap.

Gonzalez didn't so much as spare it a look. He never took his gaze off McCabe. "Tell him de la Reyes wrote the order for his imprisonment himself," Cael instructed. "The special seal is the one Gonzalez himself suggested used for times such as these to prove the missive isn't written under duress."

After Ava translated, the man's eyes lowered to the paper on his lap. It was tri-folded, like a letter. With his bound hands he clumsily turned it over, then stilled when he saw the seal securing it. And when he opened it, scanned the short message, he paled. Then he looked at Ava and spoke heatedly.

"He believes someone, probably you, has convinced the president of his guilt."

When she stopped then, Cael's brows rose. "I didn't catch all of it, but I know he said more."

She cocked a brow at him. "He also questioned your parentage, your manhood and sexual preference."

"Perhaps you'd like to address those last two issues with him," he murmured meaningfully.

Since the words were meant to embarrass her, she refused

to give him the satisfaction. "I can't say I have proof either way, so I'll pass."

"We could always rectify that," he suggested, ignoring Gonzalez for the moment. There was a light in his eyes, a dangerous heat. "What the hell, give you a bit more firsthand information to share with Samuelson."

"I can't imagine who'd be less impressed with that sort of information, Samuelson or me."

A corner of his mouth kicked up at that. But he said only, "Tell him we have proof he is working for Ramirez. That he's a traitor to his president. To his country."

When Ava obeyed, Gonzalez's reaction was fierce and immediate. When the man had halted his speech, trembling with fury, she translated, "You impugn his honor with your accusations. He has risked his life to keep the president safe. He wants to know what proof you could possibly have." She paused, smirking. "He also suggested that you spend your nights engaged in illicit activity with farm animals."

He slanted her a glance, the humor fading from his expression. "Let's keep the translation focused on the facts involving Gonzalez's involvement."

Her tone was innocent. "I thought you wanted to hear everything."

"I did. But you're enjoying this a bit too much." Withdrawing another paper from his shirt pocket, he handed it to Gonzalez. "Let him know that we have proof a large sum of money was deposited into his account recently. Ask him to deny that's his signature on the deposit slip."

Gonzalez made no move to unfold the paper until Ava had finished speaking. Then he opened it with the air of a man perusing his own death warrant. He shook his head violently, speaking to Ava in rapid Spanish.

"He says the signature looks like his but he did not sign such a slip. He denies all knowledge of it and claims someone is trying to make him look guilty." She paused while the man spoke again. "On the date listed on the slip, he was engaged in all-day training sessions with his men. He has hundreds of witnesses."

"And he must realize we know he didn't have to go to the bank himself to deposit that money. He could have filled out the slip and sent it along with someone else. Tell him to quit jerking me around." Cael's tone had grown hard. "If he has nothing else to share, he's wasting my time. I want information about the job Ramirez paid him for. The one he had Cabrerra try and carry out. What is Ramirez planning now that de la Reyes is back in the country?"

The man's protests to Ava's translation increased in volume. His black heavy mustache fairly quivered with outrage.

"He says one of Ramirez's men approached him once, not long after the election. He offered Gonzalez money—far more money than that deposit—to provide them with information regarding de la Reyes's security and schedule. Gonzalez says he refused. He suggests that perhaps they next approached Cabrerra with a similar offer."

"And that's where his story breaks down for me. Head of the president's security force and he didn't report the offer to de la Reyes? Did he tell anyone?"

Ava relayed Cael's questions, could tell Gonzalez's answer in the shift of his gaze from hers. His response was a long time coming.

"He says he was afraid telling de la Reyes he'd been approached would shake the president's faith in him. Perhaps regard him as a weak link in the security. He took efforts to warn his guard unit continually to report to him if they were contacted."

"Bullshit." Cael lurched from his chair, frustration rife in his movements. "So is that what Cabrerra did? Run to him and report that he'd accepted five thousand dollars to assassinate the San Baltes president when he was off-continent?

Because that's the amount we found in his account. Half what we found in Gonzalez's."

Her voice quiet, Ava leveled the questions in Spanish to the guard chief. The man only shook his head. He appeared smaller somehow since they'd started. As if the evidence against him and mention of his trusted second in command had carved away his defiance.

"No tenia ninguna idea que Cabrerra era corrupto. Habria estacado mi vida en su lealtad. Estaque el presidente vida de s en el. Y lo casi mataron consecuentemente."

"I had no idea that Cabrerra was corrupt," Ava translated softly. "I would have staked my life on his loyalty. I did stake the president's life on it. And he was almost killed as a result."

Cael stared hard at the man for a long moment. She wondered if he was as close to believing him as she was. The evidence against him looked damning. But it would be easy enough to forge a signature, wouldn't it? Especially with Cabrerra working so closely with the man. Simpler still to deposit money in an account to frame Gonzalez.

"We'll look at the security tapes for the day of the deposit," Cael said finally. "He remains in custody until we have positive proof of his innocence." He got up, leaving Ava to translate, and walked to the door.

She joined him outside and he reengaged the security system. "Anyone could have made that deposit to point suspicion toward Gonzalez." She holstered her weapon, although she kept the grip unsnapped.

"They could." He turned to regard her, his expression thoughtful. "But we're left with the question of why. Say Cabrerra had gotten away with the assassination. U.S. police would think the killer was one of the wackos who'd called in a death threat, or someone like them. There was no reason to point suspicion at Gonzalez. Not when Cabrerra also had a smaller deposit to his account. It makes them both look guilty."

"And muddies the waters for any investigation of their bank funds."

"I'd say they're sufficiently muddied at this point. He could also be a convincing liar, faced with evidence of his guilt, trying like hell to make it seem like Cabrerra was in on it by himself." He surprised her then by asking, "What's your read on him?"

"He was convincing," she admitted. Her gaze scanned the area around them, taking note of the off-duty guardsmen coming and going from their barracks. "But I'm stuck on the motivation issue, too. Ramirez might hate Gonzalez enough for turning him down that he wants to ruin him. But to what end? That money was put in their accounts while de la Reyes was still in America. The assassination hadn't yet gone wrong. Who did Ramirez think was going to look in the bank accounts and why bother when the plan was to make it look like an American citizen had killed the president?"

"It might have been blackmail, I suppose." Cael leaned against the doorjamb with a nonchalance that Ava didn't share. Call her paranoid, but she didn't intend to touch the house he'd wired with explosives unless absolutely necessary. "Maybe Ramirez was hedging his bets. If the assassination is successful, he's only out ten thousand dollars. If not, they could have been planning some way to cast suspicion on Gonzalez and away from a U.S. citizen. We may have even thwarted those plans by getting the forensic accounting done so quickly. De la Reyes would be persuaded to choose another chief of security."

"Maybe," she said. If there was another explanation for the deposit, it involved a plan they could only speculate on. It was far more likely that Gonzalez was as guilty as he looked, despite his convincing act earlier. "We can't afford to trust him at this point."

"Agreed. Trust is in short supply on this trip, at any rate." It wasn't so much the tone of his voice as the meaningful look in his eye.

"Something tells me you don't exactly overflow with the quality on the best of days." She was through feeling guilty for her duplicity. His motives in relation to Samuelson weren't exactly pure. "You know you and Samuelson have a lot in common." She didn't noticed the stillness that came over him at the words. Not then. "Both of you are bullies. Both will use your position to strong-arm people into giving you what you want. And both of you deserve to be taken down a notch."

"An interesting observation." The bleakness in his eyes stemmed the temper that had prompted her outburst. "But any similarities between us are purely coincidental."

Cael turned away as a thought hit him with a force that nearly sent him reeling. He and the DHS agent had been dancing around this antipathy for years. It had gotten steadily stronger on Cael's side with the man's consistent efforts to undermine him.

What if Samuelson knew him better than he thought? Ava might be more than the latest attempt to damage him and his credibility. Could Samuelson have sensed she was a woman he'd react to?

What if she'd been selected as the very personal weapon of Cael's destruction?

Chapter 6

Cael pored over the painstaking directions Reynolds had written down to the rebel camp, comparing them to the topographic map of the country.

"And you saw it for yourself? How many stationed there?"

"Hard to say," Reynolds responded laconically. "I counted over a hundred. But there's no way to be sure how many were inside the buildings." He leaned forward to point to a map he'd drawn of the place. "It's well guarded and well equipped. Some real money has been funneled into their hands. I saw enough rifles to outfit half the country."

"So if Ramirez is the source of the money, the rebels report to him now. He uses them to destabilize the country and undermine de la Reyes's government."

Coming to a realization, he straightened and looked at the other man. "We're not going to find Ramirez there, though. He's too smart to be caught with the rebels." He wasn't sure how he could use this information yet, but he'd file it away.

It was the sort of intel DHS or CIA might be interested in. So he'd make damn sure Ava never got close to it.

Just the thought of the woman left a burning sensation in his chest. He'd left her standing at Gonzalez's quarters earlier this evening without a word, too troubled by the thought that had occurred to him. Every moment he spent alone with her, even professionally, was dangerous on some level. It weakened his resolve. Made him soften toward her, and he couldn't afford even that small weakness.

His special ops background had left him with a black-and-white view of the world. And the number-one lesson he'd learned from his time in the military was that you didn't go into danger with people at your side you couldn't trust.

You damn sure didn't go to bed with them.

He hadn't taken Ava to bed, but he'd wanted to. And if he were honest, the thought lingered in the back of his brain at every second of every day. Memories of the moments spent pressed up against her in that damn take-me bed learning for himself the softness of her skin and the scent of her hair.

A soldier didn't lower his defenses when under attack, and his entire relationship with Samuelson had been just that. Ava was one more tool in the man's arsenal. Cael had to remember that, because she represented his best opportunity to destroy the man.

And, he thought grimly, he'd shed this conscience that seemed to be working overtime whenever he thought of using her. She'd displayed no such sensitivities about undermining him.

But as quickly as the thought occurred, he was forced to temper it. She'd come here all too willing to spy for Samuelson. But he was betting she'd been duped about the man's purposes. Hell, he knew from personal experience just how convincing the agent could be. His jaw tightened as he recalled just how far the man would go to get what he wanted.

He also knew how easily the facade would drop when he

was crossed. And Cael couldn't waste time worrying about the fallout for Ava once Samuelson realized she'd misled him, at Cael's direction. She deserved whatever twists came her way for going along with the man in the first place.

He told himself that. Tried to believe it.

"We can't do anything with the information right now," Reynolds was saying regretfully. It took a moment for Cael to follow the line of conversation back to the rebel camp. "We don't have the manpower. Could be close to two hundred in the camp…we'd need at least six guys."

Cael gave a quick grin of appreciation at the man's confidence. But it was close to the truth. He'd teamed with Reynolds in the military. The man had been at his side in more than one deadly situation. "That's not our mission here. At least not right now. When we get the whole team together… then we'll see where we're at on the investigation for de la Reyes. Who knows? Maybe he'll want to turn this information over to his military at some point."

Reynolds shrugged, but Cael could read the regret in his expression. "Camp probably won't be there much longer. You know as well as I do how mobile they are."

"We'll have to take that chance. Keeping de la Reyes safe is our priority. If we can find whoever is working for Ramirez, get to the man through them, the rebels will be no threat. Their enemy is whoever they are being paid to battle. And we may have gotten a valuable lead."

Carefully, he folded up the maps and the directions Reynolds had written to the camp. "Perez checked in earlier tonight. The Jeep driven by the men who fired on us on the way to the palace was reported stolen a week ago. Dental records have been matched on both of the victims. One is a brother of one of the air traffic controllers working at the airport the day our flight came in."

"We figured something like that," Reynolds commented.

"Perez is with the police right now for the interrogation."

And he doubted it was going easily on the controller. South American countries' police weren't bound by the same protocol American police were. The interview could get brutal, given what the man was suspected of.

Shrewdly, he studied the man who was as close to him as a brother. "Get some sleep. We can use some help covering the shifts on de la Reyes and Gonzalez."

"I wouldn't mind taking a shot at Gonzalez."

"Let's wait until we have the security cameras at the bank. Maybe we'll have something to hit him with later." Cael's cell phone rang, and he reached into his pocket to draw it out, read the number on the screen.

It was the information broker he'd called this morning. The one he'd charged with digging up Ava Carter's secrets.

"I have to get this. Have Sibbits show you where your room is." As Reynolds retreated, Cael answered the phone, anticipation swirling in his gut. Not even to himself would he admit that the thought of learning more about the woman was appealing in itself. She'd been maddenly closemouthed about anything remotely personal.

But fifteen minutes later Cael finished the conversation, a much different emotion careening inside him. It was, he thought bleakly, like getting an inadvertent peek at someone's dirty laundry. Except in this case not so inadvertent.

But he understood her now far better than he had ever thought he would. Understood why she hid her past. The impact the secrets could have on her career.

The only questions that remained were whether he could follow through and blackmail her with the information, in an attempt to gain her cooperation with Samuelson.

And whether he could live with himself if he did.

Because her shift came early the next morning, Ava turned in right after she'd eaten and showered. She came awake before dawn, fully alert.

Eyes getting used to the darkness, she saw what had awakened her. Each of them had been given a wrist communicator. It would vibrate and light up when there had been a breach in the security at the palace.

It was glowing and vibrating now.

Ava rolled out of bed and shrugged into her vest, fastening it with one hand as she grabbed her weapon with the other. Racing to the door of her room, she unlocked it and was speeding down the hall in less than ten seconds.

The perimeter of presidential guard was three deep inside the palace, she recalled, forgoing the elevator for the stairs. But it was impossible to tell from the wrist unit whether the inner or outer perimeter had been breached. And for some reason, the radio element didn't seem to be working.

On the main level she saw Reynolds, looking grim and dangerous with his Luger ready. Shouts sounded in the distance, and she could hear the rush of the presidential guardsmen.

"Inner or outer perimeter?" she called to Reynolds.

"Outer. Coming up through the front gate." He headed toward the front door, which already was crowded with guards.

The drive from the gate to the palace was at least a mile. When it got closer to the structure it swung in a wide semicircle. She let Reynolds cover the front and veered off to sprint toward the side entrance. If she could get to it in time, she could stop the driver before he ever made it to the palace entrance.

Elbowing her way through the guards, she had a moment to recognize they were holding their position, three deep inside each door, twelve feet apart, just as Cael had told them.

But then she was racing by them to the door, yelling to the closest guard closest in Spanish, "What's the visual?"

"Black limo, unidentified occupants."

"Open the door."

The door was unlocked and swung open as Ava hit it, taking the stairs at a leap and racing across the lawn. The lawn was soft as velvet beneath her bare feet. She could see the headlights first, spearing through the darkness. Recognized the shape of the vehicle slowly rolling up the drive before her.

She came to a sudden halt, raised her weapon. Took one deep breath and then fired two shots, one each into the front and back tire.

The limo came to a shuddering halt.

Ava was aware of the guards running up toward her, but it was to Reynolds she called, "Order a check of the undercarriage." The man snapped out an order in Spanish and several guards ran to fetch the equipment to carry out the search.

In a louder voice she shouted to the driver, *"Camine del coche con sus brazos levantados."*

But the driver and his passenger—she could see at least one in the backseat through the tinted windows—remained inside the car.

"Usted tiene treinta segundos para vaciar el coche antes de ques comencemos a tirar."

Ten seconds ticked by. Adrenaline spiked higher with each passing instant. Twenty seconds. Ava bit out an order to the nearby guards in Spanish. "Weapons loose." The surrounding guardsmen sighted their rifles.

Then slowly, the driver door inched open to frame a Hispanic man who looked to be in his mid-thirties, wearing a chauffeur's uniform in the same midnight black as the car.

"Don lanzamiento de t! Don lanzamiento de t!"

"Get out of the car with your hands in the air," Ava instructed in Spanish. When he did so, she gestured for two of the guards to search him, as a team of others, under Reynold's supervision, began inspecting the undercarriage of the vehicle for explosives.

She took position at the open door to point her rifle toward the lone occupant in the backseat. But before she could utter another order, the back passenger seat swung open and a petite whirlwind of fury exited, along with a spate of rapid-fire Spanish.

"How dare you! Who are you and what have you done with Tonio? I demand to be taken to him at once." The enraged woman slapped at a rifle barrel held by a nearby guard and spun to advance on Ava.

"If you have harmed my Tonio, I promise you will pay. I will kill you myself!"

Coolly, Ava stood her ground, not lowering her weapon even as the guard's voices sounded behind her.

"Marissa Mejido y Fuente. *Es el presidente novia de s.*"

The president's girlfriend? Ava exchanged a look with Reynolds, who also had turned at the words. His expression looked as blank as she felt. McCabe hadn't mentioned a girlfriend to contend with. For that matter neither had de la Reyes.

But the guards all seemed to recognize her.

Ava lowered her weapon. "Search the interior of the vehicle," she directed two of the men in Spanish. She switched her attention to the woman, continuing in the same tongue. "We are here to protect the president. He hasn't told us to expect you. He will be alerted of your presence here, but before you go inside I will have to search you."

Fuente's reaction was immediate and vitriolic. "You will not touch me! I demand to be taken at once to Tonio."

Ava engaged the safety and handed her rifle to a nearby guardsmen before approaching the woman. Fuente flexed her fingers and leaped at her. Ava jerked her head back, but felt the woman's nails rake down the side of her throat. Irritated, she grabbed Fuente's arm and yanked her off balance, using the woman's own weight against her as she took her down, keeping her there with one knee to her back.

With Fuente screeching, Ava swiftly and professionally frisked her for weapons. The short black cocktail dress had a plunging neckline and not much fabric to hide a weapon. Ava got up, took the woman by the arm and pulled her upright, giving her a little shake. "Behave yourself and we'll take you inside," she said grimly in Spanish. "Touch me again and I'll dump you in the fountain. Understand?"

"You will be sorry for this!" Fuente shook her hair back out of her extraordinarily beautiful face and balled her fists. "Tonio will see that you pay for your mistreatment of me!"

Ava felt the trickle of blood on her neck. Retrieving her weapon without relinquishing her grip on the woman's arm, she nudged her forward toward the side entrance of the palace. "*Your* mistreatment? And yet I'm the one bleeding. Go figure."

"This is an outrage, Tonio!" Marissa Mejido y Fuente paced the president's opulent personal living room and pointed her finger at a silent Ava, standing just inside the door. "That…that she-devil attacked me! She threatened me and pushed me down. Held a gun on me. I demand that she be imprisoned!"

"English, please, Marissa." De la Reyes crossed to hand her a glass of red wine, patting her hand. "Not all of our guests speak Spanish."

"Guests!"

Even Cael could feel the venom in the look she tossed at Ava, but she'd switched to English as requested, and sipped at the wine de la Reyes had supplied. "What is she doing here, dressed like a rifle-carrying *puta* and terrorizing your visitors?" Fuente shot him a distrustful look, as well. "What are any of them doing here? Why do you have so much security? You assured me the danger was over. Why are these foreigners here?"

But rather than answer her question, de la Reyes asked one of his own. "I didn't expect you back in the country for another two weeks. What of the modeling competition in Buenos Aires?"

The woman studied the man shrewdly before unexpectedly striding up to Cael and demanding, "Tell me what is going on. Tonio will try to hide things, or tell some but not all. You, I think, can give me the answers I seek."

Cael flicked a glance over at his operatives. Perez hadn't reported back yet, but besides Ava, Sibbits, Reynolds and Benton were all there. Next his gaze moved to de la Reyes, who gave him a little shrug.

"The president's would-be assassin in the States was killed before he could injure Antonio. The person who saved him, you might be interested to know, was Ava Carter." He nodded in her direction, noted that while the woman glanced at Ava, her focus was on the president.

"A lieutenant in the presidential guard was killed in the act," Cael continued. "Pedro Cabrerra. My company was hired by the president for added security in the States. When it became apparent that his presidential guard had been compromised, our contract was extended to accompany him back here until his safety has been secured. A second attempt was made on the president's life when he returned to San Baltes."

The woman gave a great shuddering breath before launching herself into de la Reyes's arms. The man managed, barely, to catch her wineglass before it drenched them both.

Cael looked away as the man held Marissa close, murmuring in her ear. He caught sight of Ava then and observed welts on her throat, red and raw with dried blood congealed on them. Relatively minor wounds. So it was ridiculous to feel this edge of worry for her.

Fuente's earlier description of her had been scathing, but Ava's appearance would have caught the attention of anyone new on the scene. At first glance it appeared as though she wasn't wearing anything beneath the armored vest, but he recognized the stretchy camisole and loose-fitting shorts below. She'd been wearing something similar the morning he'd accosted her in her bed.

He pushed that thought away before it could heat and distract him. But the scene Fuente had described was all too easy to visualize. He could picture a scantily clad armed Ava taking down the ultrafeminine model. And he didn't possess near enough determination to wipe *that* image from his mind.

Gently, de la Reyes set Marissa away from him, presenting her with a handkerchief taken from the pocket of his robe. He'd retired to his quarters with Benton on guard outside his door when the alarm had sounded. Cael had gone immediately to the president's side, handling communications from within the quarters.

"You still haven't answered my questions, Marissa," de la Reyes was saying. "Why are you back so soon? And why did you not call first before arriving so late this evening?"

The woman wiped daintily at her tear-streaked face. "My agent is quite displeased with me, but I insisted he cancel my appearance in Rio de Janiero. I've been so worried, I could not bear to be away from you any longer. I felt an urgency here." She touched a fist to her stomach as she gazed up at him. "I could think of nothing but seeing you as soon as possible."

"What I want to know is how she bypassed the security system on the gate," Cael said bluntly, his gaze drilling into the president. "We were led to believe you had retained the only remote access that would open the entrance."

A slight frown marring his brow, de la Reyes took a step away from Fuente. "I did. And Marissa has never been given a remote."

Her eyes flashing, she retorted, "No, Tonio has never offered one to me." And it was clear to everyone in the room that she smarted from the slight. "It was Captain Gonzalez who gave me the remote before I left the country last time. At least he recognized that a woman in love should not be kept waiting outside the gates like a servant, begging for entrance."

The room had gone deadly quiet. Cael felt his operatives' eyes on him, but his mind was racing furiously. Why would Gonzalez want an extra remote access to go to Fuente? How would that help him? If he wanted to double-cross the president, he was inside the grounds himself.

But security could be locked down by the president, he reminded himself grimly. And if de la Reyes had used the master security passkey, no one would get in or out of the palace grounds without a remote, the only one of which de la Reyes retained.

Until a spare had shown up in his girlfriend's possession.

Marissa was looking from one person to another, uneasiness in her expression. "Tonio, are you angry with me? I know I should have spoken to you about it first. I thought only to surprise you when I came back, not to cause this *alboroto*."

"I understand." De la Reyes was charming, if firm. "But your surprise entrance tonight caused a great deal of trouble for many people. I am happy to see you, of course. But I must ask that you give me the remote so we can be certain of our security."

"It is with my regular driver who brought me here," she said in a small voice. "You may retrieve it from him."

With a look, Cael directed Sibbits to do so. The operative crossed to the door and slipped through it.

"I will send my men to get your bags. Please wait for me upstairs."

Fuente nodded submissively at de la Reyes's suggestion, but Cael had the distinct impression that the fiery beauty would not stay subdued for long. She surprised him, however, when she stopped on the way out the door in front of Ava.

"I wish to apologize."

From Ava's expression, she appeared as shocked as the rest of the occupants in the room.

"I thought only of myself, my own outrage. But you saved my Tonio's life, and for that I owe you a debt of gratitude I can never repay."

Cael watched Ava accept the woman's hand. Before she continued to the door, Marissa gave her an arch look. "But as his *novia* I must suggest that perhaps you put on more clothes for this job, *si?* Perhaps a uniform—" she made a graceful gesture indicating throat to ankle "—that covers up far more. A jealous woman can be very dangerous."

Ava touched her throat. "I'll remember that."

After one long smoldering look toward de la Reyes, Marissa glided out the door. And when it closed behind her, de la Reyes let out a sigh. Reaching for the glass of wine she'd left behind, he took a sip, holding up a hand to Cael. "I know what you are thinking."

"You left some pretty major parts out of your story when we were planning your security," he said shortly. Diplomacy be damned. The man's lack of candor could have turned into a real security nightmare. "You certainly never mentioned Ms. Fuente."

"Because she was not part of the immediate picture here." The man's tone held an imperious edge. "I could not forsee she would be back so soon or I would have warned her to stay away, as I did with my family. And I assure you, I had no idea she had a remote to the gate."

Another thing Gonzalez had to answer for. Cael sent Reynolds a meaningful look and the man inclined his head. The man's quarters would be searched again. They'd thought the remotes were all accounted for. Which meant someone had had another copy made, the one that had ended up in Marissa Fuente's hands.

"What else do you need from me tonight?" the president asked him. And Cael knew he wasn't imagining the exhaustion in the man's expression. He kept a grueling schedule and tonight's events would have disturbed the first full night's rest he'd attempted since his return.

"I'll finish briefing the guards. What do you want done with Ms. Fuente's limo driver?"

De la Reyes was already moving toward the door. "His background was thoroughly checked when we arranged for him to drive Marissa. He may stay until she leaves."

Cael felt a clutch of impatience as the man left the room.

If nothing else, the woman's presence here was bound to be a nuisance. So far the president had willingly curtailed his outside activities to make it easier to check his security. Based on the taste they'd gotten of Fuente tonight, something told Cael she wasn't going to be content to hang around the palace day in and day out without entertainment.

He'd need to make de la Reyes see that the woman's presence here was an unnecessary risk, a distraction they couldn't afford. But until then, he had to lock down the security and debrief the unit that had, for the most part, done a decent job of protection this evening.

"Benton, you're back on shift outside de la Reyes's quarters. Everyone else, with me for the debriefing session with the National Guardsmen."

It promised to be a very long night.

Chapter 7

Ava's long strides ate up the hallway. It was all Cael could do to keep up with her. "I don't know why you're embarrassed. Those security tapes revealed that you and Reynolds showed exemplary decision making out there tonight."

"Embarrassed?" She whirled with a suddenness that took him by surprise. When she approached on him, her finger stabbed him in the chest. "You're damn straight I have nothing to be embarrassed about. What I am is *pissed*. I did my job like the professional I am. I didn't appreciate having my appearance on that tape treated like fodder for a bachelor party."

"What?" Stunned at her temper, he could only stare at her. But a sneaky sliver of guilt stabbed at him. Because yeah, the image of Ava's long legs racing across the expanse of lawn, the armored vest hiding most of her clothing beneath was…unforgettable. And the sight of her, bare limbs gleaming in the moonlight, dark hair mussed, wielding the assault rifle with a deadly certainty, was going to be the subject of some sweat-drenched dreams for some time to come.

But damned if he was going to admit that to her. "Everybody in that room is a professional. I can assure you, our only thought was to review our security procedure from the time the gate was breached."

She stared at him, fire lighting her eyes and shooting color to her cheeks. "If you didn't notice the reaction of the guardsmen in there for the briefing, you're dangerously unobservant. I spent all day today dealing with their response to me because I'm a woman. And finally, finally at the end of the day I earned a bit of respect. Now…" She made a rude sound. "I'm going to have to start all over again tomorrow and I'm giving you fair warning, the next one of them that touches me will be nursing broken bones."

"One of them touched you? Why didn't you report that? I'll make sure—"

"I don't need your help," she said, punctuating each word with a finger jab to his chest. To avoid injury, he reached up to capture her hand in one of his. "I need respect. I want that tape confiscated before every guardsman in the unit has a copy."

"I'll take care of it." He didn't particularly like the idea of that himself, although his mind shied away from examining the reason too closely.

She stared at him suspiciously, but something in his expression must have convinced her, because the tension in her muscles eased infinitismally. "Men are stupid."

He caught up with her as she turned and started walking rapidly down the hallway again toward her room. "Well…yeah."

An unwilling smile tugged at the corner of her mouth. "Present company not excluded."

Given that his reaction to the tape had been exactly as she'd described, that was hard to argue with, as well. "Conceded."

"Don't be so agreeable, McCabe. It's creepy."

He grinned, punchy with a combination of sleep deprivation and adrenaline crash. "What can I say? We're a primitive lot, conditioned to respond to certain, ah…shall I say stimuli?"

"I'll agree with the primitive part." Reaching her door, she seemed to remember something. "I should give you this." She shifted her weapon to her other arm, fighting to loosen her wrist communicator. "It vibrated and the alarm worked, but I wasn't able to use the radio."

Frowning, he took the device from her. "You couldn't hear the orders?"

"No. I wasn't sure why the limo had been allowed through without halting it, but I met up with Reynolds and he passed along the orders."

"The guards on outer perimeter made a tactical error assuming the limo held Fuente." The security breach still burned. "The vehicle should have been stopped far earlier. Those responsible will be released from duty. All in all, though, most of them did their job. The silver lining is, at least now we know where our weakness is and can regroup." He reached by her to push open the door she'd unlocked. "Mind if I check the base?"

Without waiting for permission, he strode across the room, his gaze unerringly going to the bedside table, which held the communicator radio base that regulated the channels on the unit. Propping her rifle against the wall, he knelt beside the base and began fiddling with the knobs. Moments later, he hissed out a breath in disgust.

"Damn thing isn't on the wrong channel, it isn't working at all."

"I believe I mentioned that."

Her tone was dry. And very close. Glancing up, he saw she'd come to stand next to him after shedding the armored tac vest. "Yeah, but they should have been checked and in working order prior to our dispersing them." He unplugged the base unit and placed the wrist communicator on top of it before rising. "I'll take this back to my room and switch it with another. Maybe it has a short in it."

His position when he stood placed him very close to her. Too close. She was caught between him and that wide expanse of bed, the mussed turquoise covers looking like ripples in tropical lagoon. And his pulse, as if on cue, began to drum. His thoughts to fragment.

After the last time he'd been in this room, it was all too easy to imagine lying on that bed with her beside him. Beneath him. He could still recall the feel of her, supple muscle and soft curves. Could still taste her, that unique flavor that fired his blood and wiped his mind clean of instinct and suspicion, leaving only passion in its place.

As if recognizing his thoughts, she took a step back. Was brought up short by the bed pressing behind her knees. "No." Her voice was firm. But in her expression he saw a reflection of the desire he was trying desperately to stem in himself. "We aren't going to make the same mistake twice."

"That's good to hear." His mind splintered into two dueling parts, logic and temptation, the latter fueled by a horned, sharp-tailed demon spurring him on to insanity. His hand reached out, as if devoid of conscious decision, and cupped her jaw.

Her hand came up as if to push it away. Lingered to stroke. "You don't trust me."

The skin beneath her ear was baby soft. When he brushed his fingertips over it she shuddered. "I can't."

"So why should I trust you?"

He replaced his hand with his lips, tracing that delicate jawline with a string of whisper soft kisses. "You shouldn't."

Her response was muffled by his mouth over hers. And the jolt at her taste was enough to ignite his system.

He ate at her hungrily, anxious to get his fill before one of them, both of them came to their senses. This wasn't smart. She was right about that. And he, who was used to quantifying every risk, assessing every danger, was deviating from hard-learned experience by ignoring that fact.

His arm snaked around her waist and he drew her closer. He'd taken plenty of chances in his lifetime, after he was assured he controlled the situation. But he wasn't so sure he could control his reaction to her.

Ava wound her arms around his neck and kissed him back with a reckless fervor that had his heart beating a heavy tattoo in his chest. And when her tongue swept into his mouth, bold and demanding, hunger lunged inside him.

Cael hooked a finger in one strap and dragged it over her shoulder until her breast was freed from the fabric, then cupped it in his hand. The nipple was taut, a testament to her desire, and he teased it with his fingers even as his free hand swept inside the elastic of her shorts to cup her butt.

The tantalizing twin pleasure of bare flesh had flames licking through his veins. She was sleek softness with the whisper of muscle beneath. And his mouth went to her breast in a primal quest for flesh.

The taste of her rollicked through his system. With a few swift moves he could have her naked, and under him, this time free to taste and stroke and touch freely. He was a man who assessed danger for a living, and he faced it now, of a sort that was more lethal than usual. This woman made him forget his convictions. To set aside the cool calculation that had been instrumental to his survival. She represented a danger of a different sort.

And was all the more tempting for it.

He became aware of her fingers between their bodies, trying to undo the straps securing the vest he still wore. Rather than moving to help her, he squeezed the fullness of her bottom, his fingers grazing the cleft. He sucked from her nipple urgently, dimly aware that he was approaching the point of no return. Ready, damn ready, to dive over the edge and think about the consequences later.

She was only a few inches shorter than him, and he could still intimately recall from the time he'd spent on top of her how well they'd fit, every inch, every angle and hollow. Skin heating against skin.

The alarm shrilling in his mind barely registered. But her stillness did. With savage reluctance he raised his head and only then did he become aware that the sound was all too real. But rather than a mental alarm, it was a cell phone.

Hers.

Blinking to regain focus, he saw the cell on her bedside table. The international one he'd provided her with, along with every other member of the team, when she'd gotten on the plane. The screen was lit up now, as it gave one last burst of sound before falling silent.

It took another moment for understanding to filter through the fog of passion. He recognized the number showing on the screen before it went dark. Had seen it on his own cell screen a few times.

He released her with a suddenness that sent a chorus of protests from parts of his body that shouldn't get a vote. And comprehension rushed in, nearly rocking him off his feet with the enormousness of his miscalculation.

Ava still looked dazed. And when she reached for him again, God help him, it was all he could do to take a step back and scramble for the logic that had deserted him like a paratrooper from a flaming chopper.

"Better call him back," he said tersely.

His words must have registered, even if his tone didn't. She picked up the phone, fumbling with it as if she wasn't in total control of her muscles yet, and the evidence of her response nearly had him throwing back his head and howling his frustration.

Tension, of a far different sort than that of a few moments ago, shot his muscles with steel.

"I don't recognize—"

"I do." His jaw was clenched so tightly it ached. "It's Samuelson's."

She dropped the phone then with a clatter, but he knew he wasn't imagining the guilt flickering over her expression. "So does he have you reporting in on a regular schedule? If you missed a time, I wouldn't keep him waiting. He isn't known for his patience."

Ava straightened her clothing, then took several strides away from the bed. And farther from him. "I left him a message with my number when I got here. I haven't spoken to him since."

Cael didn't bother to sift through her words for truth and fabrication. His stupidity drumrolled in his head, hammered home just how colossal an error he'd almost made.

The irony was she'd warned him of just that before he'd reached for her.

The fury pumped through him in waves. He knew from experience what happened when you wanted something, someone too much. That depth of feeling inevitably blinded him to the truth, made him reach decisions based on emotion rather than logic.

It had him risking more than he should. And later, when reality slashed through longing, it made the crash brutally resounding.

"Maybe it's best you wait to call him later," he agreed. "I haven't ironed out all the details, but you can start feeding them to Samuelson each time you report in."

He noticed the rise of her chest. The effort it took for her to compose her features and face him with a dispassion to match his own. "I already told you I won't be part of that."

"I think you will." He cocked a derisive brow, saw her flush with the first tinge of annoyance. "My information broker is at least as thorough as the government databases."

She went still then, and the color that had so quickly flared to her cheeks leeched just as swiftly.

"It's always a crapshoot to figure the lengths people will go to hide something from their past, but I'm figuring you'd go pretty far to make sure no one knows Calvin Julson is your father."

If he hadn't reined his conscience in with a vicious grip, her expression might have caused him to soften. To take a step toward her and stroke away the flash of pain on her face.

But the last few minutes had taught him the danger of softening toward her. Of ignoring reality in favor of dreams.

She walked a few feet to grasp one of the four posters to the bed frame, as if in need of its support. Her tension was evident in her deathly pale face, in the white-knuckle grip she had on the frame.

"I figure Samuelson discovered that, too, and used it to force you to accept this assignment." He was willing to grant her that much. Ava would have needed powerful incentive to change her mind to join his team temporarily. The money might have been part. But not all.

She remained motionless. "He intimated. I thought he must know. But he didn't come out and say it."

Of course the man wouldn't. Cael reeled in his temper, forced himself to think clearly. The agent would reveal only enough to get what he wanted. He was a master at playing people, using their vulnerabilities against them in a manner guaranteed to have them falling in line with whatever he asked of them.

Cael had been suckered himself, once upon a time.

Steeling himself against the sight of her, shocked and dismayed, he said, "Well, I don't blame you for not wanting anyone to know of your relationship to Julson." And watched her, hawklike, for her reaction.

She swallowed. Seemed to search for words. "I haven't spoken to my father in over fifteen years. He isn't part of my life. And I can hardly be held accountable for genetics, can I? It's not like I had a choice in my parentage."

Her last statement struck a chord, but he refused to let it alter him from his course. "Good line. I wonder how your

SWAT commander would feel about it. Or your captain. I think we both know what the press would do if they were fed the information. Local legendary SWAT sniper and detective affiliated with the most infamous white supremacist in the country? Every arrest you've ever made will be suspect. Every target you've ever taken out will have family pouring out of the woodwork. The city will be buried in discrimination lawsuits for decades."

Her deer-in-the-headlights expression gave him pause. He half expected her to toss his veiled threats back in his face. To invite him to do his worst. And he wondered, still, when push came to shove, if he'd be able to follow through.

But she did neither. She just looked at him with those dark and haunted eyes. And her words were like a knife twisting deep inside him. "Explain again how I'm supposed to tell you and Samuelson apart. Your tactics are the same. You go after a person's emotional jugular and hold a knife to it. And you...you're threatening to shred everything I hold dear. To destroy my life to get what you want. I used to think you two were carbon copies. But now I think you're worse than he is."

With every word she uttered his throat tightened until it threatened to strangle him. If she'd wielded a machete on him, she couldn't have wounded him more deeply.

He had to force himself to move. To round the corner of the bed where she still clung for support, and stride to the doorway. "The choice is yours. You cooperate with me and your secret is safe. But if you refuse..." He halted at the door, his hand on the doorknob, and looked over his shoulder back at her. "...then I'll destroy you along with Samuelson."

The rap at his door was unwelcome. Cael was on his balcony nursing a neat whiskey and battered scruples. He considered, for the space of a second, not answering it. Professionalism won out over surliness, and he shoved away from the railing, carrying his drink with him to the bedroom door.

He exchanged the glass for his weapon before he opened it. Found Reynolds standing on the other side.

The man didn't bat an eye at the gun. "Saw your light. Figured if you were still up you must have…" Obviously spying the drink setting on the dresser, he amended, "…and you do have liquor. What is it? Whiskey? Got another glass?"

Swinging the door open, Cael allowed the man to enter. He went to the bathroom and returned with a water glass. Pouring two fingers into it, he said, "I'm out of ice."

Reynolds reached for the glass. "Have you ever known me to be choosy?" Without another word he headed out onto the balcony Cael had deserted. Retrieving his drink, Cael followed him.

"Couldn't sleep," the man told him laconically, propping a hip against the balcony.

Cael nodded his understanding. Adrenaline did odd things to a person's body. Sharpened nerve endings to such a keen edge that rest was impossible until the effect was worn off. And Reynolds was an adrenaline junkie. So he'd pursued the type of life he was best suited for, as Cael had himself.

The two men were silent for a while as they sipped their drinks and stared out in the darkness. They knew each other well enough for the quiet to be companionable. They'd had each other's back more times than Cael wanted to remember. He couldn't think of anyone he trusted as implicitly.

"Could have been worse tonight," the other man mused. "Major screwup not stopping Fuente's limo sooner, but the inner perimeter held and the interior security looked solid. What'd you decide on the outer perimeter?"

"They've been terminated."

Reynolds nodded. There was no other choice. The men had proven that their judgment was flawed. That given a split-second decision, they made the wrong one. Whether a stupid mistake or a more calculated one, they needed to be weeded out before they made another error in judgment that could prove costlier.

"Carter was solid."

A knot fisted in the pit of Cael's belly. "Looked like it."

"Good nerves. Sharp decision making." Reynolds paused a moment to drink. "Took both tires out with one shot each, no night-vision goggles. Not too shabby."

"I saw the tape," Cael said shortly. His gut was starting to burn now. It suited him to blame the whiskey.

The other man grinned, a flash of white teeth in the near darkness. "Wouldn't mind seeing it again. Hell, wouldn't mind having that tape in my private collection. I got a thing for dangerous women. It's a sickness. And then that wrestling match with Fuente." He gave a suggestive whistle. "Worth the price of—"

"She's working for Samuelson."

The abrupt words successfully stemmed the rest of that sentence. Wiped the humor from Reynold's face with a swiftness that would have been comical under any other circumstances.

"How long have you known?"

"Long enough."

Cael felt Reynolds stare at him searchingly as he took another drink, welcoming the scorch of the whiskey down his throat.

"Do we have to watch for sabotage?"

We. The word had appreciation flickering. Cael looked at the man, closer to him than any brother could be. "No, she's solid for this assignment. He fed her a bogus line about wanting information on the government here to get her to agree to come. I figure he'll reveal his true purpose when she gets back to the States."

"He'll pump her for every fact observed about you and your handling of this mission, then twist that to suit his own purposes. Rat bastard."

It was no coincidence that their minds ran along such similar paths. "If he wants to manufacture a crap storm, the political climate is well suited for a reputation assassination, don't you think?" The performance of the private security contractors in Iraq had Congress looking at similar firms with a magnifying glass. And high-risk missions such as these were rife with opportunity for something to go wrong. It wouldn't take much spin from a man in Samuelson's position to lay the blame for any bloodshed squarely at Cael's doorstep. A congressional inquiry could tie him up for months. Close his business down. Ruin Cael's career.

"Well, if he just wants you destroyed instead of dead he's modified his objective. Any chance that's Carter's true purpose here?"

"She's a sniper, not an assassin."

Reynolds took a long drink. "Person's occupation can change given enough motivation. The way Samuelson works, he'd have provided her with some decent motivation."

"You could say that." Cael stared broodingly into the night, swirling the amber liquor around in his glass. "I imagine he's discovered the same thing I did. She's Calvin Julson's daughter."

The liquor in Reynolds's glass sloshed precariously as he jerked toward Cael. "No shit? How deep was that buried?"

"I doubt it was something she put on her job application," he said drily. Julson was, in his estimation, emotionally unbalanced. He'd seen TV clips of the man, lean and tough as shoe leather, spouting the sort of hateful vitriol that incited violence against whichever minority he was railing against at the time. He'd narrowly managed to avoid a conspiracy conviction two years ago for the murder of a homosexual couple living in Montana.

It still astounded him that the man's blood ran through Ava's veins. Little wonder she'd disavowed him.

"We can use this," Reynolds said surely. He was deep in strategy mode now. "Samuelson doesn't know it, but he's handed us a weapon in Carter. You're already figuring on using her, right?" He didn't wait for an agreement. Their minds worked similarly most of the time. "Carter doesn't want this out, she'll have no choice but to agree. We manufacture a carefully edited story about circumstances down here that put you in a less than stellar light of course."

"Of course."

"Samuelson takes the bait, mounts a full-fledged inquiry, leading the charge, discovers too late that he's been had and ends up with his reputation in shambles." Reynolds cocked a brow at him. "Is that what you're thinking?"

Useless to deny it. "Something along those lines."

"But here's the death blow for that prick." Propping his forearms on the railing, Reynolds drained his glass. "We can still kill his entire career just by letting this spin out. Getting proof of him working with Carter. Then we leak who she really is, and any credibility he has is shot. This is a win-win for us." He raised his empty glass with a grin. "Congratulations, buddy. We've finally been handed a way to give that son of a bitch a figurative bullet between the eyes."

"Destroying Carter in the process."

His tone apparently wasn't quite as even as he'd strived for. Reynolds's look sharpened. "Well, yeah. But she's collateral damage, right? You can't afford to worry about her when an opportunity like this falls into your lap. You take it and do what you have to."

"Right."

"It'll be a pleasure helping you plan just how to paint that pock-faced bastard into a corner and finish him off." Reynolds clapped him on the shoulder before setting the empty glass down and cheerfully saying good-night.

Moodily, Cael finished off his drink as the door closed in back of the man. There was nothing Reynolds liked better than plotting strategy. He'd have two or three lines of action to suggest in a matter of hours. Given their affinity for this sort of thing, Cael would be very much surprised if whatever his friend came up with didn't match pretty closely the tentative strategy he'd mapped out.

She's collateral damage, right?

No matter how he tried, he couldn't get Reynolds's words out of his head. They shouldn't burn and char a hole through his system. It would be a mistake to forget Ava had signed on for this. To spy, if nothing else, reporting details back to Samuelson that would be twisted to hang Cael.

Okay, maybe she had no way of knowing what the man was. What he'd use her for. But she was a cop. A sniper. She knew few missions went as planned. How easily they went awry and how quickly something black and white could be painted with shades of gray. She assumed that risk every day on the job.

Toying with the empty glass, he shifted his attention to Samuelson. There was little he wouldn't do to bring the man down. He'd been a malevolent force in Cael's life since they'd met. The agent had done his best to destroy him. Certainly he'd destroyed his mother. So there was little he wouldn't do to return the favor. Even if it meant using Ava Carter.

But his conscience was like a noose, strangling him from the inside. He'd have to find a way to set it aside. He couldn't afford to be soft now, when everything he'd worked for was being handed to him on a platter.

He couldn't afford to let concern for Ava sway him from the most important act of his life.

Ava sat on the bed, propped on the pool of pillows staring into the shadows. Sleep was out of the question.

It seemed obvious that it had only been a matter of time until her past became known. Odd how that thought seemed so clear now, when she would have violently disagreed with it weeks earlier. Certainly she'd never taken particular efforts to conceal it. She'd been seventeen when she stopped trying to contact her father. Stopped begging him to allow her back into his life. She was too numb to experience the familiar twist of shame at the memory. And then she'd met Sammy, married him and moved to California. Kept his name after they divorce, and even that had had as much to do with her and Alex sharing the same last name as with hiding her relationship with Calvin Julson.

Shoulders slumped, she turned her thoughts to damage control. Because she was through being manipulated. First by Samuelson and now by Cael. The past could only be used to hurt her if she wanted it kept hidden. Remove the secret, remove the power of using it as a weapon.

But the thought of what she had to do made her stomach tangle in greasy knots. She'd lied to Alex all his life. Ironic that she'd been scrupulously honest about the boy who'd gotten her pregnant. She had every intention of going through with her promise to her son that she'd allow him to contact the man if he wanted to when he was eighteen.

But she'd told him since he could ask that he had no grandparents, other than Sammy's father. No cousins. No living relatives on her side at all. She'd been protecting him by shielding him from the truth. It wasn't easy confronting who and what her father was.

But she'd been protecting herself as well. Because she hated, *hated* considering what she'd been on her way to becoming before her father had kicked her out.

The hours ticked by as she wrestled with the rationalizations and the sick fear that her son would detest her for the lie. Despise her for the truth. But as dawn tinged the sky outside the window, she knew exactly what she had to do.

Reaching for the phone, she dialed Alex's cell number.

Chapter 8

Ava exchanged a look with Sibbits and Benton as they walked into the conference room. If all of McCabe's operatives were in one place, who was guarding de la Reyes and Gonzalez?

All of them took chairs at the table. And it occurred to her, surveying Cael's grim expression, that the last forty-eight hours hadn't been kind to him. She refused to spare him any sympathy. She hadn't spoken to him alone since the scene in her room. When he'd had her in his arms one moment, threatened her the next. Nor was she looking forward to their next conversation. But for now, she focused on what he had to tell them. It was obvious from his expression that it was urgent.

"You know that Perez never returned from the police interrogation of the airline dispatcher."

Ava and the other two operatives nodded at McCabe's terse words. She knew Cael had gotten more and more concerned, especially after talking to the police captain. Perez had left headquarters after spending nearly twelve hours on the interrogation. The police claimed they hadn't seen him since.

"How do we know we can trust the policia in this country?" offered Sibbits. His rubbed his hand over his graying crew cut. "Everyone else is suspect. Why not them?"

"The interrogation did convince them that the dispatcher was in Ramirez's employ. And they may or may not be corrupt. Or others working for Ramirez could have been watching. We have to consider that Perez might have been followed and scooped up by them after leaving the police headquarters."

The mood in the room turned grim. "The hospitals have been checked?" Ava asked.

Cael nodded. "He's not in jail, he's not in a hospital. He's not in the morgue."

She wondered if she imagined the bleak unspoken "yet" at the end of that statement.

"I sent Reynolds out to sniff around last night. See if he could shake some information loose from any of the informants he's worked with. He hasn't reported in."

Uneasiness filled her. Protocol dictated reports at least every eight hours. Reynolds appeared to be a consummate professional. If anyone could find Perez, it'd be him, or Cael himself.

But his being out of communication for so long was extremely worrying.

"What this means to us is we're down two men for the time being. I've got two guardsman on Gonzalez right now. God knows they can't get him out of his quarters without blowing themselves to hell and back. And de la Reyes is in the next room having breakfast with Fuente. It's going to take the four of us to rotate between shifts. But being shorthanded is dangerous, too. I want each of you to give me names of guardsmen that have impressed you. Ones you trust more than the others. We're going to have to start giving a few of them more responsibility, at least where they can be supervised."

"Where are we on their bank account audits?"

Cael reached for a mug of coffee sitting in front him, took a drink. "No other unexplained sums of money showed up in any guardsmen's accounts. Of course they wouldn't have had to deposit a bribe, either. But there was a large deposit made to the airport dispatcher. Hopefully this means we can afford to trust the presidential guard more in the coming days."

"What have you learned about the remotes?"

There was a lethal edge to Cael's tone. "I'll be talking to Gonzalez again in a few minutes. Reynolds and I spent the last thirty-six hours interviewing the National Guardsmen. More questions about him have arisen." He glanced at his watch. "That's it. Sibbits and Benton, get some sleep. Carter, you're on de la Reyes. I'll take Gonzalez. We'll have another briefing this evening."

Ava slid her chair back and rose, turning toward the door. Cael's voice stopped her. "Carter, I'd like to speak to you for a minute."

She was tempted, sorely tempted, to continue out the door. She'd managed to evade being alone with him for two days. It hadn't been easy to tamp down the trepidation and antagonism their last scene together had fostered. Even now, her chest was going tight and nerves were clutching in her belly.

The reaction annoyed her. Cael McCabe wasn't going to be given this kind of power over her. Not anymore. Not on any level.

She forced herself to meet his gaze, hoping none of the welter of emotion showed in her expression. When the door clicked quietly behind her, leaving the room empty except for the two of them, she could feel the walls shrinking in, crowding her.

Cael was silent for a moment. But his gaze, fixed on hers, was searching. She wasn't going to remember what had happened the last time they were alone together. That path led to betrayal. Instead she'd recall what he'd said after he'd released her.

A man ready to take her to bed one minute and issuing threats the next exuded a kind of danger that owed nothing to the physical. And a woman who was still attracted in the face of his ruthlessness was nothing short of stupid. He wouldn't be allowed to slip under her guard again.

But that vow felt hollow alongside the sliver of concern that pierced her as the silence strung out between them. He looked like the last two days had been long on worry and short on sleep. Certainly the disappearance of Perez would be weighing on him.

Unwilling to break the taut silence, she waited for him to speak. When he did, his words helped stiffen her will even as they flayed her feelings.

"I'm hoping that the last couple days have given you an opportunity to reevaluate your position."

Deliberately misunderstanding, she said, "You mean professionally? Because I have to admit, dealing with Marissa Fuentes's theatrics every day does test my patience. If she orders me to fetch something for her one more time I may have to place her in a choke hold."

As a diversionary tactic, it failed miserably. The look in his pale green eyes remained intent. "I don't want this thing to end up hurting you. Whatever else happens, I don't want you being…" A muscle jumped in his jaw. "…collateral damage."

"Perfect. We're agreed, then."

She turned toward the door and he was at her side before she could reach for the handle. With a hand on her elbow, he spun her around to face him again.

"Dammit, Ava, be reasonable." His face was shoved too close to hers for comfort. His voice terse.. "Do you honestly think you can walk away from this? It's easy to say you're washing your hands of the whole thing, but Samuelson will never allow that. He's a dangerous son of a bitch and vindictive as hell. He'll destroy you."

She ignored the quick shudder down her spine. "Or you will?"

He let go of her suddenly. Took a few steps away as if by establishing a physical distance he could achieve an emotional one as well. "I've been all around this thing for the last forty-eight hours. There's no way out for you. If you tell Samuelson you won't cooperate, first he'll persuade, then he'll threaten. Don't kid yourself about him. His standing gives him a certain amount of power and he uses that to get what he wants, damn anyone in his way."

"I have only your word that what he wants isn't exactly what he presented to me—a report on the government's stability here."

He gave a humorless smile. "Did it ever occur to you to wonder what brought DHS to Metro City?"

She had, in fact, wondered that very thing in Sanders's office. "The assassination attempt," she said, with more certainty than she felt. "The terrorism being sponsored by Ramirez and his men."

"There is no terrorism in San Baltes that endangers the U.S." Cael made a short dismissive gesture with his hand. "That was all bogus to explain Samuelson's interest here. It was my involvement with de la Reyes that had him following us from D.C. to California. Me being on the same continent as the man is powerful temptation. The assassination attempt must have given him the idea to use this contract against me." His smile was bleak. "It wouldn't be the first time."

That the two had a history had been apparent from the beginning. But Ava didn't ask the questions that were trembling on her lips. Because reasons didn't matter. "Neither of you is going to be allowed to use me. And both of you are going to have to deal with that."

She suspected he was grinding his teeth. "You are dangerously naive," he muttered. "You can't play a human Switzerland here. You won't be allowed to remain neutral. Everything

I threatened you with, you can be damn sure he's already thought of. Planned for. And he won't hesitate to follow through if you refuse him."

"But you would?"

Something flickered across his expression, there and gone too quickly to be identified. He looked away. "The only way out for you is to help me. By the time he realizes the part you played in his downfall, he'll be defanged. He won't have the power to hurt you or to plot revenge. He'll be too damn busy trying to keep his ass out of a federal court for misuse of his position."

It shouldn't have hurt, to listen to him reach for any tool to elicit her assistance. She'd already learned the lengths he'd go to get it.

But it did hurt. Intensely. "I can't tell you how much I appreciate your concern for me." She made no effort to keep the sarcasm from her tone. "But I'll take my chances."

"Don't be stupid." Cael slammed the palm of his hand on the conference table, making her jump. "I can't protect you from him, don't you get that? I've been all over this thing and I can't figure a way to keep you out of it, even if I wanted to. You either let him use you to destroy me or you help me bring him down. There is no third option. The man is treacherous."

She squelched the warmth that threatened to bloom. His supposed worry for her was a sham. Nothing about the man could be trusted as genuine. Except for his hatred of Samuelson.

There was an unfamiliar tightness in her throat. "Did the thought ever occur that you might have misjudged the man? That your hatred for him has blinded you to who and what he is?"

The stillness that came over him was lethal. His fist clenched at his side so tightly that the knuckles turned white. She had a moment to wonder at his reaction before his next words, uttered in a flat, bleak tone, scattered any formal thought.

"I know exactly who and what is he. Better than most people could. He's my father."

* * *

Cael's mood was dangerous as he strode up to Gonzalez's quarters. With a terse jerk of his head, he indicated for the guardsman on duty to step aside before turning to the security device on the door. Using his body to shield his actions from any interested eyes, he tapped in the code and drew his weapon. It would be careless to let his temper affect the upcoming interview. Unprofessional to allow the scene with Ava to color his judgment.

The woman had been allowed too much control over him already.

What other reason could there be for him blurting out the truth about his relationship with Samuelson? He'd done his damnedest to forget it over the years. What other reason could explain the direction of his strategizing for the last couple of days? Every plan he and Reynolds had plotted out for bringing down Samuelson had all had the same flaw. They all meant Ava would be ruined in the process.

Even if he didn't use her in the man's demise, she'd get caught up in the fallout. That was unavoidable. And why the hell, he wondered bitterly, gesturing for the guardsman to leave his weapon at the door, should he care about that? Now, when Samuelson's destruction was within reach, why would he start worrying about a woman he hadn't even known two weeks ago?

It couldn't be allowed, he thought grimly, opening the door to allow the guardsmen to precede him. He stepped inside the quarters, weapon ready, and surveyed Gonzalez's familiar contemptuous expression. He couldn't afford to be weak when he could imagine what Samuelson was planning. He was through playing defense with the man.

And he was through—he'd have to be through—worrying about Ava Carter.

"You will interpret for us," he told the guardsman tersely. The man, Eduardo Vasquez, looked uneasy. But when Cael gestured for him to pull up two chairs the man did so, sinking slowly into one with a nod from him.

Remaining standing, Cael surveyed Gonzalez. The man stared back unrepentantly. He made a short remark that had Vasquez fidgeting, sliding a glance toward Cael but not quite meeting his eyes.

"The captain…he say that you are…uh…"

"I'm aware of his opinion of me," Cael said drily. He lowered his weapon but didn't reholster it. "Believe me, it's reciprocated."

Vasquez screwed up his brow, but Cael didn't bother to explain further. Instead he took the free chair and turned it around so he could sit on it backward, resting his arms on its back.

"You are a liar," he said clearly to Gonzalez. "And now we have proof of that." He waited for Vasquez to haltingly interpret before reaching in his shirt and withdrawing a stack of photos. He handed them to the guardsman, who looked through them, clearly puzzled.

"Give them to the captain," Cael directed, watching carefully as the younger man approached Gonzalez. But he did as directed, dropping the batch of pictures in the man's lap before returning to take his seat again.

"I assume you will recognize the man in the picture."

Gonzalez stared at him a moment longer, insolence etched in his expression.

"You ought to, anyway. He's your nephew."

When Vasquez translated, Gonzalez's eyes widened. He picked up the pictures awkwardly with his bound hands and looked down at the top one. Any doubt Cael might have had was erased when he saw recognition and shock flare in the man's expression.

"The date and time he was caught on camera at your bank coincides with when the deposit was made into your account. You remember. The deposit you don't know anything about?"

Cael's tone was caustic. Vasquez spoke in rapid Spanish, his earlier unease seemingly dissipated in the face of the news.

"The chief…he say his nephew would not do such a thing. There must be another…how do you say it…explanation."

"I have a real good idea what that might entail," Cael put in grimly. "We've got unexplained cash appearing in Gonzalez's account and his nephew at the scene at the same time. Couple that with the fact that his nephew seems to have disappeared, and I'd have to be an idiot to believe his protests of innocence." He grinned sharkishly. "I'm not an idiot."

After a swift give-and-take in Spanish, Vasquez reported, "The chief cannot explain that. He worries about his nephew. That perhaps he was made to do something and now a bad thing has happened to him."

"You know what worries me? That maybe his nephew is working for Ramirez. That Gonzalez is, too. And that he's still lying about it, hoping to avoid a firing squad for his betrayal of his president."

Vasquez was silent for a moment. His expression, when he turned back to the captain, was forbidding as he translated.

"You are wrong about him. He say he would protect the president with his life."

"Sure." Cael nodded, tapping the side of his Luger with his index finger. He watched Gonzalez's eyes track the movement nervously. "That probably explains his giving an extra remote to Fuente and keeping its existence from the president. Who else has he given a remote to? How many copies has he made?"

Vasquez translated in a rapid spate of Spanish and Gonzalez shook his head vehemently as he answered. His protest was cut short when the younger man heatedly responded again, his retort effectively silencing the chief.

"He denies that he ever gave Marissa Fuente a remote. Or that he made any extra copies of them. I told him what I told you. That I saw him give it to her one day in the palace. That I had left something in the hall and had come back for it."

Vasquez's tone was bitter. "He lies now. Because I saw that with my own eyes. It is hard not to think he lies about everything."

Gonzalez looked from one of them to another, his expression growing panicked. He spoke pleadingly, his earlier bravado vanished.

"He admit it now. That Miss Fuente pleaded so prettily for a remote and he only agreed because he thought the president knew. She promised him so."

"Hard to know what to believe," Cael said in a hard tone, staring at the man with antipathy rising. There was little as despicable as a man who sold out his own to line his pockets. "Should I believe him a traitor or merely an incompetent fool? What would he believe, if all this evidence was gathered and implicated one of his men?"

When Vasquez translated, Gonzalez remained stubbornly silent.

Cael fought to rein in his frustration. "Ask him what he was plotting. Did Ramirez plan for the next assassin to use Fuente and her remote to get him inside the palace walls? Or was he going to send a little present along in the trunk of her limo sometime? Given the bullshit security Gonzalez was providing, it wouldn't have been too difficult for Ramirez to pack an explosive in a car that would be given access to the palace's inner perimeter."

The chief shook his head violently as Vasquez translated. A moment later the guardsman reported, "He say he was guilty of an error in judgment but not of betraying the president. He would protect the president with his life."

The chair clattered to the floor as Cael lunged from it. Closed the remaining distance to the captain and pressed his weapon against the man's temple. "You put de la Reyes's life at risk." He struggled to rein in the temper surging. "By doing so you put your country's stability at risk. You're either a miserable excuse for a security professional or you're collaborating with a scumbag drug dealer. Which is it?"

Gonzalez went very still, his eyes squeezing shut. And for a moment, for one dangerous second, it wasn't the captain of the presidential guard sitting there, waiting for death. It was Dennis Allen Samuelson. A lifetime of resentment became a cauldron of frothing emotion. He hauled in a breath, fought for control.

And slowly, slowly tipped the barrel of the gun up. Stepped back. When he was sure he had his restraint on a leash, he spoke again. "The satisfaction of your death belongs to your president, not to me. It's him you'll answer to. Him and your country."

It was with great care that he left the quarters. Locked the door behind them. Reset the security system. His actions were automatic. They didn't require thinking. Right now, Cael desperately didn't want to think.

Because he didn't lose control. Not ever. And it was staggering to consider just how close he'd come in there to doing just that.

"I thought Chief Gonzalez was a great man."

He started a little. He'd half forgotten that Vasquez was still there. The younger officer's gaze lit on his face for a moment. Slid by him.

"He hired me for this position. Impressed on me how important it was. My duty to protect the president. I thought he was a hero."

Vasquez headed in the direction of the guards' barracks, a dejected slump to his shoulders. And Cael knew the officer had learned a valuable lesson that day. He'd never have a case of hero worship again. No one would ever be regarded without a tinge of cynicism.

His disillusionment might strengthen him in the long run. Maybe then he wouldn't disappoint himself the way Cael just had earlier.

With his free hand, he rubbed at the knot of muscles bunched in his neck. Perspective was deserting him, at the worst possible time. The absence of Reynolds and Perez left them more shorthanded than they'd already been. They still had several more days before the other expected operatives would be joining them.

And Ava just might be right after all. Maybe he was allowing his hatred of Samuelson to blind him. In more ways than one.

Or maybe it was his growing obsession with her that was blinding him. Settling in for a long stint, he leaned a shoulder against the exterior wall of the house. He needed to clear his mind. Think like a soldier instead of a hormone-ridden teenager. He had Samuelson in his sights. He couldn't afford to be distracted with worries about fallout for her. On a mission, nothing could detour him from his target.

He had to remember that. And he needed to regain his famed dispassion, quickly. Before this whole thing went to hell around them because he was wasting time focusing on her.

"Ms. Carter."

The imperious tone grated Ava's nerve endings. She slid her gaze to Marissa Fuentes, who was gliding up to her wearing a gown more suited for life in a brothel than a quiet day at home.

"I am quite parched. You will bring me flavored water."

Ava read the gleam in the woman's eyes. She knew damn well Ava wasn't going to do her bidding. The same way she hadn't obeyed any of the last hundred commands the woman had made since she arrived. She issued them for one reason only. To get on Ava's nerves.

Since she'd learned it was the surest way to return the favor, she looked away and assumed a bland expression. The woman was bored here. Ava had known she would be. De la Reyes had resumed his schedule of meetings and teleconferences during the day, leaving Fuente at loose ends.

Of course, she amended silently, the woman rarely rose before noon so she didn't have all that much time to fill. It was unfortunate for Ava that she'd decided baiting the only female operative on the security detail was her favorite pastime.

Fuente snapped her fingers, dangerously close to Ava's nose. "Did you hear me? I want it now." When Ava still didn't answer, the woman smirked and turned to the guard nearest her. In Spanish she said, "Perhaps she is deaf as well as dumb. She will not be of much use to my Tonio if that is so."

From the corner of her eye Ava saw the guard start to smile before he caught her looking at him. He quickly sobered, saying nothing. And there was no ripple of reaction from the other guardsmen, either. Something had changed since she'd chewed them out the other day. She could at least be thankful for that.

Tiring of the game, the woman changed tactics. Surveying Ava critically from head to toe, she said, "How does a woman such as you hope to interest any male dressed as you are? You look like a man, I think, with clothes that hide any curves you might have." She paused, but Ava remained quiet. Her expression grew sly. "Or maybe you are a woman who is not a woman. Maybe it is not a man you are wanting to attract, *si?*"

Temper spiked through Ava's system. Leaning forward, she murmured, "You want to know what kind of woman I am? I'm the kind of woman who's going to kick your ass if you don't get out of here and let me do my job."

Fuente quickly took a step back before catching herself. Smoothing a hand down her gown, she tossed her hair. "I will speak to Tonio about your attitude. You are nothing but the help and you would do well to remember that." With that she swept away and out the door. De la Reyes, on the other side of the room on the phone, didn't seem to notice.

But some of Fuente's words had left a mark. Because Ava was increasingly wondering what kind of woman she was, too. She'd never been one to make excuses for a man's behavior. Had no patience for women who did. She'd learned at fifteen how to cut her losses and move on. Her boyfriend's

profession of eternal love had died a quick and brutal death
when she'd told him she was pregnant. She damn well hadn't
hung around begging for more.

So it was pretty hard to understand the chemistry that,
God help her, still flared to life whenever she and McCabe
were in the same room. He'd threatened her. Tricked her.
Stated his intention to blackmail her. She ought to be wondering how to get away with shooting him, not speculating
about the bombshell he'd dropped earlier.

DHS agent Samuelson was Cael McCabe's father.

It was hard to wrap her mind around that. And even
more difficult to keep questions from skirting the edges of
her concentration, when she should be focused totally on
de la Reyes.

But her mind kept creeping back like a thief in the night
to worry at the pronouncement. Because there was a whole
lot that Cael had left unsaid. Far more that Samuelson had ne-
glected to mention than she'd originally believed.

Their relationship didn't explain—not by a long shot—the
antipathy that apparently existed between the two men.
Because if McCabe hated his father, it had been apparent at
the meeting in Sanders's office that Samuelson harbored no
tender feelings for Cael, either.

A knock sounded on the door then. De la Reyes looked up
from his phone call as a guardsman poked his head inside,
caught Ava's eye. She strode over to the half-opened door to
watch as Vice President Quintero, his expression long-suffer-
ing, was frisked by two of the guardsmen. Satisfied, Ava
nodded and the man was allowed to enter the room.

A moment later the president ended his phone call and got
up to greet the man, before the two of them sat at the table in
the far side of the room, conducting their business in undertones. Immediately her mind began to wander again.

She'd do well to stop contemplating the relationship and
hatred between Samuelson and McCabe and start worrying

about herself. About her son. Cael may have been exaggerating things to win her assistance, but she suspected there was a small kernel of truth in his professed concern for her. Namely that Samuelson would retaliate against her if she refused to help him. It wasn't difficult to believe that he'd learned of her father's identity.

There was a slight rise in voice level from the two men at the table, and Ava diverted her attention sharply, assessing the scene for possible risk. A moment later they were back to near whispers. Her instincts heightened, she pushed aside personal distractions to focus on the task at hand.

Although she wasn't yet sure how, she was going to make damn certain this whole thing didn't come back to touch Alex. Resolve steeled inside her. He'd sounded so shocked on the phone when she'd told him he had a grandfather. So angry when he'd accused her of lying. She'd refused to tell him her father's name yet. That couldn't be done over the phone. But when her son learned the truth it'd be from her. Not from Cael or Samuelson.

With dark humor, she considered that at least the earlier conversation with McCabe had forewarned her. She just needed to come up with a way to protect her son from a powerful government official and a dangerous ex-special ops soldier, in between the task of guarding the president of San Baltes with a shrinking security force.

Piece of cake.

"Miss Fuente has announced her plan to go out for an evening of nightclubbing." Cael's voice was carefully expressionless. "I've suggested to the president that it might be best that she not return, at least until we get a better handle on security here. He was initially reluctant, but eventually agreed."

The details of that particular conversation came as no surprise to Ava. She'd been within earshot of the heated exchange. Marissa had spent dinner arguing with de la Reyes about her "banishment."

"Our job," Cael stressed with noticeable inflection, "is to make sure the exit from the compound goes smoothly and that the guardsmen are aware the limo won't be allowed to reenter. We want to minimize our risks here." He looked at Sibbits. "You'll be on duty with Gonzalez so you won't be able to help us out with that. Benton will stay on shift with de la Reyes, but I'll update him on the plan." His gaze switched to Ava. "That leaves both of us to prepare the guardsmen on duty. You take the outer perimeter and I'll take the inner."

"So you want me to be sure the outside perimeter is clear before opening the gate for the limo. And ensure it doesn't get back inside until further notice." Cael's nod had satisfaction flickering. It wouldn't be a hardship to see the end of Fuente for a while. Ava wasn't sure how much longer she could take of the woman's baiting without decking her. "Any word from Reynolds?"

She could tell Cael's answer from his expression before his answer. "No." A muscle twitched in his jaw. "But there's nothing we can do about that until the rest of the team gets here."

She could read the concern behind the carefully dispassionate tone. Had the fleeting thought that it was only when his emotion was directed at her that she distrusted it.

"I had a conversation with Emmanuel Ortega earlier today," Cael informed him. "There are military teams covering every residence that Ramirez owns. They've turned some informants who are giving them valuable information about the man's operation. Once he has been neutralized the danger to de la Reyes will drastically decrease." He smiled humorlessly. "We just need to keep him alive in the meantime."

Ava wondered if she was the only one in the room unconvinced. If the government had known how to get to Ramirez, he'd have been arrested a long time ago, wouldn't he? Hopefully the informants could lead the way to the drug lord. At any rate, their job here hadn't gotten any easier.

Which made Fuente's upcoming departure the hands-down highlight of her day.

The woman was taking her sweet time. Ava consulted her watch. After nine thirty. She supposed the nightclub scene didn't get really started until much later. Hard to imagine someone wanting to spend a night in a bar full of drunks with an assault of earsplitting music, but she imagined Fuentes went more to be seen than anything else.

The limo had pulled up to the front entrance fifteen minutes ago. Ava had supervised the mandatory body search of the driver, which the man had endured good-naturedly. The vehicle had been cleared before being released to him. Protocol was being followed without a hitch so far. The driver had gone into the palace to retrieve Fuente's many bags, leaving the driver's and left passenger doors and trunk open. She'd lost count of the number of trips he'd made out to the waiting vehicle, taking great care to stow the bags in the trunk.

It occurred to her that someone had changed the tires on the car she'd shot out during its stay on the compound. She suspected that task had been left to the driver.

Ava spoke into her wrist transmitter. "Prepare for departure within fifteen."

"Inner perimeter, check." Cael's voice sounded on the radio. He must be in back of the palace, as he was out of sight.

"Outer perimeter, check." She recognized the voice of the guard at the gate she'd spoken to earlier.

She waited another few minutes, but neither the driver nor Fuente emerged. Rolling her eyes, she spoke into her wrist mike again. "Benton, are we prepared for departure?"

Her skin prickled in the ensuing silence. She heard Cael's voice next. "Benton, what's your—"

The rest of his words were lost as a mighty blast rocked the area, sending Ava sprawling.

Chapter 9

Disoriented, Ava rolled swiftly to her feet, her rifle in position. She half expected to see the palace engulfed in flames. Was momentarily confused to see it still standing, relatively unharmed.

In the next moment she saw the plumes of smoke rising in the distance from behind the palace and comprehension slammed into her.

Gonzalez's quarters had been triggered.

Fireballs hurtled like rockets skyward. She muttered an epithet and started running for the house. "Benton, what's your location?" she shouted into her mike.

"Maintain position." Cael's snapped order halted her progress. "I'm in a jeep right now heading toward the captain's quarters. Benton? Benton?"

After several moments, Cael spoke again. "Carter, check inside. See what the hell's going on."

But in the end she didn't follow that order. She didn't have to. Because the door to the front of the palace swung open. Dropping back, she took refuge in the meticulously landscaped bushes that surrounded the opulent structure.

The scene on the steps filled her veins with ice. Quietly, she spoke into her mike. "Limo driver is exiting side one, opening one. He's holding two weapons. One on de la Reyes. The other on Fuente."

"Do you have a shot?"

She sighted, felt a surge of frustration. "Not yet," she whispered back. "But I might get a clear head shot as they move past me toward the vehicle."

"If it's clear…take it."

A deadly calm settled over her. As silently as possible she inched farther back into the shrubs, sinking to a crouch. All she had to do was wait. Ignore the pound and spike of adrenaline and calm her speeding pulse. Give the man time to head to the limo. Once there he was faced with placing two captives in the car. The diversion might provide the clearest target.

A head shot was her only option. Breathing deeply, Ava kept her mind clear of everything but the task before her. With his weapons trained on the two captives, her only chance of avoiding a reflex shot from the driver would be to sever his brain stem. She didn't doubt her ability if the opportunity arose. She'd had plenty of practice. But first she needed the driver to walk down those stairs. Take several steps toward the vehicle.

He spoke loudly in Spanish. "Weapons down. Pile them at the base of the porch. Or your president is dead."

With a sinking heart, Ava watched as one by one the guardsmen in the vicinity lowered their weapons. Moved slowly to add their rifles and handguns to the growing pile.

"You two." He singled out a couple of guardsmen. "Take all of them and throw them in the fountain. Your obedience is all that is keeping de la Reyes alive."

Move. Just down the steps, you bastard, Ava urged silently.

Let's see what you're made of when you're not the only one armed.

"Where is Carter? I want her out here now! Throw your weapons down and hands in the air." Translating effortlessly, Ava remained hidden, her mind wheeling with alternatives. The driver had seen her earlier. He knew she'd been out here the entire time he'd waited. But he couldn't be sure she remained here after the explosion, could he?

She sighted again, silently cursing the way he held both hostages close to him, with the muzzles of his weapons pressed against their temples.

"I'll shoot Fuente first," the man promised in his native tongue. As if on cue, the woman stopped sobbing and began to scream. "Throw down your weapons, Carter. I will give you three seconds before I shoot her. One."

Coolly, she weighed her options. De la Reyes seemed frozen, but she couldn't see his expression. If the driver pulled the trigger, the crumpling of Fuente's body would provide the clear shot she needed.

"Two."

But the man hadn't progressed any farther down the steps. Which meant her only shot was above the ear, taking the chance the bullet could pass through his skull and into de la Reyes's.

"Three…"

"I'm here," she shouted. Lowering her rifle, she rose, feeling supremely vulnerable. Her handgun was holstered across her chest, easily visible. She was otherwise unarmed.

"Step out where I can see you. Keep your hands up!"

She obeyed, circling the porch as she emerged, waiting for an opportunity to dive for cover and take a shot if it should present itself.

"Disarm her," he instructed the guardsmen nearby.

None of them moved.

"Disarm her, or one of them dies now."

Slowly, reluctantly, a guard moved toward her. His face was grim as he took her rifle. Unholstered her Luger.

"They go in the fountain, too." After the order, the driver looked at her, his expression cocky. "We do not want to chance having Carter shoot our tires out again, do we? Where is McCabe?"

Ava was wondering the same thing. Her wrist transmitter was on. If he was listening, he should hear enough of the scene to have him heading back.

The question was whether he'd back in time to make a difference.

"He went to check out the explosion site. That's what you intended, wasn't it? To divide us?"

"Get up here," the man instructed in Spanish.

Warily, Ava remained where she was. "Why?"

"Now!"

It's what she didn't see in his expression that had her moving forward. There was no fear. No reservation. This man would kill without hesitation.

Once she was on the porch, he ordered her to take up position several feet behind him. With a sinking feeling in her stomach, she did so. "Stay back that far, but follow us to the limo."

Fuente had subsided to wild keening noises as she stumbled alongside the driver. Ava did as ordered, following them from a short distance, scanning the tableau around her.

The guardsmen seemed frozen. A few of them looked at her, as if for guidance. She gave a short shake of her head. There was nothing any of them could do that wouldn't put the president at risk.

McCabe, however…if he'd returned from the captain's quarters… if he were in the vicinity…he might try for a shot.

How good a marksman was he? Ava wasn't sure. It took well over average skill to make a head shot. It took outstanding skill and luck to make it without killing a hostage as close as de la Reyes and Fuente were to the gunman.

Her stomach plummeting, she recognized they were short on both.

The gunman shoved Fuente toward the open passenger door. *"Entrar."* She scrambled in, for once lacking the grace and dignity she usually displayed. The driver nudged de la Reyes toward the driver's seat and Ava silently cursed. A driver presented a constant target. But the gunman would be hiding low in the seat. Still a danger to the hostages he'd taken.

But providing no shot.

The gunman ordered de la Reyes to close his door, and the president obeyed. Then he turned to Ava and shouted in Spanish, "If a car follows, they die. If I hear a helicopter overhead, they die." With one gun still trained on the president, he slammed the door. A moment later the limo began to move.

Ava got one last look of de la Reyes as he slowly drove by.

He looked like a man going to his death.

"He says Benton must go to the hospital."

"Bullshit," the operative said weakly from the couch he was lying on in the president's private quarters. "Tell the quack to patch me up and I'll be good to go."

The presidential physician looked at Ava expectantly. But it was Cael she was watching.

"Ask him what a hospital can do that he can't do right here."

Without relaying his question she responded, "He should go." Ignoring the weak protest her words brought from Benton, she continued. "This isn't a war zone where you slap on a field dressing and call it good. He could have internal damage. And there's nothing he can do here."

"The hell there isn't!"

This time it was Cael ignoring the man. "Okay."

"McCabe, come on. This isn't necessary." The doctor waved two white-clothed medics to lift Benton's makeshift gurney and carry him toward the door. "McCabe!"

Ava gestured to the man at her side, speaking rapidly to

the doctor. *"Y ahora usted necesita mirarlo. Vea como es serio sus quemaduras son y los tratan."*

As the man came toward him, Cael looked at her warily. "What'd you tell him?"

"That your burns need to be treated."

"I'm fine."

"Yeah." She didn't bother hiding her skepticism. "You look fine." He looked, in fact, like he'd emerged from the depths of hell. His hair was singed, and so was one eyebrow. Black soot covered every bare inch of skin, except the patches on his arms and one palm that were pink and oozing.

The doctor told her in Spanish, "He must wash. Dirt is the worst thing for a burn. Then I can treat him."

"You need to shower." Queasiness filled her just thinking of the pain he must be in. "Then he can put ointment on the burns."

The expression on his face was fierce. "We've got a helluva bonfire south of the palace and the president has been kidnapped from under our noses. The vice president will be here at any minute. I've got a little more to deal with than a few scrapes."

"Not being treated isn't going to put the fire out or get de la Reyes and Fuente back. And the vice president isn't here yet," she replied calmly. "Standing around acting macho is stupid and accomplishes nothing. Risking infection is even dumber. So give me your room key. I'll go fetch some clothes for you while you shower and let the doctor treat you." There was a gleam in his pale green gaze that spelled danger. Ignoring it, she cocked a brow. "I'll let you take it from there."

He was silent a moment, his eyes searching. Then he gave a short nod. "I've got a plan."

Adrenaline, recently tamped, flickered to life again. "You always do."

An hour later Ava was seated at a table next to Cael, who was dressed in a fresh T-shirt and fatigues. Vice President

Quintero sat opposite them, his expression grim as he listened to their terse recital of the events of the evening.

"I alerted Ortega at Justice to track down the identity and affiliations of the limo driver," he said in English after they'd finished. "But I don't understand where he got the weapons. It was your job to protect Antonio. The man should have been searched. He should have been—"

"He was," Ava said flatly. "I oversaw it myself. He had no weapons on him when he drove the car up to the front of the palace. The vehicle was clean, too."

"Then I do not understand—"

"He may have stolen them from the barracks and secreted them inside the palace. Hell, he may have bribed one of the guardsmen to do it for him. It would be easy enough then to retrieve them when he was carrying out the luggage."

Ava had her own suspicion on the matter, but decided to remain quiet for now. It was all supposition at this point, anyway. "At any rate, he had the weapons the third trip he made up for the luggage, because that's when he shot Benton and marched de la Reyes and Fuente down the stairs and out the door."

"And no one could stop him." It was clear Quintero wanted to blame someone for the president's disappearance. "All the armed security, and your team, Mr. McCabe...and no one could shoot this bastard when he was standing right in front of you!"

"Have you ever tried to sever a man's brain stem when he's holding two hostages on either side of him?" Ava asked evenly. "It's a tricky shot. I've accomplished it a few times, but I have to have a position behind the gunman. The target didn't expose himself. I assumed you'd prefer I didn't risk blowing away the top of the president's skull in the process. Maybe I was wrong about that."

The vice president opened his mouth. Shut it again.

Cael put in, "I called you immediately as things were going down. Did you contact the military?"

Quintero nodded. "The espionage plane was dispatched as

you requested. As you suspected, the limo was abandoned a few miles away and the president and Miss Fuente then were transported by a Land Rover. The vehicle entered the jungle southeast of here."

Ava's gaze jerked to Cael's. He looked unsurprised. "I'm confident they'll keep de la Reyes alive, at least for now. But your government should expect a communication from the rebels."

"You are more confident that I am myself." The man's tone was heated. "Ramirez has tried assassination before. What makes you think Antonio isn't already dead?"

"If Ramirez wanted him dead, he'd have been shot here," Cael said simply. "The fact that they bothered to take him means they need him alive, at least for a while."

The vice president frowned. "But why? What has changed that he…" Comprehension dawned on his face. "The frozen assets."

"Exactly." Cael nodded. "Only the president can order Ramirez's assets to be unfrozen, so it follows that he'll be allowed to live until he does so. However, once Ramirez can drain his accounts, de la Reyes is dead. So we don't have much time."

Stiffly, Quintero said, "There is no we, Mr. McCabe. I will take over from here. Already I have the military preparing rescue teams to go into the jungle."

"That would be a mistake."

The man's earlier politeness, Ava noted, had disappeared in the face of Cael's bluntness. "Many mistakes have been made here today, but none of them were mine." Cael reached for a rolled-up bunch of maps he'd been perusing before Quintero had arrived. Choosing one, he laid it out, tracing an area on it with his finger. "You have approximately ten thousand square miles of jungle in San Baltes. It would take hundreds of men weeks to cover all of it. You have a matter of days, not weeks, to get your president out safely."

"And what would you have us do in that time? Nothing at all?"

"You might talk to your minister of finance about ways to bog down the unfreezing of assets," Ava suggested. From Cael's look of approval she knew they were on the same track. "You also may pretend that there's a breakdown of communication within the government in the president's absence. Inter-cabinet bickering. Anything that will buy the president some time." Because one thing was clear. The moment Ramirez got his hands on his money, de la Reyes would be dead.

Folding his arms over his chest, Quintero said tersely, "This is all well and good. But how will the president be rescued if you say the military should not go looking for him?"

"That's easy enough," Cael said evenly. "I'm going in myself."

"You can't seriously be considering going in alone." Ava matched Cael stride for stride down the hallway to his room.

"Actually I'm through considering."

She eyed the patches on his arms covering the burns he'd sustained earlier that day. Delirium from pain might be responsible for such a risky illogical move, but he looked far from delirious. Determined. Lethal. But no less dangerous for his injuries.

"You can't even be sure where he's being held."

"The fact that he was taken into the jungle is a pretty big clue," he said dryly. They were at his door now. He unlocked it and pushed it open.

She followed him inside, an argument still on her lips. "You're thinking he's been taken to the rebel camp Reynolds located."

"Seems logical." He went to the closet in the room and pulled out a duffel bag, from which he extracted a backpack. Unrolling it, he tossed it on the bed. Then he went to the dresser and started pulling drawers open.

"You said yourself they change camp locations frequently."

Swiftly he crossed back to the bed with some clothes. Another pair of black fatigues. An extra tank undershirt. Several pairs of socks. A couple of changes of underwear. Ava averted her eyes. She definitely didn't need a mental picture of McCabe wearing only those dark briefs emblazoned on her mind.

But it was already too late. The image wouldn't be easily extricated.

"You could give the map Reynolds gave you to the military. What do you think you can accomplish that they can't?"

"I can not screw it up. I can't be sure they won't."

It was annoying to have to talk to his back. Now he was on the way to the adjoining bathroom, gathering up a toothbrush and paste.

"I'm sure they have trained professionals for just this sort of—"

"Are you?" His interruption cut her short. He paced back into the room and dropped the objects into the bag. "Because I'm not. I have no idea what this country's military capabilities are. How could I? I don't know if they have active recon and special ops teams or how well they're trained. I also don't know if Ramirez has someone embedded in the military reporting to him. What I am certain of is that it isn't worth taking the chance. I'm going in alone. Once I've located the camp and come up with a plan for getting our people out, I'll radio the military for backup, just like I told Quintero."

Ava felt a compelling desire to bounce something off his thick head. He wasn't being reasonable, and every protest seemed to slide off him. "At least take Sibbits. You trust him, right? Between the two of you…" Cael had gone still and an awful feeling of certainty came over her. Followed with a flood of sorrow. "Oh God."

Because of course the man had been on guard at Gonzalez's quarters. And no one standing that close to the house when it went off would have survived it.

Without conscious thought she closed the distance between them, laid her hand gently on his arm between the
gauze bandages. "I'm so sorry, Cael."

She saw his throat working. The muscles in his jaw were
clenched tight. But she wasn't prepared for the arm that
snaked around her waist. Pulling her tightly against him.

He held her there, his face pressed against her hair, and she
could feel his heart thudding against hers. Imagined she could
feel the heaviness in it. "Ah…shit," he muttered. His arms
held her so tightly she could scarcely breathe. And it seemed
completely natural to slide her own around his waist and hug
him, as if from the pressure she could release some of the
pent-up emotion he was holding in.

It seemed like a long time before he spoke again. "It was
like something out of hell. I knew it was him when I started
to the quarters. Like a human torch, rolling around to put out
the flames. I couldn't help him. When I finally got the flames
out, he was…"

"I know." It was easy enough now to guess how he'd gotten
those burns on his arms. She could imagine the scene vividly.
And her heart ached. Both for the fallen operative and for the
man who couldn't save him. And the grief he bore because
of it. The muscles in his shoulders were trembling under the
weight of sorrow. And she wanted, quite simply, to wipe it
away. To relieve him of the burden of remorse that she knew
he'd carry to the end of his days.

She understood what it was to fail. To watch in horror and
misery as an assignment spun horribly out of control. She'd
seen hostage takers do their worst before she could get a
clear shot. Seen strung-out estranged husbands do un-
speakable things to the women they claimed to love while
children stood in petrified terror as the scene unfolded
before them.

Ava had been part of far more successful missions than not,
but it was the ones that went wrong that haunted her. So she

knew what Cael was going through. And realized there was nothing to say that would ease his pain.

They stood like that for several minutes, fused together in a way that had nothing to do with passion and everything to do with the very human need for comfort. She didn't wonder—not then—what it was about the man that stripped her defenses so easily. Touched her emotions so deftly.

When he spoke his face was still resting lightly on her hair. His voice was muffled. "I won't lose another one." He took a breath and released her. "I figure there's a chance Perez and Reynolds will be there, too. They've been the most exposed of any of us. They were on the ground before we arrived and they've spent the most time outside the palace compound. Ramirez may have learned their identities. It's still fairly common down here for foreign contractors or their family members to be kidnapped and held for ransom. They might be in the same place the rebels are keeping de la Reyes and Fuente."

Because it seemed cruel, she didn't point out the obvious. That they could just as easily be killed as spies if captured. That they might already be dead.

"What good will you be doing anyone if you get caught yourself?" she asked in a shaky voice.

"I won't."

"You can't know that!" Ava stopped, unsure where the fervor in her voice had stemmed from. When she was sure she'd calmed it, she tried again. "At least take a couple of the soldiers. You have a better chance if you're not in there alone."

"I never go into battle with someone I can't trust. Better to go alone than to have to watch my back the entire time."

Her breath seemed strangled in her lungs. She stared at him with futile frustration. He acted as though he were indestructible, but just the opposite was true. He had the bandages on his arms to prove it.

"I have to go." He checked his watch. "If Ramirez is expecting someone to come after them, they'll be easier to evade while it's still dark."

"All right." A numbed sort of acceptance had come over her. "Give me ten minutes to pack. I'm coming with you."

Chapter 10

"You can let me out here," Cael told Vasquez tersely.

"You can let both of us out here."

The look Cael threw Ava was blistering. She pretended not to notice. Opening the door of the jeep, she got out and reached in for her pack, shrugging into it. Then she slipped the rifle strap over her head and straightened.

It had taken longer than the ten minutes she'd promised before she'd been ready to leave the palace. But that was only because Cael had spent half an hour alternating between arguing and pleading with her to see reason. His anger now was just as ineffectual. She wasn't letting him go into this kind of danger alone. He needed someone at his back, even if that someone was suppressing an increasingly strong urge to brain him with one of her boots.

The night was lit by a slice of whitewashed moon pinned low in the sky. The hem of the jungle loomed across the road at the foothills of the mountains, its depths dark and unwelcoming. Its canopy would shut out any illumination from above.

A chill skittered over her skin. Cael had no idea just how little she wanted to enter it with him. Or how determined she was to do just that.

It wouldn't do to examine her reasons too closely. Given his plans for her future once back in the States, she certainly didn't owe him any favors. And if it occurred to her that her problems would be over if he didn't return from the jungle, the thought brought panic, not relief.

So she was going in. She'd deal with the future later.

He was glaring at her now, temper radiating off him in waves.

"I only go on missions with people I trust. You certainly don't qualify."

"Given your attitude, you *shouldn't* trust me. I'm ready to punch you already."

"You can still go back with Vasquez. Supervise the handling of Ramirez's demands."

"You're wasting time." She walked by him, across the lonely strip of deserted gravel road. Ava was fairly certain she could hear him grinding his teeth behind her.

A quick muttered conversation sounded behind her. Then a few moments later he caught up with her. Passed her.

"Stay behind me," he snapped, fixing the goggles over his eyes. "And for chrissakes try to move quietly."

The sound of the jeep driving away gave her a momentary flicker of panic. But in the next minute she squared her shoulders and plunged into the jungle behind him, adjusting her own night-vision goggles.

It was slow going at first. Cael hacked and sawed at strangler vines to clear a path for them. He'd clear a foot and then stop and begin sawing again. She wondered silently how they would ever make time if they had to do this the whole way. But after several yards the ground cleared even as the trees crowded in, effectively closing around them.

The goggles lit the blackness to an eerie green. She concentrated on keeping her footsteps silent and remained as close to Cael as she dared. The sudden screech that sounded above her nearly had her jumping on his back.

"Shit!" She remembered, barely, to whisper.

"Howler monkey." His voice sounded laconically ahead of her. "They can raise a heckuva racket."

For the first time she became aware of the night sounds playing all around them. She could hear the deep croak of frogs, and in the distance a coughing sound she thought would belong to some sort of big cat. A jaguar? Every once in a while there'd come a faint animal scream, as predator vanquished prey.

She hoped they'd escape the same fate.

After they'd been on the move about a half hour Cael abruptly stopped. He slipped off the bag he wore on his back easily, although she guessed it weighed a good forty pounds. Going down on one knee, he opened it and withdrew something, which he handed to her. "I'm going to let you hang on to this. Turn it on, but keep the light pointed downward."

Ava snapped on the heavy mag light and saw him take something from his pocket, smooth it out on the ground before them. She recognized the map Reynolds had brought back of the rebel camp. He spent several minutes studying the coordinates and comparing them with the wrist GPS he wore. Finally he rose, folding the map back up and tucking it away. "We need to start adjusting our path a bit to the west, but we should reach the camp within a few hours."

Without waiting for his directive, she switched off the light and fell in behind him as he started to move again. "It'll be full light by then."

"We'll get as close as we can and remain hidden. Wait for night for a full recon. See what we're dealing with."

Ava waved away a mosquito roughly the size of a Volkswagen. "I can already answer that. Based on Reynolds's estimate, we're going to be dealing with at least a hundred-to-one odds."

"Not necessarily." It seemed curiously intimate to be alone

together in the darkness, conducting a conversation in near whispers. "If Reynolds and Perez are there with de la Reyes and Fuente, it'd be closer to thirty-five to one."

The mention of the woman's name reminded her of something. "About Fuente…I don't think the limo driver was acting alone."

He stopped so suddenly she ran into the back of him. "Will you stop doing that?"

"You have reason to suspect her?"

"I never saw the driver near the house, did you? When would he have had the opportunity to hide weapons in there?"

"Where would she have gotten her hands on weapons?" She barely could make out his head shake as he began moving again. "She's hardly the type."

Ava rolled her eyes. Men could be unbelievably obtuse about women sometimes. "She got her hands on a remote, didn't she? Think about it. If the driver is working for Ramirez, what reason would he have for killing Gonzalez?"

"Maybe Gonzalez failed in whatever Ramirez hired him for. Or maybe he just doesn't like loose ends. He might have believed the man was going to talk since we had him dead to rights on the deposits. And you have to admit." His voice turned bleak. "Triggering his quarters was a hell of a distraction."

"Something about Fuente's reaction didn't ring true," she insisted stubbornly. Aside from her dislike for the woman, there was something there she hadn't trusted from the first. "When the driver had her and the president on the porch she was crying and carrying on. But remember how she acted that first night when the limo was surrounded by armed guards and I had a gun on her? She wasn't scared, she was furious and disdainful. Where was the fury this evening?"

A woman like Marissa Fuente had an air of entitlement that would make it difficult to believe anything bad could befall her or those she cared about. If Ava had to guess which was the woman's real persona, she'd pick the haughty one, not the sobbing, trembling woman who had crawled into the back of the limo seat. "There was no reason to take Fuente along. He had the president. Two hostages are harder to control than one. I think she's in on it."

"And I think you're letting those scratches she left you with color your perception." Ironically, there was a note of humor in his voice. "I don't think she'd have any part of endangering de la Reyes. She seems to be in love with him."

The words were jarring, coming from him. "I never would have pegged you for a romantic."

"Hardly. Any illusions I had about most people's intentions became pretty jaded at an early age."

Her mind returned to the bombshell he'd dropped—was it only yesterday? "By your father?"

Cael's stride seemed to grow longer. His voice more terse. "He's not my father in any way but biological. He wasn't in my life until I was fourteen."

There was that familiar bitterness tingeing his tone. And for once, Ava was determined she'd hear the origin of the antipathy between the two men. "You resented him for not being around when you were growing up?"

He was silent so long she didn't think he'd answer. When he did, his voice was flat. "I resented him for coming back. But not right away. At first I watched how happy my mother was. She'd never married. Had always refused to name my father, too. I have her name. But I knew when I saw them together that she'd never stopped loving him. I worshiped my mother. But she was blind when it comes to Dennis Samuelson."

"How long did he stay this time?"

"Long enough to convince her to take me to the hospital for a tissue match. Seems he had another son. Two years older than me, with the wife he must have been married to even when I was conceived. A real prince, that guy is. John, his son, had liver cancer. His parents weren't matches. He had no other siblings."

But he'd had a half brother. The sick realization filled her. She could already imagine what had brought Samuelson back to the woman and child he'd abandoned. And it hadn't been some long-awaited familial devotion. "He convinced your mother to have you tested."

"He didn't have to. By the time he was done with the whole sad story—a story that glossed right over the details of the wife he'd lied to her about—my mother offered. I didn't really know what to expect but I went along with it. And I was a match."

Something swooped low, almost touching her shoulder, and Ava ducked defensively. Although there were few things she hated as much as bats, her mind was elsewhere. "So he should be grateful to you. The surgery was successful?"

"At first. And I can see now, looking back, that Samuelson was already edging his way out of our lives as John looked like he was recovering. But months later his body rejected the transplant. He died a year after the operation."

"He was in and out of our lives after that. My mother grew increasingly distraught when she wouldn't hear from him for months at a time." His voice was heavy with irony. "Of course he never left contact information. Watch out here."

She nearly missed the shift in conversation. It was at the last second that she ducked beneath the heavy vine he was holding out of the way for her. "What brought him back after that? I mean…"

"After he'd abandoned us once?" Cael was quiet for a moment, wondering why he was bothering to tell her all this. It was ancient history. Belaboring it had never solved anything. "I suppose for a short time he entertained notions of molding his remaining son into a copy of himself. That didn't happen." He'd been a smart-ass kid with a mile wide chip on his shoulder toward the man who consistently wreaked havoc in their lives. The more Samuelson pushed, the more Cael had resisted. And it wasn't long before they discovered that they hated each other's guts.

"He left for good the summer I graduated. I was determined to join the navy. He was just as determined to pull strings and get me into West Point. My mother sided with him. But I was eighteen and didn't need parental permission. I left anyway. He never went back to my mother after that." And Cael would always blame the man for his mother's eventual suicide. The familiar bitterness lodged in his throat, threatening to choke him.

He cleared his throat. "He resurfaced several times over the years, mostly to throw a wrench into whatever plans I had going on." He'd damn near kept Cael out of the SEALs. Would have, if his commanding officer hadn't shared Cael's disdain for bureaucratic bullshit. "He was actually pretty high in military intelligence at the time. When he decided to tamper, he could usually get results."

The man had managed, over the years, to get Cael assigned to more than his share of high-risk missions. He wasn't sure what he'd been hoping for, that he'd screw up or get himself killed. But he'd never minded in one sense. That was why he'd become a SEAL. And he'd gotten experience fast, built a reputation for being a solid soldier more swiftly than most. Cael figured his survival was the best way to get back at the old man.

"He contacted me once more, after I didn't reenlist last time. Tried to get me to dish dirt on the military commanders I'd had. Missions I'd been involved in that hadn't gone according to plan. I told him to go…" He amended the sentence in the last possible moment. "To forget it. He offered to get me a job working military intelligence reporting to him. I turned him down flat. Told him I was going to start my own company."

"When did he join DHS?"

"Almost at its inception. And believe me, his position gives him plenty of opportunity to make trouble. We've seen his hand in more than a couple of deadly turns an assignment has taken. He wouldn't mind seeing me dead. But barring that, he wants to see me ruined or in prison. The way he sees it, the wrong son died. He won't be happy until he's erased a part of his past that he doesn't care to remember." Their voices were low and wouldn't travel far. But he never stopped assessing the jungle around them.

Their surroundings offered ample hiding places, but he didn't expect to see rebel guards posted this far out. Not until they got closer to the camp would there be a need for an outer perimeter.

They walked for a couple more hours, mostly in silence, stopping only to check the map and coordinates. He hadn't meant to tell her the whole pathetic story of how Samuelson had screwed over his family. But maybe now she'd recognize the man for what he was. Realize that returning to the States carried its own kind of danger. One he still hadn't figured a way for her to avoid if she continued to refuse the one plan he did have.

And there was no use asking if she'd changed her mind about that. If there was one thing he'd learned about the woman, it was that she was immovable once she'd made a decision.

"Let's take a water break." He drank from his water bottle and figured she was digging in her pack for hers. But instead she pulled out a small bottle and started spraying the contents on her hands. Rubbing them on her face and neck.

"What are you doing?"

"Reapplying bug repellent."

He nodded. His own hadn't provided as much protection as he'd hoped against the mosquitoes and flies they'd encountered. "Mud's probably the best protection. We can scoop up handfuls of it and rub it on any exposed area. Not too appealing, but it works."

"I prefer my repellent. I haven't been bitten yet."

That stopped him in midswallow. "You haven't been bitten?"

"Nope."

"Gimme that."

She handed over the bottle and he brought it to his nose, sniffed suspiciously. "What is this? It smells all girly."

"It may have escaped your attention," she drawled, "but I am female."

"Believe me, that has never escaped my attention." There were many times over the last several days when he would have given anything to forget it. He sniffed again, wrestled briefly between the two choices, shrugged. What the hell? It would wear off. He spread a liberal amount on himself before handing it back to her. "Give me the flashlight, would you?"

When she did so, he switched it on aiming the beam at the map he'd spread out on the jungle floor. "It's nearly dawn."

"What?"

He heard the surprise in Ava's voice. The secondary canopy of the trees would block out any light that managed to filter through, at least until full day. "It's four-thirty. And by my estimates we're only an hour away from the camp. We'll need to be more careful from here on in. No talking. I'm guessing they'll have guards posted on the outer perimeter maybe as far as an hour from the camp." If the president was being held there, more precautions would be taken than normal. "We need to do a recon before we go any further."

"And exactly what does that entail?"

He grinned at the suspicion in her tone. "How are you at climbing trees?"

She was silent behind him for a moment. Then, "As long as it's free of howler monkeys, I can manage."

He didn't tell her the monkeys were the least of her worries. It was the snakes and slug rats she'd need to watch out for.

"You'll get a visual from above. Once we're in sight of the camp I'll get closer on the ground. We'll use the whisper mics to communicate. We need to get a visual of the layout and more importantly, location of all posted guards and their scheduled rotation. Get a count of the hostages and the soldiers."

A thought then had him cursing. "I only brought one pair of field glasses."

"I packed a pair."

A measure of respect tangled with pride filtered through. Of course. She'd probably packed as carefully as he had.

He checked the trees carefully, continuing on until he found one that would work. It had to be large enough that it towered above the secondary canopy, or she wouldn't be able to see anything anyway. One with stout vines would be best, so she could walk her way up the side of the trunk to the limbs.

"I'll hold your rifle."

She slipped the strap off her neck and handed it to him while donning the binoculars she'd taken out of the pack she left at the bottom of the tree.

Cael laid the rifle against a nearby tree and grabbed a vine, yanked on it testingly. "It should hold your weight. But take this with you." He handed her the sheath containing the large bladed knife he'd been using to clear their path when they'd started that night.

Ava looked at him and then at him. Her eyes narrowed suspiciously. "What do I need that for?"

"It's just a precaution in case you disturb someone's home."

"Why do I have a feeling there's something you're not telling me?" she muttered. But she buckled the knife belt around her waist.

"You might see a toucan. Or a macaw."

"Uh-huh. What else lives in these trees? No, don't tell me." She took the vine from him and placed both booted feet against the huge trunk, leaning her weight back to keep the vine taut. Then, with an athletic grace that had him blinking in astonishment, she scrambled up the side and disappeared into the low-hanging branches.

He waited for what seemed an interminable amount of time, but was probably no more than ten minutes. While he waited, he consulted the map again. Then her voice sounded in his mic. "I've got a good view but I don't see the camp. I'm coming down." A few moments later he heard a rustling sound and something came whizzing down at him, in two pieces.

Cael ducked out of the way and the things thudded to the ground. Bending closer to check it out, he grimaced distastefully and moved away. At least the woman knew what to do when she encountered a slug rat.

A couple of minutes later he could see her making her way carefully down the tree again. Her long, slender legs encased in the dark fatigues were scrabbling for purchase as she slowly lowered herself to a branch that would support her weight.

Cael found a stout vine and walked it around the trunk until it was within arm's reach of her. Then Ava grasped it and descended the trunk, as easily as she'd walked up it.

The look in her eye when she stalked toward him was lethal. "I have a little bone to pick with you, McCabe."

"Ah…" If he smiled he'd be as dead as the slug rat. "I guess you didn't see a toucan."

She gave him a shove. "Next time you do the visual from the air and I'll take my chances with the guards."

He did grin then, earning himself another push. "You're lighter. Better chance of the branches holding your weight. And I'll admit it, I'm more practiced on the ground."

He handed her weapon back to her, noted that she didn't offer to return the knife.

"Just remember, I owe you one."

Cael continued onward. He was certain that before this mission was over, she'd find a way to repay him. In spades.

Fifteen minutes later they repeated the process, minus the dead slug rat. And fifteen minutes after that, Ava shimmied up another tree, with a noticeable lack of enthusiasm, while Cael worried beneath it. They had to be getting close. If she wasn't getting a view, maybe he should…

"I can see it from here."

His attention jerked to the sound of her voice in his mic. "How far?"

"Couple miles. They just cut down newer vegetation to make a good-sized clearing. Blends right in."

It took effort to keep his voice even as he asked, "Do you see the hostages?"

There was silence for a minute. Two. Then Ava's voice sounded again. "I don't see live hostages. Cael, I don't see anyone. I think the camp has been abandoned."

Chapter 11

Ava remained silent as they walked through the makeshift camp. Cael's expression was grim. The rebels hadn't moved hastily. There was nothing left behind but trash. No food supplies. No weapons.

Just flies buzzing over four bodies.

She'd held her breath while he turned each of them over. Felt vaguely guilty at the relief she felt each time she didn't recognize a victim. They'd been hostages at one time, that was clear. Each was still bound. And riddled with bullet holes.

Sickened, she turned away. She couldn't allow herself to wonder if the same fate awaited the newest hostages.

The makeshift buildings were constructed of the saplings and trees they'd cut down. But there were other structures consisting of similar young trees sharpened into points and pounded into the ground. She knew without asking that the structures had served as cells.

"They've been gone a couple days, I'd guess."

She looked at Cael askance. "How can you possibly know when they left?"

"Without getting too graphic, I checked the decomposition on the bodies." He shrugged, his gaze sweeping the area. "Good news is if they are holding the hostages, they probably aren't located that far away. No more than a few hours, anyway. Probably sent a team ahead to prepare a new camp and moved out when it was ready."

"And we're going to follow them." He didn't have to say the words. Ava was beginning to know the man very well indeed.

"Shouldn't be too hard. A hundred or more people moving through a jungle are going to leave a trail. And they moved out recently enough that the vegetation won't have hidden the path they took yet."

Ava was amazed, however, at just how faint the trail appeared in spots. It had been easy enough to see which direction the camp occupants had followed. But there were places where they had to stop so Cael could search for traces of the faint trail. She imagined the shadowy confines of the jungle would swallow up their own path in mere days. The lush vegetation sprawled everywhere. It was humans who were the trespassers here.

The sun slanted in wherever it could pierce the double canopy above them. But that didn't affect the humidity. By midmorning Ava had sweat through her clothes and had a constant stream of perspiration running down her neck. The backpack seemed to grow heavier with each step she took.

She was in good shape. The department's annual fitness test was never a problem. But hiking through a jungle in a tropical climate tested her in ways the department obstacle course didn't begin to. The heat turned the jungle into a steamy sauna, and it was sapping more energy by the second.

They stopped every half hour to find a tree and see if she could get a visual of the new camp. Each time she scrambled down to report in the negative. To her relief, she didn't encounter another of the disgusting creatures she'd killed this morning, but did disturb a gibbon once, which gave an ear-splitting scree·:h before it swung to a nearby tree and continued its tirade from there.

She also learned more than she'd ever wanted about the slime mold that grew up some tree trunks. Distaste filled her at the memory of her earlier encounter with it.

Wiping her dripping forehead on the long sleeve of the shirt she wore, she slanted a look at Cael. He seemed tireless. His unshaven jaw was bristled with whiskers a couple of shades darker than the hair on his head. He had a black bandana wrapped around his forehead keeping his hair out of his eyes. And his clothes were as soaked as hers were.

Mutinously, she stopped, glaring at his back. "You might be powered by Everready batteries, but some of us need an occasional break, Attila."

He looked back over his shoulder, his expression impatient. A moment later there was a visible thawing in it and he turned to head swiftly back to her. "You're right. We need fuel and we have to stay hydrated." Rejoining her, he slipped out of his pack and set it down. She did the same, restraining a moan of relief when she got rid of its weight.

She cut a couple of ferns and laid them down on the ground before collapsing on them with little grace. "Last time I got a visual I could hear water nearby." Just the sound had uncorked a yearning to find it and submerge herself in it. Her last shower was a distant memory. It helped to imagine that any body of water would be as suspect as some of the other things she'd encountered in the jungle.

"Must be a creek or small falls nearby." He was checking the coordinates again, his head down. "Might be a good place to hide out later, if the camp isn't too much further."

She swallowed. Once they found the camp, they'd need to do surveillance before retiring to make a rescue plan.

Ava didn't even want to think of what the odds were of them

succeeding. Instead she pulled her pack toward her, unzipped it and started rummaging around in it. "Want a sandwich?"

"When did you have time to make those?" He took the food readily enough, though, unwrapping it to bite into the thick ham between toasted buns.

"I didn't. I called down to the kitchen while I was packing and had them prepare some and send them up." She took a bite of her own sandwich and washed it down with a large gulp of water. The heat sapped the liquid from her body almost as soon as she drank each time. But at least that meant she didn't have to stop and pee very frequently, for which she was decidedly grateful.

"Beats the field rations I brought," he agreed, devouring the sandwich in a few bites.

"Why would you bring…" She stopped midsentence, and watched a brilliant blue butterfly the size of her fist flutter in back of his shoulder into the thick vegetation. It was like being in a different world, she reflected. And certainly it was as far removed from her experience as it was possible to be.

"Habit. Never occurred to me to raid the kitchen." He took a long pull from his water bottle. "But they don't take up much space, and after your food is gone you'll be happy enough to have them."

She'd brought a dozen sandwiches. Ava was sincerely hoping they'd be safely back at the palace before their provisions gave out. But since their safe return seemed rather dicey at the moment, she said nothing.

Their long dark clothing made it seem hotter than it was. But, as Cael had explained hours ago, it was a mistake to bare any more skin than necessary in the jungle. And so far Ava was inclined to agree. She'd reapplied repellent several more times, but mosquitoes and other stinging insects still swarmed and lighted, even if she had managed to avoid being devoured so far.

"As long as we're stopped we may as well change your bandages."

He shook his head. "They're fine."

"They need to be changed daily and be kept dry. Given the state of our clothing, they're probably soaked." From her pack she took out a plastic bag filled with the medical supplies the doctor had left behind for him.

He stared at her, arrested. "What all do you have in that pack?"

"I'm sure the contents are much more innocent than what you're carrying," she said dryly. She looked up from her preparations quizzically. "You'll need to lose the shirt."

His eyes remained fixed on hers, heated. Silently he started working buttons through buttonholes. An answering warmth suffused her, one that owed nothing to the humidity.

There was nothing remotely sexy about their situation. Or her request. But that didn't stop her pulse from churning to a faster pace with every button he released. It didn't stop her throat from drying, despite the drink she'd just taken. And it didn't prevent her imagination from painting this as a strip-tease, rather than just as a matter of first aid.

The shirt was completely undone now and he was working on the cuffs. Because it seemed safer, Ava busied herself tearing open the packages of gauze pads, being careful not to expose any portion of them to possible contaminants.

He squatted down next to her, one bare arm held out. "Okay, Doc. Do your worst."

She rose to her knees, moved a bit to take advantage of the slight light nearby where it was slanting through the dense foliage overhead. She'd been right; the bandage was sweat soaked. Loosening the adhesive, she peeled it away, stifling a gasp of pity. The burn was pink and angry looking, still oozing at the edges. She coated the fresh gauze with the medicated ointment and reapplied a fresh bandage. Then she repeated the action for each of his wounds, taking great care to keep her touch gentle.

"I suppose I don't need to ask whether you took any of the pain medication the doctor left you."

He was inspecting her work closely. "Can't afford to. I need to keep my head clear."

"Last time I checked, pain wasn't exactly the best thing for clarity of thinking." When she'd been shot, it had been a toss-up whether she got fuzzier from the prescription pain pills or the agony of the injury itself. But she wasn't going to nag him. She'd stopped the medicine within a couple of days, choosing to suffer the twinges and aches rather than cope with the drowsiness and nausea.

She placed the sterile first-aid supplies back in the Ziploc bag and put it away. Then she dug for a plastic trash bag she had folded up in her pack and withdrew it to shove the wrappers and used bandages in.

He was watching her with a slight smile on his face. "You believe in being prepared."

"Don't you?" Their gazes locked and the smile slowly vanished from his lips.

"Usually." He shifted a little and the width of his shoulders blocked out that single ray of light. "But I gotta admit, I wasn't prepared for you."

Her gaze searched his. There could be several meanings hidden in those words. But what she saw on his face decided the question for her.

Desire.

The recognition had her thoughts splintering. Because she had a strong sense of self-preservation, inner alarms were shrilling like a three-bell fire. There was no basis for a relationship here. She still recalled exactly what the man was capable of.

But thoughts of the future, of what awaited her in the States seemed far away now. Everything around her was so foreign it was difficult to get her bearings. Difficult to concentrate on anything outside this moment.

His shirt was still crumpled in one hand. He wore a

ribbed black tank undershirt that clung to his powerful torso and left most of his shoulders and his arms bare. She'd traced the muscles roped there. Kneaded the well-developed pecs. Felt the length and breadth of him stretched on out on top of her, limb to limb, muscle and sinew against curves.

The jungle seemed to fade away. The danger that they should be focused on intermingled with danger of a far different type. And it beckoned with a wild siren call that was the ultimate temptation.

Ava didn't consider herself a risk taker. But she was teetering on the brink now of a perilous choice. One she'd have trouble forgiving herself for later.

Drawing in a breath, she sat back on her haunches, busying herself tucking things back into her backpack. She could feel him watching her, sensed the control he was trying to exert over his own emotions. "Are we still being smart?"

Her lungs felt strangled. "We have to be."

He muttered an oath she pretended not to hear and then rose. Pulling his shirt back on, he buttoned it before going to his own bag and swiftly replacing things inside. "Bad timing. But this isn't over, Ava." The look he gave her was a searing promise.

Shaken, she stood, slipped her arms back into her pack. Retrieved her rifle. He was right about one thing. This wasn't the time to be distracted by the chemistry that flickered to life whenever they were together.

But she wasn't taking him up on his promise, either. A shudder of disappointment shook her. Despite the fact that they were on the same side for the moment, she hoped she had just enough self-respect left to refrain from sleeping with the man who'd threatened to destroy her.

"I see it."

Adrenaline spiked through him as Ava's quiet voice sounded in the whisper mic.

"How far?"

"Another hour-and-a-half trek, I'd guess."

Thunder rumbled overhead. Any stray rays of light that had been piercing the jungle canopy were gone. With a feeling of resignation, he figured they were lucky they hadn't been rained on before. This far into the mountains, there was bound to be heavy precipitation daily.

"I see four cells."

Hope flickered. That would account for Perez, Reynolds, de la Reyes and Fuente. Maybe they were all alive. But they'd have to be prepared for the possibility that at least one of them would be too badly injured to make it to safety.

Unless he arranged one hell of a diversion for the rebels.

"I've got a visual of Fuente." Ava's voice sounded strained. "No one else I recognize. I'm coming down."

By the time she was on the ground again, Cael had a sheet of paper unrolled from his pack and a marker in his hand. "Draw it out for me."

Ava crouched down beside him, but not, he noted, before checking the ground carefully for anything that crawled or slithered. Taking the marker from him, she began drawing a diagram. "The cells are at the back of the camp, situated similarly to the last location they deserted. Smaller buildings are up and dotted around the area." She drew them in. "A main structure is being constructed in the center. Really, by the time they're done, the whole setup will be a carbon copy of the one they vacated." She made some *X*s around the drawing. "These indicate where I saw guards patrolling."

Cael studied the drawing intently. Six guards for an inner perimeter. Six for outer. They were taking no chances with a high-profile prisoner like the president.

She was looking at him, something in her expression warning him.

"What?"

"I couldn't see who was in the cells. But I could see who *wasn't* in them."

When he frowned, she went on, "Cael, Marissa Fuente was out walking around, chatting with rebel soldiers. She's certainly not wearing the dress she was 'kidnapped' in. And she's looking remarkably at home."

"She was in on it," he said, stunned.

There was no reflection of his surprise in her grim expression. "Bitch. I should have hurt her when I took her down that first night."

Ava had suspected the woman had a hand in it, he recalled. But he was more than a little bemused. Fuente's talents were wasted on the runway. She should have been in Hollywood.

He said as much and Ava snorted. "Men. Big boobs strike you all blind. She played us. Well, she played de la Reyes longer," she amended. "But now we know what really had her cutting her trip short."

"So was she working for Ramirez all along or did he get to her after the assassination attempt failed?" he wondered aloud.

She lifted a shoulder. "Does it matter? She's in this up to her scrawny neck."

He pursed his lips, considering. "Then who's in the fourth cell?" They looked at each other, silent for a moment. As mobile as the camps were, the rebels weren't going to waste time constructing something that wasn't immediately needed. "Maybe she was locked up but, uh…traded some favors for better treatment."

Grimacing, Ava looked back at the map. "Either way, we can't trust her not to sound the alarm when we're getting the others out."

He nodded. The one positive thing was that they could be fairly certain de la Reyes was there if Fuente was.

He tried not to worry about his operatives. If they weren't there, he had another search-and-rescue mission ahead of him. Because he wasn't leaving the country with two of his men unaccounted for.

"It'd be best if you stayed here while I go on ahead to recon." With a sinking feeling, he correctly interpreted the flinty glare she fixed him with. "I need to assess the security and this is outside your area of expertise. It makes sense—"

"It makes sense for you to have someone covering your back when you're entering enemy territory."

He eyed her unblinkingly. "You didn't sign on for this. Think I don't realize that? You're in uncharted waters and I can guarantee you things will deviate from the best plan we come up with. And I have to react to those deviations. It would be best if you could disavow all knowledge of such actions."

Cael expected her temper. He expected an argument. He wasn't prepared for the flash of hurt that flickered across her expression. "Because you think I'll give the information to Samuelson. Help him twist things to hang you." She rose in a lithe, boneless move he couldn't have imitated if he tried. She tried for a careless shrug. Didn't quite pull it off. "You're wise to be cautious, I suppose, given your history."

He felt exceedingly dim-witted. His mind was grappling to connect that flicker of pain he'd seen in her expression with the matter-of-fact tone he heard now. The one that rang false on about a dozen different levels.

"Wait a minute." She strode rapidly ahead of him, just as he felt the first splat of rain on his head. "Dammit, Ava, wait, would you?" He caught up with her as just as the sky opened up in earnest, a torrential downpour that was only minimally blocked by the canopy overhead.

Grabbing her elbow, he halted her, turning her to face him. "You're way off base here."

"Am I?" She gave him a tight smile, yanked at her elbow. He refused to release her. "You told me the same thing last night, remember? You didn't want me along because you couldn't trust me. Not like it's the first time I've heard it."

The temper inside him ignited like a lit fuse. But it wasn't directed at her but himself. "Dammit, will you listen? I don't want any of this touching you! I'm not going to give Samuelson ammunition to be used against you in this. I'm having a hard enough time figuring out a way to keep him away from you once you're back in the States."

"I'd be a fool to believe you."

"Yeah? Well, the joke's on me, sweetheart." The fury was churning in him now. "Because I'm the one who's been the fool all along. I've made excuses for you since the beginning, do you know that? And now when I have Samuelson in my sights, instead of planning for the killing strike, all I can worry about is how to keep you safe from him. I can't afford the luxury of worrying about you. The man's a threat as long as he's in a position of power."

She met him glare for glare, temper for temper. Their argument was none the less fervent for being conducted in near whispers. "Luxury? Who asked for your concern? Not me. I've been taking care of myself since I was fifteen years old. Before that. Forget any plans as they pertain to me. I don't need your protection. Not here. Not when I get back home."

"Don't you think I'd like to forget it?" he said bitterly. "It'd be a helluva lot easier if I could do what's the smartest without considering how it affects you. But I can't." She was staring at him now, the rain pouring over her, forming rivulets to trace down her exquisite features. Frustration pumped through him. "This is a whole new way for me to think, and believe me, I'd give anything to be able to switch it off."

Abruptly he let go of her, and brushed by her to take the lead, almost welcoming the downpour of rain in his face as he strode in the direction of the camp she'd spotted.

Forget about her. He swiped the moisture off his face and plunged ahead. Damned if he didn't wish he could.

* * *

The rain stopped as quickly as it had begun, the clouds parting for the sun to turn the jungle into a vat of steam. The back of Ava's calves ached with exertion. The precipitation had turned the ground into slippery oozy mud. Every step she took the mud seemed to suck at her boot, vacuuming it back to the earth. By the time they'd walked a half mile, the muscles in her legs were trembling like leaves in a windstorm. It was getting more and more difficult even to reach out to hold a large fern or vine out of the way to duck under it.

The bone-deep exhaustion she felt was almost a relief. It made it almost impossible to think about the revelation Cael had made earlier.

Almost.

Her mind skittered uneasily away from his declaration, before creeping up to it again, afraid to examine his meaning too closely. Temper had stripped them both of subterfuge, that was clear. But she still had a difficult time believing concern for her was was the source of his frustration.

She couldn't recall the last time anyone had been worried about her.

When she was growing up, she'd quickly learned that her father had no patience for emotion, so injuries were downplayed. Tears were swallowed. And Danny had always been less focused on the dangers of her job than with the choices she had to make on it, especially as a sniper.

This…this was personal. And she didn't quite know how to deal with it.

Her mental meanderings were halted when Cael threw an arm out to stop her. He had a finger raised to his lips and she understood. They were close to the outer perimeter. Obviously he wasn't leaving anything to chance. He pointed at her, at a tree several yards away and made a crouching movement. He wanted her out of sight. She waited until he finished his signals, understanding that he was going to try to get closer for surveillance.

He got down on his hands and knees and scooped up mud to cover his bare skin. Ava melted back into the trees, choosing a different one to scale than the one he'd indicated. She tucked her rifle into some nearby vegetation. Halfway up the tree she came face-to-face with a revolting spider that was twice as big as her hand.

Fear was a powerful impetus. She fairly flew the rest of the way up. When she got close enough to the top that she could get a view, she rested for a moment, her whole body shaking with distaste and exertion. Then she reached for the binoculars and began scanning.

She was close enough to see the men in the cells, since the structures had no roofs, leaving the prisoners at the mercy of the elements. And all four cells were occupied. She recognized de la Reyes in one. Reynolds in another. She couldn't make out the faces of the other two.

What she could see had her breath strangling in her throat. Cael was inching toward the camp clearing, on his elbows and knees.

And twenty yards from him, a San Baltes rebel soldier stood, rifle raised, pointed right at Cael's head.

Chapter 12

Ava's throat closed. "Rifle twenty yards to your right," she said into the mic, voice strangled.

Even as she spoke the words, he was a blur of motion. She lost sight of him for an instant or two as he rolled, then came to his feet a few feet from the soldier. Everything slowed to still frames. The rifle barrel swinging to follow him. Cael's arm pulling back. Then shooting forward. A blade she hadn't even seen him holding whirling through the air, striking the soldier. Burying to the hilt itself in his heart.

As she watched, the soldier swayed, began to crumple. Cael caught him before he hit the ground, then dragged him deeper into the jungle. He came out alone a moment later. Commenced his recon as if nothing had happened.

Ava didn't recover nearly so quickly. Reaction set in, a giant shudder working over her body. Dropping the glasses for a moment, she just rested her forehead against the limb and waited for the shaking to stop.

He could have been killed. The body amid the fronds and ferns could have been his. It was going to take a while to recover from that knowledge. And the response it was wreaking in her system.

But then, shoulders squaring, she took up position again. Because there was only so much surveillance that could be accomplished on the ground. Aerial intel was her specialty.

And it just might be the only thing that would save Cael from the next soldier who happened by.

She scanned the area carefully, pausing on the scene taking place in the middle of the compound. The man standing in the center seemed to be shouting at two of his soldiers. Frowning, she adjusted her glasses to get a closer look. The two men seemed to be protesting or explaining something. In the next moment the man in charge pulled out a handgun.

The sound of the shots could be heard faintly in the distance. First one body crumpled. Then another. The officer—because clearly this person appeared in charge of the rebels—gestured to another couple of soldiers, who moved rapidly to do his bidding.

Ava held her breath. Because this time the soldiers were heading toward the cells.

She looked for Cael. Had difficulty finding him. If she hadn't been searching for him she never would have spotted him wearing that lightweight gillie suit. As if was, after straining for several moments she spotted him a hundred meters to the right of where he'd encountered the first soldier.

"Guard at left, twenty meters," she breathed into the whisper mic. She figured he saw him. But why he was maintaining that proximity rather than doing recon from farther out she couldn't guess. But she was beginning to believe the man did everything the hard way.

She switched her attention back on the events in the camp. One of the prisoners had been dragged across the compound and was on his knees in front of the officer, who was beating him with the butt of a rifle.

De la Reyes.

Ava released the glasses and picked up her rifle. Sighted. Nerves clutched in her stomach. Because there was no commander making the decisions from a nearby command post. No one issuing the weapons tight or weapons loose command. She didn't dare another communication to Cael as close as he was to that soldier. She'd have to make the split-second decision herself.

But what would be the right decision to make? Saving de la Reyes by shooting the officer would alert the camp and endanger the other prisoners, making a rescue attempt likely unsuccessful.

In the end, it was a decision she wasn't faced with. At least not yet. After beating the president unmercifully, the officer kicked hard at his prone body and had him dragged back to his cell. Ava's throat was tight. De la Reyes appeared unconscious. But he was still alive. And for now, that was going to have to do.

Her muscles were tight with tension. She slid the safety back on her rifle and exchanged it for the high-powered glasses again. Fuente wasn't anywhere in sight. And no matter how hard she scanned the proximity, she couldn't pick up Cael's location. She assumed he'd be making a huge circle well outside the outer perimeter of the compound. And because of the risk of detection, his progress would be slow.

Ava settled herself more comfortably in the notch of the tree and prepared to wait.

"Reynolds was right," Cael reported tersely as they made their way swiftly away from the camp several hours later. "Any infusion of cash they've received from Ramirez has gone into weaponry. For a ragtag bunch of rebels they're packing state-of-the-art rifles. No reason not to believe they've got even more gadgets stored in their artillery shed."

"That must be the structure on the front left of the camp," Ava said. She was moving like an automatom. She'd long since passed the point of simple exhaustion. Her entire body ached from perching in that tree for so long. Her pack seemed to have taken on an additional twenty pounds. And now her boots each seemed to weigh a ton as she slogged through the slick mud of the jungle floor. "I saw a soldier go into it and exchange a rifle for the officer or captain or whoever is in charge." She hesitated a moment over the memory. It had been after the man had violently beaten de la Reyes.

"That's what I figure, too. That's par for the course with an outfit like this. They'll spend the money on weaponry, but they aren't going to use it to update their countersurveillance methods. They're more concerned with keeping the prisoners in than with keeping people out. And that's good news for us."

"I spotted at least three trip wires." She hadn't asked where they were headed. She hoped, *prayed,* it was back to a spot where they could summon the military and then rest safely waiting for reinforcements.

He turned and cocked a brow at her. "Good eyes," he murmured. The admiration in his tone had warmth flickering, proving that everything inside her wasn't numb. The involuntary response made her impatient with herself. Because of him she'd had to learn to pee in a tree. That wasn't a skill she'd ever wanted or needed to acquire before now.

"Actually I found a total of six, all of which I dismantled, and about a dozen booby traps. Strictly low tech. Sentries posted at each of the cells. A half dozen others staggered around the perimeter. Makes it a challenging extraction, but not impossible."

"I spotted de la Reyes being beaten," she said. The image flickered across her mind again, but she firmly pushed it away. It was dangerous to have a connection to one of the parties inside. Made it difficult to maintain the objectivity needed to make sound decisions. "He's not in very good shape."

"I saw it, too." His voice was grim. "Figured maybe those two soldiers that got shot had been posted sentry at his cell. Their infraction might have been minor. Absolute obedience is demanded in these types of camps. Maybe they were heard talking to de la Reyes. Maybe they accepted something from him. Hard to say."

Whatever they'd done had cost them their lives. And had earned the president a serious beating.

Cael stopped to readjust the weight of the pack he was carrying before forging ahead again. "They're savages. Remember that. The rules are different here. The only laws governing these people are those imposed by their leader, who sells their services to the highest bidder. Right now it happens to be Ramirez. But when the past president was in power, this same group made it a habit to kidnap and ransom family members of government officials, often women and children. Fewer than forty percent were returned alive."

A small lizard skittered over the toe of Ava's boot. It was a measure of her exhaustion that she gave it only a glance before kicking it aside with her other foot.

"The soldiers probably won't have had any special training, but you can bet their commander has been trained by PSB Chinese Intel or former SpetzNatz. He'll be one to be careful of. Take him out of the equation and we'll have neutralized the brains of the outfit."

"What happens when the guards' shift changes and the soldier you took out is missed?"

"The shift already changed," he reminded her. "I figure they're rotating on three shifts of eight hours. I'd feel better if I could be sure, though. But unless someone stumbles over his body we'll be okay. Desertion is a constant problem with these groups. The life is hard. They'll likely chalk up his disappearance to that."

But her attention had splintered. She recognized the place they were heading toward. She'd longed to stop there only hours earlier. "Water," she breathed reverently. She could hear it again, the sound of a creek running fast nearby. The thought of cupping her hands in it, dribbling it over her face beckoned like a mirage in a desert.

"Yeah. We need rest. And food. And I have to communicate with Quintero about military intervention."

The rest sounded inviting. So did the thought of food. But nothing could compare with the lure of the water itself. Ava could barely contain herself while they climbed up increasingly steep inclines, which made the muscles in her calves weep. She had a focus now. Something to push through the tiredness for.

But fifteen minutes later when she caught her first sight of the water, she stood, transfixed. She'd hoped for a small stream. Perhaps even deep enough to bathe in. But she'd never expected the beauty she was faced with now.

The water tumbled over a rocky wall perhaps ten feet overhead and pooled between twin towering boulders before continuing in a stream that grew increasing narrow as it continued to the east. Stray rays of sunlight sent rainbows dancing across it as it cascaded into a narrow pool.

"Please tell me there are no piranhas or snakes or anything else creepy to worry about in there."

"Probably not deep enough for piranhas." It didn't escape her that he hadn't addressed the rest of her concern. "But just to be on the safe side, you should probably content yourself with a shower rather than a bath."

She paused impatiently as he stopped and examined the area with his set of high-powered binoculars for five minutes. Ten. Fifteen. Finally, when she was ready to give him a push back down the steep slope they'd climbed, he moved forward. "It looks clear. No reason for the rebels to come this far east for water. They had a lagoon several yards to the south of the camp."

She pushed him to the side and took the lead, stumbling over the roots and rocks that thrust across the jungle floor.

"Okay, you're filthy, I know that. But I'm still calling dibs on the first shower." Fairness went by the wayside after tromping through a tropical jungle for hours. She rationalized that he was probably used to it, so the mud he'd slathered on his body could wait another fifteen minutes to be cleaned off. Or twenty. "I promise not to use up all the hot water."

Ava reached a hand forward and caught a drizzle from the falls in her palm, nearly swooning with delight. She took off the glasses still hanging from a strap around her neck. Shrugged out of the strap holding her rifle, and carefully set it nearby on a pile of stones. Then gracelessly, she let her pack slide off her back and unzipped it, digging around in it for the fresh set of clothes she'd brought.

"The most important thing to remember is fresh socks. Dry your feet thoroughly before putting them on," Cael cautioned. He'd stopped, too, letting his pack slide to the ground, although he retained his rifle. "Check your boots before dressing again in case an unwelcome guest takes up residency in one."

But even as she was stripping off her long-sleeve shirt, enjoying the air on her shoulders, left bare by the stretch camisole, a little sliver of guilt was niggling through her. "On second thought, why don't you go first?"

He looked up, surprised. "First time a woman's ever suggested I use the bathroom first."

And the fact that he'd obviously had plenty of experience in that department almost made her reconsider her offer. "I'll use extra Ziploc bags to cover your wounds. Then we'll need to change the bandages again."

Cael looked amused. "I don't need a nurse. But I appreciate the thought."

He should appreciate it. He had no idea what the offer had cost her. "C'mon. The sooner you get in, the quicker it will be my turn."

Ignoring his continued protests, she stooped to retrieve the first-aid bag she'd brought. It took a bit longer to find the spare plastic bags she'd tucked away amid the food and equipment. One thing her experience camping had taught her was that Ziplocs and rubber bands came in handy at least as often as any other piece of regular camping gear.

Her fingers closed around the plastic and she withdrew what she needed. Then she rose, with the spare plastic bags and tape, and turned to Cael.

Her breath abruptly strangled in her lungs.

He was stripping off the gillie suit, carefully rolling the pieces up and inserting them in his pack. For someone supposedly reluctant to go first, he wasn't wasting a lot of time demurring. His undershirt went next and his chest looked as rock hewn as the boulders near the water. She remembered in intimate detail what it felt like under her fingertips.

Her earlier exhaustion drained away. Nerve endings felt unbearably alive and alert. She became aware of the constant background noise. The gurgling of the water. The chittering of the insects. The squawk of the colorful birds. The jibbering screech of the gibbons and monkeys.

The scene was primitive. Elemental. They were the foreigners in this environment. The jungle life would continue unmarred when they were gone, as if they'd never been here at all. It was dangerously tempting to think anything that happened here occurred without the promise of consequences and regrets.

"Ready?" He was holding out his arms for her to cover the bandages. No wonder he hadn't protested too loudly at the thought of going first. Mud was still caked on his face, neck and hands. The suit had to have acted like a internal oven, elevating his body temperature to unbearable degrees.

Ava swiftly wrapped the plastic bags over the bandages over his arms, securing them in several places with rubber bands.

"I'm not fussy," he said meaningfully, looking at her with an expression she didn't trust. "There's plenty of water for two showering at a time."

Under no circumstances was she going to let him know that she'd noticed that herself. "Maybe *I'm* fussy," she said tartly. And obviously too easily tempted. She ducked around him and grabbed her weapon, strode several yards in the opposite direction, taking great care to keep her gaze from returning to him.

But in the absence of the visual image, her other senses seemed unbearably heightened. She could hear the heavy thud of his boots dropping to the soft ground. The scrape of his zipper sounded, and she knew he was stripping off his pants. Several moments passed before she heard a different pattern of the water hitting the heavy stones. And she knew he was stepping onto the rocks. That he was now standing nude and powerful below the spray.

Ava gritted her teeth, willed her concentration off the man a few yards away and on to any foreign sounds that didn't belong there. But it was difficult to keep her eyes moving over the terrain, yet skirting the one area they most wanted to stray.

She'd done harder things, hadn't she? Held position on assignment for hours while the negotiators tried to talk a hostage taker out. Done overnight surveillance in beat-up cars in front of the apartment of whatever drug dealer they happened to be tailing. Boredom was the enemy on those assignments. Keeping senses sharp for that split second when everything could change.

And she needed sharp senses here, too. In case he'd been wrong about anyone else coming here.

But as the minutes ticked by, no sound marred the drone of the insects. Nothing was heard that didn't belong in the jungle chorus. And her nerves stretched and tightened taut as piano wire. Her blood began to throb with a primal sort of beat in keeping with the elemental setting.

A twig snapped behind her and she spun, bringing up the rifle and sighting with one smooth motion. The large wild pig that had started for the stream froze, stared back at her. In the next instant it turned and plunged back into the jungle with surprising speed.

Even as she lowered her rifle her gaze went helplessly to the man standing under the water. Found him watching her. He made no attempt to hide his stirring interest, and the sight of his masculinity weakened her earlier resolve.

It was a moment out of time. As if the rest of the world spun on its axis, leaving this place, this minute untouched. And if the world couldn't intrude on this space, neither could the worries that followed it.

He held a hand out to her then, a silent entreaty she knew better than to accept. But her feet were moving of their own volition, her gaze never leaving his.

He'd slicked his wet hair back with careless fingers and his pale green eyes were alight with a hunger that staggered her. She fumbled a little with the rifle, resecuring the safety and setting it aside.

The task of unlacing her boots should have given her several moments to come to her senses. Would have, if he didn't present a carnal picture of arousal. To have that searing intensity focused on her was its own sort of temptation. One she was no longer interested in battling.

She couldn't remember the last time she'd stripped for a man. The act was less seduction than functionality. She wanted to be as naked as he was. Wanted, finally, to feel every inch of his slick skin pressed against hers.

The dark fatigues were removed next. A muscle jumped in his clenched jaw and she enjoyed his reaction enough to slow her movements. Make them more deliberate. If this was to be a stolen moment, it should be one worth remembering. The urgency drawn painfully tight inside her loosened a notch.

So she drew out the task of removing her top. Hooked her fingers beneath the hem to bare one inch of flesh at a time. Watched his gaze scorch her with a primitive hunger she didn't remember ever eliciting from a man before. It made her feel exquisitely attractive, heady with feminine power.

It was too easy to feel at one in the primitive setting. To

feel as basic and elemental as the wildness around them. Especially with this wild pagan tattoo beat in her pulse.

Cael's face could have been chiseled from the stone he stood upon. But his eyes were alight with a savage promise that sent little spirals of thrill up her spine. And when she dropped her top to the pile of her clothes, the leap of desire in his expression turned her muscles to warm wax.

One arm snaked out, still wrapped in plastic, and took her hand, tugging. She swayed, trying to retain her balance, but landed right where he'd intended, in his arms.

The water spraying over them was colder than she'd expected. But it couldn't come close to cooling the heat that seemed to scorch her from the inside out. When he set her on her feet, she stepped closer and snaked her arms around his neck, her lips going in search of his mouth.

Their kiss rocked her off balance for a moment, and she clung to him even more tightly to right herself. His kiss was a demand she fully reciprocated. His mouth crushed down over hers, as if something wild had been unleashed. Something she welcomed. Something she returned.

Their lips mated, twisting together, tongues and teeth clashing in a tangle of need. The taste of him was hot and wild. Addictive and intoxicating. It sped to her veins and turned her blood molten.

Desperate need fueled them. As if each was anxious to forget all the reasons they'd denied themselves this. All the reasons it would never happen again. Ava was dimly aware they should slow down. Savor every brush of skin. Every sigh.

But there was no slowing with lightning jumping and flashing to life between them. No thought of drawing this out, one delicious moment at a time when sensations bumped and collided with each glide of a tongue. With each deliberate stroke.

His hands streaked over her, leaving liquid fire in their wake. She was just as greedy in her need for the feel of flesh.

Her palms swept up his sides on a rollicking exploration. There was pleasure in testing the firm pecs. The heavy shoulders, with their sculpted muscle. The strong, bulging arms. The hair-roughened chest. The flat, firm abdomen. Stopping to caress the hard straining length of him, thick and engorged.

She wasn't a woman who indulged in pretense or coyness. With something so important to hide in her life, it seemed imperative to be up-front in all her other dealings. Sex was a simple, natural act, and if it was one she hadn't bothered to indulge in recently, that was by choice. It was easy to turn away from the urge when it didn't rage like a fire through her system, a burning demand for release.

She tore her mouth from his, took a deep breath. And lost it in the next moment when he cupped her breasts in his hands, fingers teasing her nipples. Leaning forward, she dragged her sensitive lips over the stubble on his jaw, enjoying the slight abrasion. Her fingers traced the triangular patch of hair across his chest, to where it narrowed to a thin trail on his belly, then skated to his sides, exploring the smooth skin stretched over muscle.

His mouth lowered then and took one nipple in his mouth, his tongue lashing it before he suckled her strongly. Colors wheeled beneath her closed eyelids, sensation bursting forth in a tidal wave of need.

Ava arched her back, exulting in the freedom afforded by raw unvarnished passion. There was no room for pretense here, no deception. He touched her like he was staking a claim, as if he sought to brand himself on her memory.

She felt him drawing her panties down her legs and he raised his head long enough to rasp, "Step out of them." She obeyed, even as she took his heavy masculinity between her palms and lingered to caress.

Cael's breath hissed in and his eyes slitted closed and she tortured him with long, slow strokes, fingers tightening in a motion meant to drive him just a little mad. She enjoyed watching him as passion worked over him. Enjoyed seeing hunger stamp itself on his tough warrior exterior. He looked no less savage lost in passion. And she exulted in that, too, the image releasing fireballs of lust through her veins.

He was no different in need than he was in battle, she thought dimly, as his hand slid up her thigh, cupped her feminine mound. Tough, aggressive and slightly ruthless. She didn't know what that said about her to find the combination so arousing.

She traced his collarbone with her lips, exploring the intriguing hollow where sinew met bone. There was pleasure to be had in just looking at him, broad and hard, with faded scars scattered over his chest. His mouth left her breast and she felt his lips on the still pink and puckered scar above her left breast. Knew he'd recognize it as a gunshot wound. Would acknowledge it without the fascinated horror most would react with.

And in that way they were alike. Their lives, their choices on the job put them in danger, which was accepted rather than feared.

Then conscious thought deserted her as his touch grew more intimate. His voice in her ear was ragged, and the evidence of his fraying control would have been exhilarating if hers hadn't fragmented already.

"You're like wet silk here." His fingers parted her folds, rubbed against the taut bundle of nerves hidden there. "And here." One finger stroked inside her, and Ava gave a little cry as her knees went to water. "Tight and hot." His forehead rested against hers even as his arm tightened around here, taking more of her weight. "I want to be inside you. But not before I see you come apart for me." He probed more deeply, while his thumb rubbed rhythmically at her clitoris.

Every teasing stroke sent sensation arrowing to her womb and desperation clutched there, mingled with desire. She wanted him with her, every inch of the sensual journey. Wanted to see him staggered and shattered, as defenseless as she against the sensual assault.

Her touch became less teasing than demanding, and a part of her thrilled at the low groan coming from his throat. But in the next moment he drew her hands away from him with his free hand, keeping them clasped easily.

A surge of frustration pierced her. "You don't play fair," she gasped.

"Just evening the playing field," he muttered, his mouth stringing a line of stinging kisses up her jaw. "There's been nothing *fair* about my reaction to you from the beginning. You make me crazy." He drew her earlobe between his teeth, worried it gently. "I'm just returning the favor."

She twisted ineffectually against him in an attempt to free her hands, moaned when the motion embedded his finger even more deeply. His touch grew more deliberate, his thumb tapping at the tight bundle of nerves between her thighs. And when he took a nipple between his teeth, scraped it intentionally, sensation rose up and slammed against sensation, catapulting her to a bone-shattering release.

Long moments later she became aware of the band of steel at her back where his arm braced her. Still dazed and trembling, she slid her freed hands around his neck as he withdrew his touch. Shudders were racking his powerful body like a stallion on the scent. She dragged her lips across his mouth even as she felt him lifting her.

Legs folding around his waist, Ava dragged her eyes open, fighting off the stupor of satisfaction to watch him. Her pulse stuttered to life again. His face was flushed with arousal, the skin pulled tightly across his cheekbones. And his eyes…the heat there sent little flickers of answering flame licking through her veins again.

The water coursed over them, leaving tiny streams on his cheeks, which could have been carved from granite. She was half surprised when it didn't leave a trail of steam in its wake. And when she lowered a hand to touch his manhood again, it strained to her touch.

She shifted in his arms, guiding him to her softness, intent on drawing it out. But Cael grasped her hips in frantic hands and surged upward, seating himself fully inside her with one desperate stroke.

Impossibly, the fire began again in her blood, in her pulse. He was all she was aware of, this man and each individual sensation he elicited. Desire, so recently satiated, leapt forward like an uncaged tiger. Ava wrapped her arms around his shoulders, her lips searching for his as he began to thrust within her.

Heels digging into his hips, she joined him in a race toward satisfaction. Sensation collided with sensation. The water pouring over them, doing little to cool their fevered flesh. The slickness of their skin as their bodies pressed together. The wild pounding in her blood that threatened to erupt with every deep thrust.

Their bodies strained together, each movement aimed at getting closer, deeper. And she felt a clutch of satisfaction when she saw his face as he crested. His fingers grasped her hips more desperately and he pounded into her as the madness took him. And when she heard his ragged groan, heard her name on his lips, the sound triggered her own release and she followed him headlong into pleasure.

Chapter 13

At Cael's suggestion they didn't fully dress while they rested. And it was much more comfortable to sit on the bedding he'd constructed of cut ferns with the gillie suit on top, dressed only in a tank and fresh underwear.

It also felt a bit decadent to lie there against his bare chest in the dim sunlight of the jungle around them, feeling at one with the primitive surroundings.

Cael was propped up against the pile of boulders with one arm around her waist, keeping her close to him. Ava had never been a cuddler. And sex this mind shattering left her feeling exposed and vulnerable, scrambling for defenses. But they were difficult to summon with her head lying on his chest. Listening to the strong thud of his heart beating in her ear. The position was too intimate. Too tempting to believe there was more between them than the act that had left them shaking and breathless.

His breathing was deep and even. He was silent so long she

thought he slept. But then he spoke, and his words had ice abruptly forming in her veins. "I've seen your father on TV. Heard bits of some of his speeches. You're nothing like him."

Tension shot into her muscles. She stiffened, meaning to move away, but his arm kept her close.

"Not for lack of trying on his part. He raised me, or tried to, in his own image." And that's what had the shame rearing its ugly head. Recalling how she'd made the posters. Typed the speeches he'd dictated. Accepted as truth the hatred he'd spewed with little question.

"So he's always held those views?"

"Always." She thought, she hoped, that her terse answer would stem any more questions. His next words proved her wrong.

"You said once he'd taught you to shoot."

"We were living on a white supremacy compound in Montana," she recalled quietly. Surrounded by people who shared the same beliefs. Espoused the same views. "We used to have competitions. As I got better he started enrolling me in contests all over the state." It was the most normal memory she had of her childhood. Striving to improve in the one area in which she could impress her father. Winning, if not his love, at least a measure of respect.

"When I was in eighth grade I started riding a bus to public school." It was then, she recalled, that she first started experiencing questions about all she'd learned from her father. For the first time she began forming some of her own opinions. And she'd paid, dearly, every time she dared utter them at home. He'd once given her a black eye for daring to disagree with him about biracial dating. "I started seeing him differently. Questioning his views. He didn't like that. And when I got pregnant at fifteen he beat me so badly I almost lost the baby. Then he threw me out. I haven't seen him since."

Every muscle in his body seemed to tense. "He deserted you?"

"I'm lucky he didn't kill me. Alex's father is Hispanic."

And Eduardo had been the first human being in her life to offer her love, or what she'd interpreted as such. From the distance of age she could see now how panicked he was when she'd told him. How afraid for his own future. At the time she only felt deserted and betrayed.

And completely alone.

His voice sounded strained. "How did you manage?"

"A guidance counselor helped get me placed in a foster family. Assisted in getting services for me and the baby." And it was through going to church with the foster family that she'd met Danny. Two years later they were married and moving to California where he was going to seminary.

As always the ancient history left her feeling depressed. "I'm not proud of the fact that I spent two years trying to get my father to see me. Even convinced myself he'd want to have a relationship with Alex, since he was a boy. I should have known better." And what a narrow miss that had been, she thought with an inner shudder. How horrible it would have been for Alex to have been exposed to the same sort of intolerance she'd been raised with. To have been made to feel that he was somehow less simply because of the color of his skin.

"It worked out for the best." At least she'd always thought so. Had often congratulated herself on how she'd kept the Julson name from ever tainting her son. Her career. Her life.

Until now.

Earlier thoughts of the future had seemed distant and foreign. Now the worry crowded in again, insistent and troubling. She tried to sit up, to edge away. Cael kept her firmly in place.

"I won't use him against you," he said quietly. "Your father. After what I imagine you went through with him, I could never do that to you. But I still believe Samuelson will. And I've had a couple ideas, but still don't have anything foolproof planned that will protect you from him."

Lead coated the bottom of her stomach, and a feeling of resignation filled her. "I know. I called Alex before I left." And he'd been angry, vehemently so, when she confessed she'd lied to him all these years. But even in the face of his fury, the disappointment in her that he hadn't tried to mask, she hadn't disclosed her father's name. She needed to be there with him for that. Ava couldn't stand the thought of her son researching Calvin Julson on his own and discovering what the man was. "I'll tell him everything when I get back. He's furious with me right now. I hope he'll come to understand. He's pretty great."

"I'm not surprised. His mother is rather outstanding herself."

Ridiculous to feel this warm glow at his words. Ridiculous when so much between them was tenuous and built on misunderstanding and distrust. Because she didn't know how to respond to his words, was afraid to read too much into them, she continued. "Alex made it easy. He hasn't ever been much of a problem. He's scary smart. Athletic." She gave a little laugh thinking of their last argument before she'd left. "The biggest problem he gives me is getting all weird about being seen in public with me. He has a fit about going to the mall. Something about his friends calling me a MILF. I figure that's probably some derogatory teen slang for cop or something."

When Cael made a choking sound, she turned in his arms to look up at him inquiringly. "What? Do you know what it means?"

"I do. And it most definitely doesn't have anything to do with your occupation. At least not with the department."

She didn't trust that light in his eyes any more than she did the humor in his voice. "What's it mean, then?"

He ducked his head to drop a kiss under her ear. "MILF, my naive Ava, stands for Mothers I'd Like to…" The last word was whispered in her ear, and had her jerking upward in indignation.

"You're making that up!"

"I most definitely am not. I believe the term was coined in a movie, one starring a bunch of horny teenaged boys."

Fuming, she gave in to the gentle pressure he was exerting

to get her to relax against him again. "The little jerks. If I ever hear one of them saying it, I'll slap cuffs on him and throw him in juvie."

Laughter sounded in his voice. "Just more fodder for an adolescent boy's porn-filled fantasies, but hey, whatever works."

She reached behind her and grabbed a tuft of chest hair, gave it a tug, satisfied when he gave a quiet yelp. "Your whole gender is seriously depraved. Maybe I should lock my son up before he gets corrupted by it."

"Believe me, if he's…what? Fifteen? He's corrupted already."

She didn't share his amusement. What mother wanted to think about her son's development into a man? Although she had the sneaking thought that if Alex grew up with a few of Cael McCabe's qualities, he'd be quite a man indeed.

"Better try to get some rest." He stroked a hand down her back. "We'll take turns."

"I can take first watch," she objected even as heaviness began creeping into her limbs.

"I need to finalize the plans for the rescue." As if in recognition of the questions on her lips, he soothed her. "Go to sleep. We can talk about them later."

It was a measure of her exhaustion that she put aside the nerves and uncertainty about the night ahead. She felt herself sliding down the slippery slope toward sleep. Dreamless except for a green-eyed man who was ruthless and tender by turn.

Although the sun hadn't completely slipped behind the mountains, the jungle was already shadowy with the approach of night. "We need to discuss this further."

Cael finished donning the gillie suit and bent to inspect his pack. "There's nothing to discuss."

Ava stared at the back of him, her teeth grinding with frustration. "We could start with this idea of yours. And your totally incomprehensible refusal to use the military for assistance."

"We can't trust them." His voice was the measured one an adult used with a child who refused to take no for an answer. And made her want to smack him for it. "We don't know who all Ramirez has gotten to. We can't afford chancing that someone will tip him off about the raid tonight. We'd be walking into a trap then."

"So it's a risk." With furious movements she finished dressing, any lingering softness she'd felt as he'd slept with his head in her lap long since gone. "It's also a risk to depend on Reynolds and Perez being in good enough shape to help you once you release them. Hell, you'll probably be killed trying to get to them. Not to mention how you figure on getting out with all the hostages."

"I've explained the plan. It has a fair chance for success. The military should be standing by, per Quintero's orders. When everyone is safely released we'll arrange a diversion and radio for help. Chopper should be here in fifteen, twenty minutes."

Every time he mentioned the plan her veins filled with ice. "That can be a lifetime when we're being chased by over a hundred soldiers!"

He rose, shot her a feral grin. "Well, I'm gonna try to make sure most of them are otherwise occupied."

"It's too risky," she said stubbornly. The thought of him sneaking into the camp, alone, had panic slicking down her spine.

His expression sobered. "If you can't do this, you need to tell me now. I'll have to think of another way. But I still won't alert the military until it's too late for the commander of that camp to get tipped off."

She stared at him in frustration. It was like trying to reason with a slab of granite. Her logic bounced ineffectually off him. And she didn't like walking into any assignment with this fear circling frantically in her belly. Fear for him.

"If things look impossible we'll abort," he said, his voice muffled as he squatted to the ground and started rubbing mud on his face. "And if things go FUBAR, you know what to do."

The nausea that rose at the thought nearly choked her. Fade back into the jungle. Make her way to safety and radio Quintero with the coordinates to chance a military rescue.

Leave McCabe's body where it fell.

Just the thought was very nearly paralyzing. He thought she was considering the risk to herself. Ava didn't bother to inform him the thought of him dying in the attempt was closing her throat with fear. It was impossible to consider how she could feel so deeply for the man when she hadn't even known him two weeks ago. When the majority of their relationship had consisted in subterfuge and deception.

She watched him numbly as he made his preparations, trying to calm the nerves jumping and skittering inside her. She was of no use to him with this kind of emotion roiling inside her. Her experience on SWAT had taught her that. If she couldn't reach for calm, she could endanger him with an overreaction. She could get him killed.

He crossed to her then, and scooped up more mud, rubbed it gently across her cheeks. "Seems a shame to cover up this face," he said huskily.

She swallowed hard, her hands coming up to clasp around his wrists, stopping him. "McCabe."

Stilling, he surveyed her somberly. She drew a deep breath. Let it out in a slow stream. "If you get killed tonight, you are seriously going to piss me off."

His mouth kicked up in a one-sided grin and he leaned in for a hard, thorough kiss. When he lifted his mouth, he said huskily, "I know how dangerous your temper is. So I'm going to do my best to stay on your good side."

They moved silently through the darkened jungle. Cael looked over his shoulder to check on Ava's progress, found her close behind him. And probably still not thrilled with the plan he'd come up with. But he'd come equipped for the type of rescue he had planned. Not Hollywood's idea, of course, with mercs carrying clanking ammo belts and Uzis strapped across their chests. But for a silent deadly entry into the camp and hopefully an unnoticed escape, the idea was fast, silent and deadly.

He halted and handed her a single-bladed knife, keeping the larger, more deadly blade for himself. She took it without comment and slipped it into her belt.

"We can't risk using the wrist communicators from here on in," he cautioned her in a barely audible whisper. He could barely make out her features, darkened as they were with the mud he'd rubbed on them. He knew he looked just as alien with his face blackened and fading into the hood of his gillie suit. "Only shoot if it becomes absolutely necessary. I know you've got a flash and sound suppressor, but we don't want to take any chances."

"You mean because you're already taking such a huge risk yourself?" she muttered.

He was smart enough to ignore her. "You take up position here. You're behind and in the center of the three guards who have the best view of the cells from the perimeter. I'll take care of them before going in." And anyone else who happened to notice him and tried to sound an alarm.

"What are you going to do if Reynolds and Perez are in no shape to help once you get them out?" she demanded in a furious whisper. "Unless you're planning to don a red cape and tights, I don't think you're capable of hauling three prisoners out on your back with no one being the wiser."

"Let me cross that bridge when I come to it," he responded evenly. But he knew it wasn't a matter of *if* something went wrong on these assignments but *when*. And he questioned himself whether he could maintain the objectivity needed to abort if necessary, leaving his client and friends to the mercy of the rebels.

"Just be sure to stay down and out of sight." He studied her in the darkness, most of the words he wanted to utter remaining unspoken. Hell of a thing for a man to finally figure out what he needed saying at the worst possible moment. "We've got some things to iron out when this is over."

"When this is over I'm still going to be harboring a serious grudge over this whole mess," she said. "It's going to take some pretty smooth talking on your part."

Something lightened inside him as he fixed the night-vision goggles over his eyes. "Smooth's my middle name."

The first sentry was sloppy. Propped against the trunk of a tree, he was lighting a cigarette when Cael took him out. He dragged his body a little ways away and divested the man of his rifle and ammo. Then he belly-crawled to the next sentry, one excruciating inch at a time. This one was more alert. More of a challenge. When Cael finally reached him and rose, the man, seeming to sense his presence, started to turn, his rifle raised.

Cael sprang then, the wire in his hands held tight. Their battle was short, vicious and in the end, one-sided. When the guard's body went limp beneath him he started to rise. Heard a sound not much louder than a polite cough.

His focus snapped toward the direction of the third guard in time to see him jerk midstride in his race in this direction. Watched him drop to the ground, lie motionless.

The first thing to go wrong tonight almost had. Chalk one up for Ava.

He disposed of the bodies and collected the weapons. Dropping to his belly, he crawled a few yards and stashed them in some brush, hoping he got a chance to come back for them. Then he took several minutes to get a look at what was going on down below.

Two guards were on duty outside the cells. Neither man gave any indication that he'd noticed anything untoward a hundred meters from the camp. This was where the plan got a bit dicier.

Cael had a moment to hope that Ava was keeping an eye on the guard on the northeast corner of the perimeter. If the man moved to just the right position at exactly the right time, he might get a glimpse of something going on in the camp.

Cael had to move faster than caution dictated. He couldn't afford to wait long enough for a shift change. The perimeter guards would notice when three of the soldiers they went to replace were gone.

Close enough now to hear the occasional murmurs of the sentries standing guard over the cells. He couldn't catch their words, but their tones were relaxed.

The first cell held de la Reyes. After the beating he'd taken that day, he'd need assistance getting out of here. Cael bypassed the cell and moved stealthily to the next. Scooping up some of the mud beneath him, he rolled it into little balls and tossed one against the side of the first cell hoping to draw a guard's attention. Then he waited, muscles alert to an almost painful pitch.

But nothing happened.

Swearing silently, he deliberately scuffed a heel on one of the wooden slats on the back of Reynolds's cell. Heard the guards' low conversation stop. He saw one rise, round the first cell to check out the noise.

Knife in hand, Cael was waiting for him. The silent attack was swift and deadly. Holding the man's limp body in front of him, he waited quietly for the second guard to come looking for the man when he didn't return.

"Que usted esta haciendo? Tomar un escape?"

The other sentry's low whisper sounded after several minutes.

Cael waited, barely breathing. A shadow moved across the slats of the cell he leaned against. If Reynolds were in decent shape, he'd be alert to what was transpiring outside his prison. He'd be ready to move at a moment's notice.

Cael could hear the other guard's approach. Cautious. He'd be wary now, since his colleague hadn't answered. The trick was keeping him from sounding an alarm before Cael could disarm him.

He drew farther into the space between the first two cells. Leaned the guard's dead body against the first structure. Waited for the footsteps to round the corner. Cael backed up stealthily and took a quick look at the area in front of the cells. Deserted.

With one arm he extended his rifle while backing around the front of the president's cell. Listened for the guard to approach stealthily. He gave the body a jab with his rifle and it fell at the second guard's feet even as he dodged around the first cell.

He was behind the second guard even as he crouched to catch his colleague. With a flash of his knife, he dispatched him as quickly as he had the first one.

Dragging both bodies to the far side of de la Reyes's cell, he let them lie there before going to Reynolds's cell, keeping a wary watch on any undue activity in the camp. His face close against the slats of the second cell, he whispered, "Kill zone."

There was a moment of silence. Then a barely audible reply. "Hell box."

Cael knew better then to reveal his location with a flash of teeth, but he grinned inwardly, relief washing over him. It was Reynolds inside all right. The code was derived from their first experience after BUDS training, arranging ambushes for guerilla rebels.

Staying low, he reached up and unlatched the cord holding the cell door shut. Reynolds came out low, and the two of them squatted in between the first two cells. Cael handed him the extra rifle he'd taken off the first perimeter sentry he'd taken out. "What's the lowdown?"

"Fuente's in on it."

Ava had already called that. She'd suspected as much from the beginning.

"The rebel captain sent a small squad out late this afternoon to take the bitch back to town. Probably to get her reward from Ramirez. He executed two guards today who were on duty last night. Accused them of giving de la Reyes preferential treatment."

"I saw it."

"The squad is supposed to come back with word from Ramirez about something they want de la Reyes to do." Reynolds was already picking up the soft mud from the ground and rubbing it on his hands and face.

"Unfreeze Ramirez's assets."

"If it's done, he'll be a dead man."

"Not if we get him out of here first. Is Perez here?"

"In the cell at the far end. I don't know who's on the other side of me, but I know he's an American."

They'd take him with them when they left. And it was high time for them to leave. Cael dug into his pack, withdrew two grenades. He handed one to the other man. "We'll get as far as we can first. The structure in the front left corner is the weapons shed?" He saw Reynolds nod in the shadows. "What about the middle structure? The big one?"

"Barracks. Captain sleeps in the small building to its right."

Cael thought for a split second. It was demoralizing to a unit to lose their commander. And it could send the rebels into disarray. But he was one man. They needed to get rid of as many as possible.

"If this thing turns into a goat screw, take out the barracks. I'll take the weapons shed." In a perfect world they'd release the other prisoners and make their way undetected out of the camp. Some distance away he'd call for military backup and let the choppers provide aerial firepower to take out the camp.

He'd never encountered a perfect world yet.

"Carter's out there providing cover for us." He belly-crawled around the cells, divested the two guards of their weapons and crawled back, handing one extra rifle to Reynolds. "For Perez." He took a moment to sit propped up against a cell next to his friend, and looked at him. "Let's do this."

He took the first cell, unhooked the door and ducked in. De la Reyes was slumped inside. He barely stirred at his entrance. There was no time to check on his injuries. Cael got down and lifted the man's arm around his neck so he could support him and rose again, swiftly exiting the cell. He saw Reynolds give a rifle to Perez, and signal the unknown man to follow them.

The stranger ran in a crouch toward Cael. "Give me a weapon," he whispered.

"Not a chance." Without knowing exactly who they were dealing with, there was no way he was going to trust him. Instead, he had the man support the president, who seemed only half conscious. "Keep down and stay with us."

He led the way, all of them staying low to avoid detection. When he got to the trip wires he signaled the group behind him of their location. The booby traps he'd dismantled earlier on recon.

As a matter of fact, the lack of problems was almost eerie.

He'd no sooner had the thought than he heard the faint pop of Ava's silencer. Turning to look behind him, he saw the body of another perimeter sentry crumple.

In the next moment all hell broke loose.

Automatic gunfire sounded. The sentry posted on the front corner perimeter closest to them had opened fire on Ava. Cael saw her hit the ground. Saw the bullet spray kick up mud all around her. His heart stopped.

He returned fire on the sentry, just before Ava's rifle sounded again. And a crazy fireball of hope spiraled inside him. "Go, go, go!" Cael waved the others by. He ran in a crouch to Ava's side, aware that the camp was coming to life behind him.

"Are you hit?" He ran his free hand frantically over her body, barely registering her answer.

"I'm fine."

"Then move!" He nudged her after the others and turned to find Reynolds alongside him. Each of them pulled the pins of the grenades and heaved them high.

Soldiers were pouring out of the barracks. Some were already returning fire. He and Reynolds turned and ran, staying low with hands over their ears, wanting to put as much distance between them and the camp as possible.

Seconds later the grenades exploded and turned the night to flame.

It was a motley looking crew in on the debriefing, Cael noted, gazing around the table. De la Reyes swayed slightly as he sat at the head of the table, his physician hovering around him, trying to conduct a thorough examination. Quintero sat at his side, casting worried glances at the president.

As for the rest of them…Ava and Reynolds still wore blackening on their faces, as he did himself. Perez's face was swollen and bruised, although he wasn't in as bad a shape as de la Reyes. And the stranger they'd rescued looked gaunt, as if he'd been starved for a time. There were fresh-looking scars, healing badly, marring his hands and face.

Cael looked at Ava. "Tell the doctor when he finishes with the president to look at him." He jerked his head toward the stranger. He waited for her to translate before adding, "Then he can check you out."

She lifted a brow coolly. "I'm fine."

"Damn straight," murmured Reynolds, earning himself a quick look from Cael. The man shrugged. "Dangerous women. It's a weakness, like I said."

Apparently it was a weakness they shared.

"You took an unnecessary risk with the president's life," Quintero said imperiously. "You should have used the militia earlier for the rescue."

It was a moment before Cael could shift his attention away from Ava. He wouldn't be satisfied she was all right until he could check for himself, going over every inch of that exquisite skin again, inch by inch.

But for the time being, he had to deal with the matter at hand. "I wasn't going to divulge the coordinates until after we were out of there. I couldn't risk them coming in too soon and catching us in the cross fire." And he hadn't wanted to chance going in with ground units he wasn't sure he could trust. But he knew better than to say that.

"That is ridiculous. Our military is highly trained. They could have—"

"Enough, Ernesto." Although he was looking much the worse for wear, the president's voice was authoritative. "Senor McCabe executed the rescue mission flawlessly. And our military handily provided some aerial firepower that helped us leave our pursuers behind."

It was an abbreviated explanation for their escape, Cael conceded silently. The choppers hadn't arrived for well over a half hour after they'd detonated the camp. A harrowing half hour in which they'd had to make their way to freedom hauling injured prisoners while returning fire against the rebels chasing them.

The president looked at him. "My military commander reported that they rounded up nearly seventy rebels who were not killed in the blast. The police picked up Miss Fuente and her driver. They are in custody."

Cael had a moment to wonder if the regret in the man's voice was for the woman's fate, or for placing them all at risk by trusting her in the first place. It was doubtful the man would be nearly as trusting of the next female he became involved with.

"Tell us about the demands Ramirez made. You didn't release his assets?"

Quintero shook his head in response to the president's question. "We drew out the process, as Miss Carter suggested. Pretended there was much bureaucracy to cut through." He looked at Ava. "The green tape you mentioned."

Ava gave the man a slight smile. "Red tape. But yeah. That was exactly right."

Cael glanced back at de la Reyes. "We need to check with Justice. Ramirez will be forced to make a move soon. With his assets frozen and your escape, he's out of options. You might also want to put heavy security on the airport, borders and harbors for the time being."

The president nodded. "I will put the call in right away."

"I'd hesitate to include the local police force in any final plans for his capture," Reynolds put in bluntly. "I went to them when I was looking for Perez. Talked to some of the policemen involved in the interrogation of the airport dispatcher. I was approached by a uniform in town an hour later, saying they had information about Perez's whereabouts." He glanced at the silent operative. "Got blindsided. Knocked me over the head and threw me in the back of a truck. Drove me to the edge of the jungle and handed me over to the rebels."

"Carbon copy," muttered Perez. "They grabbed me up about an hour after the interrogation ended. Claimed there was a break in the case and they were to take me back to the headquarters."

The look on de la Reyes's face was thunderous. "You can identify these men?"

The two nodded.

"This, too, will be dealt with immediately. There is disloyalty all around us." There was a flash across his expression, and Cael knew he was thinking of the woman who had betrayed them. "Each of these untrustworthy individuals put lives at risk. And they will be dealt with harshly."

Cael's gaze went to the stranger sitting at the table who had been listening silently. It remained to be seen whether the man would end up in a San Baltes prison or be sent back to the States. "You're up, Jonny. What's your story?"

The man had been sitting back, taking it all in. And Cael knew he'd been as distrustful of his "rescuers" as they had of him. "Jonny Streich, NSWU-Eight."

Cael straightened, narrowed his eyes at the man. "Son of a bitch," he murmured. Without looking at him, he knew Reynolds was just as alert.

Although American law prohibits the country's military from active combat in allied countries, there were quiet deployments to support the antidrug efforts in South American countries. The Naval Special Warfare Unit Eight was one of those teams. Their task was to provide Mobile Training Teams to train the South American host personnel.

Like most South American countries, San Baltes had an extensive river system. Ramirez, along with a lot of his drug dealer counterparts in neighboring countries, used the rivers as a highway for his drugs.

"Another U.S. Special Boat Squadron member and I were assigned to military boat twenty-seven. We were ambushed and overrun by rebels ten days ago. Those who weren't killed in the battle were taken prisoner." He looked at de la Reyes. "I regret to inform you, sir, that your military personnel who were captured were killed in captivity."

Cael exchanged a look with Ava. That explained the pile of bodies they'd discovered at the deserted camp.

De la Reyes swallowed, gave a slow nod. "I had heard of the ambush while I was in the States. I want to thank you for your service." His gaze found Cael's. "And I owe a debt of gratitude to you, Senor McCabe, and your team that cannot be repaid. Anything that I can do for you, anything at all, you have but to ask."

But Cael's mind had started working the first moment

Streich had explained his presence there. His gaze landed thoughtfully on Ava, while he answered, "As a matter of fact, President de la Reyes, there is one thing…."

The first hint Ava had that she wasn't alone in the bathroom was when the shower door opened. She whirled around, found her defensive blow deflected when Cael caught her wrist in one of his hands.

The man was silent as a snake, she fumed. Twisting free, she asked truculently, "What are you doing in here?"

"I'm dirty," was his innocent reply. She watched, her ire splintering, as he stripped swiftly. It wasn't fair, she reflected dimly, that the sight of all that bare skin over bulging muscle and sinew should turn her bones to mush.

"You have a shower in your room," she pointed out as he crowded in with her. Immediately the stall grew smaller. She felt surrounded by the breadth of him. Felt the kick start to her pulse as her body responded accordingly.

"But yours was already running." He leaned in then and, guessing his intent, Ava dodged around him, nudging him under the spray.

"Like you said, you're dirty."

He reached out a hand to snag her wrist, ensuring that she didn't go too far while he washed the mud and grime away. And Ava was content to remain in place.

The rest of his team would be flying in tomorrow and her time here would be through. The thought brought a cold bolt of dread that she strove to shake off. She had plenty of regrets over choices she'd made in the past, choices that she was going to have to answer for when she got home to her son.

But she wouldn't regret the time spent with Cael McCabe.

"What were you talking about with the president after the rest of us left?" She'd noted his thoughtful gaze on her before he'd answered de la Reyes at the end. Didn't much appreciate not being in on the conversation if it pertained to her.

"Believe it or not, I've got a plan." His voice was muffled since he was scrubbing his face with her washcloth.

"There's a news flash."

She dodged his fingers when he released her for a quick retaliatory pinch, and took the soap, running it over the broad expanse of his shoulders. There was power there, in the muscles that jumped and worked beneath her fingers as she smoothed her soapy palms over his back. A strength that was all the more devastating when it was tempered by tenderness.

Just the memory had heat flooding her belly. She'd promised herself she wouldn't indulge in regrets, so she'd tuck the memories away for the future when memories were all she had. But her touch slowed purposely to savor the tactile sensation beneath her fingertips. It'd be one more image to add to her mental scrapbook and she was fiercely determined that their parting be unmarred by remorse. Of any kind.

When he turned to her his face was clean, save for the day's growth of whiskers. They made him look tougher somehow. A bit uncivilized. She raised a hand to brush his stubbled jaw with her palm. He slid an arm around her waist to pull her closer.

"Normally I like to keep details of my security missions under wraps, for a host of reasons. But this time I've asked de la Reyes to make some phone calls on our behalf."

She stopped midstroke. "What kind of calls? To whom?"

"To the Pentagon, for starters. He'll verify Streich's identity and then he'll be talking to everyone he can contact, both there and in the White House, to sing our praises for the rescue of both him and a U.S. military officer." He made a slight grimace, as if the thought embarrassed him a bit. "Like I say, not my usual thing. When the national media get hold of it later in the day it's going to be a free-for-all. So I'm going to arrange for private transport to fly you back and to get you from the airport. You might want to plan for you and your son to stay elsewhere for a few days. I'm guessing reporters will be camped on your doorstep."

The desolation that pooled in her stomach at his easy talk of her departure was alarming. She couldn't afford to react emotionally. Not now, when there was so much at stake. Protecting Alex had to be her first concern and there were a few details missing from his "plan."

"And what is all this supposed to accomplish?"

His grin was roguish. "It's called deflection, baby. And it's a preemptive strike that will make it politically impossible for Samuelson to strong-arm you. Even if he did expose your parentage to the public or to your superiors, your heroic stature is going to make you untouchable. If anything, the news stories will just shift to contrast your character with your father's. Not exactly pleasant, I admit," he added, when she made a face. "But you still come out of it undamaged, with your reputation and your career intact."

He free hand slid up to cup her breast, toy with the nipple. He was, she thought, with a hitch of her breath, a bit too easily sidetracked.

"And what about you?"

One broad shoulder lifted. "Basically the same thing. Timing won't be the best for the smear campaign I assume he has planned. He'll have to wait until the next opportunity arises. It'll drive the son of a bitch crazy."

She eyed him knowingly. "But it won't help you destroy him."

The humor abruptly fled from his expression. He shifted so the water continued to cascade over his shoulders, making little rivulets over his arms and chest. "No. It recently came to my attention that there might be more important things to concentrate on than to one-up my biological father."

There was a jitter in her pulse. His green eyes were alight with an emotion that she couldn't identify. Was afraid to identify. But it sparked spurts of answering heat in her veins.

"And when did this moment of enlightenment occur?"

His arm around her waist tightened. "Might've been when I saw you standing there providing cover for us, as bullets kicked up the dirt all around you. But it started before that. I just didn't realize what the hell had me so distracted where you were concerned."

Her feminine smile of satisfaction curled her lips. "Her distraction, was I?" Linking her arms around his neck, she nipped the side of his throat ungently. "I didn't notice that you were particularly diverted when you were threatening me."

"I should have been tipped off when I became more concerned with protecting you from Samuelson than I was in destroying the prick for good," he murmured, tipping her chin up to brush her lips with his. "As it is, you played hell with my intentions, because I became more worried about protecting you than getting the best of him. I don't have a whole lot of experience in the area, but I figure that means I'm crazy in love with you."

Her heart did a slow, lazy spin in her chest. "I'm not going to quibble with your definition. Especially since I haven't been able to get you out of my head since we first met. I love you—" The rest of her words were lost when his mouth came down more firmly on hers. Her fingers curled into his hair as little thrills of pleasure skipped up her spine.

By the time he lifted his head, her thoughts had scattered. "This is going to be complicated," she said faintly as he scored her earlobe with his teeth.

"Simple," he disputed, his mouth busy. "Very, very simple."

She tried to gather her fragmented logic. "Our jobs...I can't move. I wouldn't do that to Alex. He has three more years of high school."

He leaned back to smile at her then, as he skated a possessive hand down her back. "Don't worry about a thing. I'll make a plan."

Epilogue

The wedding organist was just beginning to play when Dace Recker stepped out to stand alone at the altar, looking decidedly more jittery than he did on an incident response. A moment later, Cael and Alex joined Ava in the pew. She sent Cael a reproving look, but he just winked at her. "We got stuck in traffic," he whispered loudly.

Beyond him, Alex grinned. "Yeah, traffic."

She lifted a brow to indicate she didn't for a second believe either of them. Unless traffic was the latest euphemism for extra batting practice these days.

But it was hard to be annoyed when she saw daily how well her son got along with the man she loved. And she and Alex were back on an even keel now, although there'd been some rocky days when she'd first returned from San Baltes. He'd been accusing and disappointed by turns, and she'd accepted the blame for not being honest with him about his grandfather. He'd deserved to know the truth at some point, although God help her, if this hadn't happened she still didn't know when that point would have come. It was difficult to balance her son's right to know with her overwhelming need to protect him.

But the more Alex had read about Calvin Julson, the more he'd understood her reticence on the subject. And the more his ire had faded. The man's past was ugly enough to dim any burgeoning thoughts of long-lost reunions. And that was a disappointment she couldn't shield him against.

Lindsay Bradford and Jack Langley walked up the aisle arm in arm. As maid of honor and best man respectively, they would be the only attendants in the wedding. And judging from the rock on Lindsay's finger, Ava would be attending another wedding sometime in the near future.

She gave a slight shake of her head. It was difficult to imagine Langley, the dark-haired charmer with the devilish grin, as marriage material, but judging from the way he was looking at Lindsay, he'd finally met his match.

The music changed, and Ava turned to see her friend Jolie Conrad walking down the aisle. There was a dizzying sense of bemusement at all the changes that had taken place in the last few months for some of the members on the Alpha Squad.

Cael's hand slipped into hers and their fingers interlocked as Ava turned to smile at him. It seemed fitting somehow that this man was at her side as she watched her friends begin their future together.

Because whatever the future had in store for her, she knew Cael was going to be part of it.

* * * * *

INTRIGUE

 **INTRIGUE**

Coming next month

2-IN-1 ANTHOLOGY

SECRET AGENT, SECRET FATHER
by Donna Young

Left for dead, spy Jacob had no recollection of who he was or who had tried to kill him. The only thing he responded to was Grace – and her seriously sensual touch!

THE CAVANAUGH CODE
by Marie Ferrarella

Private investigator JC finds detective Taylor's tough-as-nails demeanour a turn-on. And her stubborn refusal to accept his help makes him want her even more.

SINGLE TITLE

HUNTING DOWN THE HORSEMAN
by BJ Daniels

Stuntman Judd has never given a thought to marriage, yet he starts to reconsider when adventurous trick-rider Faith catches his eye.

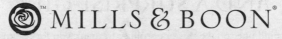

2 FREE BOOKS
AND A SURPRISE GIFT

We would like to take this opportunity to thank you for reading this Mills & Boon® book by offering you the chance to take TWO more specially selected books from the Intrigue series absolutely FREE! We're also making this offer to introduce you to the benefits of the Mills & Boon® Book Club™—

- **FREE home delivery**
- **FREE gifts and competitions**
- **FREE monthly Newsletter**
- **Exclusive Mills & Boon Book Club offers**
- **Books available before they're in the shops**

Accepting these FREE books and gift places you under no obligation to buy, you may cancel at any time, even after receiving your free books. Simply complete your details below and return the entire page to the address below. You don't even need a stamp!

YES Please send me 2 free Intrigue books and a surprise gift. I understand that unless you hear from me, I will receive 5 superb new stories every month, including two 2-in-1 books priced at £4.99 each and a single book priced at £3.19, postage and packing free. I am under no obligation to purchase any books and may cancel my subscription at any time. The free books and gift will be mine to keep in any case.

Ms/Mrs/Miss/Mr _____ Initials _____

Surname _____

Address _____

_____

_____ Postcode _____

E-mail _____

Send this whole page to: Mills & Boon Book Club, Free Book Offer, FREEPOST NAT 10298, Richmond, TW9 1BR